NO LOVE LOST

A FAITH MCCLELLAN NOVEL

LYNDEE WALKER

SEVERN RIVER PUBLISHING

Severn River Publishing
www.SevernRiverBooks.com

This is a work of fiction. Names, characters, businesses, places, events and incidents are either the products of the author's imagination or used in a fictitious manner. Any resemblance to actual persons, living or dead, or actual events is purely coincidental.

ISBN: 978-1-64875-467-8 (Paperback)

ALSO BY LYNDEE WALKER

The Faith McClellan Series

Fear No Truth

Leave No Stone

No Sin Unpunished

Nowhere to Hide

No Love Lost

Tell No Lies

The Nichelle Clarke Series

Front Page Fatality

Buried Leads

Small Town Spin

Devil in the Deadline

Cover Shot

Lethal Lifestyles

Deadly Politics

Hidden Victims

To find out more about LynDee Walker and her books, visit

severnriverbooks.com/authors/lyndee-walker

For Justin, with many thanks for being both a great partner and my best friend. You made it easy to understand this one.

"And ever has it been that love knows not its own depth until the hour of separation."

— *KAHLIL GIBRAN*

1

It's surprisingly easy to get used to cutting people up.

Most folks don't like to think about how fragile humans can really be—the lurking dangers even inside our own bodies that can wreak havoc, sometimes tragically so.

He thinks about little else these days, even when he dreams. How cruel fate can be, and how he can help balance the scales. Heal the deserving.

Save the world.

He rolls the woman to her left side, his eyes on the monitor beeping softly behind her. She's young. Her heartbeat is strong and regular, her blood pressure a perfect, textbook 119/73. Her eyelids don't flutter. It's go time.

A deep breath settles him. He can do this. He has to do this.

He drenches her pale skin with rust-colored disinfectant. Lifts the scalpel from its tray.

Ten inches, hip to armpit, and please God don't let there be a rib in the way. That's too complicated for the time and equipment he has. The scalpel slides, easy and sure under his touch. He ignores her blood as it wells and spills over, looking past it to the next step.

Skin, muscle, fascia, fat. Resect ureter. cut blood vessels. Clamps.

The ice box is open and ready, vapor rising into the cool air. He slides a healthy pink kidney carefully into a bag half filled with Celsior and seals the top. The second bag is full of saline, as is the third, each sealed up in turn like the nesting doll of saving lives. He places the whole package into the ice box and seals it, checking the temperature on the outside. Five degrees Celsius.

"Perfect." A sigh of relief leaves his chest feeling a touch lighter. He turns back.

His hands, always steady and sure, nearly drop the cauterization wand.

He catches it. Takes two breaths. Whispers a prayer of gratitude.

The blue surgical mask covering his nose and mouth doesn't save him from the stench of burning flesh. Lap pads soak up the blood. He drops them to the dingy brown, threadbare comforter that's the hallmark of every American no-tell motel, this one already soaked through with her blood. He leans closer, his eyes on severed tissue and cleanly-sliced vessels.

Sweat beads on his forehead even with the thermostat set at fifty-nine. He tries to blot it with his sleeve, careful not to touch his skin with his gloved hands.

Minutes tick by slowly, his eyes burning as he stares into the cavity where her kidney was.

When five have passed and he's sure the bleeding has stopped, he puts the wand down and reaches for the sutures, backing out step by step, just the way he got in.

The car is already assed-up to the rear door of the room—the back doors are one of the reasons he picked this place. He moves the ice box carefully to the backseat, strapping it down with the shoulder belt before loading the monitors into the trunk.

Wearing clean gloves, he steps back inside. The IV tube has to be the last thing to go—she'll wake up in a matter of minutes when he pulls it. She'll scream, and he won't be able to stand it.

He gathers his tools and his bag before surveying the blood-soaked king-size bed. No way around buying a new one.

He pulls the phone from the night table and lays it near her head, then he reaches to pull out the IV.

Grabbing his bag, the pump, and the trash, he books it for the back door. Manages to get it shut before she stirs.

In the car, he changes his shoes, dropping the comfortable but bloody ones into a plastic grocery bag and pulling on clean, stylish leather boots.

He speeds away, the clock ticking on the kidney in the backseat.

There's no going back now.

2

"Attention all units, shooter in sight, north wing. I repeat, shooter is in sight in the north wing. WPD in pursuit near pretzel stand, suspect is armed and dangerous."

I glanced at the map of the Bluebonnet Hills shopping mall on my phone when the alert came through our radios, screams punctuating the words.

"We're in the east wing," I said, keeping my tone low. "But we should be able to head him off if we keep going this way."

Heart pounding in my ears nearly as loud as the *pop-pop-pop* of shots fired just yards from where Graham and I were standing, I tugged the sleeve of his Travis County Sheriff's Office uniform and zig-zagged around a wooden kiosk, running in the direction of the chaos.

Keeping stride next to me, Graham pointed to a narrow hallway that wound toward the north wing of the mall. "If I were running, I'd go back there," he said.

"Me too." I kicked the speed up a notch, focusing on my breathing as I reached for the weapon in my holster.

We rounded the corner just as a barrel-chested man dressed ski-mask-to-shoes in black raced into the near end of the space.

He paused, eyes going wide, before he leveled his weapon at me.

"Gun!" I shouted.

Graham took aim and shouted in a commanding baritone, "Police! Put your weapon on the floor now!"

Footsteps echoed from the other end of the hallway. The shooter turned to look over his shoulder, his hands shaky.

Graham's green eyes slid to me. "No," he muttered.

I shook my head as I sprinted forward anyway, the heels on my Laredos *thwacking* the floor three times before I launched myself at the shooter's center mass, my hands out to grab the arm brandishing the weapon. The guy barely had time to get his head back around before we were tumbling to the cold tile. My breath went out in a *whoosh* on impact, and I heard Graham muttering "stubborn woman" behind me as I slammed the guy's right wrist into the floor.

"Drop it." The words slid through my gritted teeth as he writhed and tried to kick under me.

The fifth time his wrist connected with the tile, he dropped the weapon and yelped. "Dammit, McClellan, get off!"

I snatched the very realistic-looking paintball gun off the tile and stood, sticking a hand out to help Bolton off the floor.

"You put up a good fight, kid," I said as he pulled the ski mask up and the contingent of pursuing officers and paint-spattered victims at the end of the hallway burst into applause.

A big hand landed on my shoulder. "Nice work. Except that if he'd had a real gun you might be bleeding out at our feet."

I spun and smiled up at Archie Baxter. "Come on, you're the first person to admit I'm too damn stubborn to die, Arch."

"Not funny, McClellan. Nobody is invincible."

I looked over Archie's shoulder to see Graham scowling at me. "I told you it wasn't safe," he said.

"And I knew it was." I put both hands on my hips. "I've sparred with Bolton, remember? He's strong as a Mack truck, but that doesn't translate to speed. As soon as he started to look over his shoulder, I knew I had him." I patted the rookie's arm. "No offense."

"I'm not as quick as she is," he agreed, pulling the ski mask completely off and running a hand through his close-cropped hair.

Graham took both of the black plastic paintball pistols from me and handed them to an Austin patrolman with a box full.

I stretched my arms backward and gently rotated my shoulders, checking the ache from the impact with Bolton's solid wall of abs and looking around. Nearly four dozen officers from six different departments mingled and chatted, most in uniform, some in street clothes splattered with paint. Behind us, dingy tile lined the front of what used to be an Orange Julius, though the sign was missing the "O" and both "u"s. Even the air was sad: stale and slightly moldy, tinged with faint memories of corn dogs, cinnamon rolls, and department store perfume spritzer girls that had seeped into the plaster during the mall's heyday.

"But you were supposed to treat this as a real-time, real-life event," Archie said, nodding to Lieutenant Boone, who was trying to extract himself from the crowd of admiring junior patrolmen. "Orders didn't include tackling the shooter because you have prior knowledge of his weaknesses in hand-to-hand."

"He's right, McClellan, and you know how much I fucking hate admitting that," Boone said, waving one hand at the throng of cops. "Jesus, Baxter, you have a fan club over there. Those kids think my Rangers badge is a star on the Hollywood Walk of Fame, hand to God."

"They have some good recruits at WPD this year," Archie said, shaking Boone's hand. "It'll be nice to have someone to hand the reins over to when we're too old to tackle folks anymore."

"Which will be a long time from now," I said brightly. He'd made so many comments lately about getting old he'd made me paranoid there was a retirement announcement hanging over my head. Which would be all my mother's fault, and I had enough reasons to dislike Ruth McClellan without her forcing the man who made me want to be a Ranger into retirement barely a year after I took my commission.

Archie patted my shoulder.

"It was a ballsy move," Boone conceded, something that could've been mistaken for a proud smile turning the corner of his mouth up slightly.

"And in real time, I'd have saved countless potential lives by heading him off." I turned to Bolton. "How many rounds do you have left, anyway?"

"Close to a hundred," he said, counting clips.

"A hundred more shots." Triumph dripped from my words. "Shots that weren't fired because I disarmed him." I folded my arms across my chest and rubbed them through my jacket. "Anyone else freezing their ass off?"

"Only the emergency lighting is available for this place," Boone said. "The WPD SWAT captain said the owner group who lost their shirts when it shut down a few years back were happy to have a bit of cash from the city, but wouldn't pay to have the power cut back on so we'd have heat."

"We shouldn't need heat in late March," I said. "I'm ready for summer. The cold can go now."

"It better get warmer next week," Archie said. "Your mother tells me your dress isn't fit for an outdoor wedding in the cold."

"It will," I said, squeezing Graham's hand. "If we've made it this far, Mother Nature will smile on our day."

Boone flashed a little smile that actually looked like a smile instead of his usual smirk. "Good for you, McClellan. Congratulations."

I opened my mouth to thank him and everyone's radio crackled to life. "Attention all units, Travis County K-9 Officer Costen with a dog alerting on a door. A locked door. South wing, near the JCPenney sign."

Archie glanced at Graham, who was already running. I took off to catch up, the chill fading under a surge of adrenaline.

"Which dogs did y'all provide for today?" I huffed, even though I was pretty sure I remembered him telling me the answer earlier, and it would fit with why we were running again.

"The cadaver ones."

Graham and I pulled up when we spotted the dog, who was eyeing a closed gray door like it was made of steak.

"He doesn't look bothered." Graham's words were slightly winded as he gestured to the dog after we introduced ourselves to his handler.

"That's his signal, Lt. Commander Hardin sir." The handler's spine was ramrod-straight. He might have saluted Graham if he hadn't been holding the dog's leash.

"Military?" I asked.

"Marine Corps, ma'am," he confirmed. "Two tours in Afghanistan."

"I appreciate the sentiment, but I'm just Hardin," Graham said.

The deputy relaxed. "Tom Costen."

"And your partner here?" I really did know better than to scratch the German Shepherd's gorgeous head while he was working, but I still had to fold my hands behind my back.

"This is Louis," he said. "He's the king of body discovery. He's never been wrong."

"Never?" Graham and I exchanged a glance.

Costen shook his head, his eyes on his partner.

"How long have you worked together?"

"Going on four years now," Costen said. "I trained him from the time he was a puppy. That took a year and a half, and he's the smartest dog I've ever seen—I swear on my grandmomma's butter biscuits, he understands every damn word I say."

"How many finds last year?" Graham asked.

"Thirty-four."

I let out a low whistle. "How many jurisdictions do you cover?"

"All of Travis, Wilkerson, and Bell counties, some of Bexar, and part of McLennan. People ask for us because Louis is the best."

"Did they put training scent in the building today for the dogs?" I asked.

"Not in there," he said. "We all had maps of everywhere scent was used so we'd know how to work the dogs through the simulation. The idea would be for us to come behind everyone else to make sure all the victims were found, but my CO said it'd be a good opportunity to expose the dogs to working around a crowd of loud, live people, so Louis and I came toward the tail end of your event. But before I could even get him to the part of the building we were assigned, he alerted on this door."

Archie and Boone walked up behind us, a tall woman with a dark bun threaded through with silver in a vest and tactical gear behind them.

"Liz Yeager, Waco PD SWAT," she said. "What're we looking for, Deputy?"

"Louis here is a cadaver dog, ma'am."

She waved her team into place. We scattered so three officers in vests and face shields could take a battering ram to the door.

Even the squeal of metal on metal didn't deter Louis, who sat alert with his eyes on the door, Costen standing at his side.

I glanced at the map on my phone. "It's a hallway. Back doors, bathroom, storage, cleaning closets." I turned the screen so Graham could see.

"And dead people, according to the best dog in the state." He sighed. "Maybe it's a bird or a possum or something?"

Costen shook his head. "He can tell the difference. He's well trained to only alert to human remains, sir. I mean, Hardin. I can't promise you there's still a dead body in there, but if Louis says so, there at least was at one time.

"He can pick up traces down to drops of fluids and fragments of blood. Last month he identified a murder scene at a restaurant even though the killer dumped the body more than fifty miles away. Forensics sweep confirmed blood and small bone fragments."

"It never ceases to amaze me how smart these dogs really are," I said.

The door gave, and Archie and Boone followed Yeager over it before they picked it up and moved it to one side.

Louis waited patiently, trotting into the corridor when the officers all stepped aside.

He sniffed the air, his nose working faster than Ruth McClellan moves through a sale at Saks, before he went to the floor, leading Costen to another door about halfway to the first bend in the hallway.

Louis sat.

Captain Yeager tried the door. It, too, was locked.

Her guys hauled the ram back in, a more difficult task in the smaller space.

Four whacks took the door down, first glance revealing a commercial water heater with mangled plumbing surrounding it, plus what looked like a couple of wooden broom handles.

Louis barked twice.

"Y'all are going to want to move that door," Costen said.

Graham stepped forward and helped one of the SWAT officers pull it free and toss it aside.

"Good dog," Boone said, waving me close enough to see the distinctly human-shaped plastic-and-duct-tape rollup on the floor.

3

"It doesn't look like she's been here long, but a body that's wrapped this way can subvert some indicators." Jim Prescott stood, his knees crackling like a bowl of Rice Krispies, and pulled off his exam gloves, dropping them in a garbage bag before he waved two assistant McLennan County medical examiners over to load and remove the corpse Louis had happened upon. "If they can let me into the lab, I'll get started tonight and let you know what I find."

Graham jotted notes while I continued a methodical scan of the entire area all the way back to the mall's main corridor.

"How long has this place been closed now?" I asked.

"Nearly three years," Archie said. "The guy who manages it for the owner group is on his way up here. Took me a bit to track him down and it sounded like he was in a bar when I did, but he's coming."

I glanced at Jim. "Whatever else we know, she hasn't been in that closet for more than two years, right?"

"I wouldn't guess she'd been in here for more than two weeks with what I can see right now," he said. "But let me get her to the lab. The lack of insect activity is weird." He pulled out his phone and pecked at the screen with one index finger.

"Insects? This early in the spring?" Archie asked.

"Inside an essentially abandoned building? Even this plastic wrap shouldn't have kept them out perfectly," Jim replied, pocketing his phone.

I waited three beats, watching Louis enjoy the rest of the chicken Costen was feeding him.

"It's been chilly, but not cold enough for it to be freezing in here with so much insulation in these old walls," Jim muttered, almost to himself.

"And?" I asked when he didn't elaborate.

"Y'all didn't notice the smell?"

I turned to Graham, eyebrows up. Archie cleared his throat.

"It's not sunshine and roses, Jim," he said.

"No, but it isn't as bad as normal, either," I said, stepping closer to the door and peering down.

It had taken me months to get used to the body-recovery part of working homicide, and I'd become a vegetarian my second day on the job. I couldn't believe I hadn't noticed, but Jim was right: this body didn't smell any kind of good, but it didn't smell as bad as every other one I'd ever come across that wasn't already bones.

"What's doing that?" I asked Jim.

"Sometimes a combination of freezing and being sealed up like this makes the tissues decompose differently. The worst of the smell always comes from putrefaction that starts in the gut."

"That's why bodies float in the water," I said.

"Right. The bacteria in the intestines flee as the cell walls give way after the heart stops, and it's a free-for-all, but the gasses they make as they consume the tissue of their former host puff up the abdomen and make a corpse float." Jim waved a hand at the woman's body, still mostly wrapped in the plastic from the chest down. "Her belly is still flat. I've only ever seen that happen with bodies kept in cold storage, so I'm wondering how it happened here. I just checked the degree days for the past four weeks and it hasn't been cool enough out to cause freezing of tissues in here, even if you assume she was here during the snowstorm last month."

Graham jotted that down while I examined the frame around the door.

I was intrigued, and in a rare lull between cases I suspected Archie had orchestrated at my mother's request as we came down to the wire on wedding planning. The ceremony was set for the gardens at the Driskill in eight days, and I was counting down to being done with the prep work for it almost as much as I was to being Graham's wife.

"I'll know more by this time tomorrow," Jim said.

Archie stepped forward to shake his hand while I plucked a tiny flashlight from my pocket and clicked it on, aiming for a scattering of faint scratches in the black paint on the door frame.

Wife. It wasn't a word I ever thought would apply to me. Then Graham Hardin walked into Marshall High School looking for information on a dead track star and landed back in my life, and nearly a year later, I was thinking things I'd never allowed myself to. Since I was fourteen, my only goal in life had been to earn my coveted silver star Rangers badge, which would allow me to move through the homicide unit to the cold cases so I could finally figure out how my sister died.

"What're you so interested in?" Graham leaned over my shoulder.

I pointed. "These marks look like someone was trying to get into this closet." I touched the shiny silver of the exposed metal beneath. "Relatively recently."

Archie and Boone both stepped over to have a look. "Your eye for the little things is the damndest I've ever worked with, McClellan," Boone said.

Archie shot me a grin. After months of carrying files and getting coffee, I'd earned the lieutenant's respect, and while I couldn't help thinking that would've been easier if I were a man who wasn't related to Chuck McClellan, I was happy to have it all the same.

I moved to the twisted metal door and crouched to look at the handle and the edge. "Harder to see here because of the damage from the battering ram, but they only hit it a couple of times—these small marks on the handle and the edge here near it don't fit with the damage SWAT did."

I pulled out my phone and snapped photos of both surfaces before I pointed them out to a petite blonde in a WPD forensics windbreaker with "Miller" embroidered on it over her heart.

"What are you thinking?" Graham asked when she started snapping photos and I stepped back.

I shrugged. "That those marks might prove interesting when we know more about what happened here and who she is. Just trying to make sure I get everything."

He leaned close to my ear without being obvious. "It's really sexy that you're so smart," he whispered. "Just in case I haven't said it today."

I smiled at the floor, my skin tingling from my earlobe to my toes.

Yeager turned to me. "Are the Rangers working the investigation here, then?"

"Happy to help out however I can," I said. "I work out of the F Company offices."

"McClellan here has the only perfect homicide clearance record in the state," Boone said.

I swallowed a laugh. Not that he'd given one damn about that until I pushed my way into clearing tough cases for him. "I'm good at noticing small things that are often important later," I said.

"Atta-girl"s from my superiors didn't impress me. The victims and their families had always been my motivation for digging when other detectives gave up and moved on to the next file in the stack—my "perfect record" was way more about stubbornness and perseverance than it was about any vastly superior skill. There were a lot of good cops in my orbit. It was just rare for one to be as pigheaded as I was. But the more cases I cleared, the more I wondered if my stubborn streak would be as useful in cold cases, where my ability to notice things other people might miss would be limited to notes and photos that other officers took, not to mention sometimes fuzzy memories.

"If Jim Prescott says this body is weird, I'm sure we'd welcome any help y'all want to offer," Yeager said. "I know his work—he's something of a legend. The more brains on it, the better."

I knew from experience that the reality of that depended almost entirely on the personalities and ambitions of the brains in question.

I would never give up on Charity—and I would find the people who took her light out of the world far too soon. But I was beginning to wonder if there was more than one way to go about that—and hoping Boone would stay impressed with my work enough to want to keep me happy in F Company until I worked up the nerve to ask him.

I just nodded to Yeager and handed her a card. "Happy to offer up our offices off 35 as a base for the investigation if that's helpful. We're right by the museum, so just make sure you use the right parking lot."

Her eyebrows went up. Most of the other agencies we worked with were peppered with folks who held the Rangers with some sort of mystique, and an invitation into the inner sanctum was often a quick way into another officer's good graces.

It also gave me a bit of home court advantage and more control of the investigation.

"That's very generous of you," she said. "I'm sure our detectives will appreciate it."

"Jim is as stubborn as McClellan here," Archie said. "He'll have something for us to work with tomorrow, I'm sure."

"I'll pass this along." Yeager held up the card and shook my hand, huddling briefly with the forensics folks before she gathered her team and called it a night.

I sidestepped a tech taking a swab from the floor inside the body outline and peered around the little closet Louis had discovered.

"What in the devil's handbasket is happening here?" The slur in the drawl from outside the corridor was so thick I couldn't have hacked through it with a machete. "I got an urgent page that my presence was required. I thought you people would be able to handle your own playacting."

I returned to the hallway. "We handled it fine until a dead body turned up in one of your closets, Mr. ...?" I lifted one eyebrow, fixing him with an unblinking gaze and the smallest smile in my arsenal.

"Beauchamp. Buster Beauchamp." He looked flustered, smallish eyes darting around the corridor from beneath the brim of a Stetson so big it could've escaped from a cartoon. His jaw fell open when he spotted the outline on the floor. "Are you talking about an actual real live dead person?"

Archie couldn't suppress a snort.

Graham flipped back in his notes. "A woman, probably in her mid to late twenties, dark hair, petite build, average clothing," he read from the page. "Anyone you might know?"

Buster started to shake his head. Paused. Raised one finger. "Well now, there were a few little gals who worked for a cleaning service that used to carpool from the parking lot. I saw them once when I was meeting an associate."

"How long ago was that?" Graham asked.

"Probably a couple of weeks. Guy called about a laser tag game he wanted to host for his company." He nodded, the hat wobbling. "Yeah. A couple weeks."

"And did they have the laser tag game?"

"Hasn't ever called back yet, was looking to book for the first of April," Buster said. "I get the damndest phone calls from folks like y'all who want to rent the place, but a few bucks here and there is better than nothing, I suppose. Investors can't ask for more with a property like this in today's world of internet shopping."

Graham made a note.

"Has anyone else had any kind of event here in the past two months?" I asked.

"Last rental was right before Christmas. A photographer set up a Santa set. Nobody since then, though—it gets cold in here in the wintertime."

I wrote that down. Surely she hadn't been in there since December.

"Would anyone have cause to access this hallway?" Archie asked.

Buster looked confused, staring around the half-circle of officers in front of him. "Why would anyone do that? The bathrooms in the old food court are the only open ones, that's in the contract. New wing was built after the original structure, so the plumbing is on a separate meter. I don't have the water on to the rest of the building. Limits the possibility of damage from a busted pipe or an idiot leaving something running."

"So no one would have access to this hallway?"

Buster blinked. "I'm sure I have a key somewhere, but I can't think of anyone who would want in here."

"Which is probably why whoever put that body here wanted in here," I said, half under my breath. Before Buster could process my words through the booze, I flashed him a ten-thousand-watt the-judges-are-watching smile. "Do you have security cameras, Mr. Beauchamp?"

He fidgeted with the brim of the hat. "There are cameras out there." He waved one arm at the hallway. "Technically."

"How many of them work?"

"Less than half." He settled the hat back on his head and stuffed his hands into his pockets. "It's a bear getting these investors to pay for much of anything in the way of maintenance, and when it comes to security, the standard response is that there's nothing in here worth stealing."

"So there's not a regular patrol by a private security company, either?" Archie asked.

Buster shook his head.

"Thank you for your time tonight, Mr. Beauchamp," I said, catching a small nod from Archie as I handed Buster a card. "I'm going to need a complete list of the building's investors by tomorrow morning, and any security footage you might have from the past month, as well. Any upcoming events will need to be rescheduled until the building is no longer an active crime scene."

"When will that be?" His eyes popped wide.

"Hard to say right now, but we'll be out as soon as we can."

Lieutenant Boone shot me an approving smile and hustled Buster away in the direction of the food court, asking him if he drove himself and offering to call a car for him in his "distressed" state.

"No security. Few cameras. No information on date of death." I sighed, leaning one shoulder against the wall. "Hell of a 'learning experience' we've gotten ourselves into here, huh y'all?"

"It has to be someone who knows the building," Graham said. "How would anyone else get a key?"

I raised one finger, walking back over and pointing to the marks on the door. "Someone at least tried to get into this one without a key recently." I moved to the wider door that led back out to the main floor of the mall, clicking on my flashlight and peering at the frame. "This one, too."

"But if they succeeded in breaking the lock, how were the doors locked when we got here?" Graham asked.

"True." I waggled the flashlight against my palm, turning back to the door after a minute and peering at the knob.

"I'll be damned," I said, pointing. "Because I'm pretty sure these knobs have been replaced. Recently, too."

"We should ask old Buster tomorrow if he has a key to one of these doors we can try," Graham said.

"I bet he doesn't anymore," I said.

"Decent leads for an hour's work." Archie clapped Graham on the shoulder. "Y'all ready to head home?"

"Did it strike anyone else as odd that old Buster there wasn't more concerned about the report of a likely homicide?"

"It didn't seem he was too concerned about anything but getting back to the bar," Archie said.

Graham snorted.

"Yeah. That," I said.

"Did anyone scout this location before it was chosen?" Graham asked.

I pulled out my phone and did a quick search of emails. "My invitation came from the Waco PD public information officer." I walked back down the hall and waved Officer Miller down to ask if PIO Wells was still in the building.

"Let me check." She pulled a portable radio from her hip. "Detective Wells, respond with location please."

We waited. No response. "Wells? Repeating, please respond with location at the request of Texas Ranger McClellan."

The unit crackled to life. "I'll be right with you."

Ah. He was in the restroom, then.

"Proceed to main body recovery site on second floor when possible." She hooked the radio clip back over her belt.

I thanked her and returned to the mouth of the hallway. A few minutes later a uniformed Waco officer jogged up, slightly out of breath and hands still damp from the sink when he shook mine. "What can I do for you?"

"This was your show, right?" I asked, pulling out a notebook.

Wells nodded. "It was the chief's idea, he heard about something similar being done in Virginia at a conference he went to, I think. But I organized it."

I looked around the space, toward the forensics team.

"How did you choose this location?" I asked.

"It's big enough and it was empty and available." He shrugged. "We thought having something like this at a school was a little morbid, even if it was a weekend, you know? But at the same time no matter how much we hate it, we have to be able to prepare our personnel for events like this. The vast majority of cops who have ever been called to respond to an active shooter event have never been in a similar situation. That's not the sort of thing anyone should have to learn on the fly."

I nodded. "What did you make of Mr. Beauchamp?"

"Buster?" Wells snorted. "He's a character, with his booming voice and his too-big hats. Did he kind of remind you of Boss Hogg from *The Dukes of Hazzard*, too?"

"He did." I laughed. "But you think he's harmless?" I waved one hand toward the forensics activity in the hallway.

"You mean do I think he killed that girl?" Wells shook his head. "Not that I'm an expert, but that doesn't seem likely to me. Could I see him being shady in his business? Totally. Killing people? Not so much."

I thanked him for his help.

"What happened to her anyway?" he asked.

"We'll have to wait for the autopsy report to know that," I said, crooking a finger at Graham when I saw him looking for me. "We're heading out, but if you hear anything that might help the investigation, please call me no matter the hour." I handed him a card. "My cell is on the back."

I rejoined Graham and Archie, my eyes taking a mental inventory of the entire building as we walked back toward the entrance we'd used what felt like a long time ago now.

"So much for an easy Friday," I said.

"We'll figure it out, McClellan," Archie said. "And we'll do it before your wedding. No worries."

I just nodded as I walked through the door Graham held open and followed him to my truck. Thinking over the meticulous nature of the body disposal we'd happened across, the wedding was the least of my worries right then.

4

My phone rang with Jim's assigned tone before the sun was up enough to call it morning.

"Haven't you ever heard of Saturday morning?" I asked without opening my eyes. "Any chance Jane Doe isn't still dead?"

"No," Jim said, his voice too high. "I know it's early, but I couldn't sleep."

I blinked, fatigue shriveling faster than a weed in January as I absorbed the worry coating his words. "What's up?"

Graham stirred behind me. "What? What's up?"

"She's not all here," Jim said. "Date of death is going to be a challenge on this one, because a lot of the standard decomposition rules won't apply."

I sat up, and Graham rolled and put one warm hand flat on my back.

"I'm going to need way more words than that before coffee, Jim," I said.

"Jim?" Graham sat up, too. "It's not even light outside yet."

"Her organs are gone," Jim said. "Well. Her heart, lungs, liver, and small intestine are gone."

It took me a full minute to put words to the horror show in my brain.

"So we have our own homegrown Jack or Jane the Ripper?" I asked. "Doesn't this seem like a thing we'd have noticed yesterday?"

"She was closed up and dressed before they wrapped her in the plastic," Jim said. "Y'all ought to come down here and have a look for yourself, but whoever did this has at least a working knowledge of human anatomy. These stitches aren't, like, surgical grade, but they're not bad if you consider the killer was likely in a hurry, and the cuts are precise."

Nine thousand and one questions fought to be first out of my mouth, and I couldn't pick one, so I gave up on trying. "Thanks, Jim. We'll be there shortly."

I clicked the end circle and dropped the phone to the mattress.

"Her organs are gone," I said before Graham could ask.

"Uh. Okay." He stood and stretched his arms over his head before he reached for his pants. "This is a new one on me."

"Jim said there had to be basic medical skill involved. Clean cuts." I shook my head like it would clear the thoughts jamming in from every direction and stood, ducking into the closet for my clothes.

"He didn't give you a cause of death?" Graham asked when I joined him in front of the coffee maker a few minutes later.

"Let's just both pray it wasn't this asshole cutting out her heart."

Graham winced. "That right there would be what I'm afraid of."

I took the cup he handed me and added sugar, taking a sip before I put the lid on. "Plus he said everything about the decomp would be weird because of the missing parts, which will make it hard to find out when she died."

"This just gets to be more fun by the minute."

Not another word passed between us as we climbed into my truck. No time of death made it hard to use security footage to scout for potential witnesses or suspects, because we didn't have the manpower to watch weeks' worth of tape. I pulled up the local forensic lab on my GPS and steered the truck to it on autopilot, sucking down my coffee and running game scenarios for what Louis the cadaver dog might have happened upon the day before.

Graham's fingers drumming on his knee said he was doing the same. I sighed.

"We shouldn't get too far ahead of the facts here."

"You said 'Jack the Ripper' yourself. I heard you."

"I did. Because who wouldn't? Most murderers don't go around cutting out people's hearts. But we don't know what we're dealing with yet. We follow facts. Not ghosts of dead serial killers, no matter how compelling their legends. Right?"

"Of course. And we will here, too."

I parked next to Jim's pickup and cut the engine, draining the last of my coffee before I put the cup back in the holder and hopped out of the truck, casting a glance at the wide blue sky. A slight chill clung to the air as streaks of orange crept higher on the eastern horizon, the morning promising the first truly gorgeous Texas spring Saturday we'd had this year. "I can think of about a million things we could do today that don't involve dead people," I said, joining Graham at the front of the truck.

"None of them will be more fun for you than catching whoever could do something like this, and you know it." He slung one arm around my shoulders and squeezed. "And that right there is one of the reasons I'm marrying you."

"A week from today." I smiled the kind of soft smile usually reserved for new babies and floppy-eared puppies.

"The first day of the rest of our lives never had quite such a truth to it."

I rang Jim's phone to let him know we were there, but it went straight to voicemail.

Weird.

Graham reached for the door and pulled it open, and my stomach flopped as I stepped inside, watching Graham turn the lock behind us.

"Not like him to forget to lock the door," I said.

"He probably went to get some coffee of his own if he's been here all night," Graham said. "Easy enough to skip it when his hands are full and you told him we'd be right over."

I nodded, turning for the hallway that led to the autopsy labs, pointing to the first one because the lights were on.

"I would've brought cof—" The word died on my lips as I pushed the door open to chaos: instruments and gauze littered the speckled linoleum, a pool of thick burgundy spreading slowly outward from under Jim, who was face down on the floor steps from an empty exam table.

5

My boots slid in the blood, leaving streaks as I hit my knees, my hands frantically searching my old friend for the source. Behind me, Graham barked his badge number and a call for an ambulance into his phone.

"Get me some—" I turned, and Graham shoved a wad of gauze at me before I could finish asking for it, just as my fingers found the gash—a small, well-placed incision directly over Jim's right carotid artery. "Help." I rolled my hand, and Graham knelt and helped me turn Jim to his side. I didn't want to move him more than necessary to reach the wound before the EMTs could get there.

"Jim, please talk to me," I said, pressing the gauze down hard over the wound, mindful to avoid his trachea. The gash wasn't bleeding as much as I would've thought it should be, given the pool on the floor. I knew enough about anatomy to know that while the puddle currently seeping through the knees of my Wranglers was scary, it wasn't nearly all the blood Jim had to lose.

Please God, let us have gotten here in time. It was the hardest I'd prayed since my sister disappeared, and I wanted a different outcome this time with everything in me.

Graham held a hand under Jim's nose. "He's breathing. It's shallow, but it's there."

I swallowed hard against the lump in my throat and kept the pressure in place.

"What the fuck?" I asked no one in particular.

Graham stood and walked a lap of the room. I heard the door to the cold storage, which was a big deal for Graham—historically, he pukes more often than not in the autopsy lab, and the salty, earthy tang heavy in the air was different than the usual decay smell, but no less unsettling.

"The body's gone," he said as the first strains of sirens hit our ears. "I'll go meet them at the door."

"Call Archie," I said, my eyes staying on Jim. "He stayed at the Marriott last night because Ruth didn't want him driving home tired."

"On it."

I heard the door shut behind him.

"You can't die, Jim. Sharon and your boys need you," I whispered.

His chest hitched, eyelids jumping.

"Stay with me." My voice shot up a full octave. "Help is almost here."

A long sigh rattled out of Jim's chest.

"Jim!" It came out a strangled scream, but I kept the pressure on his neck, not daring to move a hand to check his breathing.

The door slammed into the wall behind me, and Graham led a rushed team of EMTs wheeling a gurney into the room.

"Stay where you are," a deep voice said. "Keep that pressure in place."

Jim's shirt moved the slightest bit, his chest expanding with a breath. A small one. I'd take it.

The EMT team fanned out, two large men and Graham lifting Jim as a woman knelt and slid the gurney under him. I kept pressing on his neck, trying to keep panic at bay as they talked.

The guy with the velvet baritone caught my eye. "We're going to stand on three. Ready?"

"Yep." I didn't even recognize my own voice.

He counted it off, the gurney rising with us when he released the catch.

"Low O2," the woman said. "His lips are blue."

They fastened straps around him and pulled them tight to hold him still.

"I got a heartbeat," the shorter of the two men said, pressing a stethoscope to Jim's chest. "Sluggish, but detectable."

"Do either of you happen to know his blood type?" Baritone EMT asked.

"Graham, get my phone out of my pocket and call Sharon. Her cell is saved under his name as the home number."

He slid my phone from my hip pocket and pecked at the screen before he put it to his ear.

"Faith!" Archie's baritone came from the front of the building.

"In the lab." I didn't get the words all the way out before he came through the door.

"Dear God." He stopped just inside and took in the blood and the mess and Jim, strapped to a gurney and holding on by what felt to me like a gossamer-thin thread.

"AB negative," Graham said, holding the phone away from his ear. "Y'all are going to Memorial, right?"

The tall EMT nodded.

Graham relayed that before he ended the call and returned my phone to my pocket.

"His wife made the trip up with him—they were going to stay for the weekend. She'll meet you there." Graham turned to Archie. "Our Jane Doe is gone."

The female EMT did a double take, whipping her head back to look at Graham. "Jane Doe like a dead body?"

"Whoever did this to him took it, it would seem," Graham said.

"What in the ever loving hell?" Archie murmured. I could hear low tones from him and Graham until we were about halfway down the hallway. My brain wanted to be back there hashing through theories with them, but I didn't dare let go of Jim until there was a doctor in the room. Like I could hold the life inside him by sheer force of stubbornness, I closed my eyes after I was seated on a bench in the back of the ambulance. He had to be okay. I refused to consider another option.

"How long ago did this happen?" the one who sounded like Barry White asked.

"We got here about six, and found him like this." I opened my eyes. "Is he going to be okay?"

"I mean, I'd say if he's still breathing now, he's got a chance," the shorter guy said from the driver's seat. "I had a guy shot in the neck last fall, lost more blood than your guy, we thought he was a goner for sure. Picked him up just last week with a GSW to the right shoulder. So it's not impossible."

"Sounds like that guy needs a quieter life," I said, finding an odd comfort in the story as I watched the heart monitor they'd attached to Jim when we got into the ambulance.

The EMT snorted. "Dealers, man. Plenty of people hate them, you know?"

"Oh, I know," I said. I'd worked a dozen cases involving narcotics in my homicide career. But until today, I'd never had a victim who was my friend. I glanced at my watch. "How in the world has it only been twenty minutes since I got to the lab?" I blurted. "It feels like we were there all damn day."

"That's the adrenaline," the driver said. "Hang on, Officer. We're almost there."

"What was this guy doing at the crime lab so early on Saturday anyway?" Barry-White-voice-EMT asked.

"Jim is the best we've got," I said. "He had a curious case and couldn't sleep, so he went to work. It's not unusual for him."

The unlocked door at the front of the building was weird, though.

"Seems like somebody didn't want him to figure something out," the woman said, standing in a hunched pose as the driver backed into the ambulance bay.

I held my post as they guided the gurney through the doors to a waiting medical team, where a doctor in a pale yellow gown and a face shield took over the compression before they whisked Jim through a set of double doors and into an elevator on the other side. The EMTs ran to keep up, reeling off the facts they had about time since the injury.

I sagged back against the wall, every part of me shaking, and folded my arms across my chest, hugging my own shoulders. "Ma'am? Are you okay?" A willowy brunette in scrubs paused in front of me.

I glanced down at my blood-soaked jeans and hands, opening my mouth to tell her it wasn't mine.

Before I got a word out, Sharon Prescott sprinted through the sliding glass doors across the small hallway and let out a scream when her eyes landed on me.

The brunette's badge said her name was Alexis, and she recruited an orderly to help me and Sharon to chairs in a small private waiting room.

"He's breathing, they're doing everything they can," I repeated for the third time in thirty seconds as Jim's wife clung to Alexis and sobbed like he was already dead.

"How does this even happen? He was at work," Sharon blurted between sobs. "He couldn't sleep and was tossing and turning in the little hotel bed. I—I told him to go on to the lab since his friend got him a key."

I patted her hand as Alexis extricated herself and hustled back to the treatment area.

Turning, Jim's wife of multiple decades grabbed my hand in both of hers and squeezed. "He said he'd be back this afternoon. We were going to go to the Dr Pepper museum and drive up to West for kolaches. How did this happen?" She dissolved into sobs again and I put one arm around her.

"I don't know, but I will find the person who did this to him." I had never meant a sentence more in my life. Jane Doe's murder had just crossed a line from professional curiosity to personal vendetta.

I hadn't felt such rage since my sister died. But this time I wasn't a four-teen-year-old girl kept under lock and key save for going to school. I could find this bastard. Right then my biggest fear was that I'd forget my training when I did.

Sharon leaned into my shoulder, her sobs shaking her whole thin frame. I put my arms around her and let her cry, my eyes on the door. Half of me wanted to go find Archie and Graham and get to work, and half couldn't bear to leave her there alone.

Twenty minutes of soothing noises later, a younger, fitter version of Jim rushed through the sliding doors. "Mom? I got your message, what in the name of all that is holy is happening?"

Peter. I was pretty sure Jim's youngest son was Peter, and seeing him there I remembered that he was a junior at Baylor. He took the chair on the other side of his mother and she let go of me and fell into his embrace, wailing, "Petey, someone attacked your father at work."

I met his gaze over her head as he stroked the short gray hair that was filling back in after her cancer treatments. "I'm Faith McClellan."

"I know. My dad has told me all about you and what you did for our family." He squeezed his mother, his voice hoarse with emotion, tears shining behind his wire-rimmed glasses. "Think you have another miracle up your sleeve, Ranger?"

"I have the only perfect case clearance record in the state on my side, anyway," I said, handing him a card as I stood. "I love your dad. He's a fighter. My cell is on the back, please call me the minute you hear anything."

"I will."

I patted his shoulder on my way out, touching Graham's name in my favorites list before I cleared the doors to the hospital. "Can someone come get me?"

"Be there in ten. How's Jim?"

"In surgery, breathing when they took him up. Their youngest is here with Sharon. How's it there?"

"WPD forensics is here, and I called Deputy Costen and Louis in to see if the dog could pick up anything on the missing body. Turns out having a cadaver dog try to search a morgue is pretty weird."

"Poor Louis."

"He really doesn't know what to do with himself. If he gets nothing from the parking lot, Archie's going to send them on."

"We're going to find this fucker, Graham."

"That we will." The fact that he sounded like it was a foregone conclusion made me love him a little bit more, and I wasn't even sure that was possible.

"Drive safely. See you in a few."

I ended the call and turned my head to find nurse Alexis standing in a square of sunshine to my left smoking a cigarette.

For the first time in six months, I really wanted to ask if she had an extra.

"Thank you for helping my friend's wife," I said instead.

She turned, flicking ash to the ground. "No problem. That was the guy with the severed carotid, right?"

"I suppose y'all don't see those every day."

"We see them more than you'd think, but most of the time it's an accident or someone gets pissed and blindly hacks into it. I've never seen one as precise as the trauma crew said your friend's was."

"I feel very lucky we got to him when we did."

She glanced at my badge. "Any idea how it happened?"

I shook my head.

"Weird case. Our best trauma nurse said the incision—that's the word she used, like he was cut with a scalpel—was only about an inch long. So whoever did it knew right where to cut and how deep to go to find the artery, but the clean cut is probably what saved his life."

My eyebrows puckered right along with my lips. "I'm sorry?"

"When a major artery is completely severed, the separated sides retract into the sheath that surrounds it, which stymies the flow of blood. I mean, he would've bled out eventually, but you're talking about 20 minutes, not two. Most cases of a severed carotid are shallower cuts that open one side of it, but don't cut it all the way through. That's a much more serious injury because the blood keeps gushing." She paused and made a face. "Sorry. It's your friend, and you're probably not as fascinated by this stuff as I am."

"On the contrary." I pulled out my phone and clicked on the voice recorder. "Would you mind explaining all that again?"

She flashed a smile that said she used whitening strips to mask her nicotine habit. "Sure thing."

I had it all saved in my phone and scribbled in my notes for good measure by the time Graham pulled up in my truck. Thanking her, I waved as I jogged over and climbed into the passenger seat.

"No forced entry at the lab," Graham said as I blurted, "This guy has more than a rudimentary knowledge of anatomy."

We both took a breath as he backed the truck out and turned it toward the F Company offices.

6

Archie was already in the main conference room at F Company, leaned back in a big leather office chair chatting with a dark-haired man in a Waco PD polo and khakis.

"Faith McClellan, Graham Hardin, this is Sergeant Jorge Cortez. He works special victims and violent crimes at WPD and is one of the best detectives in the city."

Cortez rose and offered a hand for us to shake. "Your record is the stuff of local legend, Miss McClellan." He flashed a bright white smile under a thick, dark mustache. "It's an honor to meet you, and I'm more than a little excited to work with you."

"Archie, you're overselling me again." I returned the smile with my most confident one, feeling it was warranted for the first time since we walked into the lab that morning—one of the most decorated Rangers in history with nearly thirty years on the job, Archie had friends everywhere. Waco isn't a large city, and this guy knew its violent criminals.

We'd get our man.

"I actually hadn't said a word, that was all you, McClellan." Archie tossed me a marker. "I'm sure you're itching for the board. Check out the upgrade."

I turned to the wall and found that the extra-large hanging whiteboard I was used to working had been removed, along with a five-foot-tall section of the wall that ran the length of the large room. In its place was a flush, shiny new section of integrated whiteboard. "Consider it a wedding gift from Boone," Archie said with a wink. "All the whiteboard you could ever want."

"Wedding gift? When is the big day?" Cortez resumed his seat.

"Next Saturday," Graham said.

"You're a lucky man, Hardin."

"I'm well aware."

I pulled the cap off the marker. "Y'all are going to make me blush," I said, turning the attention of everyone in the room back to the case. "Jim Prescott is the best of the best at finding clues to why a body is on his autopsy table. Someone tried to murder him today in the process of taking a body out of the lab, and it's not a leap to say they went to the lab because they wanted to make sure he didn't have a chance to examine our Jane Doe."

Everyone murmured agreement.

"But Jim got up and went to the lab in the middle of the night because he can't sleep when there's an interesting case waiting for his attention," Graham said.

"Even when he's supposed to be on a getaway with his wife." I went to the board, putting Jim's name as the header for one list and Jane Doe for another a few feet away.

"How big is your friend?" Cortez asked. "Would it take a big guy to take him down?"

"Probably fairly big, yeah," Graham said. "Though strength and stealth are variables we can't leave out of that."

"When he comes out of surgery we can try to ask the doctors if there was a particular angle to the wound. It's not always something they even notice when they're trying to stop someone from dying, but if it was tilted egregiously either way, they should be able to tell us. That helps give a ball-park height differential. Which side of his neck was the wound on?" Cortez asked.

"The right," I said, writing it down as I went. "Assuming the attacker grabbed him from behind before he wounded him, that means he's left-handed."

"But given the orientation of the doors in the lab and Jim's tendency to favor the left side of the table, it may have been a head-on assault," Archie said.

I made another note. "That would take more of a strength and size advantage. And the killer would be more likely to have defensive wounds, too."

"We can try swabbing Prescott's nails when he comes through surgery," Cortez said. "Not sure if there's anything to be found, but my guy at the lab is pretty good and he'll give it his best shot."

I smiled a thank you everyone's assumption that Jim would be okay like a balm for my worried brain. I needed to believe it so I could focus.

"Jim's artery was severed by someone who knew exactly where to find it and how deep to cut—but didn't realize that if they cut too far, he'd actually have a better chance of survival."

"Venous retraction," Cortez said. "I've seen it save many a life."

"Here's hoping Jim makes that list," Archie said somberly.

"The nurse I spoke to said the trauma team used the word 'incision' for the cut on Jim's neck." I wrote it on the board and turned to look at Archie. "Were all the surgical implements accounted for in the lab?"

"The scalpel was missing."

I wrote that down as well, my blood pressure spiking at the thought of someone hacking into my friend with his own scalpel.

"So probably a weapon of opportunity," Graham said.

"And more for our 'the killer didn't think anyone would be there' column." I made a note, moving to the left and starting a list for Jane Doe.

"I know Jim had her on the table when he called me because he told me we needed to come see for ourselves," I said.

Archie shook his head, his lips disappearing into a grim line. "It's the weirdest goddamn thing I've ever seen. And I've seen a whole lot of weird in my years at this job. What kind of sicko steals a corpse?"

"The kind who thinks that corpse is going to give up some clues." I put that point first on my list before I turned to Graham. "Did you guys notice if

Jim's voice recorder was there? It's little and silver, just a tiny bit bigger than a pen. He's been using it since I was a brand-new deputy."

Graham pulled a notebook from his hip pocket and flipped pages. "I don't have it on my list."

I turned and locked eyes with my fiancé, my partner for so many years we often had the ability to finish each other's sentences. "This guy knew too much."

"He got into the lab without busting the door," Graham said.

"He used the scalpel like he knew what he was doing," I replied. "He took the recorder."

"The son of a bitch works there," Graham said.

"I'm thinking that's not a huge leap," I said. "It could explain what Jim said about the missing parts, too."

Archie inhaled sharply and coughed twice. "I'm sorry?"

It had been a long day to not even be nine a.m. yet.

"We didn't even get to tell you. That's why Jim called us to the lab this morning. He went to do the autopsy and found that not only had she been sewn up postmortem, but she was missing organs."

"What. In the actual fuck?" Archie's jaw hung loose and I snorted because laughing was better than crying. Or rolling up into the fetal position in the corner.

Archie Baxter was the very definition of badass. A decorated Ranger who'd solved more crimes, fought more battles, run down more suspects, and put more bad guys away than most cops see in their entire careers by roughly double, he was still going strong at fifty-eight. And nothing bothered him. Let alone scared him.

I added *Lab employee?* to the list on the board.

"Um. Y'all?" Cortez's high pitch drew my eyes from the board. His were wide.

"What's up?" I asked when he didn't say anything else.

"She's not the only one. Missing organs, that is."

7

Knowing she's going to die makes it easier, in a way.

The cuts can be slightly less precise. He can work faster. And when a procedure takes five hours and a heart is only viable for six, faster matters.

Indeed, it's everything.

He unbuttons her blouse. Pulls on his gloves. Checks the machines.

Everything is ready. He works in order of what can last outside her body the longest: liver, small intestine, lungs, heart.

His eyes burn, the heat and glare of the portable studio light harsher than the wind whipping around the corners of the empty building. His shoulders scream, his hands tire.

He keeps cutting. No cauterizing this time because bleeding doesn't matter when there's no heart to keep pumping blood. Bleeding out might even be a mercy if he got the anesthesia wrong. It was, after all, his weakest rotation.

Resecting the vessels and arteries around the heart is painstaking work even when you know this patient won't live, as you pray your recipient will. Clean cuts, a sure hand, and the ability to cope with playing God are all handy skills for this endeavor.

Just breathe.

He lifts the heart free when the last vessel is cut, packaging it carefully in Celsior and saline and placing it in the top of the ice box.

A lump fills his whole throat, panic rising as he fights for breath for a moment. Tears well and spill over. He can't tell if they're laced with regret or relief. Sometimes he wonders how much of a difference there is between the two anymore.

He turns back and sets to work repairing what he can. Sutures, bathing cloths, clean clothes. Careful to focus on his hands and his work, he doesn't look at her face. It's too much.

"I'm so sorry it had to end this way," he whispers. "Thank you."

Moving her to the plastic isn't easy, but he manages, laying her on one edge and stooping to roll from there.

He opens three gallons of bleach and dumps them on the floor, going after the blood with a mop, pushing it toward the drain. Just in case.

Almost done.

Her resting place is ready. He pulls out his phone and checks the camera. The room is dark, the door closed. Hefting her to his shoulder, he moves quickly through dark concourses that were once familiar, comforted by the memories of long-ago laughter.

He'll laugh again. When this is over.

"This is the only one. It's a fair trade if this is the only one." The muttered words hold little conviction as he places her body in the closet and adjusts the camera.

Running back to the bathrooms for his equipment, he hears voices.

Shit.

He scurries to an enclave in the wall, a rat running from daylight, laying a hand on a door that's probably locked.

Women. Four of them.

Sinks run.

Toilets flush.

Minutes tick off the heart's already short shelf life.

It feels like a thousand lifetimes come and go before he hears them talking again, carefree and too loud, their voices fading with their footsteps into the recesses of the old building.

"At least I chose the right door," he says to no one in particular.

He breaks down the makeshift bypass pump and the monitor, shouldering the bag he packs them in before he snatches up the ice box, the temperature at six degrees, and runs for the exit.

She's the only one.

Somehow he knows already that it's not the truth.

8

"Every damn time I think I've seen everything, some asshole figures out how to be more disgusting than every asshole that came before him." Archie laced his fingers behind his head. "If I wasn't already sitting down, I'd need to."

My eyes were locked on Cortez. "How much do you know? And whose case are we talking about?"

I hadn't seen a news report on a murder with missing body parts lately, that was for damned sure. Headlines like that tend to jump out at people in my line of work.

"It was my case. Dispatch thought it was a prank and hung up on her the first two times she called."

"She was alive?" I didn't even bother to try to hide my horror.

His lips vanished beneath the mustache for a second. "She woke up in a motel room with a sharp pain in her back and one leg numb. When she saw blood on the sheets, she called 9-1-1."

"Name?"

"Marcy Finelli."

I added a column heading a few inches down the wall and scribbled the details he'd already reeled off.

"How is she now?"

"Don't know. She took off about a month after I met her. At that time, her leg still didn't function fully," Cortez said. "The doctor said she was lucky the nerve was just nicked and not severed, though."

"Any leads?" Graham asked.

"Hard to come by. Prostitutes aren't used to opening up to the cops, you know?"

Ah-ha. I scribbled that down. "So the guy was a john? And a new one, I assume?"

Cortez sighed. "I wish I could say that narrowed it down, but...She swore she only remembered meeting a guy at a bar and him telling her they should get out of there after a couple of dances. It was dark, there were strobe and blacklights in the place...she couldn't tell us much except that he's probably average height. She said he was about this much taller than her"—he held one hand about five inches above his head—"which would put him between five nine and five eleven, most likely."

I added that to my list.

"And does she know how she got to the motel?"

"She said she didn't remember anything after he asked her to leave the bar. We tried having the department shrink work with her to see if we could get anything that might be more helpful back for her. I never could get a read on whether she honestly didn't remember, or was afraid to say."

"Could be either. The brain does protect itself," I said. "And if there was ever anything it would want to be protected from..." I shuddered, tapping the marker against my thigh. "Jesus."

"You said the pain was in her back," Graham said. "So he took her kidney?"

"Like right out of the old campfire story," Cortez confirmed. "That's why our dispatchers didn't believe her at first. The only thing different was that she was sewn up pretty neatly and there wasn't any ice involved. I was the second one on the scene, and it's not one I will ever forget." He shook his head. "I was shocked she was talking to us. It was a lot of blood. Like, a lot."

"She wasn't screaming?" I felt my brows shoot up.

"Adrenaline," Cortez said. "Best we could figure."

"But a doctor confirmed her kidney had been cut out?" Graham asked.

"I have the ultrasound in my report," Cortez said.

"So where did your investigation go?" Archie asked. "Did y'all drop it when she disappeared?"

All eyes stayed on Cortez, who shifted in the seat. "Do you know how many cases we have backlogged, how many victims are there and willing to talk, just waiting for help?"

Archie nodded. "I do. And I'm not passing judgment on you, Sergeant. I've heard nothing but good things about how determined and talented an investigator you are. I was simply trying to do what I seem to do best: cut through the bullshit and figure out what we're dealing with and where we're starting from."

"The case was thin—and that's probably putting it generously. The cameras inside the club were functional, but we didn't get anything we could really use. She arrived alone via the front doors a little before ten that night, we got her in the edges of the frame of the camera on the bar by the register from ten to ten-thirty, but we can't see who she's talking to. She moved away from the bar just after ten-thirty and there's nothing after that."

"She didn't leave by the front door?" Archie said.

Cortez shook his head.

"They don't have a camera on the back?" I asked.

"The landlord has one that sweeps the alley every ninety seconds. The owner said he's never had trouble out there so didn't install his own. We figure she must've left that way, but the feed doesn't show it."

I spun back to face them. "We need the feed from the two weeks prior to the incident. Everything they might still have."

Archie sent me a wink, a proud smile lighting his long face.

Cortez drummed his fingers on the table. "I checked the preceding three nights per procedure, but she hadn't been in recently and we didn't spot any suspicious behavior."

"I don't want to just see night footage, I want everything they have. Days too," I said.

"The victim said she'd never been there before," Cortez said. "Another girl told her she'd had good luck and the management looked the other way there, so she decided to go try it out. Her luck was not so good, but spending hours poring over film she already told us she's not in benefits nobody."

"I'm not looking for her, I'm looking for whoever cut her up." I fiddled with the marker cap. "Someone knew the placement of the cameras and the run cycle of the one on the back door. Which means it wasn't our ripper's first time in the place."

"Or someone spotted the camera pointed at the register and got lucky at the back door," he said. "Which is just as likely."

I took a breath. I wasn't trying to insult the guy—like he said, his desk was weighed down every day by three times the files we'd see in a month, and his point about the cameras was a logical one. "No offense intended, Sergeant. It's my job to see things other people don't, and a killer with enough knowledge of human anatomy to remove a kidney without killing someone is smarter than average. Just turning every rock, that's all."

He shrugged. "I suppose. But how is the film going to help? It's not like this guy would be shooting tequila in a shirt with a kidneys-for-sale logo on it."

I snorted. "If only it were so easy." I turned back to the board and surveyed it. "You said she'd never been in there before?"

"Correct. She said the girl who recommended she try working the place was supposed to meet her, but never showed up."

"Why not?" I scribbled on the board.

"Victim was kind of new in town, so she said she didn't know many people. Her living situation was sketchy, from what I gathered. I think she might've been sleeping in her car, but I couldn't ever get her to say."

Graham met my gaze over Cortez's head. "It would be helpful to see the file, if someone can messenger it over," I said.

"Sure thing." Cortez shrugged. "Hell, fresh eyes on it might see something I didn't." He pulled out his phone and made a call. Hanging up, he said, "It'll be here in twenty minutes."

"Thanks."

I turned my attention back to Archie. "I'm guessing you didn't get any prints from the lab this morning," I said.

"They got some, sure. But if your killer is on staff there, prints aren't going to tell us shit," he said. "Like you said, this one seems to be smarter than our garden variety slasher. I'll get a call if they found anything that's not what we expect to see."

His phone rang as soon as his lips closed.

"Baxter." He raised it to his ear.

We all watched as his brow furrowed. "Can you send it to me? I'll see what my crew can do with it. Sure thing. Thank you."

He ended the call and laid the phone on the table. "The cameras at the lab picked up someone leaving with a body bag at 5:57 this morning," he said. "No identifying characteristics other than the perp was male, average height from references on the building, and strong. He had our Jane Doe slung over one shoulder like a loaf of bread and was moving like the building was on fire."

"Because he'd just assaulted a state official," I said.

"The guy said they couldn't make out any blood," Archie said. "And that's not all. He parked in the vacant lot next door, out of reach of any camera."

"So we have no vehicle information."

"Right."

"Their cameras are old and shitty and it was still dark when we pulled up at five after six, so I'm not holding out a lot of hope, but I'd like our cyber team to take a crack at it."

"Me too," Archie said. "They're sending it."

I glanced at Cortez. "We can get a copy for your team too."

"I'd appreciate that. It's still technically my case." He caught my eyes with his warm brown ones. "I know our discussion so far hasn't inspired a lot of confidence in my abilities, but you have my promise that we will find the person who did this to your friend, Miss McClellan. The folks who work down at that lab make it possible for us to put scumbags away. I'm not looking to have word get out that they can be attacked with anything less than full repercussions."

His jaw set when he stopped speaking, indignation sparking in his eyes.

"Thank you, Sergeant. I am thrilled to have your expertise on Jim's side." I capped the marker and joined them at the table, picking up coffee that had long since gone cold and taking a long swig anyway. Before I put it down, the buzzer for the front door sounded.

"That's my file." Cortez stood, and Graham scooted away from the door so he could open it.

"Stolen organs. Missing bodies." I buried my hands in my hair on both sides of my head and barked a sharp laugh. "I admit, I'm so jaded I thought we really had seen it all, gentlemen."

"Even I've never seen anything like this," Archie said.

"I've never even read about anything like this. It's straight out of the you-couldn't-make-this-shit-up files." Graham crossed to take a seat at the table as Cortez returned waving a file that wasn't nearly as thick as I had hoped.

I put the marker on the table and held out one hand, opening the folder to the photos before I laid it in the middle where everyone could see.

An angry red welt surrounded black stitches pulled through pale skin tight enough to make it pucker, a no-tell motel king-size bed sporting sheets more than half soaked in drying, reddish-brown blood, a blood-spattered motel sink and shower, and several staging shots of the room.

I paused on one of a shoe print in the grimy motel carpet. It had measuring markers as a men's size 10. "Did y'all ever ID the type of shoe?"

Cortez reached for the report. "It's an Adidas walking shoe, sold for men as evidenced by a slightly wider width and differing tread pattern than the women's version," he read, flipping the page to a product photo from a website. I went back to the crime scene photos, finding one of the victim's ashen face pinched with pain.

"She's gorgeous when she's not miserable," I said with the confidence of a former pageant queen who had spent years seeing the most beautiful women in America before breakfast—a smoky eye, some blue-undertoned red lipstick, and clean, styled hair would make the girl in the photo a knockout. She had the brand of rare beauty that actually opened doors—and not to the kind of motel rooms in the evidence photos.

Cortez shrugged. "I guess."

"She confessed to turning tricks?" I asked, tapping the marker on the table in a slow rhythm.

"She said the girl she was supposed to meet told her it was an easy place for pickups, and she could make good money."

"But she didn't say she actually had any experience at this?" I pointed to the shoe. "A woman who looks like this one could with a little makeup and the help of a hairbrush rarely needs to trade sex for money—at least in so blatant a sense. Certainly, she's the type who would draw four figures an hour, which means if she were really in that business, she'd know better than to leave a club with a guy in dad sneakers."

I looked around the table and found three blank stares directed at me.

"What do his shoes have to do with anything?"

I flipped to the catalog photo of the sneakers. "These are not suitable club attire when you're trying to attract women like her."

"Forgive me if I'm being stupid, but...so what?" Cortez asked. "If he was paying her and he had the money, why would she care if he was wearing kind of dorky shoes?"

"Those shoes and this motel room don't match the kind of money this woman would be making as a call girl, which makes me think she was new to the game. Maybe even brand new, which probably equals pretty desperate for money. Didn't you say she had just moved here? And you got the idea she was broke?"

"Correct on both counts."

"Did she say where she moved from?"

He shook his head. "I asked and she just stared at the table. When I repeated the question, she whispered that it didn't matter, so light that the tape didn't pick it up. For the record, she said 'nowhere.' I figured she was running from something."

"Seems maybe she still is. What did her background turn up?"

Cortez flipped a page in the folder. "Not much. She has a car, a 2019 Nissan with an Oklahoma registration. We ran an all-points on it for a few days after she skipped town and didn't find it. No employment history. DOB July 19 of '99. Previous address was a ranch in a town called Broken Arrow, but the bank foreclosed on the property more than a year ago, and she didn't own it."

"Did you find whoever did?"

"Why would I look for them?" He seemed genuinely confused. "I had an assault case where the victim disappeared before we arrested her attacker. The story was wild, she was a bit of a mess, and then she was gone. Unfortunately, we have more crime in this city than we have good detectives, which is why I'm still spending fifty hours a week on investigations and another twenty doing paperwork instead of moving to the desk and running the section full time like I was supposed to when I got promoted to sergeant over a year ago. I saw no reason to try to find her if she didn't want to be found."

"The dead body that disappeared from the forensic lab this morning might prove to be a good reason." I kept the edge out of the words with a lot of effort. I needed his help more than I needed to give him a lesson in the benefits of thorough detective work. He seemed like a smart guy. If it turned out this case was pivotal to the missing Jane Doe—or Jim's injury—Cortez would notice, and I bet he'd never "move on" from a crime that weird and violent again.

I turned to make a note about the parents under Marcy's name on the board. "I'd like to copy that file so we have our own set of documents," I said before looking back at Cortez. "Because it sure seems like Marcy might be material to finding the guy who attacked Jim, and keeping track of everything that jumps out at me is how I work."

"And how you work has never missed a collar."

"Exactly."

"By all means, see what else you notice that I didn't think to." He nudged the folder closer.

"I assume this motel has no registration log?" I asked.

"Oh there's a book. But half the lines are signed with pseudonyms, whether they go with John Doe, like our guy, or try to be clever like this one." Cortez flipped to the log copy and pointed to a line that said Mya Fair.

I snorted. "Paid with cash?"

"Yep. They still had the bills, but we couldn't get a print off them."

"Damn, he thought of everything," Graham muttered.

"He missed something," I said. "They always do. We just have to figure out what it is."

I flipped pages until I found the background report with the address in

Oklahoma and the names of the property's owners: Barbie and Fred Green-field. But she went by Finelli.

"So the last known address is owned by people she may or may not have been related to." I added the names to the board and capped my marker. "Archie, can you see what you can turn up on these folks while we go talk to whoever we can find at this nightclub?"

9

"These places always look weird to me in the daylight. Like going to Disney World and having the lights come on inside Space Mountain," Graham said in a low voice as we stepped into the empty bar and looked around. Ten-foot ceilings were rimmed by thick crown molding, the flooring marble and wood, the bar polished and gleaming.

I nodded agreement. Absent the blacklights, strobes, and pulsing music, clubs like this one had always stricken me as just a shade less creepy than a dark, empty school. And we chase human monsters for a living.

"It's nicer than I would've thought from the grainy video stills," I observed, looking around the stage and dance floor, the entire room trimmed out to the kind of high-end finish level my mother would nod approval over. Not that Ruth McClellan would put a pinky toe into a night-club. The very thought was enough to make me snicker right out loud, which drew a look from Cortez.

"Nothing," I said, pinching my lips together before I cleared my throat and called, "Anyone here?"

A man appeared in what looked like the mouth of a hallway at the other end of the long, black granite-topped bar lining the near side of the room. "We don't open for a few hours yet." He stuck a pen behind one ear under shaggy, light brown hair, offering an apologetic smile.

"We're not here to party lunchtime away," I said, striding to the end of the bar and extending a hand when he rounded it to meet me with a slight furrow between his brows. "Faith McClellan, Texas Rangers. We have some questions about a young woman who was attacked."

"Another one?" His eyes, an incredible shade of blue I wasn't even sure mother nature could replicate in a Texas sky, popped wide.

"No—" Cortez started to speak but stopped when I slid the heel of my boot into his shin. Not hard enough to hurt, just a tap to let him know I wanted him to hush up and let the guy talk.

"How many have there been?" I asked. Not every assault gets reported to the police, and if this guy was here in the middle of the day, he was probably around enough to know all the recent gossip. Gossip is often more valuable to a criminal investigation than dusting for fingerprints, especially if you know what to listen for.

"I mean, more than usual lately." He leaned on the bar, folding his arms and shaking his head. "I'm damn glad to see y'all, to tell you the truth. If this gets out, no woman in her right mind would set foot in this place. And no women means no business at all, which leaves me out of a job, you know?" His full lips twisted into a rueful grin. The hair, the eyes, and the lips combined with high cheekbones and a perfect dusting of stubble made him a hell of an attractive package. I wondered if a lack of women patronizing the bar really concerned him from a work perspective, or if he was more worried about going home alone after work. I checked his hands and noted the wedding ring on the left one. Or not.

"Sure. This is Sergeant Cortez from APD special crimes. Do you mind if we take notes? Or record our conversation?"

"Whatever you need. I've been thinking of calling the cops myself no matter what Sonny said, but the stories are so weird I wasn't sure anyone would believe them. Or be able to do anything if they did."

Graham stepped forward and I introduced him.

"Where are my manners? Brian Maxwell. I'm the head bartender."

"So what kinds of things have been concerning you, Brian?" I asked, pulling out a pad and pen as Graham set his phone on the bar and clicked the recorder on.

"We've had three women in the past four weeks found in the ladies' room late at night, passed out on the floor. Every one of them had bruises on their arms, but they all said their clothes were just as they left them. So, you know…" He let the sentence trail, his eyes on his gray tasseled loafers.

"They weren't sexually assaulted?" I asked.

"Right."

"What kind of bruises?" I asked.

"Big bluish-purple ones." He held out his arm, pointing to several places on his forearm and the back of his hand. "But just on their arms. And the last girl, it was just one arm. None of them remembered falling or being hit, and none of them are sore anywhere else."

"That is…weird," I said for lack of a more fitting word, my eyes skipping from Brian to Cortez to Graham. "And you didn't think this warranted a call to the police?"

"At first, me and Sonny just hoped it was a weirdo one-off thing and it wouldn't happen again," Brian said. "Then when it did, we figured if the ladies wanted the cops involved, they'd call. Hell, the first three didn't even go to the hospital. They came to before the ambulances got here and insisted they were fine and left. But after the fourth one, well…people talk, you know? I don't want the place to go to shit. Like I said, I was going to talk to Sonny today about getting something done. We can't put cameras in the bathroom without breaking the law ourselves, but I was thinking maybe a female bouncer, you know? Like a lady we could pay to hang out in there and watch things for us. But we never settled on a plan."

"Show us the restroom where this occurred?" I asked. Not that we'd get any forensic evidence from a public bathroom days after an assault. But I wanted to look around.

He waved for us to follow him, rounding the end of the bar and disappearing into a hallway.

My eyes scanned the area as we walked. No exits, just two restrooms and a third door marked "employees only."

"What's in there?" I asked, pointing.

"Cleaning supply storage," Brian said, opening the door to reveal just that, on stacked shelves that came nearly all the way to the door frame, the foot or so of extra room filled in with yellow plastic folding "wet floor" signs.

He closed it and turned to the ladies' room, opening the door and waving us inside. It was a small room, with two stalls and one sink, hand towels stacked on a small table in one corner.

I opened the doors and peered into each stall. They were narrow, but unremarkable. The ceiling was acoustic tile. I pointed. "How large is the overhead space?"

Brian shrugged. "Big enough for the HVAC ducts, I guess. I've never looked."

Cortez pulled a penlight from his pocket and stepped up onto a toilet seat, balancing as he pushed a tile up and looked in. "Maybe three feet of clearance. It wouldn't be impossible to get up here, but it would be difficult."

I eyed the sink. "Much more likely someone hid in a stall and jumped her from behind while she was at the mirror." I turned to Brian. "We'd like to see any camera footage you have for the nights this happened," I said.

Brian held the bathroom door open for the three of us, pointing back the way we came. "The computer is in the office behind the bar."

I cleared my throat, Marcy Finelli and her Frankenstein stitches fresh in my head. "The ladies who were attacked but didn't call the police. Did they have a reason to be averse to police attention?"

Brian glanced back over his shoulder and shrugged. "Maybe?"

We rounded the corner into a surprisingly spacious office, and he fiddled with the mouse on the desk to wake the computer monitor. I gave him a few beats before I asked again. "If they were prostitutes, I need to know. I'm not going to bust them for solicitation, but it could be important to finding whoever is doing this."

Brian's shoulders tensed, then slumped. "I don't ask, you understand." He spoke to the keyboard on the desk.

"But the bartender always knows everything," I said.

A dry laugh escaped his throat. "Not by a long shot, ma'am, but I am good at watching folks. And I would say your suspicion about these ladies, wherever it came from, is very likely right on. That's part of the reason we didn't know what to make of this. Not for sure, anyway. Wondered myself if it might have been a pimp beating them up and they just didn't want to say." He clicked play on the video feed. "This is the most recent night. She was found by another customer at 11:26, so I'm starting from 10:45. That's the last time the bar camera caught anyone coming out of the hallway that leads to the bathrooms, so I'm pretty sure it was empty afterward."

"But you didn't see anyone go in?" Cortez asked.

Brian waved a hand at the screen. "I wasn't working that night. See for yourself."

Every eye stayed on the screen, mine barely even blinking, as the program ran through the 40 minutes of film at two and a half times normal speed. As Brian said, a woman came out of the hallway at 10:46, and then the area was empty until a petite, curvy woman in a sequined black dress disappeared into the hallway only to come careening back around the corner on four-inch heels at 11:27, flapping her arms. Her distress was palpable even on the grainy security feed.

"I'll be damned," Graham said.

Brian clicked pause. "After this it's just the paramedics coming in and taking her out of the building. She was out cold."

"What about before she went in there? Do you remember enough about what she looked like to find her in the crowd for me on the bar camera?" I asked.

"I can try," he said, reaching for the mouse. "I mean, yes, I know what she looked like. She'd been here a few times, I recognized it when my staff described her." He clicked the bar and dragged the feed backward in time, watching the minute reading at the bottom of the screen. "I just don't know if she was anywhere you can see. I've been telling Sonny for weeks we needed to add more cameras to get the rest of the room and not just the register."

"How long have you worked here, Brian?" Cortez asked, his tone conversational.

"About three months now, I guess," Brian said.

"And you're the de facto manager?" Cortez let one eyebrow go up. "Did the owner bring you in to do something specific? The person I spoke with last time I was here was a woman."

"Sonny isn't always the easiest to handle." The twist to Brian's lips as he paused and looked up said he was trying to be kind. "The girl who was here before me didn't last long, and the other bartenders don't want to be in charge because they don't want to have to deal with him. That's the bargain for keeping them slinging drinks: they don't have to talk to him. I play the middleman."

Sonny sounded sufficiently interesting to warrant a visit, with women being attacked in and around his club.

Brian clicked play on the video again.

"This is her, right here." He pointed to the screen. "Her name is Courtney. I haven't seen her come back in since, but I saw her a few times before this night. She drinks Jack and Diet Coke, never more than two in a night, and she leaves with a different guy every time."

I reached over him to pause the feed when the woman turned her head, studying the contours of her slightly pointed face and wishing for about the ten millionth time in my career that security footage was higher resolution.

She took her drink, handed a bartender with floppy dark hair cash, and walked back out of the frame toward the dance floor.

"Do you remember everyone who comes to get a drink?" Graham asked.

"When they turn up injured in the bathroom a few days later, they stick out." Brian's words were clipped.

Graham watched him with slightly wide eyes, but stayed quiet.

"Thank you for your time," I said to Brian, handing him a card. "If anything else happens that even strikes you as a little odd, please call me. And I'd like to get a copy of that footage to have our computer guys review, too. Every night there was an attack, the whole evening."

He ran one hand through his hair. "That will take a couple of days."

"Of course. You just give me a call when I can pick it up, and I'll come by. It would be fantastic if the owner could be here at that time."

Brian's lips settled into a firm line. "I'm not sure you'll say that after you've met Sonny, but sure. Whatever I can do to be helpful."

I pointed to a business card holder on the desk. "Can I have one of those?"

He picked up the front one and handed it to me, watching me slide it into my notebook. "I'll call you as soon as the footage is ready."

I put my hand out for him to shake and turned for the door as my phone started buzzing in my pocket.

I pulled it free, my eyes rolling back in my head as I glanced at the screen. Skye Morrow.

"She won't leave you alone until you answer her," Graham said, looking over my shoulder.

"I know." I stabbed the green talk button hard enough to hurt my finger and put the phone to my ear as we crossed to the doors and stepped out into warm sunshine and a light breeze, the kind of Texas spring day that was perfect for a park or a lake. Unless we were trying to catch a murderer.

"I'm not telling you anything," I said, not bothering with pleasantries.

Skye's throaty, entirely-too-deep-for-a-human-her-size laugh made me move the phone away from my ear.

"It's cute that you still think I need you to tell me anything in order to land my story," she said through the last peals. "As it happens, I think I might be able to tell you something about what happened to Jim Prescott this morning. Or at least, I can tell you who to ask about it. But I believe now I'm going to need you to say 'please.'"

10

Skye Morrow could get under my skin better than anyone drawing breath —including my father. She not only knew that, she reveled in it.

I tossed Graham my keys and headed for the passenger door.

"Please." It slid between my teeth, nearly against my will.

She barked a short chuckle that dripped glee. "I see all those charm lessons in your pageant days weren't for nothing, Faith."

I counted to seven as I inhaled, my nostrils flaring. "What do you want, Skye?"

"This is the thanks I get when I try to help you?"

"I'm quite sure you have never tried to help anyone more than yourself." I couldn't help the words, they slid out before I could swallow them.

There went the damn laugh again, as piercing to my eardrum as Freddy Krueger working over a blackboard.

"You have always been insightful, Faith," Skye said. "Where are you?"

"Near the university campus in Waco."

"Perfect. Meet me at Alta Vista Park in thirty minutes. I have a proposition for you."

She hung up before I could say anything else. Because as fucking infuriating as she could be, Skye was damn good at her job. She knew cops inside out, and she understood—in a way I had spent many a sleepless night considering from every psychological angle—what made criminals tick.

She knew I'd be there. I had to know what she was going to say. Just like she would if her spiky Louboutin were on the other foot. It might be the only similarity between the two of us I'd ever acknowledge.

I tucked the phone into my pocket and shook my head. "It seems we're taking a detour through Alta Vista Park."

"What did she want?" Graham asked as he unlocked my truck.

"Who?" Cortez glanced at his watch, stepping toward his unmarked WPD sedan. "I have other cases that need my attention if you two are tied up for a while."

"I appreciate all your help today, Sergeant. Do you have a couple of detectives we can borrow for a few days to conduct some interviews?"

"I'm sure I can find you someone," he said. "What sort of interviews did you have in mind?"

"I think we have enough circumstantial evidence to think there's a chance our guy works at the forensic lab in some capacity. I'd like the employees brought in for questioning. Anyone matching the limited description of our killer or displaying suspicious behavior or holes in their story, have your guys hold them over and call me." I handed him a card.

"No problem," he said. "I'll stay in the loop and update you a few times a day."

"Can you get a list and get started today?"

"Sure thing. I'll let you know what we find." Cortez slid into his car and hung a U-turn as Graham and I got into the truck.

Silence settled over the cab like a favorite sweater as Graham drove toward the park, located on the southern outskirts of town.

I flipped through my notes, circling things here and there and jotting new questions down. The fourth one I scribbled deserved to be asked out loud.

"If an ambulance took that woman Brian mentioned, the one who was assaulted, from the club to an emergency room, the doctors are mandatory reporters. Where would she have been routed from there, I wonder?"

"Paramedics would go to Sparks from there, it's too far out of downtown for Memorial," Graham said. "But the bartender said she didn't press charges. We think that's because she was working the club, right?"

"Maybe. But there should still be a routine report from a cop who had to go take her statement."

"And it would have her name." Graham's lips curved up at the corners. "Nice work, baby."

I pulled my phone out and logged into Waco's online police report portal, searching the date in my notes.

"Chloe Danielle Bremer, DOB January 28 of '97."

I scrolled. "But she didn't give an address. Or a phone number. Report says she was jumped from behind, didn't see anything, didn't want to press charges, and refused the rape kit."

"That all fits with the idea that she was there looking for johns," Graham said. "Who was the reporting officer?"

"Patrolman David King."

"Doesn't sound familiar."

"Not to me, either. But I'd like to swing by WPD headquarters at some point and see what he remembers."

Graham pulled into a space at the park, and I spotted Skye on a bench near a low, rambling oak, not a single hair on her head moving in the breeze that ruffled the baby leaves.

We strolled up to the bench and Skye pushed her wide, black-rimmed Prada sunglasses up onto her head and smiled. "If it isn't the happiest couple in Texas law enforcement."

"We like to think so." I tried to keep my tone, if not cordial, at least conversational.

Skye smirked. "Getting close to the big day for you two."

"Ever been married, Skye?" Graham asked.

"Once." Her voice softened to a tone I had never once heard from her, not even when she was afraid someone was trying to kill her and she needed my help. "Highly recommend it."

Graham and I exchanged a sideways glance at the far-off look that slackened her face from its normal hard-ass investigative reporter expression.

"Do not go making me curious about her as a person," I whispered, leaning into his shoulder to make sure she wouldn't hear me.

His shoulders shook with a laugh he kept to himself as her focus snapped back to us.

"So. What do you know?" I asked.

"Jim Prescott was examining a body, at your request, when he was attacked in the local crime lab here and the body stolen," she said.

"True," I said. "But that was in the public report."

"The fact that the body was missing a few key parts was not," Skye said, not blinking.

"You know a dozen cops and medical examiners who owe you favors, so I'm not surprised you got that out of someone." I also wasn't asking who told her. I'd prefer trying to get information out of a serial killer over Skye Morrow every day of the week. Most of them are less pathological in their narcissism. "What do you want, Skye?"

"I have an idea about who might be involved in this." She sighed, some sort of mental war with herself playing out across her face, which was weird enough to send my eyebrows up.

"Was the corpse Prescott had on the table stitched up upon discovery?" she asked.

I tipped my head to one side. Her brows furrowed ever so slightly as she waited for my answer, actually leaning forward in her seat.

"It was," I said.

"Oh sweet Jesus." She touched a hand to her face. "Do you know who the victim was or where they came from?"

"We don't have much of a background on her yet, but we'll get there," I said. "Why is this bothering you so much? I've never seen anything rattle you like this." The words were rimmed in genuine concern.

She pulled out her phone instead of answering me.

"I'm not going on the record with you on this, Skye."

"You really must think I'm stupid." Her voice was calm and professional. "It wouldn't even occur to me to ask you to, it's quite literally not worth my breath. But I think I have something you might need. And Jim Prescott is a good man whose family has been through too much in the past few years."

Graham poked my ribs, the look on his face a clear *I told you so* when I glanced at him. He'd contended for years that she wasn't as completely evil as I thought.

I still didn't buy that, but her concern for Jim appearing to take precedence over her desire for a scoop was new and different. I was interested enough in how it would play out—and what she knew—to keep standing there.

She flipped her phone around, a split screen showing a photo of two men, one older and one younger, in white lab coats. "I want to help Jim. But I have some conditions."

There was the Skye Morrow I knew and loathed.

"Such as?" I kept my tone flat.

"I do want you on the record." She licked her lips and glanced at Graham. "But not about this. I don't need you for this."

My skin flushed warm in the cool March breeze, the hairs on my arms popping to attention.

Graham's hand landed on the small of my back.

Skye just held my gaze.

"What?" I asked finally, the word coming out much sharper than I would've liked.

"I want your word that you'll sit down with me, on camera, and talk about your father." Skye's words rushed faster as my eyes widened. "It's no secret that you hate him anyway; you put him in prison, for Christ's sake. I want a half hour of your time, and your honesty. The only person who stands to be hurt is Chuck, and what do you really care about that?"

Her eyes had a pleading glimmer that was unfamiliar on her.

I sucked air through my nose for a ten count.

As much as I hated to even think it, she wasn't wrong about anything she'd said.

But I didn't want to help her. And we both knew such an interview would make the last few years of her slightly flagging career. The new producer at Channel Two wanted younger talent, and didn't care about Skye's years of experience as the most ruthless TV personality in the state.

The thing was, the white-coated guys on her phone screen looked like doctors. Given the medical bend to this case, I had to wonder if they might give us a shortcut to the person who'd hurt Jim. She really did know something, I was sure of it, because Skye is a lot of things, but a skilled actress isn't among them. She's a good liar, sure, but the body language that went along with our brief exchange about Jim and the missing body told me more than her words about how much she knew that might be relevant to my case. Something she was working on had crossed paths with our murderer.

"You won't run anything on this that might alert the killer we're onto him until we have him in custody?" I asked.

She shook her head.

"Just Chuck. Nothing else." My eyes narrowed as I said the words.

"Of course." She didn't blink, her impossibly long fake lashes not so much as wavering as she watched my face. "Do we have a deal, then?" She extended one hand, her scarlet talons making me want to recoil.

I reached for it instead. Her palm was sweaty.

That, too, was unlike the Skye I thought I knew shallow soul to fake façade.

We shook, eyes still deadlocked.

"Provided the information you have for me actually helps the investigation." I swallowed hard. Talking to the press—to Skye fucking Morrow, no less—about my family's dysfunction and the governor's bottomless narcissism wasn't something I'd ever even contemplated. It would bring its own set of issues. But I'd deal with them later if it meant she could tell me something that would actually help now. "Who are the white coats?"

"I've been following a story about healthcare access in rural and migrant communities and resulting medical malpractice for three months now, and it has spawned some dark tangents." She laced her fingers together and leaned her elbows on her knees, nodding approval as I pulled out a notepad.

"What kind of tangents?" I asked.

"I started with a lead on underprivileged and immigrant women who'd gone in for gallbladder surgery or with acute appendicitis, but woke up having had other surgeries—and missing other organs—they never consented to. From there I found a guy who had a tonsillectomy in a migrant camp when he was fifteen and woke up missing a kidney," Skye said.

I sat forward, thinking of Marcy Finelli and the bloody hotel room.

"The doctor told his parents he went into renal failure on the table and the kidney was diseased, but the guy never believed that, and now his brother needs a kidney and he's a perfect match, but he doesn't have one to donate. So I started poking around online, but it's slow-going. Are you at all familiar with the dark web?"

Graham snorted. "She's more than familiar."

I just nodded for Skye to go on.

"I've heard things about it for years, of course, but I've never had reason to do any exploring there until this story," she said.

I was genuinely shocked, which I didn't do a great job of keeping off my face.

"I'm not as evil as you like to think." Her dry tone was almost funny.

"I just figured all the cheap spyware would make it nosy reporter central," I said.

"There is still something to be said for ethics and skill in this business. I'm plenty good at getting people to talk to me," she said, almost like she knew what I was thinking. "I don't need to resort to illegal invasions of privacy."

"You're counting blackmail and badgering as skills now?" The question slipped through my lips before I could think better of it.

"Aren't they?" She raised one perfectly-threaded eyebrow and let silence fill four beats.

"Can we get back to people having their organs stolen?" Graham leaned over to try to look at her phone screen.

"This type of egregious malpractice is a horrifying problem that has plagued clinics near the border for a few years now," Skye said. "But it's spreading. Limited access to healthcare in rural and poor areas of the state is compounding it, along with a clique of doctors sporting mighty God complexes and an apparent hatred for poor and working class people."

Graham and I exchanged a glance. I'd never heard Skye sound so disgusted.

"Maybe we can help each other," I consented, jotting notes. "Do you have proof of what these people are doing?"

"Sure, but the problem is getting the women involved to go on camera," she said. "Some of them are in the country illegally, but even the ones who aren't—these are people with a strong sense of community. And the internet has given space to message boards where doctors like these trade information. They've spent years insinuating themselves into these remote practices. When the only doctor in town is arrested for mutilating his patients, who will take care of people when they get sick? So they soldier on, they grieve the children they didn't get to have, they hope their remaining kidney or chunk of liver continues to work, and they won't talk about it on the record—not to me, and not to you. They feel it's too much risk for their friends and neighbors."

Graham shook his head. "How does someone who can do this call themselves a doctor and still sleep at night? What the fuck is wrong with people?"

"It takes a lot for us to say that in our line of work," I said.

"Oh I know," Skye said. "This has been the most infuriating and heart-breakingly frustrating story I've ever run across."

"How did you find out about these women?" I asked. "If they don't talk to the press or the police, I mean."

"A nurse at University Medical Center treated a migrant farm worker's wife in November. They were following the harvest through Austin, and the woman came to the ER with abdominal pain that turned out to be an infection and internal bleeding. She told them she was pregnant because she hadn't had a period in three months. The MRI revealed that her uterus was gone. The nurse said she became hysterical when they told her, and then the husband said she'd had emergency surgery at their local clinic to remove her appendix because it was on the verge of rupture—about three months before."

"And no one at this clinic told them her uterus had been removed?" I felt a little sick.

"No. Not according to my source. She said the patient was inconsolable, but when she mentioned calling the police, she and the husband both clammed up. The nurse called our tip line because she thought I might be able to help. I've been trying ever since, but it's a rough, slow road."

"With detours, you said." I blinked, trying to keep my focus on one horror at a time.

"Right." She took a deep breath. "When I spoke with the man who lost his kidney, I was able to uncover a really repulsive black market trade. Some of the doctors are selling organs. On the internet."

Graham raised one hand. "How exactly would that even work? Are you accusing these people of murder?"

"Well, that's the thing. I didn't think I was, until I heard about what happened to Jim Prescott and why. Most of what I've been able to gather suggests they harvest organs from younger people who die or remove non-vital parts from patients during other procedures. The sort of patients who wouldn't be on UNOS's radar as donors."

"And this is done without the patients' and families' permission?"

"Yes." She scrolled through a document on her phone. "I've found evidence linking back to both of these doctors on the dark web, and I think they're running some sort of larger network." She paused. "Given your contempt for my profession, I'm not terribly worried about you talking to another journalist about this, but I have to say that I don't expect this to be shared with another reporter anyway."

"Definitely not a worry with us," Graham said.

Skye watched me. "Of course," I said.

She returned to her phone. "I never would've thought this would be a business," she said. "And I really thought I'd seen everything."

"For the right amount of money, a lot of people will turn on their ethics," I said with the conviction of a person who'd grown up seeing it happen. "Especially people who are lacking in them in the first place."

"So it seems, yes." Skye sounded genuinely puzzled, which was funny given that she'd be near the top of my personal list of unethical humans.

"But who would buy an organ?" Graham rubbed one hand over his close-cropped hair, a sign he was trying to decipher something. "Like if you need a kidney, your doctor gets you one, right?"

Skye and I exchanged a glance, and my heart filled watching the bewilderment flickering across his handsome face.

"He really is a good man." She murmured what I was thinking as I laid a hand on his arm.

"The doctor gets you on the list. But people with money and connections use them to get what they want when they want it all the time." I swallowed hard. "I hadn't ever considered this particular scenario, but I'm not sure why it would be any different now that I have."

"So they're buying their way to the front of the line?" Graham's jaw dropped, and he closed and rubbed it. "Jesus."

I let my head drop back and studied the soft, lime green baby leaves drooping off the tree branches in the still air.

"How does it work?" I fired questions at Skye as fast as they came into my head, not taking my eyes off the leaves or righting my head. "You said you think these guys are running a network? How do people find what they're looking for? How do they find a surgeon to do the transplant? Where do they do them? Rich people leapfrogging the transplant line aren't going to stand for dim rooms and folding tables like some sixties back alley abortion."

"That's why I called you," she said. "This has been slow-going, and Jim needs it to go faster. You can probably access things I can't. Like I know the organs are listed on this black market website by blood type and size and tissue markers, and that the window of viability is pretty narrow. So it has to be a well-oiled machine. I can't imagine the guys I've tracked down are the only doctors involved, because it would be way too much work for just two people. Transplant surgeries are really involved and require specific skills, and they take a whole day for one surgery."

"So how many doctors do you think we're talking about?"

"From what I've been able to figure with talking to scrupulous doctors and the listings I've seen come and go? Ten. Maybe fifteen. Scattered all over the state, not just around here."

"And how much money are we talking about?" It had to be a lot to make someone—sounded like maybe a lot of someones—risk their medical licenses. Becoming a physician is a long, grueling slog increasingly motivated more by desire to help people than the drive to amass a fortune, thanks to insurance companies.

I pulled out a notebook, jotting a note to talk to the dean at the university medical school about the possibility of young doctors or residents being lured into something like this.

"Thoughts?" Skye asked.

"Speaking of using connections: I'm pretty sure Ruth serves on a couple of charity boards with the wife of the dean of medicine at the university," I said. "I'm going to feel out his thoughts and insight into this situation."

Skye's mouth opened to object and I raised one hand. "I'll get what I can out of him without giving anything away, no worries."

"Any leads on who might be doing the purchasing?" Graham asked.

"Best I can tell, the deals are brokered by lawyers, not individuals. But I don't have names. The legal jargon in the messages I've been able to see is the basis for that assumption."

"It's a safe assumption," I said. "With the amount of cash we have to be talking about, the kind of people who can afford that would be lawyered up to make sure their investments are protected."

Graham poked at his phone screen. "Skye, you said you think the people they're taking them from are poor folks who are sick and dying?"

She sighed. "Every single thing I have right now is at least partial conjecture, but yes, matching death certificates with some of the organs I saw listed, it's the best I can come up with."

"How long before the death are the organs listed?" he asked. "Because these timeframes Google is giving me are really short. Like a heart can only be out of one body for a maximum of six hours before they need someone to put it into."

"On the ones I was able to track, it was about two or three days."

"Which means these guys have to have a place they're keeping sick people on life support for that long while they wait for buyers," Graham said. "So I guess like you said, it's a well-oiled machine."

I tapped my pen on my notebook. "And if they're moving these organs around the state, they need pilots with those timetables." I made a note. "This is getting to the realm of expensive enough to narrow the suspect pools by virtue of resources."

"But no one who bought an organ is going to admit it on the record," Skye said. "And they won't tell you, either, they'll just say they want their attorney. Which is why I gave up on the buyers as a lead a couple of weeks ago."

I tipped my head side to side. She was probably right. But I wasn't willing to concede the entire point yet. I didn't need a buyer to talk, I just needed someone who knew what happened. In a circle like the one this would have to be—like the ones I grew up in—that would be anyone from a horrified servant to a teenager—or even an adult child—with a strong moral compass and a dislike for their parents. I knew that feeling well enough to spot it in others, given the chance.

"I'll see what I can find," was all I said.

"So are you going to tell us who these doctors are and why you think they might be connected to what happened to Jim?" Graham asked.

"Was the victim ever reported missing?" Skye asked.

"Not that we were able to find," I said. "We never got a name, but WPD said the database didn't turn up anything based on her description. We're still trying to figure out who she was."

She pointed a dagger-like nail dressed in her signature blood-red polish at me. "That's why, right there." She poked at her phone screen and flipped it around for me to look at. "It was a white woman, right?"

"It was." My eyes skimmed the type on the photo of a laptop screen, getting bigger with every word.

"What?" Graham leaned in, his brow furrowing as he watched my face.

"This message was only there for forty-five minutes after I took this," Skye said. "Whoever sent it got the answer they wanted and deleted it."

"Someone desperate enough to buy a human kidney insisting it come from a white female?" Graham shook his head. "It's not like I haven't had plenty of redneck fucks say racist shit to me, but...Wow."

"And if my theory here is right, the vast majority of what these guys had available would come from people of color," Skye said.

I gestured for her to keep the phone still, reading. "There are specs in there, blood type and such." I looked at the date, flipping back through my notes. "Holy shit, Skye, I think you might be onto something."

"Did Jim ever say when he thought that woman was killed?" Graham asked. "I thought he said it was hard to tell because of the lack of decomposition."

"He did." My brain was racing to order the equation spreading in front of us. "But this post lines up with two of the weird assaults we heard about this morning."

His brows lifted. "Oh shit. Women who had nobody. Bruises on their arms..."

"I bet someone was checking their blood type," I said.

I turned back to Skye. "Can you text me that?" I pointed to her screen. "And I need to know the names of the doctors you suspect."

"What are you talking about, assaults?"

"If anything comes of it, you will have it all first," I said.

She eyed me skeptically. And not without reason, I knew.

"You have my word, Skye. And my thanks, if this pans out."

She pecked at her screen. My phone buzzed when her text arrived a second later.

Looking at Graham, she said, "Douglas Pendergast and Bryce Little. Their practice is between Cuero and Victoria."

"We'll see what we can dig up. You're staying on it, too?"

"I'm not letting this go. Especially not now."

"We'll keep in touch." I turned back for the truck.

Skye shot off the bench and followed. "Faith."

I turned back when my hand was on the door. "Yes?"

"I hope Jim is okay. And I just wanted to say thank you... you know, for coming when I called."

"I'm glad you did."

I never thought I'd say that to her and mean it. This day was turning out to be chock full of firsts.

11

"She seem different to you today?" Graham asked as I pointed the truck toward Waco PD headquarters.

"She did. Like she was actually concerned about helping these people." I put on my blinker and slid into the left turn lane. "Can you text Cortez and tell him we're coming by there?"

He pulled out his phone and sent the message. "I've talked to Skye dozens of times and I've never seen her shaken up. It was weird, right?"

"For Skye? Yeah. But so far every single thing about this case has been fucking weird."

"True."

My phone buzzed with a text.

"Can you check that?" I asked, my eyes on the road.

"It's the caterer," he said. "He says there's a recall on organic chicken breasts because of some kind of bird flu, and he only got two-thirds of our order."

"I am not getting upset about this," I said. "I am marrying you on Saturday and that's all I care about."

"I thought your mother was planning the reception."

"I thought I should be involved," I said. "She tends to go overboard."

Graham shrugged. "So what? We're only doing this once, right?"

Right. "Can you call my mother on the speaker?"

He obliged.

"Please don't tell me you're not coming to dinner tonight," Ruth said. She never bothered with "hello."

"No, we are," I said. "Looking forward to it. I was just wondering if I could ask you a favor."

"Of course."

"I know I said I wanted to be involved in planning, but you're better at dealing with these things."

"What's wrong?" Ruth McClellan didn't miss a trick.

"Something about bird flu and a sudden shortage of chicken breasts. It's too late to change the menu."

"I will take care of it."

"It's just that there's this murder case now—" I began.

"I don't need you to tell me why, Faith," she said. "I am more than happy to help. I'll call Jean Jacques now, and if any other vendors need anything, give them my number. You and Graham will have a wonderful day. I will see to it."

"Thank you."

"See you at seven."

Graham ended the call, and I felt a bit of tension leave my shoulders. Ruth McClellan could plan a party with the very best—Graham and I could focus on the case, catch the killer, and as long as we showed up Saturday, everything would be fine.

"Dinner tonight," I said. "You warned your mother about Ruth, right?"

"Momma gets along fine with everyone," he said. "She adores you. She'll be okay handling your mother."

"Not many people can handle my mother." I parked the truck on the street in front of the high rise '70s concrete office building that housed all three divisions of the police department. "But your mom is pretty great."

"Indeed." Graham glanced at his phone. "Cortez is out on a scene, but he said use his name at the desk if we need to." He jogged up the concrete steps and pulled the front door open, nodding to the officer next to the metal detector, who looked over our badges and waved us through.

My phone buzzed in my pocket. I swallowed a groan and cursed Ruth

McClellan under my breath as I grabbed it while Graham introduced himself to the weary-eyed desk sergeant and asked to speak to the patrolman who filed the report on the assault victim from the nightclub.

The message on my screen wasn't from Ruth, though. I didn't recognize the number so I touched the box, holding my breath and whispering a prayer.

This is Pete Prescott, Jim's son. My mom wanted you to know my dad is out of surgery and in the ICU. Doc said he's not out of the woods, but he is alive. My mom says I have you to thank for that. So thanks.

I blew out a *whoosh* of air and shot Graham a thumbs up when he turned.

"Jim?" he asked.

I nodded.

"Thank God."

The sergeant cradled the phone on his desk after calling back for patrolman King and glanced between us. "Y'all talking about Jim Prescott? I heard the chatter on the radio this morning about an attack at the lab. I worked in Travis County for ten years after the academy. Never met a smarter guy. Is he all right?"

I smiled. "His son says he's out of surgery and in the ICU. The doctors aren't making promises, but he's still with us after the surgery."

"Well hallelujah." His eyes brightened, a smile stretching his fleshy face. "Everyone here will be damned glad to hear it. That shit was scary this morning, you know."

He leaned forward on the desk, eyeing us with interest for the first time since we walked in. "So are y'all working on Jim's case? You think Officer King knows something about what happened to him?"

"We think there's another case linked to this one. And that Officer King might have taken a statement from a person of interest in that one a few months back."

He blinked at me. "I didn't get your name, Miss?"

"Faith McClellan."

"As in..." His face went slack for a split second.

"He's my father."

The sergeant laughed.

Graham shot me a puzzled look and I returned a small shrug.

"I didn't mean that crooked bastard, ma'am," the officer said, shaking his head. "I was going to say 'as in, the actual Faith McClellan, standing in our lobby?' but then I realized how idiotic that sounded given that you'd just told me your name, so I was trying to play it cool." He stood and stepped down, rounding the counter and extending his hand. "It is a pleasure to meet you."

Graham stood aside, a proud smile playing around his lips. "Likewise, Officer...?"

"Eric Smithers, ma'am. Glad to know Prescott has you in his corner." I shook his hand, surprised I'd never seen him before. I live and work in Waco, it's not like I'm a total stranger to the local PD.

A lanky man in a uniform came through the door that led back to the station's bullpen, his eyebrow half up. My eyes slid sideways to find Graham's doing the same. This guy was a little old to be a patrolman. "You wanted to see me?" he said.

"King, meet the one and only Texas Ranger Faith McClellan. She's working on an important attempted murder case and she needs to speak with you. Show her and her partner back to the conference room, please."

"Sure thing."

King had a lousy poker face, confusion plain in his expression as he waved us ahead of him through the bullpen doors, pointing to the left at the first hallway intersection and then directing us to the third door on the right.

He flipped the lights on and closed the door behind us. "What exactly can I do for y'all?"

"You responded to a call a little more than a week ago about an assault at the Gray Goose nightclub on Bosque Boulevard. I need to know everything you remember about the victim. Small details might be important."

"This was the chick with the weird bruises on her arm, right?" King balanced one hip on the edge of the table when Graham and I remained standing.

"Correct," I said.

"She was wired, that girl," King said, his eyes going to a spot on the wall behind my head. "Couldn't sit still. Talking a country mile a minute. The nurse said she had real trouble getting her to hold her arm still to get blood samples."

I pulled my notebook out and jotted a list.

"What was she talking about?" Graham asked.

"That she couldn't be there, she had to go, someone was coming to pick her up." King shook his head. "Sounded like a crackhead. A looker though, for sure. But something wasn't right about her. She kept repeating the same things over and over."

"Did she tell you anything about what happened to her at the club?"

"Only that she didn't feel right, and she went to the john thinking she was going to puke, but someone came in and jumped her before she passed out."

"She didn't see who, though?"

"Said she didn't see a thing. Sounded like a rape to me, you know. Somebody drugged her drink or something. Different Saturday night, same old story."

King put one finger to his chin. "She did tell me her stuff was out of her little bag, like scattered on the floor, when she came to."

"Anything missing?"

"Nope. That's another weird part of it."

"So she wasn't robbed. And she wasn't raped? You're sure?"

"She wouldn't let them do the kit. Said she'd know if she'd been raped and she hadn't." His tone took on a defensive edge. "I asked her all the questions, you know—tried to get her to tell me why she didn't want to press charges. But she wouldn't say. She told me she didn't see anything and there was nothing to charge anyone with and just kept saying someone was coming to get her and she had to go. She even slapped the chick who was trying to get her blood pressure."

"Did the nurse file a report?" I asked.

"Nah. Acted like it was no big deal. I guess crazy people go in and knock them around the emergency room pretty good." The bland look on his face as he spoke spiked my blood pressure.

"Did you notice anything else about the victim?"

He narrowed his eyes, looking past my shoulder. "She was wearing a ring. Looked really old. And like it was worth money. I noticed because the vibe she gave off about the rape kit and not wanting to seek charges kind of made me wonder if she was a whore. But that ring sort of screamed 'class,' so I wasn't sure enough to ask." He chuckled. "Didn't want the wild little thing slapping me too."

Just keep asking questions.

"Did you see who came to pick her up?"

"Nah, I got another call and left. Nothing I could do if she didn't want the police involved. She told the doctor twice she had to get back to the Cordova."

My eyebrows went up.

"So you're familiar? She didn't really look like the type, except maybe around the edges."

The Cordova was the kind of rooming house where people could pay by the hour or by the week, and the owner didn't give a shit what went on in the rooms as long as the rent got paid on time. It was popular with sex workers and addicts.

"Is there anything else you remember about her?" I asked. "Any identifying marks or anything?"

"She had a wicked snake tat on her thigh," he said. "I only saw a little bit of it, because her skirt was ripped a little." He put two fingers spaced about five inches apart on his upper left thigh. "It was high up, looked like it wrapped around her leg. Purple and black."

"Her clothes were torn?" I asked as I scribbled the details of the tattoo.

"Her sleeve, by the bruising on her arm, and the skirt on the same side, but like I said, only a little. Like enough to see the tat maybe." He glanced at Graham. "She said it got caught on the door when they wheeled her out. It wasn't the kind of rip that would've gotten anyone access to the good parts."

I choked on my own spit and felt Graham go rigid next to me.

Coughing twice, I recovered my composure and narrowed my eyes. "I understand that everyone on the job has different motivations for doing this kind of work. Personally, Graham and I both keep the safety and integrity of the victims we work for at the center of what we do. I'd recommend trying it."

King folded his arms across his chest. "I know who you are, you know. Hell of a thing you did, locking up your own daddy." The contempt dripping from the words said he didn't mean that in the complimentary way a lot of other folks had.

Graham's head snapped back around and King sneered. "You going to come at me for insulting her, big fella? I didn't say a word that's not true."

"Oh, she doesn't need me to fight her battles, Patrolman." Graham coated the word with the kind of disdain King had shown for women throughout the interview. "I'd bet everything I own that if you ran your mouth long enough, she'd put you on your ass in half a blink."

King snorted and turned to me. I held his gaze without blinking until he dropped his eyes to study his uniform shoes.

"No superior officer worth his badge wants to hear you refer to women like they're pieces of meat. And nobody I've ever worked around uses the word 'whore' in a professional context. Prostitute or sex trade worker will serve you better."

He blinked. I walked out, Graham on my heels.

We waved at Sergeant Smithers on the way out, his booming voice wishing us luck as we cleared the front doors.

"That was good work," Graham said. "We've found people with less to go on."

"If we find her and if we can get her to talk. Assuming she lied to him and she actually does know something."

"We can always get them to talk, baby." He patted my arm as I started the truck. "Jim made it through surgery. He's working on recovering. Let's check in with Archie and Cortez and see where we are, and then we'll go to the rooming house. We'll get him. We just need to work the case."

12

"Small things matter." Archie put his half-eaten burger back on its harvest gold Whataburger wrapper and dipped a fry in a tiny pot of number five fancy ketchup. "This is the perfect testament to why we don't cut corners here. I don't give a shit what this thing can tell you"—he pointed to the computer sitting unopened in the middle of the conference room table— "good old-fashioned legwork is what solves cases."

"I like to think I'm a good hybrid," I said, popping a crunchy onion ring into my mouth and chasing it with a sip of strawberry milkshake. Whataburger isn't heavy on vegetarian options, but some days that's a damned good excuse to call junk food a meal.

Graham surveyed the whiteboard. "So the most recent victim from the club bathroom's last known address is out at the Cordova. That's our next stop for legwork?"

"Right now it seems like the best bet. She's also the only one who was transported to the hospital, so she's the only one we can find. Nothing so far on enhancing the security footage from the lab?" I turned to Archie.

He shook his head. "They're still trying. Cheap ass cameras."

"I bet that changes right quick," I said, waving my phone. "What happened to Jim is all over the internet. We can't stand for medical examiners becoming targets for murderers who don't want to get caught."

"Which is why we have to put this fucker away. While people are still talking about the case." Archie finished his burger in three big bites and wadded up the wrapper, shooting it basketball style into the garbage can in the corner.

"They need to beef up security too, though." I said.

"Speaking of reporters and computers," Archie said. "What can this thing tell us about the doctors Skye is stalking?" He nudged the laptop toward me like it might turn and snap a chunk out of his finger.

I flipped it open and touched a few keys, looking for something Skye hadn't mentioned.

Pay dirt.

"One of them was investigated by a special committee at the state medical board about three years ago." I clicked the link for the hearing transcript.

Page not found flashed above a frowning face on the screen.

"What did he do?" Graham asked as I went back to the search results and checked the link.

"Hang on," I said. "This link is broken. I need to find where."

Archie tossed his empty plastic cup into the green recycle bin and left the room. I tinkered with the link for several minutes before giving up and going to the review board main page to search a different way.

I typed in the doctor's name, watching the spinning wheel in the center of the screen.

"No results found?" Graham read over my shoulder. "How can that be?"

I clicked back to the Google tab and took a screenshot, my brow furrowing as I hunched over the computer, trying to discern a way to make it cough up the information I wanted.

"Did someone delete what you're looking for?" Graham asked.

"It sure seems so, but we can't make assumptions until we find out exactly what it is that we're looking for."

"Who are you talking to? I'm the king of unassuming investigations."

"No idea what I was thinking. My apologies, love."

I grabbed a pen and wrote down what looked to be a case number, switching to the state review board's sub-page on the site.

Search.

Case file.

I typed in the number and crossed my fingers as I hit enter.

The wheel spun, a blue link appearing in the center of the screen. *Texas Medical Association v. Douglas M.H. Pendergast, M.D.*

I clicked it and scrolled through the resulting document, scanning for the charges.

"So two years ago, this guy Pendergast was running an insurance scam." I sat back, stretching my shoulders before I scrolled back to the top to read more detail. "He stole nearly a million dollars before he got busted."

Graham let out a low whistle and leaned down to read over my shoulder.

"Seems finding a way to make money dishonestly isn't a new rodeo for our cowboy doctor," I muttered, returning to the state board window and searching for my gynecologist's name.

Her photo and office address popped right up. License renewed fifteen months ago.

I tried Dr. Cowboy again.

No results found.

I went back to the other window and scrolled to the bottom of the hearing transcript.

"He lost his medical license." My fingers flew to my lips with a will of their own, everything Skye had told us flashing through my brain on fast forward.

"I thought Skye said they had a practice currently?"

"Google didn't return an office address."

"So maybe Pendergast is working there unofficially?"

I jumped out of the chair so fast I almost knocked it over into Graham, hurrying to the board and snatching up my marker. I wrote Pendergast's name in the center and circled it. "Can you print me a photo of him?" I asked Graham.

"Coming up." He leaned over the computer.

"We need to be able to connect this guy to these women." I waved a hand at the board.

"That sounds an awful lot like an assumption." Graham crossed the room and handed me a color photo of the guy's smiling face, his Stetson whiter than his lab coat and his teeth beating them both at just shy of blinding.

"He looks smug," I said before I looked up. "I know it's an assumption. But it's a pretty safe one with what we know, right? An educated assumption?"

He laughed. "You just made that term up."

"My gut says this is our guy, Graham. But we can't just show up at his place guns blazing, we need everything nailed down tighter than a whale-bone corset before we go near him. We can't tip our hand until we can make this stick or he'll be a ghost of a memory."

"Far be it from me to question your gut, but you know as well as I do that going in looking for things to point a certain way leads to mistakes and sometimes even wild leaps." He handed me the photo and watched me tape it up. "This dude is absolutely a person of interest here, but we need to follow the case, not try to direct it where we think it should go."

"Uh. What did I miss?" Archie shut the door behind him out of habit, since the office was empty except for us. Most other Rangers who worked weekends did so in the field. The office was home base during the work-week, but the Rangers tradition of working alone most of the time meant it wasn't really necessary anymore. I just preferred yellow fluorescent lighting and giant whiteboards to my cell phone and laptop in my living room—something about being in the office had an effect on my speed of thought.

"The computer had some secrets about Skye's crooked doctors—specifically that this one had his license to practice revoked after an investigation by the state committee a few years ago. Insurance fraud."

"No shit?" Archie took a seat at the table.

"It's him." I pinched my mouth into a tight line.

"Maybe." Archie shrugged. "Certainly, what we know so far appears damning. So we work the case and see."

"That's what Graham said."

"Smart fella." Archie held my gaze. I stared back without blinking for a twenty count.

"I know," I said finally. "Work the case."

"Keep him as a POI," Archie said. "He's definitely that. And we'll keep going. All this will help us get a warrant if that's where the case goes."

"Should we go talk to him?" I asked. "I'm afraid of him taking off if he thinks we're onto him."

"Not yet." Archie popped the top on a Diet Dr Pepper. "I agree, if you tip your hand too soon he'll bolt."

"Just wondering if maybe a visit from the Rangers would make him nervous enough to slip up," I mused.

"Not worth the risk," Archie advised. "It's better to wait until you know enough to hold him if he deserves to be picked up."

I nodded slowly, turning my attention back to the victims I'd made notes on at the top of the board. The photo of the computer screen from the bar I'd added above Courtney's name an hour earlier was grainy, but it was the image I needed to keep in my mind. I didn't get many cases where I could talk to someone who likely had a run-in with my killer and lived to tell the tale.

I snapped a photo of Dr. Cowboy's picture on the board with my cell and turned for the door.

"Let's go see what she can tell us."

Graham banged on the door a third time, using the side of his fist to rattle it harder.

"Courtney, are you okay?" I called. I didn't want to announce that we were law enforcement unless I had to, lest she get the wrong idea about why we were there before she came near the door.

"She ain't there." The voice came from behind me and down the hall. Graham, Archie, and I turned as one to find a stout man with a beer gut hanging bare between his gray basketball shorts and his once-white Fruit of the Loom tank undershirt, scratching the back of his head and squinting bloodshot eyes that said we'd likely woken him.

"Sorry to bother you." I flashed my most dazzling smile, taking two steps his direction. Graham and Archie hung back. "Do you happen to know where she is? It's pretty important that we speak with her."

He stared, his eyes growing wider by the second. "What does a broad who looks like you want with the likes of her?"

"I think we might be able to help her with something." I tried the smile again.

He blinked rapidly. "Never met a cop who wanted to help...well, anybody, come to think of it. Y'all here to bust her?"

"You have my word no one is here to arrest anyone," I said.

He twisted his mouth to one side. "You got some class to you. Like you don't know how to get your hands dirty."

I just held his gaze, staying quiet.

"Probably means your word means something to you." He hitched the shorts up over the bottom of his belly. "She hasn't been here in...probably a week now."

I glanced back at Archie and Graham before I focused again on the missing victim's neighbor. "You don't know where she went?"

"Vacation? Hospital?" He shrugged. "This ain't the kind of joint where people confide in each other, you know? I collect rent and put off the repairs the owner don't want to pay for if I can't do them myself. Her rent's paid through the end of April. On account of that, I figure she'll be back eventually. In the meantime, ain't nobody bitched at me this week about the company she's keeping, so I got no complaints."

"Is that normal?" I asked. "For people to pay their rent up in advance?"

"Not everybody has a regular paycheck. But everybody has their priorities. This chick, her place is at the top of hers. She pays her rent up a couple or three months in advance pretty regular. Saves her from having to worry she won't have enough to cover it if she spends the dough, I imagine."

I pulled a card from my back pocket and slid it under her door, then offered another to the building manager. "Can you please tell her I'm not interested in how she earns a living, but I really need to speak with her as soon as possible, the next time you see her?"

"Sure thing." He glanced at the card and tucked it into the pocket on his shorts. "Hope you find what you're looking for."

"Thank you."

That was proving hard to come by, but what else was new? The devil is always in the details. We just needed to keep collecting them and see where they led.

13

"Seems that this guy chooses his victims carefully," Archie said, speeding onto the I-35W onramp. "Which could mean he watches them for a while before he makes his move."

"Definitely a reasonable train of thought," I said from the backseat, adding the building manager's comments to my notes while they were still vivid in my head. "I wish we could find someone who could tell us if any of them had a stalker."

I glanced up when I felt the car slow. We couldn't be near the office yet. Archie turned into a tall concrete parking garage. He was going to the hospital. I put a hand on his shoulder over the back of the seat. "Thanks."

"I'd like to lay my eyes on him, too," he said. "Jim Prescott and I go back longer than you've been alive. Hell, I remember when he had hair."

"I thought he was born with the comb-over," Graham said.

Archie chuckled. "It's true what they say, that this job makes you family. Kids never think about the grownups around them being people or having lives before they were around—or outside their responsibilities to them, either."

My pen froze in midair as he took a ticket from the automated dispenser while his comment rattled around my head.

I had done that with Ruth. Most of my life, I'd had terribly unkind thoughts about a woman I saw as having settled for life as a political trophy wife, content to plan parties of every size down to the perfect origami napkins, hold court over an army of servants, and drive my sister and me crazy with her rigid expectations of perfection.

It was only after I found out she'd spent more than half my life in love with Archie that I began to think of her as having a life apart from duty and family at all, and any conversation we'd had about that had been limited mostly to Ruth swearing to me she'd never been physically unfaithful to the Governor, and me repeating that I wouldn't have given one tiny flying rat's ass if she had. Chuck McClellan's skirt chasing was damn near Kennedy-level legend.

So what else did I not know? What else had I assumed; what other blanks had I filled in entirely the wrong way?

For someone who makes a living in large part asking questions, I couldn't remember the last time I'd asked my own mother anything more substantive than what color wine she wanted with dinner.

"Faith?" Archie was standing outside the parked car with the door open, leaning down to peer at me. "You coming?"

I put the notebook and pen on the seat next to me, grabbing an evidence bag packaged with a sterile swab and scraper before climbing out. "Sorry."

"Don't apologize for being lost in thought," he said. "The more we pick through this, the faster we'll have our killer."

"Can't be too fast," Graham said, his hand on the small of my back as we crossed the street to the main hospital entrance. I liked the warmth radiating from his fingers through my shirt in the chill of the March evening. "This is the craziest shit I've ever seen. I'll sleep better myself when the fucker responsible for it is locked up."

"The missing organs adds a ghoulish vibe," Archie agreed. "Something so much more...distasteful...about hacking parts out of people than just killing them and moving along."

"Distasteful hell, it's fucking creepy," I said, punching the elevator button for the fourth floor, where the surgical ICU was located. "It lends the whole thing a very cold-blooded mantle. Like 90 percent of the murders that come across a cop's desk are crimes of passion. Even the weird ones that make it to us are mostly precipitated by a snap decision that went really bad."

Graham pointed at me. "Exactly. But stealing someone's organs for profit is very clearly premeditated."

"We don't know for a fact that it's for profit," Archie cautioned.

The elevator doors opened. "But we have a pretty good idea," I said. "I mean, look at just the things Skye was able to uncover on these doctors and what they're up to. It makes sense."

"Follow the money," Graham said. "At least until you can't anymore. My first and favorite instructor at the academy back in the day must've said that to us a thousand times."

"It makes people do some pretty horrible things," Archie agreed, pointing down the hall to the ICU unit doors when we stepped off the elevator. "And the bitch of it is that most of them find out after the fact that it doesn't make them happy anyway."

Archie flashed his badge at the nurse on the other side of the glass. She raised one eyebrow and made no move to open the door. "Do you have a family member here with us, Officer?"

Her tone sent my eyebrows up. Nurses are charged with protecting their patients' health, and as such, they often resent cops showing up at hospitals and causing stress. But most of them are at least polite about it.

"We're here to see James Prescott," I said.

"And you are?"

"Faith McClellan. Archie Baxter. Graham Hardin." I pointed at each of us as I spoke. "We're the officers who saved Mr. Prescott this morning. He's a close friend."

She pursed her glittery rose-glossed lips, her eyes on the evidence bag I wished I'd put in my pocket. "The regulations say family."

I opened my mouth to argue and heard a deep, unfamiliar baritone behind me. "Ranger McClellan?"

I turned to find Jim's eldest son, eyes bright with tears. Before I could nod, he enveloped me in a hug that cut off my oxygen supply. Jesse Prescott was roughly eye to eye with my five-eleven height, but the stocky build that ran in Jim's DNA was all muscle on his boys.

I let out a squeak and Jesse stepped back. "Forgive me. I have wanted to

thank you for what you did for my mom for a long time now, and today...
the surgeon said my dad would've died if it hadn't been for you, so that
makes both of my folks' lives I owe to you. I don't know that you can even
understand how glad I am to have a chance to say this: thank you, ma'am."

Jim's bright blue eyes sparkled from Jesse's face. I knew he was a senior
at Rice, earning a political science degree with an eye on law school. He
wanted to take a year off to clerk in the public defender's office and prep for
the LSAT, last I'd heard from his proud dad.

"Truly my pleasure," I said. "I'm just sorry Graham and I weren't ten
minutes earlier this morning."

Jesse waved at the nurse, who pursed her lips again, but buzzed the
doors open without further comment.

We followed him through. "How's your dad doing, Jesse?" Archie kept
his voice low, the beep and whir of machines filling the hallway even with
the sliding glass doors to the patient rooms closed.

"He's stable. He hasn't come to yet, but the brain guy told my mom
there's nothing on any of the scans or tests that makes him think that won't
happen. He said these kinds of comas are common after so much blood
loss and that kind of trauma, and it could take as much as a few days for
him to wake up."

We stopped in front of a set of glass doors in one corner of the
rectangular-track hallway. On the other side, Sharon was curled in a plas-
tic-upholstered hospital issue chair under a thin blanket, a book spread
open on her lap. She had color in her cheeks that wasn't from makeup and
her hair was growing back in nicely, even if it wasn't quite long enough to
comb. Sharon and Jim hadn't been far from my thoughts all day, especially
after we met with Skye. Graham had been so horrified at the idea of people
buying organs, but I couldn't stop thinking about the fact that I had used
Chuck's connections to get Sharon into a drug trial in Houston that was
likely the only reason she was still sitting there. I hadn't killed anyone to do
it, of course, but for some reason it rankled as much more complicated now
than it had when I'd first called the Governor about it nearly a year ago.

"I sent Petey back to his dorm. We'll take shifts sitting with them like we
did when Mom was sick," Jesse said. "She's been asleep for about an hour.
They told us this morning that they only let visitors back for fifteen

minutes out of every hour, but one of the nurses had that chair brought up for her when she noticed that his heart rate and blood pressure are better when Mom is in there with him."

"He's in a coma," Graham said. "How can that be?"

"The doctor said he can hear her and probably feel her holding his hand." Jesse pointed to the blanket covering Jim, where his parents' fingers were laced together as they slept. "She makes him feel better."

I glanced up at Graham and caught him looking at me. "I know the feeling," he said.

Jesse smiled. "Good for you. I hope someday I do, too."

He reached for the door and I stopped him with one hand. "I don't want to disturb her. She was so scared this morning, and she's been through so much the past year. Let her sleep. I just need to tiptoe in and swab under his nails—I'll be very quiet."

He smiled. "Thank you. Again."

I slipped through a narrow opening in the door and shut it softly, then tiptoed to the bedside. Sharon was holding Jim's left hand, but odds were high he would've defended himself with his right—or both hands. I opened the bag and the swab, careful to avoid touching the tip. Jim's right hand was palm up on the blanket, making it easy to reach without moving him. I swiped carefully under each fingernail and slid the swab into a plastic tube before I returned it to the bag. Pulling the paper wrapping off the scraper, I ran it under and around the bed of each nail to catch any invisible cells. With everything sealed in the evidence bag, I crept back to the hall.

"If your dad wakes up, will you text me?" I handed Jesse a card. "My cell is on the back."

"Of course."

"No matter what time it is."

"You're trying to find the person who did this, right?" Jesse said. "I looked it up, cases of medical legal lab workers being attacked are very rare."

"Your dad was looking for something this morning when he called me," I said. "He was kind of freaked out about the Jane Doe on his table, but he said he was going to check something and he'd fill me in when I got there. He had a hunch. I'd really like to know what it was."

After talking with Skye, I was hoping Jim was going to tell us the victim's organs had been removed by a doctor, but trying not to get ahead of myself. He'd mentioned medical training, but only in passing.

"A couple of reporters stopped me when I went to the cafeteria," Jesse said. "I guess Mom is right and I look like Dad after all. They wanted to know if he'd told me anything about what happened. I just told them he wasn't awake yet."

"Keep telling them that," Archie said. "Or if he wakes up and you don't want to lie, please say 'no comment.'"

"My dad has told me all my life how much he hates talking to reporters," Jesse said. "So I wouldn't tell them a thing without asking him first. I just didn't know if talking to them might help y'all. They were eating in the atrium when I came back upstairs."

"Generally speaking they're more trouble than they are help," I said. "With a very few exceptions. This doesn't seem to be one."

"You're not talking about doctors, I hope, Ranger McClellan."

I recognized the voice but couldn't place it until I turned. "The best plastic surgeon in the Hill Country," I said, smiling at Dr. Chris Gilroy. "What are you doing all the way up here?"

Tablet in hand, he jerked his chin at Jim's door. "Even a neat cut in sagging tissue will leave a nasty scar if it's not repaired just the right way. An old friend called me this morning, asked me to pretty it up while he was in the OR. Dr. Velasquez did the important part, but now he won't be reminded of the attack every time he looks in the mirror."

"Thank you. That was kind of you."

"Like I told you before—I do the nose jobs and facelifts fifty weeks a year for the two I get to spend repairing cleft lips and helping accident and burn victims. Your friend was a welcome bright spot of purpose in my day."

"Thank you for helping my dad," Jesse said. "I seem to be saying that every time I turn around today."

"Glad to be able to do it," Dr. Chris said, nodding to the door. "I'm just going to slip in and have a look at the sutures."

We moved and he opened the door.

"If you tell me you know a plastic surgeon because your mother took you to talk to him..." Graham's voice held a warning note.

"No, no," I said. "She did a lot of things, but that was never one of them. He sewed my hands up a few weeks ago when I cut them up at the big wreck scene on 35." I flipped my palms up, the scars already fading to barely visible. "He's good at what he does."

The doctor came out, Sharon on his heels. She sobbed and launched herself into my arms. Ten hours a week of TRX core training was all that kept me on my feet. She was strong for being so tiny.

"I almost lost him," she said, standing up straight and dragging the back of one hand across her face. "All this time, I never understood why he was so scared after I got sick. Now I get it—I wasn't worried because I wasn't the person who was going to have to live without my better half."

Graham's hand landed on my shoulder and he cleared his throat. "The lady makes a good point."

I tipped my head back to lean it against his shoulder, finally understanding something that had eluded me for months. We didn't argue often, but when we did, it almost always involved my tendency to see my own safety as secondary to solving the case and making the collar. Standing there looking at Sharon's blotchy face, I realized that when Graham talked to me about being more careful, all I ever heard was him trying to tell me what to do or thinking I wasn't capable of handling dangerous situations on my own. Because that was what every man had thought after five seconds of looking at me for my entire life—especially the Governor.

Somehow Sharon Prescott's tearful words seeped through to a place in my brain Graham's hadn't been able to reach. Putting myself in her shoes, it was easy to see why he worried. He didn't think I was weak, he just didn't want to lose me.

Epiphanies were just raining from the sky today.

I reached up and squeezed Graham's hand, my eyes on Sharon but my words directed at my fiancé. "I understand."

"Jesse said he's stable," Archie said.

Sharon perked up. "His brain activity is good, even high at times today, which the neurosurgeon said is really positive. It probably means he's dreaming, or maybe that he's fighting to wake up."

"I've been praying all day," I said.

"Thank you so much, Faith," she said. "My family can never even adequately express how much we value you and your friendship."

"Jim is a good man. I'm happy to help however I can," I said. "We catch killers, and no one is as brilliant as he is at finding the kind of evidence that will get to the heart of a murder—no pun intended. I mean, I need Jim to be able to do my job, and he needs you to keep doing his—so it's not like my motives are totally selfless." I flashed a grin.

"I for one don't give a damn what motivated you to save my parents," Jesse said. "Be as selfish as you want as long as I get to keep them around."

Too-loud laughter shook our little circle, drawing narrowed eyes from two nurses as we leaned on one another and tried to swallow the volume. Everyone needed the respite from stress right then.

When everyone was quietly wiping the corners of their eyes, I leveled mine at Sharon. "Did they by chance bring you Jim's bag from the lab this morning?"

Archie raised an eyebrow in my direction, but he and Graham stayed quiet.

"I think his briefcase is in there, isn't it?" She looked at Jesse, who went in to fetch it when Dr. Chris came out.

"Is there something there that could help you?" Jesse asked.

"I'm not sure," I said, taking it from him. "Can I borrow it for the night?"

"Of course," Sharon said.

I thanked her and peeked at Jim, still lying peacefully. He'd look like he was asleep if not for the half dozen tubes and wires connecting him to various machines.

"Give him my love, and please call me if he wakes up. No matter the hour." I turned a solemn stare on Sharon and Jesse in turn until they had both nodded.

Waving at Dr. Chris on the way out, I stepped into the elevator gripping the handle of the worn-at-the-corners brown leather briefcase so tightly the edges bit into my hands.

Archie reached down and took the evidence bag. "I can drop this off at the Travis lab Monday morning. There's a guy there who owes me a favor."

"Naturally." I winked. "Thank you."

"What's in there?" Archie gestured to Jim's briefcase. "Or rather, what do you think is in there?"

"I don't have the first clue," I said. "But Jim was so interested in this case he went to work in a strange city in the middle of the night. He talks to the recorder while he works, which the attacker knew or guessed because it was missing, but sometimes he writes notes, too. I'm hoping he's got a file in here. If not, we'll go back and check the lab." We stepped off the elevator and made it three steps toward the doors before shouts of "Rangers! Do you have suspects in the savage attack on Jim Prescott this morning?"

"No comment." I repeated it five more times as we moved through the lobby with half a dozen mics on our heels. One young woman followed when we left the building, calling questions in a shrill tone all the way to the garage.

We shut the car doors in her face before Archie peeled out of the garage a little more aggressively than I'd ever seen him drive.

"She's persistent. I mean, she's no Skye Morrow," he said. "But she doesn't give up easily."

"Did you recognize her?" I asked.

"Sure. She's the new girl over at Channel 9. My phone has been blowing up with texts from her all damn day, and I don't even know where she could've gotten the number."

I turned in the backseat and watched her, mic hanging at her side as she stared after us, her open mouth rimmed in the exact right shade of red lip color to complement her green eyes and not a single blonde hair daring to escape her perfect chignon.

A younger, fairly resourceful Skye with more energy and no fear.

Just what we needed while we tried to catch a killer who'd gone after one of our own.

14

The spider-silk-fine line between investigating and snooping is harder to walk than most folks think. Throw a coworker who had become a good friend over the years into the mix, and it was damn near impossible.

I put Jim's briefcase on my kitchen table while Graham flipped through the mail and pulled out three small ecru envelopes containing response cards for the wedding. "Something tells me your mother will be just thrilled with late RSVPs." He made a mock-horrified face. "I hope they're not from my family."

I laughed. "She's handled worse. She'll make it work."

Crossing my arms over my chest, I eyed the briefcase like some nasty critter with too many legs was about to slither out of it.

"You want me to look?" Graham asked. "I know you don't want to snoop."

I loved the way he could often almost read my mind. I sighed, flicking the latches open.

"You don't either. I got it." I plucked a manila folder off the top of the pile.

Autopsy report on a forty-nine-year-old male who had died of a heart attack. I put it down and went to the next one. A twenty-seven-year-old woman who'd been in a car crash.

Next: forty-four-year-old female, cause of death listed as a stroke.

I placed it on top of the other folders and shook my head. "These are all just random files, probably paperwork he needed to catch up on and was taking home."

I looked in the elastic-lined pocket in the top of the case and found a notebook. "Jesus, how can he even read this chicken scratch himself?" I flipped through pages, squinting at a poor impersonation of letters.

Graham looked over my shoulder. "Yikes. I think that's an insult to the chickens, babe. May I?"

I handed him the notebook. "You're one to talk."

He winked and moved closer to the light. "Which may finally come in handy for me. I think this says 'liver.' And 'heart' is this one here." He put a finger on the last page of notes after a minute. "These are numbers next to them. Do you have something with 4107 or 4701...or maybe 4167 or 4761? Jesus, Jim...anything with a four in it over there, babe?"

I flipped through the folders. "Got file number 4167 right here."

"See if it says the liver was damaged?"

I flipped the folder open and scanned the report. "Oh shit, it says her liver was gone." My eyes went to the bottom of the page. "This wasn't Jim's case. Another medical examiner did this one."

I grabbed the next folder, reading the full case details this time. "Missing a heart, cause of death listed as a motor vehicle accident. She was treated at a local health hospital in Goliad County and died in surgery."

"I'd imagine so if the surgery took her heart." Graham's brows went up.

"But that's the thing: young, healthy accident victims come into the morgue without organs all the time," I said. "When families donate them, they're taken at the hospital before Jim gets near a body. Autopsy is routine in the case of young people who die suddenly, though. To make sure the cause of death was what it appeared to be."

I opened the folder on the bottom of the stack and went back to the MVA victim.

"Both of these victims were treated at the same hospital. The man who died of heart failure was missing a kidney."

"Jim was bringing these files home because he thought something was weird," Graham said.

"He sounded alarmed on the phone this morning." I tapped my fingers on the table in an even staccato beat. "When he was talking about our Jane Doe."

"Murder victims don't usually get the option of donating organs."

"Exactly. So maybe neither did these people?" I waved the folders. "Because organ donors usually donate most or all of their organs. Not a liver here and a heart there. Something else was going on here." I pulled out my phone and looked up the address of the medical center where the patients had been treated, then checked my notes from my conversation with Skye.

"Skye's shady doctors are in driving distance of this hospital. I'd bet my wedding gown the one who still has a license has surgical privileges there. And I really, really love my dress."

"I wonder if this is the other weird thing Jim wanted to tell us this morning?" Graham said.

"If there's weirder stuff here, I feel like sane people shouldn't want to know."

"Except us. Weird is kind of our bread and butter." Graham went to the fridge and opened a beer, pulling a half-full bottle of chardonnay out and raising it in my direction with an inquiring eyebrow up. "It's been a long day, and we're due at dinner with your mother in an hour."

I sighed and nodded, and he pulled a glass from the cabinet by the sink and filled it nearly to the brim with wine. Handing it to me, he waved one hand at the doorway. "Let's take this stuff to the sofa and see if we can figure out what Jim was thinking."

"None of the notes here are about the Jane Doe." I took a long drink of the wine and let my eyes fall shut as warmth spread from my abdomen until it was lapping at the tips of my fingers. I was careful with booze— never more than twice a week, never more than two glasses, and only for celebrations were my hard and fast rules. I wasn't about to start breaking them now.

Perching on the sofa next to Graham, I raised my glass. "To Jim," I said. "May he make a full and quick recovery."

"And thank God he's still here to give it a shot." Graham's lips tipped up into a small smile as he touched his bottle to my glass with a *clink*. He knew my rules, and he even understood them. "You're nothing like your father."

"And I aim to keep it that way." The Governor had a notoriously shitty temper that his beloved scotch ratcheted up to stepped-on-rattlesnake-level spite. He'd been an alcoholic at least since I could walk, and knowing his DNA lurked inside me somewhere was enough to warrant caution.

Absent a whiteboard, I flipped to a fresh piece of paper and started writing.

"So Jim saw the missing organs and probably went looking for other cases with similar notes. These were the ones that came up in the search, and he pulled the files and stowed them to take home," I said as I scribbled.

"Or maybe to show us," Graham said.

I wrote that down too. Opening the folders, I spread them on the coffee table and checked the signature lines. Only two of the cases had been handled by the same ME, and he wasn't one I knew well. The downside of my preference for working with the best was that I didn't have many contacts in the medical examiners' office, which didn't matter unless my one good one was in a coma.

"I wonder why the folks who performed these autopsies didn't ask what happened to these organs," Graham mused, flipping pages in the file on the woman with the missing liver.

I put a hand on his arm, reading an additional page of notes when he stopped flipping.

"They did. At least this woman did."

He leaned over the file. "Liver noted by attending physician as too damaged to save."

"But the doctor's name isn't here anywhere." I sighed, adding the ME's name to my notes. She wouldn't be back at the office until Monday, but I needed to know if she remembered the case or had actually spoken to the doctor first thing.

"Hey, where did you say that hospital was?" Graham asked.

"Goliad County."

"You don't think maybe that JP out there with the morgue in her house —what was her name?" Graham snapped his fingers.

"Corie Whitehead!" I threw my arms around him and planted a kiss on his lips that quickly turned more involved than I might've intended. Not that I was complaining. "You're brilliant," I whispered when we paused for air.

He chuckled, tugging my shoulders until we were comfortably reclined on the sofa and his lips were moving across my collarbone. "We'll go see her tomorrow," he murmured. "And maybe Jim will wake up. And we have some time before dinner."

I sighed and tipped my head, my hand curling around the back of his neck. "When you put it that way..."

"You know what I'm, like, stupid excited about?" Graham asked, turning so we were side by side and facing each other.

"You can pick one thing?" I asked.

"I swear the first time I hear someone call you Ranger Hardin, I'm going to pop buttons right the hell off my uniform shirt. I cannot wait." His soft smile and ravenous stare brought a lump to my throat.

"Me neither, baby." I leaned into a kiss.

So much to look forward to. As soon as we had the sick bastard who attacked Jim. And assuming we survived dinner with Ruth.

15

Any greater-than-cursory concern about my hair or makeup had been long buried in a dusty carton with my tiaras and sashes. These days, I favored a sweep of mascara and a little lip gloss, ponytails, pressed Wranglers, and boots.

Until I was walking into dinner at an expensive steakhouse to meet Graham's mother and Ruth McClellan, it seemed.

"I should've put more makeup on," I said as we stepped into the gleaming walnut and brass foyer of the restaurant.

"You look gorgeous," Graham said.

"I'm wearing jeans."

"Welcome to Texas. Everyone here is wearing jeans." He put his arm around my shoulders. "It's going to be a nice evening. Archie and I are both here. Take a breath and relax and let's go eat—you've been looking forward to this all week."

I had. The place was swanky, but perfect because everyone else could have steak while I got to enjoy the best tossed salad and beer butter bread in this part of the state.

I sucked in a deep breath, and Graham pulled the door open and gave the maître d' my mother's name.

"Right this way, y'all." He moved from behind the podium with long strides, leading us to a corner near the person-sized fireplace.

"See? Jeans," Graham whispered with a nod at the maître d's denim-clad legs.

I squeezed his hand. I faced down death on at least a monthly basis. I could get through this dinner.

Archie stood as we approached the table and I was relieved to see Graham's mom hadn't arrived early. While Ruth had preached "on time is fifteen minutes late" at me all my life, she also frowned upon others showing up too early when she didn't expect it.

I leaned down to kiss her cheek and took the chair next to her as Archie and Graham took their seats.

"The bird flu is not going to ruin your wedding," Ruth announced with a wide smile. "The available chicken has been reapportioned into croquettes, and he's placed an order for brussels sprouts to bulk up the vegetables. Problem solved."

I despised brussels sprouts. So did Graham, and he eats just about anything. But she was so proud of herself, I couldn't say that. "Thank you," I offered instead. "Those will go with the whipped potatoes?" Since that was all I was planning on eating that wasn't salad or cake.

Her head swiveled my way like her neck was filled with ball bearings, her eyes wide. "I assumed that was an oversight on your part. Potatoes are so...unremarkable. I requested a change to grilled quinoa with peppers and kalamata olives. It'll present so much better."

Okay then. Who says cake can't be a balanced dinner?

"I like potatoes," Graham said in the same smooth tone he used on frightened witnesses and victims. "My whole family does, too."

Ruth shifted her gaze to him when he started talking, her face softening.

"I didn't mean to be insulting, Graham darling," she said. "I just want everything to be perfect for the two of you."

"My days will always be perfect because I get to keep your daughter with me every day for the rest of them." Graham flashed a smile. "No apologies necessary."

She sighed and reached for her wineglass. "You really are such a lovely young man."

Her free arm trembled under my hand, and I watched her face, noticing the genuine stress there in a way I wouldn't have before. Like Archie said, she was a person before she was my mother. Before she was formidable First Lady of Texas Ruth McClellan. And I was determined to start seeing the things I'd never noticed.

"Mother." I said it softly, testing the way it felt rolling off my tongue. I hadn't called her much of anything kind except Ruth for more years than I could count.

Her eyes flew to mine. "Faith?"

"I appreciate you taking this over so I can focus on work. Fine tune details. Handle problems—it's the week before, and I'm sure the bird flu won't be the last one. Do whatever you see fit." I squeezed her hand. "I trust you. Nobody throws a party like you do."

Ruth blinked, the Botox keeping the emotion in her eyes off her face, but I saw it for myself for the first time.

"Thank you," she whispered.

"For?"

"Forgiving me." Her eyelids fluttered rapidly, banishing tears she wouldn't stand for shedding in a public place.

"Back at you." I squeezed her arm.

"I told you I liked this woman, son." Graham's mother's no-nonsense drawl came from behind me, and Graham and Archie shot to their feet, Graham moving to pull out her chair.

"We didn't see you come in, Momma." He hugged her, taking her coat and gloves and passing them to the lurking server, who whisked them off to the cloakroom Wanda Hardin hadn't known to look for when she came into the restaurant.

"You look good." She laid one hand along the side of his face, a soft smile lighting hers.

"You look beautiful. It's good to see you." He returned to his seat when she was comfortable in hers.

"Faith, you look lovely as always." Wanda grinned across the table.

"Thank you, Mrs. Hardin," I said. "Ruth McClellan, Archie Baxter, this is Graham's mom, Wanda."

"It's a pleasure to meet you, ma'am." Archie took her hand and squeezed. "Your son is a fine man, if I may say so."

"He never gets tired of working with you, Mr. Baxter," she said. "You made him want to be a policeman in the first place, you know."

Archie's jaw went slack for a second, his eyes skipping from Wanda to Graham to me. I shrugged slightly, not sure what she was talking about.

Wanda didn't miss a beat. A bank teller for nearly thirty years, people were her business. "Graham David Hardin. Have you never told this man that?"

"It, uh...it never came up." Graham stared into his water glass.

"Well now it has."

Every eye around the table on him, Graham plucked at his swan-folded napkin. "I was a junior in college when my roommate was caught up in a bar fight at a road game outside San Antonio. Things got out of hand and someone died." He cleared his throat. "He was the only black man in the building, and the local sheriff arrested him before he took a statement from a single person at the scene."

Archie's eyes widened, his hand going to his chin. "Little dive bar off Magnolia, not far from the campus?"

Graham nodded.

Archie's eyes went faraway and unfocused. "I remember that case. There was a deputy in the SO out there who called the Rangers because he said he was worried they were going to let a killer walk."

"So that's why you came," Graham said softly. Louder, he added, "I never knew why, but I was so damned glad you showed up."

Archie looked around the table. "The guy who had actually fired the fatal shot—with a gun registered to his daddy, mind you, this was not exactly crack detective work—was halfway to Canada when the Missouri state patrol caught up with him. The young man who'd been arrested wrongfully spent three days in a cell and then was released and returned to school."

"He played double-A ball for a few years and now he works in the IT department for the city of Houston," Graham said. "Because you didn't look at his skin and assume he was guilty."

Archie's Adam's apple bobbed with a hard swallow. "I'm mighty glad to hear that. I had no idea, Hardin."

"I decided the world needed more good cops. So I dropped the plans I had to go to law school if baseball didn't work out and focused on becoming the kind of officer I was so glad my friend had in his corner."

I grabbed Graham's hand under the table when his voice went thick with emotion. "I never thought I'd actually get to work alongside you, though." He looked at me. "I was mad at you for leaving the SO for a long time because we were good together. But I wouldn't trade anything about the road it took to get us here."

Dammit, there I went blinking back tears.

"Hear hear," Ruth said, raising her wineglass as the server filled Wanda's with chardonnay when she pointed to the bottle of white on the table. "To Graham and Faith, and winding roads that lead to the best things in life." The last words were said with her eyes on Archie.

I raised my glass, my heart full in spite of the horrors of the day.

Two hours and as many bottles of wine later, Graham helped his mother into her SUV and closed the door as I waved from a few paces back.

"You'd think they were old friends," he said in a low tone, nodding to Ruth as Archie put his hand out for her to take while she walked down the steps. "I haven't seen my momma laugh until she cried since I was in the seventh grade and put a toad in Wallis Cook's lunchbox because he pushed a girl I liked off the monkey bars."

"A toad?" I laughed. "What did you do that for?"

"Wallis was the neighborhood asshole. Nobody liked that kid, not even the parents. Hell, maybe not even his own parents. For all his swagger, he was terrified of every kind of varmint you could name—but particularly the big bullfrog toads. So I slipped a speckled slimy one that was easily the size of my hand into his lunchbox and waited for the noon bell." Twenty-five years later, Graham's lips tipped up and his shoulders shook a little at the memory.

"So what happened?"

"Shit his pants. Right there in the cafeteria."

My hand flew to my mouth. "Did anyone know it was you?"

"I might've told a few people. Wallis stopped pushing people around after that, though."

Ruth and Archie stopped on their way to the car.

"Your mother is a true gem, Graham. No wonder you're such a wonderful young man." She was a little tipsy, but not drunk enough for me to wonder if it was the wine talking.

I beamed. "Thank you both for a lovely evening."

"Be ready to hit this hard tomorrow," Archie said. "Whatever in the hell we stumbled into, I'll sleep easier when the person responsible for it is in a cell."

"We found a lead in Jim's briefcase we're going to drive down to Goliad to follow in the morning. I'll call you when we're done there," I said.

"Good work today, you two." Archie put a hand on Graham's shoulder as he spoke. The story Graham told at dinner had really touched him.

"Speaking of work." I looked at Ruth. "Do you still know the dean at the university medical school?"

"Of course. Do you need to speak with him?"

"That could be very helpful," I said.

"I'll set it up for Monday morning." She kissed my cheek and then Graham's. "Get some rest. Archie says your friend Jim needs you running at full speed tomorrow."

"Yes, ma'am." I waved as they moved to Ruth's black Jaguar, and Graham opened the passenger door of my truck for me.

I slid onto the seat as my phone started buzzing.

I raised it to my ear. "McClellan."

"Ranger, this is Cortez at the Waco PD. Just wanted to let you know my detectives made it through five of the fourteen lab employees today. So far no matches for the physical description and everyone had an alibi for early this morning, but we'll keep plugging. It may be Monday before we run them all down, but I'll keep you posted if we bring in anyone you should talk with."

"Much appreciated, Sergeant. Have a nice evening." I ended the call and turned to Graham. "No good leads among lab employees so far, but they have nine people left to check out."

"We'll find him, Faith."

I let my head fall back so I could see the stars pin-dotting the clear night sky. Corie Whitehead was smart, and Jim had snagged files on two corpses from her neck of the woods. I was well versed in the difference between what I knew and what I could prove, but surely if someone was selling black market organs in Corie's orbit, she could at least give us an idea of what we were dealing with.

16

Perspective is every bit as important as fact to a murder investigation. A full seven hours of dead-to-the-world sleep and halfway through my second cup of coffee, I felt like I could see a wider picture—one I hoped would lead to our killer.

We had three distinct camps of victims with one really horrifying common thread.

The woman who disappeared after being attacked in the nightclub bathroom was a prostitute.

The people Skye was trying to help were immigrants with little money and limited access to healthcare.

And the people in Jim's autopsy files were accident or otherwise sudden death victims.

If I had to guess right then where Jane Doe fit, I'd have chosen prostitute, though I knew what Graham would have to say about hunches and assumptions. Which was why I would keep that one to myself until we could ID her.

"No print card anywhere in the lab yesterday?" I asked Graham again as I turned the truck off the freeway toward Corie Whitehead's place.

"We didn't find one, but we'll check with the forensic team today and make sure we didn't just miss it," he said.

Texas requires all ten fingerprints to renew a driver's license, so if we could get her prints, odds were good we'd get her name. I knew Jim's procedure. "There's no way he didn't start with that on a case like this," I said, finishing the last of my cooling coffee in a single gulp.

"Anyone who knew to take her body and Jim's recorder would also know to take her fingerprints. They still have more lab employees to interview."

"True, but I fell asleep last night thinking about what Cortez said—that there are only fourteen employees at the lab and so far the five they've talked to all have alibis—it could also be someone who watches too much TV and knows how to research shit online," I said. "I don't think those things narrow our field as much as I wanted them to necessarily. I'm beginning to see them more as something to keep in mind as we work through whatever other details we can find. The guy we're after is thorough. And he really doesn't want to get caught."

"They seldom do."

"But this guy is way smarter about it so far. He knows the tools we use to investigate, however he learned them, and he's working to remove them even at personal risk. I'm all for Cortez having his people interview the lab employees, but I'm glad we're not tied up doing that because I'm not as convinced it's the road to the killer as I was yesterday." Something nagged at the back of my brain, but didn't want to come through.

I turned onto the country road that led to Corie's home.

"You're thinking smart like a doctor, maybe?" Graham asked.

"Maybe. But there are some things that don't make sense, too. Why leave the body in a building? Even an abandoned one? If he's so smart and he doesn't want to get caught, why did he sew her up? Why not just...you know...dispose of her in pieces somewhere? Missing persons cases go unsolved every single day, and so far we haven't even been able to find a report on this woman."

Graham pulled out his phone and tapped the screen. "Because the mall is up for demolition?"

I turned my head and stared long enough to nearly run the truck off the road.

"It's what? Why didn't property manager guy mention that when we talked to him?"

"I dug in online trying to find out more about the building and who might frequent it, asked around in a couple of local police chats about it, and according to this post, it's coming down this fall. A guy from APD shared a link to an article about the demo job going to a woman-owned contracting firm. Bodies dumped outdoors or buried are sometimes recovered by chance or animals. But left to decompose—slowly, since her organs were taken—and then crushed under tons of stone and moved to a construction waste landfill? What are the chances anyone ever finds her?"

I drummed two fingers on the wheel as I turned into Corie's drive.

What were the chances, indeed.

"That would mean the killer knew no one would miss her if she disappeared off the face of the Earth," I said, saddened by the thought.

The banana I'd eaten on the way out the door sat like a quarry stone in my stomach, an itchy, uncomfortable feeling creeping over my skin until it felt hot in the truck.

I lowered the window to let in the spring breeze, white-knuckling the wheel.

"What?" Graham asked.

"Nothing I haven't already said. It's just...This guy is more brash than most. That's a bizarre chance to take."

"We haven't missed one yet."

I nodded, the unease in my gut growing instead of subsiding like it usually did when I thought about how many times I'd thought a case was impossible only to figure out it really wasn't.

I shook my head like that might clear the apprehension and hopped out of the truck, meeting Graham at the hood on my way to Corie's front door.

She opened it wearing yoga pants and an oversized T-shirt, a coffee mug in her hand. "Ranger McClellan!" Her face widened into a smile as she opened the screen door and waved us inside. "What can I do for you?"

"Sorry to bother you on Sunday," I began, and she waved one hand and sipped her coffee.

"Please don't apologize. I learned last time that your work ethic rivals mine. If you're here on Sunday, it's because someone needs your help. And if I can lend a hand with whatever you're working on, my Sunday was well spent."

We followed her to the kitchen. "I appreciate your help," I said.

"I haven't had a murder victim—or an anything victim—in my lab in three weeks," she said.

"Must be nice to be in a place where it's so quiet," I said.

"It has its benefits." She smiled. "Just like your job does, I'm sure. So what brings y'all out here? Something going on around here I don't know about?"

"I'm wondering what you might be able to tell us about Bremo Medical Center. And anything...interesting that comes to mind about any of the physicians or staff there." I watched Graham to gauge my question, putting considerable effort into being vague. I didn't want to lead her into talking about the doctors Skye had mentioned. She needed to bring them up.

Corie pointed to the full coffee pot on the counter. "Coffee, anyone? We might be here a minute."

"Yes, please," Graham and I said in unison.

Corie laughed. "Not a lot of sleep last night?" She opened a cabinet and reached for two mugs.

"Someone attacked Jim Prescott yesterday," I said, recalling the admiration she had for his work.

The mugs crashed to the counter and shattered, shards flying as Corie spun to face us with her mouth open in a round little "o" and her eyes big.

"He's not..." Her hand went to her throat.

I shook my head as Graham and I moved to clean up the mess. "I didn't mean to frighten you," I said. "He's in a coma, but the doctors expect him to recover. It'll be a long road, though. His carotid was severed."

"So someone tried to kill him. They just failed." She scurried in slippers to a small pantry and returned with a broom and dustpan.

We made quick work of the broken cups and settled around her little tile-topped table with coffee, Corie fiddling with a paper napkin she pulled from a holder in the center of the table.

"Like any rural hospital, Bremo has its issues. Lack of funding, aging equipment, and trouble attracting quality staff," she said. "But there are a

few things that worry me beyond what worries everyone who pays attention about inequality in our health system."

I sipped my coffee to keep quiet. It would be so much more credible if
she told me with no prodding.

Corie fiddled with the cup some more. "I have a lot of latitude out here
with what I do, but I try to be mindful of the fact that in a place like this,
whispers and suspicion are enough to ruin someone—personally and
professionally."

"Sure," Graham said.

Corie met my gaze. "You ever just get a bad feeling about someone?
Like, there's nothing you can point to or prove, but everything inside you
seems to go on red danger alert when you're around them?"

"I sure have." And every damn one of them had turned out to be a
murderer in one way or another. But I didn't add that last part.

"So, one of the things that makes me good at my job is that I notice
details," she said.

Sure. Jim and I had the same knack.

"I know that I watch things maybe a little closer than I should," she
continued. "But I've noticed a few things."

"About someone at the hospital?"

"There's a surgeon. I met him at an economic development event a
couple years back, when he first moved here, and right off the bat I just..."
Corie shivered. "Like my skin tried to crawl up my arm to get away from
him when I shook his hand."

We stayed so quiet we didn't dare breathe, our forgotten coffee cooling
on the table.

"Here, it would be better if I showed you," she said. "At least seeing it on
paper will prove that I'm not crazy. Or hateful."

"We don't have reason to believe you're either. Or to refuse to take you at
your word." I wanted to know what she was going to say and about whom
so badly my chest felt like someone had it in a vise grip.

"All the same." She held up one finger. "Be right back."

"That's promising," I said.

"Do you remember how Jane Doe's clothing was all straight and
fastened? And her arms were folded?" Graham's face said he was working

on a theory. That didn't have anything to do with what we'd come to see Corie about.

"I do," I said. "Why?"

"It's all here." Corie came back before he could answer, fanning a stack of manila folders across the tabletop. She opened one to a spreadsheet. "Last year alone, he had several times as many patients die on the table as the next guy on the list."

"Die of what?" I pulled the folder closer. Pay dirt. My eyes stayed trained on the "Bryce Little" in the first box of the spreadsheet row until I had to blink to stop them from burning.

"I don't know. He also has the highest percentage of families that refuse autopsies."

I raised my eyes to Corie's and found her brows up so high they were hidden by her soft wisp of copper bangs.

"Yep." She popped the P at the end of the word hard.

"You don't happen to have his stats on organ donors, do you?" Graham asked while I pored over the other numbers on her spreadsheet.

"I don't, but we can find out. We'd just have to call UNOS and ask for the numbers for the hospital itself. I doubt they have it broken down by surgeon, but I can ask a few people and get close."

It was a nice thought, but if I was right about Dr. Little, UNOS would have no record of what we were looking for.

"What time period does this cover?" I asked, not taking my eyes off the sheet.

"June to December of last year," she said.

"In a small rural hospital this guy lost almost 20 patients on the table in six months?"

Graham whistled. "I'm not a medical expert, but that seems like a lot."

"It's a whole lot." Corie refilled her coffee mug and added sugar and a splash of cream. "Most doctors lose that many people in maybe three years?"

I flipped pages in her folders, finding a printout of the staff page at the hospital for the surgery team, Little smiling from the top photo.

"He's the chief of surgery? When he kills nearly as many people as he saves?"

"I'm pretty sure he knows the CEO of the hospital system from way back, and we're the smallest facility they run," Corie said. She paused. Sighed. "I know there are a hundred possible explanations for this. If you look in the back there, you'll see I made myself a list of them a few months back. Maybe he takes the hardest cases because he's the head of the department and he's looking out for his staff. Maybe the guy is just truly shitty at his job. But there's something about him I don't trust. That's what I keep coming back to. I don't often have such a visceral reaction to meeting people. Matter of fact, it's only happened one other time in my whole life, when I was twelve. A new family moved in down the road a ways and I got whipped with a switch for being rude to the father because I wouldn't help him carry a mattress upstairs when my daddy offered to help unload the moving van." She shivered at the memory.

"Same thing. I just had this unstoppable certainty that I shouldn't be around the guy, let alone go upstairs alone with him. Seven months later he was arrested for kidnapping and raping one of my classmates. She was missing for three days and never spoke another word after she went home. Killed herself three weeks later. My daddy fired the shot that took the guy down when he charged the deputies with a gun after they surrounded the house."

"Jesus, I remember that story." I ran one hand over my ponytail. "Her name was Clarissa, right?"

"It was. She was in the choir at church. My mother played the piano and said Clarissa sang like an angel sent down from heaven to make sure people had their butts in the pews come Sunday morning, no matter what they'd been up to Saturday night."

I shook my head. "It was all over the news, and she was my age. My mother went bat shit crazy over it. My father had just been elected to his first term the year before and she assigned extra security to me and my sister, somehow convinced that whoever took that girl was coming for the governor's young daughters next. That was how I got to know Archie. Ruth had him pulled from the governor's detail to ours because everyone said he was the best." Because she'd been afraid. Ruth McClellan, afraid something might happen to Charity or me. Almost like any other mom might've been, seeing the coverage of Clarissa's disappearance.

Imagine that.

"He still is," Graham said.

I pulled out a notebook and my phone and made notes about what Corie had said and took photos of the pages in her file after I asked her permission.

"Do you happen to remember the name of the guy who kidnapped Clarissa?" I asked.

"Ronnie Dewayne Harris," Corie said. "I still have nightmares sometimes about him leering at me over that mattress."

"Always trust your gut," Graham said. "If there was one piece of advice I could make sure was given to every single woman in the world the day she turned twelve, that would be it. I have worked far too many cases where a woman ended up dead because she was trying to be polite."

"And in the course of the investigation we find out that she had mentioned getting a creepy vibe from the man who turned out to be the killer," I said. "It's a horrifyingly common story."

"Those cases are always the easy ones," Graham said.

"And men like that aren't usually smart enough to cover their tracks," Corie added.

"I would take a bumbling dumbass today," I said.

"I hope I was able to be helpful," Corie said.

"So helpful," I said. "Now if I can find out where Pendergast and Little were yesterday morning without them knowing I'm asking, we'll be in great shape."

Corie's brow furrowed. "Yesterday? They were the featured speakers at the Rotary Club breakfast. I was there. Managed to avoid handshakes, though."

My shoulders slumped enough for her to notice. "What time?"

"From seven-thirty to ten." She winced. "Not what you wanted to hear?"

"I always want to hear the truth, even when it's not what I expect." I smiled a thank you at her avoidance of asking me why we were interested in the maybe not-so-good doctors. She might not want to know any more than I wanted to share. Not that I didn't trust her, but keeping a working case close is ingrained in every good cop's DNA—the fewer people who know what we're thinking, the lower the chance the killer knows what we know before we want them to.

We thanked Corie for her help and offered to return the favor anytime at the door, descending her front steps to my truck as my phone rang. I didn't recognize the number, but it was a Waco area code, so I clicked the green circle.

"McClellan."

"Ranger, this is Jeanette Miller, Waco PD Forensics."

"What can I do for you?"

"My team is finishing up at the scene in the old mall today and they found something in the closet where the body was placed that I think you might be interested in," she said. "A camera."

"Like a 'take a picture' camera?" I asked.

"No, like a security camera. One of the ones that plugs in and runs video to the cloud. People can check in on an app from their phones. Rigged up in the corner behind the boiler. Pointed at the door. My tech squad is examining it now; it's possible that it has a motion sensor."

"Which would've alerted whoever put it there if the door opened."

"I suppose so, yes."

So much for a bumbling dumbass.

"Is there any way to see the footage it took?" I asked.

"Tech is working on that, and we'll call the manufacturer and see how far we get, but right now there's not. You'd have to know the login for the phone app it's linked to."

I furrowed my brow. 'But to feed to a cell app it would have to be linked to the internet," I said.

"True."

"Did you find a router or anything in there? Because I know there's no wifi in the mall itself."

"Not yet, but we're still processing the surrounding area, and I don't know the range on this thing, so we'll get it from the manufacturer and expand our search in a ring. If it's in there, we'll find it."

"Keep me posted?"

"Sure thing. Have a good one."

"You too."

I ended the call and looked up at Graham with a sigh.

"There was a surveillance camera in the closet."

"Seems like the only person who would've put such a thing in a locked, unused closet is the same person who put a dead body in said closet."

"That's kind of where I ended up, yes."

I turned that over in my head.

I wanted it to be the doctors, because it seemed like they'd slithered over to the dark side preying on the poor and uneducated in truly monstrous fashion, and nothing about my job is more fun than seeing scumbags who do horrible things to vulnerable people held accountable.

But Graham was right, we'd learned a long time ago that trying to lead an investigation in a certain direction was never a good idea. If the doctor wasn't an outright murderer, well...that didn't mean we couldn't nail him for selling body parts after we caught our killer.

"Buster said he handles everything for that facility himself," I said. "So if he has the only keys..."

"Maybe he thought it was a safe place to hide a body."

"Or maybe we were right about the doorknobs Friday and he doesn't have the right keys anymore. I mean, how the hell would that guy know how to remove organs suitably for transplant, or to sew someone up?" I asked. "He didn't exactly seem like the intellectual type to me."

But what did we really know about him? He drank before five—at least on Friday—he drove too fast, and he didn't seem to love his job.

I started the truck as Graham closed his door.

"We asked him for documents and keys the other night that we never got, at least that we know of," he said. "Let's go find him. Take him in, ask some questions. Maybe we can crack him."

I tried to sound more sure than I felt. "If there's anything there to crack, we'll get it."

17

Two hours and change into the three-hour drive back to Waco, my phone rang with another unfamiliar number.

"McClellan," I said, putting it to my ear.

"Hello, Ranger, this is Brian Maxwell from the Gray Goose. You came in yesterday?"

"Of course," I said. "What can I do for you, Brian?"

"We were able to get the camera footage you requested together for you. What we have, anyway. I'd be happy to bring it to you."

"Thank you so much for compiling that for me," I said. "How were things at the club last night?"

"Pretty quiet for a Saturday," he said.

"I can send you the address for my office if you'd like to drop that by," I said. "There's a slot to put materials through. As long as it's just a thumb drive, it will fit without a problem."

He didn't answer for long enough to make me check the phone's screen for a dropped call.

"I was just wondering if you had time to meet me to pick it up," he said. "I thought I might ask for some pointers on how to keep this from happening again. Sonny isn't big on the idea of going to the press, he thinks it will kill our attendance."

"Any chance he might be able to join us?" I asked.

"He's in San Antonio for the weekend," Brian said.

Damn.

"We can come by the Gray Goose if that's easy," I said.

"They're doing inventory in the back and getting ready to open for the evening," he said. "Do you know Cadence Coffee, on the south end of town?"

"Sure." I checked the GPS. "We'll be there in about 40 minutes."

"See you then."

I ended the call and returned the phone to the cupholder.

"Video footage?" Graham asked.

"Yeah. But it also seems like this bartender might want to talk. And not where it might get back to his boss. He specifically asked to meet at a coffee shop."

"I could go for some coffee," Graham said.

"Me too. Especially if it comes with a shot of answers."

"Did we look into this guy?" Graham asked.

"The bartender? Didn't strike me as the murderous type," I said. "He seemed worried about the club's business."

"I agree, just trying to cover every base. There have been several attacks that might be related at that bar in the past few months."

"We did have Cortez haul in all the employees at the lab." I plucked the phone back out of the cupholder. "Let's see if Archie can turn anything up. For someone who hates the computers so much, he's quick to dig anything worth digging out of a background check."

I opened a text, flipping in my notebook to the page where the card Brian had given me the day before was stuck. *Sorry to bug you on Sunday— can you run a history on Brian Maxwell? Mid to late 20s probably, he's the head bartender at that club we went to check out with Cortez yesterday.*

Anything I can do to help came the almost immediate reply.

You're the best.

Looking for anything in particular?

To rule him out as a possible POI, I typed. *I don't think he could be, but Graham pointed out that we should check him off the list with so many attacks tied to the bar.*

Never a bad idea. Let me know if you want me to check anyone else.
Thanks, Arch.

I put the phone down and watched the roadside blur into a camouflage palette of greens and browns outside the window. Before long, bluebonnets would transform the highway shoulders into seas of cobalt beauty. And hopefully long before then, we'd have our Jack the Ripper wannabe in custody.

Brian was at a back corner table in the coffee shop when we walked in, looking at his phone.

Graham pointed to the mug on the table in front of Brian. "Go get started, I'll get coffee."

I smiled a thank you and crossed the mostly-empty space. Not many folks wanted to be in a dim little coffeehouse late in the afternoon on a gorgeous spring Sunday.

"Hey there," I said when I stopped in front of the table.

He clicked the phone off and slid it under the table, looking up with a charming smile. "Didn't see you come in. Thanks for meeting me."

He pulled a plain white envelope from an inside pocket on his jacket and laid it on the table. "I hope that has something that will help you," he said.

"I appreciate you getting it together for us so fast."

"I figured if y'all are trying to find out what's been going on and put a stop to it, it was worth losing a little sleep," he said. "I've been trying to think of anything else that might help you." He fiddled with the edges of a napkin.

I watched his face. His eyes dropped to the table, his mouth twisting to one side. Curling one arm slowly behind my back, I held up one finger to let Graham know to hang back for a minute. Brian wanted to tell me something. And I didn't want him getting rattled by Graham walking up and chickening out.

"There's a group of...well...um, prostitutes that work the bar," he said finally. "I know you asked about that yesterday and I said I try to ignore it, and I do, but some of them really don't like each other."

"I'm pretty sure the person we're looking for is a man," I said.

He plucked the corners off the napkin. "I'm not trying to argue or tell you how to do your job or anything. Just wanted to let you know that they get pretty nasty with each other. Since you asked if the woman who was attacked was one of them. And at least one of them is as tall as I am. Maybe taller."

I pulled out a notebook. "Do you know any of their names?"

He shook his head.

"How about where they live?" I asked.

"I try to avoid talking to them, which works for us both because they don't talk to people they can't make money off of." He paused. "Has to be too far from the bar to walk, though. The one with the red hair drives a small car they all pile into to get there."

"Has your boss ever asked you to keep them out of the bar?"

"I'm pretty sure he knows at least some of them." Brian plucked more shreds off the napkin. "Like knows them, knows them. So I wouldn't mention it to him. But if you wanted to talk to them, I took a picture of the plate on the car they drive last night." He pulled his phone out and flipped the screen around. A fuzzy photo of a gray Toyota Corolla that probably last had all its paint when Clinton was president filled the screen, the plates slightly blurred, but not such that we couldn't make them out to run them.

"Thanks, Brian," I said. "Can you text that to the number you called me on earlier? I'll see what I can turn up."

I wasn't convinced it was a lead worth following given the video footage from the lab and Jim's words, but he didn't need to know that.

"Have you found out anything useful since yesterday?" he asked as he sent the photo to my phone. "Should I be worried about it happening again?"

"We're working on several leads. I can't tell you not to worry yet, but hopefully soon."

Graham ambled over and handed me a coffee. "Took a minute, but it's just the way you like it."

Something flashed across Brian's face and his fist closed over the remains of the napkin. I held his gaze, and his eyes weren't angry. They were sad. Maybe a little worried in the lines at the corners he seemed way too young to have.

"Is there anything else you want to talk about?" I sipped the coffee.

Brian blinked. "I don't think so." His eyes went to my ring. "You're engaged?"

"Only until Saturday." Graham put a hand on my shoulder. "We'll be married after that."

Brian's lips curved into a small smile. "Congratulations."

"Thank you." I watched him for a few beats. "You okay?"

"Oh sure. Bad breakup, but I'm getting past it."

"You never know what better things might be in store," Graham said. "Trust me."

Brian stood, tossing the napkins in the trash and draining his mug. "I hope the video helps," he said. "Just let me know if you have any more questions."

"The number in my phone is your cell?" I asked.

"I never bothered to set up the voicemail, but yes." He smiled.

"We appreciate your help, Brian. I'll let you know when we have someone in custody."

I pocketed the envelope as we watched him leave.

"Seems like a decent enough guy," Graham said.

"I guess if he's not, Archie will let us know shortly." I stood too, grabbing my coffee to go. "In the meantime, I'm sure Buster has some interesting things to share. If we can make him talk."

Buster Beauchamp wasn't home. He also wasn't at his office, housed in a building that clearly used to be a Diamond Shamrock station in a better lit, less moldy life.

I rattled the steel and glass door in the frame for good measure before I sighed and pulled out my phone. The parking lot's concrete cracked and crumbled in more places than it didn't, pushed aside by early season dollar grass and dandelions seeking the sun.

Graham and I climbed back into the truck as I tried Beauchamp's number again, checking the clock.

"How the fuck is it almost six already?" I asked, rubbing one temple. The day was one of those that somehow felt like it took twelve years and flashed by in a blink, all at the same time.

Buster didn't answer his phone, either.

I opened my maps app and searched for nearby bars, clicking the little red pin on one that was about halfway between where we sat and Buster's home.

"Take a left at the next light and then a right on Faulkner. He smelled like booze last night—if he won't answer the phone, we'll check the local bars until we turn him up."

Graham started the truck and turned on the radio. "Anything new from Jim's family?"

I opened my texts. "Jesse sent an update about an hour ago. He's stable, the neuro guy was back in and said his brain activity is really good. But they're still waiting for him to wake up before they can tell anything for sure about how much damage the blood loss might have done."

I pointed to the left at the intersection and Graham turned the truck onto a short dead-end street that held a contractor supply yard and a squatty pink building with a flat roof and a gravel parking lot full of cars.

"Talk about a neighborhood dive," he muttered.

Half-working lights lit up one side of a cracked plastic sign over the door, christening the place "Maxine's" in big blue letters and advertising cocktails, beer, and something that had been blacked out with spray paint across the bottom. Upon close inspection, I could just make out enough letters to realize the third word was "girls."

"Dive is too generous a word," I murmured. "My grandfather would've called this place a beer joint."

Our thanks for pulling the door open was a racial slur screamed over the clatter of wood meeting wood and floating out on clouds of stale smoke and the reek of cheap beer mixed with just a hint of vomit.

"See?" I arched one eyebrow and checked the security strap on my holster. I could get my weapon out of there in half a second, but didn't want anyone getting any bright ideas if we were walking into the middle of a fight.

Graham put one hand on the door over my head and held it as I stepped inside. In the time it took my eyes to adjust to the dim, hazy interior, the unmistakable sound of a blunt object connecting with bone came from the back corner, followed quickly by more shouted epithets.

"Keep back, you lying motherfuckers, or you're next."

Graham and I exchanged a worried glance and parted ways, flanking the crowd gathered in the far corner, which included everyone in the place except a weary-looking bartender who wiped a pint glass clean while keeping one eye on the situation. The muscles bulging under the guy's black T-shirt as he did the dishes said he doubled as a bouncer—one who'd probably been at it long enough to know when to step in and when to avoid risking personal injury to save idiots from themselves. If a place like this called the cops every time there was a fight, they'd lose their license to operate in a month.

"Jerry, man, easy." A lanky guy in a Señor Frogs shirt so faded it was practically transparent and jeans sporting the kind of holes that come with age and wear, not fashion, took a step forward, his hands raised and his voice cool. "It's just a misunderstanding."

I kept my hand resting on the butt of my Sig, thumb on the strap and my eyes on the man on the far side of the crowd wielding what looked like a hunk of broken chair leg like a baseball bat.

"That fat fuck called me a liar." Jerry's eyes were wide, his voice high and strained. "I ain't saying I'm no saint, but I ain't a liar. Not over a goddamn game of darts and a bet for buying a round of beer."

A dart board hung on the wall a few feet behind the crowd. The way Jerry's eyes flicked to the floor when he said "fat fuck" made me think someone probably needed medical attention, but I didn't want to cause a situation that might be defusing to erupt again by trying to help whoever was down there before Jerry had put his club down.

"Enough of this horseshit." I couldn't see where that came from, but the voice was on Graham's side of the circle. "You're a cheating sumbitch, Jerry, and we all know it. About damn time somebody said it to your face. Now put that thing down and get the hell out of here."

Jerry was in no state to be insulted. He launched himself, club raised, at the far side of the crowd, and a black felt cowboy hat went flying as he tackled the man wearing it. They fell into three others—two stumbled backward into guys who shoved them away, and one fell, which earned him a sharp boot toe to the ribs from a guy who spilled his beer on account of being jostled.

In one blink, the situation went from contained but concerning to out of control. I glanced at Graham. He didn't want to step into it any more than I did. We had more important things to do than break up a bullshit brawl in a sad little beer joint.

"Dammit, someone's liable to really get hurt," I muttered as the four guys closest to the rack on the wall holding the pool cues all grabbed one, and at least three people drained their beer bottles and then flipped them around to grip them by the neck as weapons. I scanned the edges for the easiest route into the middle of the mob.

"You going to stop this or you want me to?" The deep voice came from over my shoulder as the first pool cue connected with a skull and a flurry of punches were thrown, tables tipping and glass crashing to the floor. I slid my eyes to the burly bartender, who looked way more tired than annoyed.

"Happen often?" I asked.

Before he could answer, a screech and a ray of fading sunlight came from a door that led out the back of the building. "You cheating, lying bastard!" the woman howled, running on unsteady feet that made me wonder if she'd already tied a few on. A skinny redhead in a denim miniskirt and red stilettos, she leapt onto Jerry's back, knocking his ball cap to the sticky floor and pulling his graying blond mullet with both hands hard enough to snap his head back and let black felt hat guy land a good punch square to Jerry's chin.

This dude was just catching hell from all corners tonight.

"Once a week when things are good and folks are working. More when they're not. Jerry ain't had a steady paycheck in going on a month now." Shaking his head, the bartender stepped forward and put his thumb and finger in the corners of his mouth, blowing out an earsplitting whistle that silenced the shouting for a few beats.

"Knock it the fuck off, folks," he boomed in a rich bass. "The cops are already here, so unless any of you assholes want to spend the night in the can, you can return to throwing darts and shooting the shit right fucking now. You got me?"

Every head in the place swiveled to Graham and me in turn.

"Travis County Sheriff's Office." He held up his badge.

"We ain't in Travis County," Jerry snarled, tossing the woman over his shoulder. She hit the floor with a low *oof*.

"Texas Rangers," I barked, the words ringing through the space. "Are we in Texas, Jerry?"

He muttered something I was sure Graham and I didn't need to hear as his makeshift weapon clattered to the floor next to his girl and he fell into a chair.

Shoulders slumped and people reached to help others off the floor. The peacemaker in the Señor Frogs shirt righted a table and picked up pieces of a broken pitcher.

"Thanks," the bartender said as he turned to return to the bar.

"I didn't do much."

"I usually have to pull a couple of them up and chuck them out when they get that worked up." He rubbed one shoulder. "That shit's not as easy now as it was when I was 25."

I glanced at Graham and he nodded as he moved through the small, dispersing crowd to haul Jerry to his feet and check on the redhead and whoever had started the whole mess.

"You get a regular crowd here?" I asked the bartender, turning to follow him and hoping to get a bead on Buster.

"Same guys every day. Women come in occasionally, but only the sort who reek of desperation." He gave me a once-over.

"Do you know Buster Beauchamp, by any chance?" I asked.

He jerked a whisker-darkened chin at a stool toward the middle-end of the bar farthest from the door. "That's Buster's seat, there. Drinks cheap shit whiskey and thinks he's better than the other guys because they drink beer. Currently probably still laid out on the floor over there judging by how hard ol' Jerry swung that chair."

"Faith!" Graham's shout came as I was spinning back. He was kneeling alongside Buster, the Señor Frogs guy next to him, and an alarming amount of blood seeping across the floor under Buster's head.

"Shit," I muttered, sprinting across the sticky, threadbare red paisley carpet as I pulled out my phone and called an ambulance.

"He's breathing, but not well," Graham said as I reeled off our location to dispatch.

"He's been picking at Jerry all week long," Señor Frogs said. "But he was in a real foul mood tonight."

"Which 'he?'" I asked as the peals of the sirens said the paramedics were getting close.

"Buster." Señor Frogs waved a hand over his unconscious form. "Jerry said he hit the triple eighteen when he was probably in the single, and Buster called him a lying…" He glanced at Graham and then back at Buster. "Uh. Well, you see, it's like this, the gal Jerry had with him last night was uh…she was of African descent."

My eyes went to the redhead, who was stomping her foot a few yards away, gesturing to the door as Jerry tried to grab her hand and she repeatedly shook him off, pointing to the bartender and Señor Frogs and a couple of other guys.

"We heard that part when we opened the door," Graham said.

"So Jerry grabbed a chair and swung for Buster's head, and Buster went down like a sack of potatoes. The chair broke. That's how hard Jerry hit him. You think he'll be okay?"

The paramedics came in the back door before I could say he'd be fine. I was busy being annoyed that we'd found him but he couldn't tell us anything.

We all stepped back so they could work.

"Where are you taking him?" I asked the one closest to me.

"County," she said, watching the screen on a portable blood pressure machine. "His vitals are okay, but he needs a few stitches and some fluids."

"Thanks." I turned to Graham. "Now what?"

He waved for me to follow him to the table nearest the dart board, where we watched Señor Frogs toss two bullseyes and a twenty.

He saw us after he pulled the darts and handed them to the guy in the black felt hat.

"Y'all can't be here looking for a game," he said, glancing between us.

"We were actually looking for Buster when we got here," Graham said. "You said a minute ago he was picking on Jerry all week but he was in a bad mood in particular tonight. You know why, on either count?"

"Jerry used to work for Buster. Nobody here knows why he don't anymore, but they were tight for a long time and now they can't stand to look at each other without talking horseshit." He took a swig of a Miller Lite and put it back on the table, wiping his lips on the back of one hand. "And I didn't hear what had Buster quite so pissed off, but something went terribly wrong for him since he was here yesterday, that's for damn sure."

18

"My grandfather had some sayings, too." Graham's voice was low in my ear. "Chief among them was two and two ain't always four, but don't question it without damn good reason."

"Truth." My eyes roved the room for Jerry's Shiner Bock trucker-style ball cap, or the woman's stringy scarlet hair.

I found both at the same time—just as they stepped out the door into the twilight.

I tugged Graham's sleeve, Brian's comment about a redheaded sex trade worker frequenting the Gray Goose fresh in my thoughts, and gave chase with him on my heels. I had to move a couple of decent-sized men out of my path to the door when "no thank you, excuse me" didn't deter their offers of a dance. A yelp followed a few seconds after I heard the second one mutter "uppity bitch" when he hit the floor, but I didn't look back.

Graham kept stride with me all the way to the truck as I recited the plate number on the beat-up Trans Am Jerry and his lady friend rolled out of the parking lot until I was sure I wouldn't forget it.

I tossed Graham my keys at the tailgate. "You drive, I'll run that plate and get an address."

He slid into the seat and started the engine as I clipped my seat belt and tapped into the DPS computer system from my phone. "Did you kick that guy?"

"What guy?"

"The one who called me an uppity bitch when I shoved him out of my way because politely declining his offer to dance didn't work." I tossed a smile his way as I waited for the results to load via a one-bar cell connection.

"I wouldn't kick anyone." Graham did a pretty good impression of sounding insulted. "I can't promise his hand wasn't on the floor in my path or that the heel of my boot didn't land on it as I ran past." He cleared his throat. "But I did not kick him."

"Well. Thanks." I glanced at my phone. "Car is registered to Ellen Marie Helmsley, last known address is—" I paused, putting it in the map. "Five blocks that way." I pointed east.

Graham pointed. "Well then he's not taking the lady home."

I followed his gaze out the windshield and saw the Trans Am three cars ahead of us on the right.

"We make a good team," I said.

"Always have."

I kept my eyes on the Trans Am. It was definitely listing to the right.

Graham changed lanes when he saw the car veer onto the shoulder and then right itself.

The Trans Am zipped along at a decent clip, managing to keep between the lines even if it did still look unsteady. There was another light ahead, already yellow, no way either of us would make it through the intersection. Graham put one foot on the brake.

"Hey, I was thinking about Jane Doe—" he began.

The rest of the thought disappeared on a sharp inhale as the Trans Am's engine gunned and the car caught just a bit of air running off the road, spinning a 180 in a cloud of dust and weeds before coming to a stop with the back end resting against a speed limit sign.

"Shit." Graham swerved to the shoulder and brought the truck to a stop.

"So much for not letting on that we're following them."

I reached for the door handle and Graham put one hand on my arm. "Um."

With the Trans Am flipped around, we could see Jerry and the woman, who I assumed was Ellen of the vehicle's registration.

She straddled his lap in the driver's seat, her spine bent at what had to be an uncomfortable angle around the steering wheel.

She was definitely bouncing up and down.

I stared for a full five seconds before I started laughing. "They're. Um. Right there in the front seat of the car, huh? I suppose that would be a reason to lose control of your vehicle."

"This is a first for me." Graham coughed around a laugh. "I've seen people do what I thought was every kind of crazy shit I could think of while driving; I even pulled a guy over once who crossed the center line because he was getting a blowjob, which I know because they didn't see a need to stop just because I was at the window. Never had anybody so happy to take a ticket. But I've never seen anyone..." He shook his head. "We write this up as distracted driving, right?"

"I think the real question is do we break it up now or do we wait until they're done?" I swiped at tears leaking from the corners of my eyes, turning to survey the traffic. "They could legitimately cause an accident with the intersection right there if anyone looks over at them."

"Eh. It's dark enough." Graham cut the headlights on my truck, which were spotlighting the Trans Am's interior. "I don't want to go over there right now, do you? Besides, he might feel more like talking if we don't interrupt."

I leaned my head back against the seat, my shoulders still shaking. "Damn, I almost want to thank them. I needed the laugh today."

Other cars passed us for a good two minutes, none the wiser, before the driver's door of the Trans Am flew open, the woman pitching out onto the dirt at the foot of the speed limit sign.

"That's our cue?" I let the last word go up, like a question. Inky country darkness crept in deeper by the minute, but I could still see just well enough to tell she didn't look happy.

I hopped out of my truck and turned on a flashlight, approaching the driver's door with caution since we knew from earlier that Jerry had a temper.

The woman's legs splayed out of a denim skirt hitched up to her waist, one surly patrol officer away from an indecent exposure charge. She was coughing, rubbing at her throat, which was where I fixed my gaze. "You selfish son of a bitch," she spat back toward the car, oblivious to or ignoring me, and it was impossible to tell which.

"What seems to be the trouble here, folks?" I let the words ring loud in my most practiced, authoritative cop voice.

"That bastard tried to kill me, that's what!" She scrambled to her feet, thankfully tugging her skirt down as she stood.

Graham quickened his stride and rounded the hood of the car, his hand on his weapon and his eyes on Jerry. "Sir, we're going to need you to step out of the car please."

"I didn't do shit to that whore she wasn't already doing to me," Jerry bellowed.

"We can sort that out after you step out of the vehicle." Graham kept his voice calm.

"I'm trying." One boot-clad foot appeared. "I think she broke something." He stood slowly and turned his back, sucking in a sharp breath as he fidgeted before he turned back around with his jeans buttoned, dirty white T-shirt hanging down over them. He shot the woman a glare. "Bitch."

"Don't you call me names, you lowlife loser," she screeched, lunging. I grabbed her shoulders with a grip that made her wince.

"Stay put," I warned.

"He ain't got nothing to break, anyway." Her eyes were on me, but the loud, clear tone was clearly meant to goad Jerry.

"Go to hell," he called, but he didn't make a move toward her with Graham standing between him and me.

"You first," she muttered, still rubbing at her neck.

I glanced at Graham. Divide and conquer. We didn't know enough to know if anyone needed to be arrested, so it looked like we were stuck in this little detour until we did.

I herded her backward until I had her seated on the tailgate of my truck. Her face scrunched as if with pain when she raised both arms over her head and stretched to either side, her crop top riding up almost too far in the process.

"I'm Faith." I smiled, a small one I had practiced in the mirror for years to perfect. *You can trust me,* it said, much more effectively than me so much as whispering a word. "Ellen, right?"

She shook her head. "I'm Rosie."

I put out one hand. "Nice to meet you."

She shook it reluctantly. "Yeah, same."

"Can you tell me what happened?"

She gazed warily at my badge. "We had a disagreement."

"About what?"

"Money."

"Does Jerry owe you money?" I remembered the way she'd run into the bar and jumped on his back.

"Not exactly." She shifted her weight from one foot to the other, putting my mental lie detector on high alert.

I resisted the urge to fold my arms across my chest, tucking my hands into the back pockets of my jeans instead and leaving my body language open.

"Listen, I'm long past my days of writing tickets or hauling people in for minor indiscretions. This will go a lot faster for both of us if you level with me."

"Cops aren't usually the nicest or most trustworthy people around, in my experience," she said.

"I'm not most cops. My area of expertise is homicide, and at the moment, it's pretty much my only area of interest." I raised both eyebrows and curved my lips into a half smile. I knew the expression gave just the right hint of conspiratorial friendship, much more effectively than words ever would, and without me having to promise her anything before I heard what she had to say.

"Jerry ain't never killed nobody," she said, maybe a little too quickly, but she was nervous. I watched her for signs of a lie. She shifted again, left foot to right and back again.

"Of course not."

"Then why are you following us? I saw you at Maxine's."

"I was there looking for Buster Beauchamp because I need to ask him a few questions about a property he manages. It seems Jerry is put out with Buster, and as a result, Buster is unavailable for questioning at the moment.

I thought Jerry might tell me why he's upset with Buster." I kept my voice even and calm, delivering the facts as I wanted her to see them.

She tipped her head to one side. "Jerry used to work for that old bastard. I didn't see what happened tonight, but I'm sure Buster had it coming. Hell, I can name ten regulars at Maxine's who would lay that asshole out given the chance."

Yet when Graham and I walked in, Jerry was at the center of a circle of people he seemed to be holding off with a stick. I knew better than to argue, though.

I switched gears instead. "What did Jerry do for Buster?"

"Fixed shit." She wiggled her index and middle fingers in a scissor pattern. "Like when stuff broke at the properties. Buster inherited that company from his daddy. He pushes paper and takes the majority of the profits every month, plus the kickbacks. He did Jerry dirty with pay, though."

I kept my face blank, holding her gaze. "How so?"

She glanced over her shoulder at the car, where Jerry was waving his hands animatedly as he talked to Graham.

"I'm not sure I ought to be telling you things. He might get pissy about it."

"I thought you were mad at him."

"I stay mad at him." The smile that tugged at the corners of her mouth seemed to contradict that. "It's what we do. But I don't want him to be in trouble. Or to be really mad at me."

"I don't want you to tell me anything you don't want to." It was a flat-out lie, but sometimes the best way to keep someone talking is to tell them it's okay with me if they stop.

"I mean it's not like Jerry was the one skimming the cash or anything."

The revelation that Buster was skimming cash was probably the least surprising thing I'd ever heard. I didn't say it, though, offering a flicker of a nod and waiting for her to keep talking.

She sighed. "Buster Beauchamp is a cheating, no good, rat bastard scum ball. Whenever something needed to be fixed, he'd call someone about it, but then tell his client the price was more than whatever the contractor said. Then he just kept the difference."

Simple. And really not all that uncommon. I waited. Let her talk.

"We were playing darts one night at Maxine's and Buster and Jerry got to talking. Jerry never had the money to go to school, but he was in the service and he's real handy, you know? He can fix almost anything. So Buster asked if he'd be interested in a few jobs. Once Buster figured out that Jerry was reliable and cheap, but he just couldn't charge as much as someone with a license, he was thrilled. Jerry took over most of the repair jobs, and Buster charged his property owners whatever his overinflated professional rate was and kept the difference."

"How long did Jerry work for Buster?"

"Almost a year."

"And why doesn't he anymore?" I asked.

She stared at me with big, haunted eyes. "I guess he finally got sick of being taken advantage of. Listening to Buster brag about how rich he's getting got old quick when Jerry was the person actually doing the hard work."

"Did he ask Buster for more money?"

"Sure. Not that it did any good. But Jerry knows stuff Buster would really be better off with other people not knowing. Said he was going to remind Buster of that today. He said Buster came at him, but he was ready."

Now that she was in the mood to share, I tried a question. "Did he say what that secret was?"

She clamped her lips shut, shaking her head.

I changed lanes swiftly. "Do you want to press charges over...whatever happened in the car?" I asked.

"Things just got out of hand." Her cheeks flushed bright red. "He said the spark was gone out of our relationship, that he went out with that bitch yesterday because I wasn't as spontaneous"—she made air quotes with her fingers—"as I used to be. I showed his ass spontaneous." She smirked and smoothed her skirt. "But then he started choking me, and then..." She waved one hand at the car. "You saw the rest."

I looked over her shoulder and caught Graham's eye.

"Rosie, do you know a nightclub called the Gray Goose?" I asked.

She twisted her mouth to one side and shook her head. "Don't sound familiar." She squinted at me. "Is that the place someone got murdered?"

"No, no one died there." I raised one finger in Graham's direction and wound it in a *wrap it up* gesture. "You cool now?"

"Yeah." Rosie tugged on her hair.

We ambled back to Graham and Jerry.

"Everyone good here?" I asked.

"Yes, ma'am," Jerry said.

Graham nodded.

"Y'all drive safe," I said as Graham and I turned back for the truck.

Pausing, I looked over my shoulder. "One more thing: who is Ellen?"

Jerry looked from me to Graham to Rosie and dove into the Trans Am. Before any of us could move, he revved the engine, ripped a one-eighty, and sped away.

Our jaws hanging open, we watched the taillights fade into the night.

19

"Rosie says Jerry told her he won the car in a card game." I clicked back to the address DPS had on file for Ellen Helmsley in the GPS after we dropped Rosie at a diner where she said she had a friend who could take her home. She refused to press charges against Jerry for assaulting her, and we had no reason to detain her.

I went back to the results page on the plate and scrolled down. "It hasn't been reported stolen. Take a right up here."

Graham drove to Ellen's home while I hunted background on Jerry from the scan Graham got of his license.

"He's 46, did six months for felony assault five years ago. One DUI more than a year ago, no traffic or moving violations in the past six months. No legal connection to either Ellen or Rosie. Rosie said he did handyman work for Buster that Buster scammed money out of his clients, but Jerry wasn't involved other than getting paid under the table."

"Jerry swore he didn't know why Buster was in such a lousy mood today," Graham said. "He told the same story as the guy at the bar—said he laid him out after Buster accused him of cheating at darts and called him a foul name, but that Buster had been there long enough to be slurring his words and he was acting out of character."

"Did he say anything about asking Beauchamp for money?" I didn't think he would've, but it was worth asking.

"Nope."

"So the big question right now is: why did Jerry run when we said Ellen's name?"

Graham stopped the truck in front of a small house with dingy yellow clapboard siding and bars on the old wood windows.

"Maybe Ellen knows?"

We picked our way up a cracked, uneven concrete sidewalk and a set of cement steps sporting several layers of peeling paint, the most recent of which was green. No doorbell. I raised my fist to rap on the metal frame of the screen door.

Graham turned to survey the neighborhood, rows of small, neat houses and chain link fences facing a narrow asphalt street with high curbs and strips of weeds running up the center of nearly every concrete driveway. The yard next door was scattered with plastic toys: a red and yellow car with pedals to power it, a blue sit and spin, a small plastic basketball hoop.

Across the street, the fence came all the way to the road with a gate at the sidewalk, and beer cans crept across or dangled from every surface like silver and blue locusts. The whole display was lit by half a dozen floodlights placed strategically around the yard.

"How long you figure it'd take to drink all that?" Graham murmured, taking in the scene.

"With just one liver?" I asked, rapping on the door again.

Graham snorted over a laugh. "Right?"

I leaned closer to the door, listening for signs of anyone inside.

"No lights on," I said.

"I don't think she's home," Graham said.

I opened the screen and tried the door. Locked.

"We don't have a warrant," Graham said.

"I don't know that she's coming back," a voice called from beer alley across the road.

I turned to Graham and raised my eyebrows, nodding toward a stocky guy in a blue tank top who leaned on the fence opposite Ellen's porch.

"When did you see her last?" I asked, jogging down Ellen's steps and crossing the street.

"About two weeks ago maybe?" He rubbed at graying stubble on his chin as I stopped on the other side of the fence.

His eyes flicked to my badge. "I been wondering when you people were gonna show up over there."

I smiled. "We try."

"People coming and going all hours of the night in different cars," he said. "Like all hours. Three, three-thirty in the morning, she has people knocking on her door. I watch TV. She's dealing drugs, right? And this neighborhood don't need that shit. We got kids around here." He jerked his chin at the house next door to Ellen's.

Graham pulled out a notebook and started jotting things down. I knew he was thinking that seemed like a hell of a good reason for Jerry to not want us to link him to Ellen.

"Did you see anyone get drugs from Ms. Helmsley?" I asked.

"She was careful about that part," he said. "I mean, nobody can call the cops if they don't see what she's doing, right? But also means those little ones couldn't see if they happened to be awake, either. So that was good. Cars pull up, dude gets out, goes to the door and goes inside. Comes back out a few minutes later."

"How many minutes?" Graham asked.

"Ten? Maybe? I wasn't, like, running a timer."

"And how many times a night did this happen?"

"I'd see five, sometimes ten cars go by in a night. Never there for long. A lot of times they left them running."

Graham made a note.

"Did you know Ms. Helmsley at all?" I asked.

"I mean, she waved when she was outside," he said. "She never sat out in the yard, and the lady next door with the kids really didn't like her. I imagine because she's up in the night with little ones and put the same pieces together there I did. But she wasn't unkind or anything. Just kept to herself. I imagine most of those kind of people are pretty closed off."

"Was there anything unusual that happened before she disappeared?"

He shook his head. "Nah, I mean, her car is gone, too, so it's not like there's a big mystery there. She left." He looked from Graham's flat expression to my badge and back again. "Right?"

"Her car disappeared the same time she did?"

He shrugged. "I guess right? That's the thing makes the most sense."

"Did the night time visitors stop when she disappeared?" Graham asked.

"After a couple days. I guess word gets around." He finished his beer and tucked the can into a section of the fence links.

"This is quite a display you've got here, Mr. ..." Graham let it trail.

"Perry. Mark Perry." He grinned. "Taught my old lady a lesson about nagging me about beer cans, that's for damn sure. You married, Officer...?"

"Commander Graham Hardin, TCSO." He pointed. "Faith McClellan, Texas Rangers."

"I knew I'd seen you on TV." Mark's face lit up. "You found the missing mom up in Dallas. My old lady followed that story for weeks. She cried when we saw the little boy got his momma back."

"That was a good day." I smiled.

"So you think something maybe happened to her?" He waved one hand at Ellen's house. "I mean I guess when you lay down with dogs you're damn bound to get bit by some fleas, but...I mean, I don't want nothing bad to happen to nobody."

We didn't know enough to hazard a guess. On one hand, this web we'd fallen into when we found that Jane Doe at the old mall seemed to keep spinning out and ensnaring new people and bits of stories, all of whom were at least somewhat connected. On the other, if she was dealing, she might've pissed off a junkie, a rival dealer, or a supplier enough to get herself killed—or she might've taken off to lie low for a while in an effort to stay alive. Hell, for all we knew she'd asked Jerry to drive her car around in an effort to camouflage her absence.

I pulled a card from my back pocket and slipped it through the fence between beer cans. "I really appreciate your help, Mark. If you wouldn't mind giving us a call if you see anything out of the ordinary, or remember anything else, that would be fantastic."

He took the card, running his thumb over the raised star-shaped Rangers logo. "Sure thing, ma'am." He tipped his baseball cap.

Graham and I crossed back to Ellen's side of the road, and I paused to snag a flashlight from the glove box in the truck.

"How long you think Mark there has been holding this beer can grudge against his wife?" Graham whispered.

"He's walking around spying on his neighbors and talking instead of being dead of liver failure, so I'm guessing a while."

He waved one hand at the dark, silent house. "Does it strike you as odd that so far everyone we've tried to talk to about this case is missing or in the hospital?"

"It strikes me as smart. On the part of the killer."

"But neighbor Mark said this woman has been out of pocket a while. No surveillance camera warning about us being in that maintenance closet made someone get rid of her two weeks ago."

I glanced at his arched eyebrow and pretended I didn't see it. "Good point."

Graham looked from the flashlight in my hand to the house and back at me. "You want to snoop. Warrant be damned."

"We know nobody's home," I said.

"And Jerry having her car is weird," he agreed, like he was trying to talk himself into justification for looking around. "Maybe she was his dealer?"

"There are about a thousand possibilities based on what we know so far. All I want to do is narrow them enough to try to figure out if these people had anything to do with what happened to Jim. I won't break anything," I promised, tugging his sleeve and heading around the side of the house to look for an open window blind or door she'd forgotten to lock —though if neighbor Mark was right and she was dealing, there wasn't much chance of that.

Near the back of the house, I spotted the shadowy outline of a detached garage in the darkness and pointed. "That might be unlocked."

Graham sighed and we crossed a narrow expanse of weeds. I pointed the flashlight straight down and squatted outside the door to examine the sprouting leaves on a milkweed. "I don't think anyone has driven over this in way more than two weeks."

"But we're not the only people who wanted in here." He pointed to a rust-riddled chain wrapping the handles of the old-fashioned double doors. It was tucked in at one end and had a heavy antique padlock hanging from it, but the chain had been cut.

"I'll be damned," I said.

"It's likely that anything interesting in there is gone if someone broke in," Graham said as I started pulling the chain loose.

"Sure," I said. "But likely doesn't mean certain. For all we know Ellen lost the key and was hoping the illusion of it being locked would be enough to keep people out."

Graham shrugged. "If we suspect Jerry stole her vehicle, her garage would be a reasonable place to check out."

I grinned. "Indeed."

The hinges squealed a protest when we pulled the door open wide enough to slip inside. I held the flashlight high and swept the space with the beam. "Texas Rangers," I said. "Anyone in here?"

Graham's chuckle floated through the dark. "The door was chained from the outside, babe. I think we're safe from squatters."

It had been a decade since Graham and I were sent to a call about an intruder when we were partners at the Travis County Sheriff's Office. We arrived to find a woman who lived alone holding a baseball bat on an obviously mentally disturbed man who had taken up residence in the garage behind her house. She wanted him arrested for trespassing. He brandished a piece of paper and claimed some long lost king of America had given him rights to her property. When I didn't buy that, he claimed squatters' rights. When we moved to cuff him, he split Graham's lip and landed a good punch to my right eye that left a shiner before we managed to subdue him.

The woman had called me twice more over the following weeks because he kept going back, until a judge sent him to a correctional facility two hundred miles away on the third strike, adding a harassment charge.

"That was one of the weirdest calls we ever took," I said. "I have never looked at a detached garage the same way since."

"Me neither," Graham agreed.

Satisfied that there wasn't anyone sharing the space with us, I lowered the light and poked around. Shelves lined the perimeter, most of them stacked with cardboard boxes and a few holding gardening tools. The center held a vehicle that wasn't the Trans Am.

"A single woman with more than one vehicle?" I asked.

"More than one vehicle she left behind when she disappeared?" Graham's tone said he didn't buy it.

I moved the light over the back of the small sedan, noting the Nissan emblem and the late-model style. "This one is about as far as you can get from an aging, souped-up Trans Am."

I knelt on the concrete floor and looked under the car. Fluid stains darkened the concrete, but none of them appeared fresh enough to still be wet. "I can't tell how long this has been here other than to say cursory evidence points to a while."

Standing, I tried the driver's door. Locked.

Shining the beam through the windows, I peered inside. Gray uphol-stery, black interior. It had been kept clean and neat, not so much as a tissue littering the floorboard. I checked the other doors and moved to the front to note the plate number before turning to Graham. We couldn't force our way into the car without more good reason than we had right then.

"I wish we'd asked Rosie how long Jerry'd had the car. Maybe he traded this one for the cooler one," Graham said, pulling a box out from a low shelf and looking inside. "Christmas ornaments."

I grabbed a different box. "This one is full of books." I yanked a school yearbook free and tucked the light between my ear and shoulder, tipping my head to one side. "She went to high school up in Fort Worth," I read from the book's title page before I flipped to the student photos. "Gradu-ated in 2012."

Ellen Helmsley was a pretty teenager, her round face lit up with a bright smile that showed off even teeth, and her hair carefully curled for her photos. I checked the index for her name and flipped more pages. "She was in the choir and on the student council. Says here she wanted to be a singer or a hairdresser and she was planning to move to New York City after graduation."

"So how did she end up in northeast Waco with a neighbor convinced she's been slinging dope, and a scuzz ball like Jerry running from the cops in her beat-up old car at the mention of her name?" Graham asked, leaning over my shoulder to look at the choir photo. I pointed to Ellen.

"Things don't always work out like you think they're going to," I whispered, thinking of my sister's gorgeous smile the day Ruth arranged her high school graduation photos at the governor's mansion. Charity would've surely conquered the world by now, if she'd lived to try.

I snapped a couple of photos of the book's interior, including one of a page where Ellen had drawn a heart around a boy's photo. He'd signed above it: Luv u 4 ever babe. Returning the book to the box, I slid it back into place and pointed to a large white chest freezer on the back wall, taking the flashlight off my shoulder.

"Let's see what's in there."

"My mom keeps frozen pizzas and biscuits in hers," Graham said.

We stepped toward it and a long, high squall reverberated off the thin wood walls of the garage. I flinched and dropped the flashlight, plunging us into darkness.

20

Adrenaline is a funny thing. When fight or flight kicks it into high gear, it can be counterproductive when the "flight" part of the equation isn't possible, causing sweat-slicked hands to shake.

Fumbling in my pocket, I clicked on the little LED light on my phone just as Graham did the same. My flashlight had rolled across the floor and come to rest near the freezer, the top of which was now occupied by a fat orange tabby cat with green eyes. He yowled again as if to confirm that he'd scared the hell out of us once already, flattening his ears and baring his fangs in a strange combination of a hiss and a growl when I took another step toward the freezer.

"Behold the reason I hate cats," Graham said.

"I thought you hated cats because your grandmother's cat was useless and mean?" I didn't take my eyes off the one on the freezer lid.

"They're all useless and mean."

"Mine wasn't," I said. "I had a white Persian cat when I was little, and she was cuddly and soft. She had a pillow on my bed where she slept. It was like hugging a cloud."

"Figures you'd get the exception to the rule." Graham turned and grabbed a pool noodle from a shelf, prodding the cat with it. "Move along, please," he said.

The cat hissed and lay down, scooting his back legs in.

"He's going to—" I didn't get the words out before the cat sprang off the lid of the freezer. "Jump."

Graham's athletic reflexes hadn't faded in the years since his playing days. He stepped gracefully out of the cat's path and snickered when the thing landed not quite on its feet, hissing once more from the floor before it seemed to sense we weren't as scared now that we knew what we were up against. We watched as the cat let himself out of the garage with a soft clatter of the door.

"Well that was weird," Graham said.

"My nerves can't take much more today." I picked up my flashlight and turned it back on before I slid the fingers of my free hand under the edge of the freezer's lid and lifted.

Shit.

"Not frozen pizzas," I said as Graham closed in behind me and peered over my shoulder at the corpse in Ellen Helmsley's freezer.

"What the hell?" Graham whispered.

The body was face down, and blood had frozen pinkish-red in streaks down the freezer's walls. The victim was folded unnaturally into the box, her torso bent in half above the hips in a way even yoga masters don't normally bend. Her head was tucked down at an odd angle, the hyperextended back of her neck and waves of long, dark hair comprising most of what I could see.

"I guess we know what we're doing for the rest of the evening." Graham pulled out his phone and called in the body discovery. It took about thirty seconds for the dispatcher to assure us that WPD's crime scene and forensics units were en route.

I closed the freezer and we picked our way back to the doors, more conscious of the possibility of disturbing evidence. Outside in the spring evening chill, I spotted the cat sitting on the metal lid of a garbage can near the little porch on the side of the house. He looked me in the eye and licked his chops, displaying teeth that looked yellow in the sickly glow of the porch light.

A van painted in blue and white with "forensics" in all caps running up the side pulled up at the curb, followed quickly by a tricked-out RV with a five-foot Waco PD shield painted on the side.

Miller was the first up the driveway, her step faltering slightly when she saw us. "We just keep meeting like this," she said.

"Believe me, I wish we could stop." My lips tightened into a grim line.

"What've you got?" She pulled on gloves and offered us each a pair before a lanky officer who looked like he wasn't old enough to shave ambled up the drive with a box of booties for our shoes tucked under one arm.

"Caucasian female in a chest freezer in the garage," I said. "I couldn't see much, but it looked like there was quite a bit of blood loss."

She threw a glance at the house. "Do we know who the owner is?"

"Neighbor says the single female who lives here has been missing for about two weeks. I'm thinking it's possible we just found her."

"In her own freezer?" Miller's eyebrows went up. "Yikes."

I stood aside and waved an arm at the door. "Trying to avoid the obvious leap to a conclusion," I said. "I suppose this woman could've disappeared because she killed someone and stuffed them in the freezer."

"Though you'd think she would've made sure the chain on the door was actually fastened," Graham said. "If that were the case."

I tipped my head to one side. "You would." I dragged the words out, my eyes darting around the space that was suddenly lit up like planes were going to land on it as three more officers carried large floodlights in and set them up.

"What're you thinking?" Graham asked.

"That you make a good point regardless of who the killer was. Why didn't they make sure the door was chained? Who goes through the trouble to hide a body this well—I mean, unless there's a power failure or a missing person's investigation, nobody's going to find her for months, except that we happened in here snooping—and then just leaves the chain on the door cut? There are kids next door, for fuck's sake."

"Someone who's in a hurry," Graham said.

Miller went immediately to work, her crew dusting the freezer for prints. When I saw the silver nitrate react near the rim of the lid in the center, I stepped forward. "Some of those are going to be mine," I said. "Sorry. I had no idea there was a body in there."

"Why did you open it?" she asked.

"We got a tip that she was dealing. I was just poking around looking for evidence because the door wasn't locked."

"Is this related to the attack on Jim Prescott or the human remains discovered at Bluebonnet Hills?" The question came from the doors behind me.

I spun to find the young reporter who'd chased us to the car at the hospital.

"This is an active crime scene," I said. "Which means I'm going to need you to leave." I didn't bother to try to sound polite.

She smirked and held up a small HD camera. "I'm outside your crime scene, Ranger McClellan. But your history of being uncooperative and secretive, keeping the public from knowing what's happening with your investigations, is well documented. So I'm not surprised at the request."

I blinked three times. Slowly. Did she really think I felt a flicker of remorse at keeping the press out of my cases until I had answers? If she was trying for a guilt trip, I was really not her girl.

"It wasn't a request." I let the timbre of my voice fall, which added a dangerous steel edge. "It was an order. I can't keep you from reporting the story, but you will do it from the curb"—I was a breath from saying across the street when I remembered chatty, beer-guzzling neighbor Mark—"and the official reply of law enforcement is no comment on open investigations. Have yourself a nice evening."

She stood there holding my gaze for a full minute, her camera still recording. I had to give her points for guts. But I didn't have to like her.

"Fine." The door clattered when she stalked off.

"She's a pain in the ass," Miller said. "You made quicker work of that than anyone I've ever seen."

"I have a bit of practice," I said.

She smiled, using a tape card to lift a print off the top right quadrant of the unit.

Another ten minutes passed while Miller's team took every print visible on the freezer.

"Schaefer, grab that drill and let's get the lid out of the way," Miller said.

The lanky officer leaned over the top of the unit with a power drill and unfastened the hinges on the lid. Miller got on the opposite end and they made easy work of lifting it away.

"Collins, Gregory," she called, getting the attention of two officers who were methodically painting every inch of the shelving units with finger-print medium. "We're going to take this out to the van. I want every inch of it examined with a microscope before we get her out of this box."

"Yes, ma'am." They followed her outside.

Graham and I both folded our hands behind our backs out of habit and leaned over the uncovered freezer, peering closely, scanning for details.

"Is that?" I leaned closer, my eyes on a blood smear on the back wall of the unit.

"No way." Graham's words sounded slightly strangled and miles away.

I closed my eyes for a brief second and swallowed hard as I heard Miller come back in talking to Officer Schaefer.

"See anything interesting?" she asked.

She was the forensics expert. I stepped to the side and pointed. "Back wall, just to the left of the middle."

The sharp intake of breath said she saw it too.

"Jesus Christ," Schaefer muttered. "Is that a handprint?"

21

I snapped a photo of the bloody handprint with my phone.

"Could that be the killer's?" Schaefer asked. A short line appeared between Miller's brows, telling me she was frustrated by the question. But the tone of her voice when she opened her mouth would've won her preschool teacher of the year.

"Technically we never rule anything out at a fresh scene," she said. "But step in and look at this closely and tell me why I think that's not correct."

He leaned over, blocking my view of the body. "It's not very big," he said.

"True, but we don't know who the killer is or their size," she said, ever patient.

He rested two fingers across his lips, not blinking as he stared, his brow furrowing under shaggy hair.

Miller watched his profile, the line between her brows willing him to figure it out.

"Is it because it's facing up? Like the fingers pointing up there, I mean," Schaefer said.

"Exactly. Whoever left this print most likely did it from inside the freezer."

"And why would the killer get into the freezer?" Schaefer crowed, proud of himself. He faltered. "Wait. Does that mean she was um...was she alive when someone put her in there?"

"We don't know anything for sure until we examine the entire scene," Miller said. "But I can't rule that out."

She was a good teacher. She turned to me. "Did you all notice anything else out of the ordinary in here?"

"There was a cat that nearly scared us out of our skin," I said. "Orange tabby, foul disposition. Seemed for all the world like he didn't want us near the freezer."

"Maybe he belonged to the victim," she said.

"The number of times in my career I've wished animals could talk is second only to the number of times I've wished I didn't know the worst things that humans are capable of doing to each other," I said.

Everyone in the room paused to mutter agreement.

"Hey, Sarge," a petite blonde in uniform called from the door. "I think there was blood out here."

We trooped outside to the weed-riddled backyard, where another young officer held a UV light over the ground. He swept it side to side, revealing a glowing splotch about five feet in diameter.

"Soil samples?" the young officer asked.

Miller nodded. "Thank you, Reynolds."

We turned to go back to the garage and she leaned toward Graham and me. "What the fuck kind of person are we dealing with here?"

"We don't know the murders are related," I cautioned.

Her left eyebrow shot up. "Waco isn't exactly the big city, Ranger McClellan. We get maybe two murders in a month here when things are really hopping. Two young women discovered chopped up in two days pretty much has to be related."

While I tended to agree, we didn't know anything about Jane Doe thanks to the body thief who'd attacked Jim, and we did know that at least one nosy neighbor thought Ellen was moonlighting in a dangerous line of work. So I was trying with everything in me not to jump to conclusions. I couldn't rule out that I still wanted it to be the doctor Skye had tipped us to, and I wasn't even sure I could point to a good reason for the pull that held anymore.

"One was wrapped and the other was in cold storage," Graham said. "While they might have been killed weeks apart for all we know, it does seem on the surface like we're looking for one killer here."

"Exactly. Just trying to make sure all our ducks are lined up straight, especially given what we don't know."

I stopped at the edge of the house and looked toward Mark's front porch. The light was off, but I made out his form in a rocker, the orange glow of the tip of his cigarette moving in the darkness, his eyes probably following our every move.

"He didn't like her living here," I said, almost to myself.

Graham snorted. "The beer guy? The biggest thing that dude ever killed was a twelve pack of Natty Light."

"It was obvious he was watching her," I said. "And it wouldn't be the first time we spoke to someone who was convincingly concerned about a victim and had them turn out to be the perp."

"If that dude is a serial killer, I'll walk into your mother's perfectly planned wedding buck ass naked."

"I think that's my cue to get busy getting this woman out of the freezer," Miller said.

I poked Graham, my shoulders shaking with laughter. "I can't believe you said that."

"Hand to God, I will."

"Ruth would skin you alive right there in front of God and the Who's Who of the Texas social register."

"I bet my momma could take her."

"Let's not find out."

He put one finger under my chin and tipped my face up to his. "The neighbor didn't do it, Faith," he said. "You're grasping, which isn't like you."

"I want it to be easy." I sighed. "Jim is hurt and still in a coma, a body is missing—a body, Graham. Stolen from the fucking crime lab. We're hunting a real live ghoul here. We're supposed to be happy this week—to get a break from the darkness that sucks up most of our days. And organ theft is pretty damn dark."

He put an arm around my shoulders. "I get that, baby. I do, too. But if that Mark guy across the way was responsible for a string of brutal murders, we'd have had him cuffed in five minutes. He was easier to read than a British spy novel."

I nodded, turning to the garage doors. "A handprint...How could someone cut her up and stuff her in there before she bled out?"

"We've seen a lot of crazy shit, but this definitely ranks near the top of the list," he agreed, dropping his arm back to his side as we stepped back into Ellen's garage.

"We're jumping ahead again," I said. "We don't even know for sure that it's Ellen in the freezer."

"True. It's easy conjecture, but there's no proof that Ellen herself didn't put whoever that is in the freezer, give Jerry her car, and take...Ow." He shook his arm as I sank my fingers into his bicep, my eyes popping wide. "What?"

"Jerry has her car."

"Yeah." He paused. "Oh, shit. And he took off at the mention of her name."

I called into WPD dispatch. "Texas DPS Ranger Faith McClellan, I need an all-points on a Trans Am, plate number AMZ 5728, approach with caution, driver may be armed and dangerous."

"Yes, ma'am," the dispatcher said. "We'll alert you of any possible hits."

"Thank you." I clicked the end button.

"Surely to God we didn't talk to our guy for twenty minutes today and then let him drive away," Graham said.

"We didn't let him do anything," I corrected. "He just did. But I for damn sure never suspected that guy of being a criminal mastermind."

"I mean, he has the ability to be violent if he put Buster in the hospital. But removing organs to sell seems like it'd require a special skill set that might be beyond Jerry's intellectual ability."

"You're saying he's too stupid to be our killer?"

"I didn't say anything. I offered an observation and said 'may.'"

I slipped back into the garage, watching Miller and her small team work. Photos were taken from every angle before a power saw was brought in from one of the vans to cut away the side walls of the freezer. The work was painstaking, the dust dangerous. Officer Schaefer passed out face coverings so we wouldn't inhale any particles before Miller began cutting through the appliance, which had been unplugged.

Every inch took several minutes, fine white and yellow particulates flying until the whole space looked like it had been engulfed in a blizzard.

Schaefer leaned over Miller's shoulder, but we couldn't hear their conversation over the whine of the saw. He pointed occasionally, probably helping her watch to make sure she didn't damage the remains.

"We have officers in Austin she'd put to shame." Graham's voice was muffled by the mask covering his nose and mouth.

"She is really thorough," I said. "I like her."

I pulled out my phone and texted Archie: *I need more background on a suspect than I was able to get through regular channels. You know anyone who can help?*

Archie always knew someone who could help.

I checked my watch. It was after eight, and these days that meant he was probably already home. While he still met any psychological definition of a workaholic, I had to admit my mother had been good for his work/life balance.

My phone buzzed in my hand. Archie wrote me a novella of a reply: *I have a friend at the FBI who's pretty good with digging up details. He ran that bartender for me this afternoon when I didn't find anything—he's a choir boy in the flesh. Not so much as a ticket. Two years of community college and then started tending bar because his father was sick and his mom needed help during the day.*

Poor guy. I wondered if that was the reason he lost his girlfriend, not that it was my business. *That's some specialized info, though. I'd love to know what he can get on this definitely not choir boy I think might be a POI.*

Send me what you know so far?

You're the best. Fair warning: what I've got isn't much on the guy, but he's driving a car that belonged to a woman with a dead body in her garage freezer, so I'd sure like enough to know where to find him.

Sounds like what you need is to know where to find this woman.

She might be here in the freezer. We're waiting to see.

Damn. You have an all-points out on the vehicle already?

Yep, thanks.

I'll do my best. You watch yourself. Big day coming up.

Of course.

I copied what I'd managed to gather about Jerry from my notes and pasted it into a text I sent to Archie just as my phone started ringing, Corie Whitehead's name at the top of the screen.

"McClellan." I put it to my ear, walking to the doors.

"Sorry to bother you so late." I could hear the distraction in her voice through the buzzy connection and wind whistling around the corners of the garage.

"Not a problem," I said. "What can I do for you?"

"I have a weird thing. And you were asking about some weird things this morning, and I thought this one might be of interest to you."

I rubbed one hand over tired eyes.

"I'm afraid I'm having a little trouble following you, Corie."

Was that a nervous laugh? My eyebrows shot up.

"I didn't ask many questions this morning on purpose," she said. "And then this shows up on my table tonight." She blew out a slow, controlled breath.

"What's on your table? Are you okay?" I asked.

"I'm pretty sure Chester Henning has a kidney he shouldn't." Her voice was small. "Had, I guess. Not doing him much good now, with a bullet hole through it."

My free hand floated to my head as my eyes fell shut. A billboard flashed on the back of them, one we'd passed twice just this morning. "Chester Henning, of Henning Automotive Group?"

"Second largest car dealership in the state," Corie quoted from the commercial Henning himself starred in, his trademark black Stetson always slightly askew. "But we won't be beaten on price or service here at Henning's car and truck bonanza."

"Someone shot him?"

"His wife. Caught him in her bed with his mistress. She's a good shot, the sheriff said she fired four rounds from Chester's Glock 33—got him in the kidney, the heart, and the back of the head, and hit his secretary in the gut."

"Is she dead too?"

"She'll live, but she's going to hurt like hell for a while."

I blew out a long, low whistle, moving the phone back. "Tell me about this kidney. What's wrong with it?"

"There's clear scarring indicating it was transplanted, and not more than probably six months ago," Corie said. "I have tissue samples here ready to go to the lab to confirm DNA, but I'm sure of what the results will say. His right kidney is more calcified than any other I've ever seen—even dialysis patients don't get this far along that road before they die. This one is pink and healthy as it can be. Plus, someone was either in a hurry or really tired when they did this; the sutures weren't anything resembling even."

"Is Dr. Pendergast usually messy with his sutures?"

"What? Not that I would have ever noticed."

"I'm trying to figure out what made you think to call me," I said.

"Oh. Well, the thing is, Chester shouldn't have had a kidney transplant," she said. "He was only 48, but he was a boozehound who drank like a fish and smoked anything you could light on fire, and this autopsy shows it. The level of damage to his lungs and liver would have disqualified him from a transplant. There's no way UNOS would approve this."

I didn't bother asking if she was sure. If she wasn't, she wouldn't have called me.

"Is his wife in the county lockup?"

"She is." Corie paused. "Do you really think Chester...bought...this kidney?"

"Sure seems like he might have." I rubbed at my temple. "Tell the sheriff to hang onto the wife. I want to talk to her in the morning."

"Sure thing."

"Thank you, Corie," I said.

"Have a nice evening."

I ducked back into the garage, stepping around the back end of the red Nissan before I raised my phone and searched the DPS database for the plate number. Force of habit—checking under every available rock is how you find the one hiding the truth. I didn't expect the red box that popped up in the center of my screen. I jabbed Graham lightly with one elbow when he turned toward me as I walked up behind him. "That Nissan has a bulletin out on it," I said. "Issued by Waco PD in October." I clicked the box and damn near dropped my phone. "Oh my God."

Graham leaned over my shoulder. "No way."

"I want to see inside the vehicle." I found Cortez's number and opened a text, typing *We found Marcy Finelli's car.*

"I'm going to ask the folks in the van outside if they have a slim jim for that car door." Graham turned and jogged outside as Miller shut the saw off at the far end of the bottom of the front freezer wall and Schaefer and Reynolds moved into place to pull it out.

"Slowly on three," Miller said. "The contents are starting to warm up."

She counted, they lifted.

Nothing happened.

Schaefer leaned over with a flashlight, examining the bottom seam—what he could see of it, anyway, which wasn't much—from the top of the freezer.

"It may not be cut all the way in a few places," he said through the face mask. "It's really hard to tell because the space is so tight."

"I can't press harder without risking damage to the remains." Miller sighed.

"What about a crowbar?" I asked.

"Yes!" She pointed at Schaefer. "Get both of them, they're in a bin on the right-hand side wall in my van."

He hustled out the door.

The warming of the remains meant decomposition, hints of the sickly scent of decay sneaking through the mask on my face. We needed to get the victim out of there while we could still keep her in relatively the same shape we'd found her in.

Schaefer returned with the crowbars, Graham on his heels with a slim jim he passed to me before taking the second crowbar from Schaefer and moving to the far end of the freezer.

Everyone else stepped back as they slid the ends of the metal bars into the sliced places in the freezer.

Graham counted.

They leaned, both hands gripping their bars, pushing until Graham's considerable biceps strained against the seams of his uniform shirt.

Just when I was about to move to help, a sharp, plastic cracking sound reverberated through the garage. Half a second later, the freezer gave way.

The victim's melting intestines spilled onto the concrete floor.

I heard retching behind me. And Miller gasped from her crouching vantage point angling off the end of the freezer.

"We've got more than one corpse here, folks."

22

Death is a constant presence.

Three hundred and thirty billion cells die in an average adult every single day.

Thankfully, every one of them is replaced with a new, fresh cell ready to take on the work of keeping the body's systems moving.

At least, that's what's supposed to happen. That's what happens when a person is healthy.

Homeostasis—the delicate balance that keeps our lungs breathing, hearts beating, and muscles moving—is really terrifyingly easy to disrupt. Even people who understand this don't like to think about it—it's unsettling in the same way most of us don't really want to know the CIA secrets of how close the world comes to disastrous conflict on a fairly regular basis. We go about our lives, drinking coffee, sending texts, running errands, working late, not giving cellular biology a second thought.

Until it stops working the way it should, that is. A few dead cells a day that aren't replaced, over time, break the rhythm that keeps a person's systems moving in the same way a major trauma or heart attack would.

Missing cells disrupt the body's processes.

The problem manifests in small ways at first. An upset stomach. Burning in the chest. Ready bruising. Easily brushed off, every last one.

Even when they pile on at virtually the same time.

It was all his fault, of course.

Youth imbues most of us with a terribly misguided sense of immortality.

A mind consumed with studying all day and working most of the night has time only for a few scattered daydreams of a bright future: picket fence, black shutters—no, maybe yellow—a red tricycle with streamers and a bell on the concrete sidewalk.

Behind it all, a big, loud, messy house, because aren't those the very best kind? And love. So much love it seeps out of his pores, threatens to consume him if he doesn't concentrate on something else.

He has to focus, though. Everything he wants is so close now. Thick books full of long Latin words that are familiar now, never mind that he never thought he'd learn them once upon a time; fat binders full of case studies that are nothing but puzzles to solve—and he's always loved puzzles. Midnight oil burns right along with his eyes as he reads, watches, takes notes. Three more years. With twenty behind him, it sounds like nothing—but everything waits on the other side of it.

He's happy. Busy. Stressed.

The perfect formula for missing things he should've seen.

By the time he notices, the scale is tipped way too far toward the dead cells.

But there has to be a way to balance it again. To save that shining future.

There has to.

No matter how unimaginable the cost.

23

A basic tenet of human psychology is that the brain tries to blot out horrifying experiences almost as soon as they register. It's a protective mechanism. One of the things my psych degree does for me on a daily basis is help me fight against that natural impulse, because allowing my mind to block the evidence of the worst among us means I might miss something important.

Miller and her team went to work retrieving and separating—as best they could, at least—the remains of two women. Two officers photographed the freezer and floor from every angle as Miller leaned in contortionist fashion with an ink pad and a card to take fingerprints from both corpses before bagging their hands for further examination at the lab. "Just in case," she said, flashing a grim half-smile and handing the cards to another officer.

As she and Schaefer moved to lift the first body off the second, I donned gloves and raised one hand, stepping to the far corner of the freezer and raising the woman's shirt to expose her bare back.

The shiny pink scar raced six inches up her side from her pelvis. "Shit," I muttered.

I stepped back. Schaefer looked a little green around the edges.

The second woman was stuffed into the chest with her forehead resting on her knees, a crimson lake of blood still pooled beneath her. Miller waved Schaefer off and shook her head.

"I don't suppose either of you feels like lending a hand?" she asked. "My team is good, but these kids haven't ever seen anything like this."

I stepped forward. "I got it." Graham doesn't do well with human remains.

Miller counted off and we lifted on three, transferring the body to its thick black rubber bag.

"You want to check her too?" Miller asked, one hand on the zipper.

"I'm sorry?"

"You looked at the other one's back."

"I found what I needed," I said.

"I'll call Cortez." Graham scrambled for the door.

Schaefer returned from puking in the side yard and helped Miller carry the body bag to the van.

Graham stuck his head back in after they left. "He's meeting them at the lab." He waved a hand at the Nissan. "If you want to snoop, now would be the time."

I moved in for a closer look at the interior walls of the freezer.

Officer Reynolds leaned over one end, carefully applying fingerprinting medium to the top four inches of the plastic. I pulled out my phone and snapped three more photos of the blood smear that looked so much like a handprint I couldn't see how it could be anything else.

Miller appeared at my elbow and pointed to the long marks that looked like fingers. "It drags down and slightly back, which would fit with how her arm was in there."

"Who's the best you've got at the crime lab here?" I asked.

"Regina Eastman," she said without missing a beat.

"I'd like to get privileges for a JP from Goliad County to join her on this case," I said, hoping Corie Whitehead would be game for helping. I was particularly interested in whatever experience she might've had with folks who'd died on Dr. Little's table at Bremo, and any similarities she might notice here.

"Shouldn't be a problem, as long as our lab isn't a crime scene anymore by tomorrow," she said, a wrinkle forming in the center of her forehead as her voice softened. "I'm really sorry about your friend."

"Thank you. He's strong. Could be a long road, but he'll be okay." I gave the words more confidence than I felt because they simply had to be true. I couldn't accept any other scenario.

She leaned into the freezer box with several swabs and test tubes and took samples of the blood from the handprint, the bottom corner of the unit, and the end walls, handing each to Schaefer, who was pale and sweaty but standing ready with a Sharpie to label the samples.

"I'll rush these and then we'll at least know for sure if that belongs to one of these victims." Miller's eyes went to the handprint.

"I'm going to poke very carefully through this vehicle and then I want it moved to your lab so someone can comb through every millimeter of it," I said. "Sergeant Cortez said he'll meet y'all there."

A flicker of annoyance creased her forehead so briefly I might have imagined it as she nodded.

I grabbed the slim jim from the shelf I'd set it on and slid it into the driver's door.

"How long has it been since you've done this?" Graham asked.

"A thousand years." I moved the tool carefully. "And I was never good at it back then."

Schaefer blotted his still-sweaty head with his sleeve and stepped forward. "I was a patrolman until four months ago," he said. "May I?"

I let go and stepped back. "All yours."

He had the door open in thirty seconds.

I thanked him and donned fresh gloves, leaning into the vehicle and opening the small center console.

A pack of Trident, two hair ties, and twenty-nine cents.

"She kept her car clean," I said.

"Cortez said it was the only thing she owned," Graham said.

I pressed the trunk release. "So was she living in it?"

Graham changed his gloves and went to the back of the car. "Bingo."

I joined him and surveyed neat stacks of clothing, a laundry bag, a plastic bin of canned food and plastic utensils, and a small gray zipper bag. I opened it and found soap, shampoo, and a razor.

"Sure looks that way," I said. "I wonder for how long?"

"I wonder how the guy still found her," Graham said.

We closed the trunk and I went to the passenger side of the front, opening the glove box and pulling out her registration receipt. "She registered this car in McLennan County just a month before Cortez put out the bulletin on it." Laying the card on the dash, I kept looking. A user manual, a business card for the salesman at a dealership in Tulsa that I snapped a photo of, and a cell phone charging cord.

Graham pointed to the charger. "She had a cord, but I don't see a phone."

I checked the backseat. "I don't, either."

He jotted it down.

I straightened, my back protesting the long day, and started to close the door when a scrap of pink near the edge of the floor mat caught my eye. Careful to touch only the edges, I pulled a Post-it-sized square of notepaper free and flipped it over. In purple ink, it read *Bluebonnet Hills 1:30*.

I laid it on the seat and snapped a photo of it, too, before I returned the registration to the glovebox and showed Graham the photo of the note. "Maybe this has something to do with how she ended up here?"

"Goddamn, this thing just keeps folding back into itself." He sighed.

"Let's go see if we can still catch Buster before they let him out of the ER," I said.

"What about Jerry?" Graham asked.

"Archie's making some calls to see what he can find out about Jerry."

"He never comes up empty-handed."

"Hoping that holds here. And fast." I turned to Miller. "Can you make sure they fingerprint everything in the car including the pink paper on the passenger seat?"

"You got it."

"You still have my number from yesterday?" I asked.

"I do. And I will call you with more updates than you'll probably end up wanting."

"Trust me, I want every single one. Assuming related cases as you said earlier, multiple victims mean we're on the clock now—the longer it takes us to figure this out, the more people could die."

"I've never worked a serial before, but it does add a new layer of urgency."

"I appreciate your understanding and your help." I looked around the room. "All of you."

"Was your father really the governor?" Schaefer asked as Graham and I turned for the doors.

"He was. And now he's really in prison."

"Why do so many politicians end up in prison, anyway?" I couldn't tell from the thoughtful tone if the question was really directed at me, but I shrugged and answered anyway.

"I've known more politicians in my life than most people. Some of them were wonderful folks who ran for office because they believed they could make a difference in their communities or the world. Others were more like my father—interested in the power associated with the offices they sought, and what sorts of material gains could come with that power. Not all of the good ones end up making a difference, and not all of the bad ones get caught. A lot like police work, when you get right down to it."

He raised his eyebrows. "Well, for what it's worth, no matter what your father did, it's pretty easy to tell you're one of the good ones, Ranger." He tipped his hat.

"That's kind of you, Officer Schaefer. Stick with Miller here, she'll teach you well and make sure you get to make a difference."

"That's why I'm here," he said.

"Definitely not for the great hours or fantastic pay," Graham said.

"You forgot about the seeing nightmares come to life that actually make you puke up your dinner," Schaefer said.

By the time we made it back to the truck, I had the GPS on my phone set for the county hospital. "Hopefully if nothing else, Buster can tell us where the hell Jerry might've gone."

"Now you listen for just one goddamn minute, missy, I don't want any more medication, and I don't need another X-ray. I am fine, and I want to get the hell out of this godforsaken place." Buster's twangy drawl met us at the sliding double doors to the emergency room, saving me an argument with a nurse over who was allowed to see him.

"I'm guessing he's going to be okay," Graham said.

"I'm thinking we better go corner him before he busts out of here." I quickened my steps in the direction of the noise.

A fresh-faced nurse in puppy dog scrubs threw up her hands and let them slap against the sides of her legs as we stopped in the partially-open doorway of the small room where Buster lay in a narrow bed, covered with a knit blanket and hooked to three different machines by various wires and tubes. "Mr. Beauchamp, you have an internal injury that needs to be monitored to ensure it doesn't kill you. Are you really going to leave against the doctor's advice with that hanging over your head?"

"I'm sure Mr. Beauchamp can be convinced to see reason," I said from the doorway.

"Officers." Buster's complexion lost what little color it had, and his eyes dropped to his lap. "What're you doing here?"

"Wondering the same about you," I said. "We have a few questions for you if you feel up to talking."

"I didn't do shit to him." Buster's words were sharp with defensiveness.

"Nobody said you did." I didn't figure a kindergarten lesson in fighting words and not calling others names was prudent right then.

The nurse watched the exchange like we were volleying a tennis ball until I turned my gaze to her and flashed my most dazzling runway grin. "Is he in shape for us to have just a few moments?"

"Oh! Sure. Sure thing." She snatched a tablet off the rollaway side table and ducked out the door.

"He busted a chair off in my side, and then broke the goddamn thing over my head." Buster softened his voice, adding quite a dose of victimhood to it. "After I gave him a job and trusted him."

"Why was he angry with you?" I asked.

"Because I fired his lazy ass," Buster said.

"What did you do that for?"

"He was in charge of maintenance at Bluebonnet Hills."

I held his gaze as his eyes got increasingly bigger. He didn't speak.

"And?" I couldn't lead him into telling me anything. The ideas had to be his own.

"Well, there was a dead woman in the closet there," he said, faltering like he wasn't sure exactly what he wanted to say. "He should've known that. He was the only other person with a key to that closet, and I damn sure didn't put her there."

But the bartender and Rosie both told me Jerry hadn't worked for Buster in a while. I noted the discrepancy but moved on, keeping my face carefully blank, my voice flat. "Is there a reason you didn't mention that when we asked you yesterday who had keys to the building?"

Buster plucked at the blanket. "Jerry don't exactly have a contractor's license. And the government don't exactly know he works for me."

He fell quiet.

Graham and I waited him out.

"Well, I didn't see how it did me any good to tell you he had the keys until I had a chance to talk to him myself, did I now?"

"I don't suppose you did." My voice was way calmer than I felt. If this jackass could've given us a name and stopped Jim from getting hurt, but didn't because he was afraid of the IRS...well. I should let Graham and Archie handle booking him for aiding and abetting and accessory after the fact and anything else I could think up to charge him with.

"Damn right," he said.

"I'm going to need your key to that closet, Mr. Beauchamp," I said, "and one that will get us in the main doors."

"What for?"

"It's evidence in a murder investigation." I kept my tone even. I wasn't really lying. It was evidence: of whether or not someone had changed out the lock set.

Buster pointed to a plastic bag on the room's lone chair. "My pocket. Left side."

I handed him the keyring and he pulled off one labeled 45 in orange marker and another marked 49 in red. "Food court exterior entrance." He passed me the 49. "Closet door." That was the 45. I tucked them into my pocket.

"So what happened with Jerry today, Buster?" Graham asked.

"I went to Maxine's today and picked up a dart game with him because I wanted to talk. He was pissed at me, and the only way I could get to him was to put money on a dart game, so I did. But then he cheated like he always does, so I didn't want to play no more. I tried to just ask him when the last time he checked the boiler closet was, he went apeshit, grabbed a chair and started in about how I didn't know how to run my business, I was a thief and a lazy good-for-nothing who was living off what my daddy left me, and I...well, I lost my temper. I said something that wasn't very nice." His red-rimmed eyes flicked to Graham. "And I paid for it, too. Damndest thing. I wouldn't have pegged Jerry for violent."

"Do you know anything about his past?" Graham asked.

"Why would I have cause to ask about that? He could replace light bulbs and repair sheetrock, and he was decent enough with plumbing and electricity to get by. It ain't like we were girlfriends or anything. We didn't spend Friday nights painting each other's toenails and talking about our feelings."

I tried to muffle a snort with a cough.

"Have you ever heard Jerry talk about a woman named Ellen Helmsley?" I asked.

"She was his dealer." Buster's voice ticked up an octave, like he was excited to have something he thought I'd be interested in to dish on. "Woman sells everything you can think of, according to Jerry. He got me some of them pain pills the doctors don't give you anymore when my back went out last year."

But they weren't friends. Except maybe when it was convenient for Buster. The more he talked, the more he reminded me of the Governor. And the more I disliked him.

"Do you know why he was driving her car today at Maxine's? Had he said anything about her loaning it to him, maybe?"

"We hadn't talked in a while before I called him Friday night," Buster conceded. "I can't remember the last time I saw him, or when I would've seen what he was driving, either. Has to be weeks ago."

But he just fired him. Sure. I knew he was lying, I just couldn't figure out why, and now didn't seem the time to press him.

"You'd likely remember this vehicle," Graham said. "A Trans Am with a matte finish and a mismatched fender."

Buster shook his head. "No, I hadn't seen Jerry in anything like that."

He leaned his head back against the pillows, a fine sheen of sweat covering his face and neck. "I don't feel so good."

I reached over and pressed the call button for the nurse. "One last question and we can be done for now," I said. "Do you know where Jerry lives? Or if there's anywhere he'd go if he didn't want to be found?"

"Lived with his brother last time I asked." Buster's fist closed around the blanket and the heart monitor started blaring an alarm. Graham and I stepped back as a team of medical personnel rushed in.

"Try his girlfriend, Rosie, if the brother got tired of his shit," Buster said. "If his whore has a place to stay right now, you'll probably find him with her."

24

Archie had Jerry's brother's address in my text messages by the time we got back to the truck. I clicked it in the GPS and pointed to the parking lot's south exit. "Advantages to a smaller city: Jerry's brother's place is about four miles that way," I said. "We might as well stop by."

"I know you like the doctors as our bad guys here, but I'm still trying to figure out why someone murdering a woman to harvest organs takes the time to sew her up, dress her, wrap her, and place the body in a very strange hidey-hole." Graham put the truck in gear and backed out of the lot. "I think that's much more ceremonial or sacrificial behavior than greedy, ghoulish organ thief behavior."

"But Corie said she has a body on her table right now with a kidney that could've been bought," I said. "I can see why you might think we have a very weird serial, but I don't think you're right."

"Even with two more victims added to the tally tonight?" he asked. "One of them very likely an assault victim from months ago—maybe even the original victim that the killer couldn't bring himself to kill just yet? There's a lot pointing to serial tonight."

"The venues and M.O.s are different, though. You just said sewing up and dressing Jane Doe made you think serial, but then we have two women with their guts literally spilling out of a freezer, and you still think it's a serial. You know the criteria. The scenes were too different."

"They are," he conceded. "I can't figure that part out. But I'll keep working on it."

"And I'll keep working on Buster," I said. "He knew the guy had a fucking key, Graham, and he didn't tell us."

"How could Jerry have taken Marcy's kidney and left her alive, though?" Graham asked. "Removing an organ isn't in the same league as repairing plaster and sheetrock or wiring an outlet."

"Odds are pretty good she's not alive now," I said.

"But Cortez spoke to her after she lost the kidney."

"If it's really a network maybe someone decided they wanted another... um...piece of Marcy," I said. "After the motel thing."

I shook my head. "I can hardly believe we're even having this conversation, and we've seen some crazy shit. How the fuck is there a black market for human organs?"

"For the same reason there's one for plastic surgery and abortion and a million other things," he said. "I did a little reading after we talked to Skye. You were right: people with the means to work around the UNOS list buy organs just like people who can't afford a high-end plastic surgeon buy back alley boob jobs."

"So you think maybe a real doctor stole the prostitute's kidney at the motel, but good old Jerry is just hacking shit out of people based on YouTube tutorials or something?"

Graham snorted. "Or something. It seems like the more frightening of the two options here is someone who lacks the finesse to put people back together and sew them up, based on what we saw earlier. The way the women in that freezer were sliced open, I'd bet they're missing some organs."

He stopped the truck in front of the address Archie had given us. The house was small and neat, with pale blue shingle siding and metal awnings in a dingy white over the front windows. A lamp was on in the front room, with more light spilling in through a doorway that probably led to the kitchen.

"I don't see the car." My shoulders slumped.

"Could be a garage out back here, too," Graham said. "Let's just see what's what."

I jogged up the narrow concrete sidewalk and the four steps to the small stoop. No doorbell. I raised a fist and rapped on the metal rim of the screen door.

A curtain moved in the window with the light seconds before a porch light came on.

The front door cracked open, a chain keeping it from moving more than a few inches. "What do you want?"

"Good evening, Mr. Blanchard." Assuming the person who opens the door is the homeowner is easier: when someone opens their door after dark and a police officer asks who they are, they tend to get nervous whether they've done anything wrong or not. If he wasn't Jerry's brother, he'd say so in a minute. "We have a few questions we'd like to ask your brother Jerry."

He kept the chain in place, but moved so he could look directly through the crack at me. His white tank top undershirt was yellowed around the rims of the armpits and rode up slightly above where it was supposed to meet his gray sweatpants. "Who's asking?"

"Faith McClellan, Texas Rangers."

"The fucking Texas Rangers?" Eyes popping wide, he slammed the door and for a second I thought we were going to have to get a warrant. But then the chain scratched along its metal track and the door opened wider. Tommy Blanchard leaned against the doorjamb, keeping his other hand behind the door and hugging it close to his side. "What has that little fuckup done? I knew something wasn't right. I should've tried harder to find his stupid ass." He muttered the latter like he was talking more to himself than to us.

"You don't know where he is?"

"I wish I did, the little weasel owes me money, but I'm afraid I can't help you. He disappeared." He shook his head, touching one finger to his chin. "Has to be a couple weeks ago now. He crashed here for about a month, six weeks, maybe; it's hard to keep track of the days this time of year."

I raised my eyebrows but stayed quiet.

"I work construction," he said. "When it starts to warm up, it gets crazy, people wanting everything done they put off all winter. I've pulled sixteen-hour days for a month. Jerry was here for part of it, but I barely saw him, I'm usually only here to eat and sleep. I wanted to watch a little baseball tonight or I'd be in bed even though tomorrow's my only day off. I think the Astros are going to have a great year." He directed the last words at Graham, leaning into the screen and squinting.

"Hey, man, are you..." He let it trail, twisting his mouth to one side. "Are you Graham Hardin?"

Tommy really was quite a baseball fan, it seemed.

Graham grinned. "I am. Commander Graham Hardin of the Travis County Sheriff's Office these days."

Tommy opened the door, waving us inside. "Can I shake your hand?"

Graham obliged and Tommy pumped his arm like fresh Texas crude was bound to pour from it any second.

"Can you just stay..." Tommy put his hands up, palms out. "Just stay right there for just one minute, please, sir?"

He rushed from the room.

"Look at you, still all famous," I said.

"I've watched you work your last name over on people for years, but that's got to be the first time baseball ever got me an in with someone who didn't want to talk to us."

"You don't hear me complaining, do you?" I winked. "I'll take a Graham Hardin fan over a Chuck McClellan one any day of the week. I happen to be in the Graham Hardin fan club myself, in fact."

Tommy came back with a UT baseball jersey and a ball. He shoved them at Graham and opened a drawer in the front of a small wood veneer TV stand, rooting around for a few seconds before he came up with a black Sharpie.

"Could you sign those for me, please, sir?"

Neither of us had been asked for an autograph in more than a decade. I watched Graham fumble with the marker, a proud smile playing around my lips. I'd seen old videos of his playing days. He'd have been in the Hall of Fame someday if his shoulder hadn't given out on him.

Graham flipped the jersey over and blinked twice at his name and number on the back. "I thought the only one of these left was in the back of my closet."

"I bought it the day I caught that ball," Tommy said. "It was a foul that came all the way back past the post. Man, you had a fastball."

Graham's jaw slackened, his Adam's apple bobbing with a hard swallow.

I couldn't have kept the beaming pride off my face if I'd wanted to. Which I didn't.

Graham smoothed the jersey out over the top of Tommy's ancient tube-style TV and turned to me. "Can you pull this tight here?" He put one hand on the shoulder seam.

I replaced his hand with mine and watched him scrawl a signature across the cotton.

He made his writing smaller and neater than I'd ever seen it on the ball, adding his jersey number underneath it before he handed everything back to Tommy.

"Thank you so much," Tommy said, his deep drawl gruff with emotion. "I'll tell you, I never thought I'd be glad to meet a cop who's looking for my worthless-ass brother."

Sensing Tommy's lowered guard, Graham slid smoothly into home base with a thousand-watt grin preceding his question. "What's Jerry's story, anyway?"

When it's possible to get a source or suspect to talk, open-ended questions are a cop's best friend. It's a hard reality to beat through to people who find their way to the job thanks to a lifetime of watching TV crime shows, but that's also one of the reasons it works: often the person we're questioning has the same limitation on experience with law enforcement. They expect the kinds of yes or no questions that populate TV interrogation rooms, so the "tell me a story" approach catches them off guard.

And gets a smart cop all kinds of information he might have never known to ask for, if the subject takes the bait.

Tommy gobbled it right up: proverbial hook, line, and powerboat.

"He's been a mess since we was kids. Never really wanted to work for anything. My momma, she worked herself into an early grave taking care of us, and I tried to do right by Jerry after she died, but he refused to do right by hisself." He shook his head, perching heavily on one arm of a threadbare olive sofa. "He skipped way more school than he went to. I'd drop him off at the front door on my way to work in the morning and he'd wave and go in, and walk right out the back and leave with one of his pothead buddies. Eventually, they said he couldn't come back. But he never graduated."

"We understand he'd been working for a property manager named Buster Beauchamp for a while now," Graham said, his voice smooth. I tried to fade into the seventies wood-paneled walls and make Tommy forget I was there. I wanted him to tell Graham Hardin, baseball hero, Jerry's entire life story. I could keep busy listening for anything that might link him to the murders or the assault on Jim.

"That crooked old bastard," Tommy scoffed. "Yeah, I guess you could call it work. Mostly, it's doing Beauchamp's dirty work. Running dope from a dealer Beauchamp knows, putting band-aids on broken shit in Beauchamp's properties and taking pennies while old Buster charges his clients hundreds for shit that didn't even get done. Jerry runs at the drop of a hat, stays gone at all hours, and can't even afford a sleazy motel room to crash in. Because believe me, he wouldn't have asked to be here if he had options."

"Why is that?" Graham asked.

"Ever since he got home from the service, he's been pissy with me. Paranoid that I'm judging him."

"Are you?" Graham's tone was conversational, his gaze unflinching.

Tommy let his gaze fall to the floor after half a minute. "Not exactly."

So yes, then.

I wanted to know more about the fleeting mention of military service.

"Which branch did he serve in?" Graham asked.

"Army. He enlisted right before he turned 21. Got himself off pot for a whole three weeks and signed up to be a soldier because he said he couldn't do anything right here, but maybe with someone to boss him around all the time, he could figure out how to make something of himself."

"Do you know what he did in the military?"

"Grunt work in Afghanistan," he said. "He was with the hospital unit, he went ahead of the doctors into hot zones and set up tents and equipment." Tommy shook his head. "He used to say it turned out he wasn't worth anything to Uncle Sam, either, since they used him as a walking land mine locator and sniper target."

"It's a shame that any soldier or their family would ever feel that way," Graham said. "Your brother volunteered to serve his country and you should both be proud of that."

I pulled in a slow breath. I'd never considered the soldiers who were first into war zones, really. Movies make it look like well-trained warriors lead the front lines. But listening to Tommy's blunt assessment of the way his brother's life had been treated with cavalier callousness made me sad for Jerry. And I didn't want to be sad for Jerry, especially not if he really was the person of interest we thought he might be here.

Tommy raised his head and squared his shoulders, a smile stretching his face at the kind words coming from someone he admired.

I focused on the part about the hospital unit.

So did Graham.

"Did Jerry ever mention getting to see the doctors in action?"

"Oh sure, he was like the secretary when they had wounded guys coming in," Tommy said. "I mean, once the hospital was set up, they stayed a while so it wasn't like he was the first-in scout every day. Most of the time, Jerry did the laundry, made sure there were clean towels and plenty of supplies for the doctors and nurses. He told me once in a letter that he got to help out with sewing people up sometimes when it was a real shit day and they had more injuries than the doctors could get to in time to save them. Said he saved them fifteen minutes on each person after the doctor taught him how to sew up wounds and surgeries." Tommy paused, his eyes soft and unfocused, looking past Graham at something no one but him could see. "It's the only time I can remember him sounding like he was happy. I think he felt like he was helping those people and it gave him purpose, you know?"

"So what happened?" Graham leaned forward.

"Same shit different day. He got busted stealing Fentanyl and needles from the drug supply. He'll lay his hand right flat on the Bible and swear he didn't do it to this day, but they booted him. Dishonorable discharge and a court martial, too, though they didn't send him to prison."

"What did the judge find?"

"That there was 'insufficient evidence' to convict him." Tommy wiggled his fingers in the air as he spoke. "But the damage was done anyway. Do you know how hard it is to get someone to hire a vet who got booted? Nobody gives a shit if there wasn't enough evidence."

"Hence, Buster," Graham said.

Tommy shook his head. "So what's he done now? Must be some pretty serious shit if you're this far from Travis County and the fucking Rangers are out for him on Sunday night and all, huh?" He sniffled and dragged one hand across his face, letting his head flop backward. "I tried, Momma. I swear I did," he murmured at the ceiling.

My heart twisted. Jesus, this poor guy.

"We don't know that he's done anything for sure," Graham said gently. "But someone has done some pretty terrible things, and his name keeps coming up. We need to talk to him to see what he knows."

The Channel Two breaking news alert blared from the TV before Graham got the last word all the way out, breaking into the forgotten baseball game. I stepped out of the corner when I heard Skye's voice.

"News Two has learned exclusively of a Texas Rangers investigation in Central Texas involving the murder of at least two women and an attack on a state medical examiner who is currently in the intensive care unit fighting for his life," she intoned dramatically. "Tune in after the game for the full update—and learn what you can do to keep your family safe."

Damn that woman. I'd gambled because I needed information she had, and she bit me in the ass. Skye didn't know any other way to be but backstabbing and self-serving. I shouldn't have expected anything different, but if she thought I was still talking to her about the Governor she was out of her fucking mind. If she wasn't abiding by our deal, there was no chance in hell I would, either.

Tommy shot to his feet, his face flushing as he pointed at the TV and then at me. He took two halting steps to the side and crumpled onto the sofa as Graham and I both stepped forward.

"Murder?" He shook his head as he murmured the word, like he couldn't process it. "Listen, Mr. Hardin, sir, you have to believe me. My brother is a lot of things, but he's not a killer. He couldn't be." He waved a hand at his surroundings. "Our momma raised her boys to be good and upstanding. We didn't have much, but she taught us to follow the commandments, to respect other people, and especially to respect women. Jerry has had his problems, and I know a lot of what I told you here tonight probably don't sound so good, but he's not a murderer. Like I said, he's never been happier in his whole life than he was when he was helping them doctors save people in Afghanistan."

"I understand," Graham said. "We just want to talk to him."

"He's got a girl, Rosie," Tommy said. "They go way back, she grew up with us on the next block over. Her grandma still owns the house over there. Rosie was a..." He looked at his bare feet, peeking out of the frayed hem of his sweatpants. "Well, she cared as much about school and stuff as Jerry did, I think he was a bad influence on her. I heard she was a prostitute, but she's always had a soft spot for my brother."

Graham glanced at me and I shook my head ever so slightly.

"Thank you, Tommy." Graham stood.

"He couldn't kill anyone." Tommy looked from Graham to me and back, not getting off the couch.

"I hope not," I said, meaning every word. I laid a card on the table. "Please call us if you hear from him. I know it's a lot to ask you to trust us, but I promise you Graham and I are looking for the truth about what happened here, not looking to have your brother take the fall for something he didn't do. It sounds like he's had enough hard knocks to last a lifetime."

"That he has." A fat tear escaped, sliding into the gray scruff along Tommy's jaw. "I'll call you if I hear from him."

We let ourselves out.

"The army docs taught him to sew people up," I said, pulling my notebook out when we got into the truck and scribbling everything down before I forgot it.

"It doesn't sound good for Jerry," Graham agreed.

I put the pen down when he started the truck and reached for my phone to check the all-points on the car with Waco PD just as it lit up with a call.

"McClellan," I said, putting it to my ear.

"Ranger, Derek Masters at the Waco PD. One of our officers found your Trans Am about twenty minutes ago."

I sucked in a sharp breath.

"Do you have the driver in custody?"

Graham slid a glance my way.

"No driver on the scene. Car was wrapped around a tree off Wortham Bend Road. Blood on the steering wheel and the door handle, but nobody in the vicinity."

Twenty minutes. On foot and bleeding. He couldn't have gone but so far.

"Officer Masters, we need a two-mile perimeter in place in ten minutes and every officer and K9 unit available to you combing the immediate area. The driver is a person of interest in the murder of the Jane Doe found at the Bluebonnet Hills center Friday and the attack on Jim Prescott at the crime lab yesterday. I want him alive and able to talk to me when he's found. Can you please send the coordinates of the vehicle to this number?"

"Yes, ma'am."

My hands shook as I touched the pin in the text and turned on the GPS. Graham floored the accelerator when the truck was pointed the right way, saying what I was thinking.

"We have to find him first."

25

Finding a person who doesn't want to be found is way more difficult than horror movies make it out to be. Michael Myers always goes straight to the whimpering girl once he catches up when she gets winded and hides in the movies, but in real life, searching an open area for a fugitive is an exacting, carefully orchestrated production involving dozens of people. And even then, it helps to have luck on our side.

My face nearly split in two with a grin when I spotted Officer Costen and Louis getting out of an SUV as Graham skidded to a stop in the gravel along the edge of the highway.

Maybe our luck was turning.

"Commander, Ranger." Costen waved as Louis sat stoically at his side. "The vehicle is right up there." He pointed. "We're going to pick up a scent and start a grid. The driver is a suspect?"

"I'm glad to see y'all. I'm anxious to speak to this guy—my gut says if he isn't our killer he knows who is. Or at the very least he knows something that'll get me closer to figuring that out. If you find him, I need him to come in capable of talking."

"Louis won't alert unless there are remains to be found, which isn't terribly conducive to talking, but my buddy Drake Simmons and his dog are headed this way, and if your fugitive is in condition to talk, they'll bring him to you." Costen tipped his hat.

"Go with him," I murmured to Graham. "See what's what up there and I'll be right behind you."

"Please do not go off alone hunting this guy when I'm right here," Graham said.

"I'm not. But I'd much rather one of us be the one to locate him and we double our odds by splitting up, plus I want to know how he went off the road."

"What?" Graham's forehead scrunched. "Why?"

"Just a hunch." I couldn't get Tommy's tearful insistence that his brother couldn't be our killer out of my head, no matter how badly I wanted to be done with this case. I had to find the person who actually hurt Jim, and while family often isn't the most accurate judge of character in a murder case, there's something to be said for listening to the folks who know people best. I've had the occasional mother look me straight in the eye and tell me she wasn't surprised to hear I wanted to question her child about a murder. And those moms have been right every time.

I sent Graham and Costen on to the vehicle while I waved down a young Waco PD officer.

"I need some traffic support on this road," I said. "One car about a mile that way"—I pointed east—"and another a mile west. Stop all traffic until further instruction."

He glanced at my badge. "People may not take kindly to that."

"You're allowed to apologize for the inconvenience, but beyond that, this is a murder investigation, and I don't really give a damn what they take kindly to."

He bobbed his head once, laying his index fingers in the corners of his mouth and blowing a wolf-whistle. "Harry!"

I stood to the side of the road while two marked cruisers took off in opposite directions, lights flashing. I gave them a minute, watching carefully for headlights, before I stepped out into the road, pulling the flashlight back out of my pocket.

I found the skid marks from the Trans Am almost immediately and followed them back a couple of hundred yards, the noise and lights of the search scene fading behind me as I walked. When I reached the starting point, I slowed and pointed the light at the pavement, turning a slow circle.

The most likely scenario was the easy assumption that Jerry had spent the last couple of hours bellied up to a bar somewhere and he'd swerved to avoid something—deer were common this time of the year—and couldn't right the car in time. The tracks even supported that. The rubber burned into the road started abruptly, two parallel tracks from slammed brakes that veered to the right. About halfway between the start point and the tree a wave pattern told me the car had fishtailed, so Jerry was aware enough to put effort into keeping it on the road. He must've been driving like a bat out of hell.

"Where were you running to, Jerry?" I looked east down the road before I spun slowly back west. "Or is it what you were running from?"

"I'm looking forward to seeing you ask him." I gasped when Lieutenant Boone's voice came out of the darkness.

"I've had trouble figuring out which end is which with this case," I said as he stepped close enough for me to see him. "But I have a feeling Jerry is a key to something. Even if I'm not exactly sure what."

Boone chuckled. "I have learned my lesson about discounting your gut feelings, McClellan. I've always thought they were an overblown myth of police work myself—meticulous investigation, finesse with witnesses, and a pinch of luck have always been the most prominent facets of my own technique. But my mother was a big believer in women's intuition, and I have to say you've made a convert out of me."

"I just hope I'm on the right trail here," I said. "You heard about Jim?"

"I went by there a little while ago. He's starting to come around."

My eyes popped wide. "Really?"

"I have no motive for lying. He's not up for questioning yet, but he's telling his wife his neck hurts, asking where he is, why his sons are there. Not that he stays conscious long enough for anyone to answer him yet. But the doc says it's all a good sign."

I felt a tiny bit of tension seep from my shoulders. Jim was talking. If the doctors could get him out of the woods, he'd be okay.

"Thank God."

"Happy to be the bearer of good news for a change."

"I don't see you in the field much." I took the diplomatic tack for asking what he was doing.

"I don't have an old friend attacked by a nut job while he's trying to do us a favor every day," he said. "I spent years in the Austin PD working homicide cases with Prescott, back when all our kids were little. Hell, we coached in Little League at the same time. I trust you to find the fucker who assaulted him, but I wanted to get my hands in this, not just push the paperwork after the fact. I wasn't far away when I heard the call out here."

"Happy to have you, sir."

"So why do you think someone ran this guy off the road?"

I smiled at his quick analysis. Boone hadn't always been nice to me, but he was a hell of a good cop in his field days, and I was proud of having earned his respect.

"I just got to thinking on the way here, Graham and I saw this guy react violently—and seemingly disproportionately—to a situation earlier. When we caught up to him, the woman who was with him, who is apparently his at least sometime girlfriend, told me he was unusually upset about something. We asked him about the woman who owns that car"—I waved one arm in the general direction of the accident scene—"and he dove for the driver's seat and sped away. An hour later, I'm pretty sure we found that woman, and another one, filleted and stuffed into a freezer in the garage where said vehicle was stored until recently."

"Sounds like a strong case for this guy being the person who put her there."

"It does. But I keep thinking there's something I'm missing. This guy was a soldier with the Army Medical Corps. His brother said the happiest he's ever been was when he felt like he was helping save people."

"I could see the twisted logic in someone convincing themselves they're helping people by selling human organs to the highest bidder," Boone said.

I tipped my head, considering that. "I can too, at least for a little while. But if he's selling organs, why is he flat-ass broke?"

Boone shrugged. "Maybe he's smart enough to sock it away to avoid suspicion?"

"Maybe. The thing is, this guy seems to have a decent amount of bad luck, too." I shook my head. "I've been wrong before—this weekend, even

—but I just can't help thinking maybe he fell into something horrifying and didn't know how to get out."

"Except to run," Boone said.

I pointed at him.

"Exactly. And that got me wondering who might chase him, especially after Skye put it on the goddamn TV that we're working this case." The last words swam in bitterness, and I didn't even bother to try and hide it.

"I learned a long time ago not to waste my energy wondering if that woman cares what she screws up in the name of breaking news," Boone said.

He raised a flashlight and clicked it on. "Let's see what we see. I still remember enough from my traffic days to be a decent extra set of eyes."

"Much obliged, sir."

We started in corners about thirty yards apart and worked in a grid around the place where Jerry had lost control of the car, looking for any other telltale marks.

"Nothing," I said when we met in the middle a few minutes later. "So much for intuition, no matter what kind it is."

We started back up the highway toward the accident scene.

"You and Hardin have a big day coming up," Boone said. "You know I have to tell you, I never thought I'd see the day anything got to Archie Baxter enough to make him cry. Didn't know that old hardass had it in him."

"He's a big softie." I choked a little on the last word.

"Seems to be going around," Boone said.

I opened my mouth to reply and my flashlight beam bounced off something in the road.

We were almost back to the scene, the pavement lit by the far reaches of blue squad car lights and the red burn of fizzling road flares that had been placed along the shoulders by the first officers to arrive.

I stopped and swept the area with my light. Boone made it a few paces more before he realized I wasn't next to him anymore and doubled back.

I picked up lighter rubber marks in the flashlight beam. They started about a hundred yards to the left of the place the tire tracks from the Trans Am pitched sharply to the right, swished in a backward "J" shape, and continued across the yellow line to the westbound side of the highway. I kept walking until they stopped. Boone caught up, his own flashlight bobbing along the marks.

"They didn't chase him," I said, turning and jogging back to the spot where the tracks got closest together, walking off a rough measurement between where the new set stopped and Jerry's began.

Boone stopped behind my shoulder. "They don't actually meet."

I swept my light over the swish where the second vehicle—the one that wasn't plowed into a mesquite tree—had made a too-fast U-turn. "This one has rear-wheel drive. The front tires wouldn't leave marks, only the back ones. Which would put the front end of the car right about here when Jerry ran off the road." I pointed the flashlight at my boots, which were on the track the driver's side tires on the Trans Am left as Jerry tried to swerve.

"They didn't chase him," I repeated. "They cut him off. In a car he recognized well enough to slam his brakes a hundred yards that way."

I ran for the accident scene, calling for Graham.

26

I ran past Costen's Travis County K-9 SUV and blinked twice when I saw Louis in the back, stretched out and gnawing on a plastic bone.

Pulling up at the back bumper of the Trans Am, I found Graham in the crowd of officers surrounding the vehicle.

"There was another car involved in this," I said, putting my hands on my hips and sucking deep breaths.

"That would explain why these marks in the dirt show that the driver was dragged from this vehicle," Costen said, pointing. "Brodie there got the scent nearly immediately from the blood on the steering wheel, but when he heard the command to locate, he followed a trail to the side of the road right up there"—he pointed to a flare about ten yards from us—"and he stopped there and signaled."

Costen pointed to a smallish black Lab sitting next to an officer in khakis and a department polo.

"He swears the dog has never been wrong, either," Graham said.

"Brodie doesn't make mistakes—not at a fresh scene," Costen said. "He's part beagle—they were bred to track for centuries. He has the most accurate nose in five states. Well. Except for Louis."

"So they cut him off, ran him into a tree, and dragged him out of this vehicle and put him in theirs. From the width of the tire tracks, I'm guessing a pickup they could put him in the back of. So we pull the footage from the past four hours or so from the nearest traffic cameras and see what we see." I jogged up the shoulder to where Brodie and his handler waited and introduced myself as I studied the ground.

"It looks here like they went east after they grabbed Jerry," I said, pointing to the faint tracks in the thin layer of dirt that disappeared at the collar of the pavement.

"Someone get me tax data on every parcel of land east of here for fifty miles," Boone said in his most commanding tone. I spent my first few months in F Company being terrified of that tone in Boone's voice. But it got shit done.

A young WPD patrolman with *Masters* on his uniform nameplate actually saluted. "Yes, sir."

I shot the lieutenant a grateful smile.

"I can push papers if that's what helps the most." He tipped his hat.

"Thank you, sir."

"Thank me when we know what the fuck is going on here, McClellan," he said.

Graham strode to my side. "Rosie?" he asked.

"Rosie." I squeezed the lieutenant's arm on the way to my truck. "His girlfriend talked to me earlier. I'm going to go see if this will scare her into giving up everything she knows about what kind of shit Jerry here is buried in."

"No pun intended," Graham said.

"Can you send the property records to my cell when they're in?" I asked. "I can scroll through and see if something jumps out at me."

Boone nodded. "Good luck."

"You too, sir."

We climbed into the truck and headed west, my eyes on the clock. "It's almost ten. You think she's still at the diner with her friend?" I asked.

"I'm not even sure anymore she actually has a friend that works there," Graham said. "For all the fuck we know she was with whoever caught up to Jerry. Or she tipped them off that we'd asked him about Ellen."

I drummed my fingers on the console as he drove, watching the speedometer in my F-150 push past 90.

"All of the victims so far have been women," I said, a tight knot settling heavy in my stomach as I pictured Tommy's face. "You don't think they'll kill Jerry?"

"I think a kidney is a kidney, and two of them have got to be more than Jerry's life is worth to whoever is behind this, especially if they think he's been talking to us."

"But he didn't," I said. "He left."

"In a car that led us to one of the victims. That he may have 'borrowed'"—he hit the word hard—"without permission. Maybe because he knew she couldn't use it anymore."

"Drive faster."

Graham stomped on the accelerator and I watched the dark fields lining both sides of the road, turning everything we knew around in my head, trying to figure out what we hadn't noticed yet.

"Why did someone assault Jim?" I muttered, tapping my fingers on my thigh. "Who thinks to go after the medical examiner?"

"We got that one already. Someone who knows enough about medicine to know what an autopsy is going to tell the medical examiner," Graham said.

"Yeah." I let the darkened landscape outside the windows blur as I sank back into my thoughts. "Corie said the doctor that Skye is on about was at a rotary club breakfast sixty miles from Jim yesterday morning, and we let that establish that it wasn't him," I said. "But what if we're looking at the whole thing wrong?"

Graham waited a beat. "Care to elaborate?"

I sighed. Whatever was floating around the back of my brain wouldn't quite come to the surface. "I don't even really know. I'm just trying to figure out what we're missing."

"Sleep," Graham said, tapping the clock that said it was coming up on ten. "We're missing sleep. We're going to see if we can find Rosie, and then we're going to go home and go to bed. We'll go back at it tomorrow."

"What if Jerry dies tonight because we wanted to go to bed?"

"The chances that we find Jerry before sunrise are small," Graham said. "I know you know that as well as I do."

"Small isn't the same as nonexistent," I said. "And this isn't just any case, Graham. It's Jim."

"Jim is resting so he can recover. You saved him, Faith. But you have to take care of yourself, too. The case will still be there in the morning."

I folded my arms over my chest. "I know."

He turned back onto the four-lane highway we'd driven with Rosie what felt like four lifetimes ago. The neon sign towering over the lot was missing a few letters, but the message got across. The parking lot was mostly full of pickups and big rigs, with the occasional sedan stuffed between them.

I swiped at bleary eyes. Hell, maybe he was right about the sleep.

Graham held the door and I stepped inside, the scents of bacon, butter, and cigarettes wafting from various corners of the establishment.

"Be right with you folks," a young woman in a pink uniform dress called from behind the counter she was wiping down. "Take a seat anywhere you like."

We crossed to the counter when we didn't spot Rosie anywhere. "We're actually looking for a woman we dropped off here earlier this evening. Her name is Rosie—she said she had a friend who works here."

I was close enough then to see that her red plastic name tag was engraved with "Lena."

I was also close enough for her to see my badge.

Her eyebrows went up. "She left."

I couldn't read whether or not she was telling the truth. "Are you the friend she mentioned to us earlier?"

"Listen, she don't know nothing about that scumbag stealing a car."

So yes, then.

"It's possible that Jerry is in danger. It's also possible that if Rosie is mixed up in whatever this is, she's in danger, as well. If you know where she is, I need you to tell me." Exhaustion and frustration made the words sharper than they would've normally been.

"What do you mean 'in danger?' If he hurts her..." Lena's eyes flashed as she flung the cloth onto the counter.

"It's not him I'm worried about." I sighed. "At least I don't think it is. I have three dead women and one close personal friend in the ICU, and no real idea what the hell is going on. I am still on my feet right now by force of sheer will. I don't want anyone else to die. I need to know where your friend is. Now."

She leaned both hands on the counter, holding my gaze for several beats. "I don't know where she went. That's the God's truth. A pickup pulled in out front at the tail end of dinner rush. She waved to me and went out and got in it. Tires squealed as it pulled out of the lot. I thought she had made a...um...a date."

I pulled in a slow, steady breath. "Do you remember anything about it?"

"It was red. I think it was a Chevy, but to tell the truth I don't know why I think that because I can't remember noticing. I was running seven tables and we're short one prep cook today."

"Did you see the driver at all?" Graham asked.

"I tried to look to make sure it wasn't fucking Jerry," Lena bit out, her eyes going wider with every word. "But the glare of the light from the windows and the sign off the windshield was too much and I didn't have more than a second to look. It could've been Jerry. Could've been Santa Claus, too, for all the fuck I know."

She reached across the bar and grabbed my hand. "Rosie is a sweet girl, but she ain't the brightest bulb there is. She puts too much faith in other people, especially loser asshole men. You'd think she'd have learned her lesson about men working the streets for years, but I guess not."

Graham nudged me.

"Is Rosie still a prostitute?" People had danced around it all evening, and I both didn't care and was tired of trying to parse the answer to a simple question with much more complicated ones looming over the situation.

"She says she stopped turning tricks months ago," Lena said. "She waits tables now."

"Where?"

"The Bluebonnet Cafe."

I pulled out a notebook and added that to my notes, jotting down the highlights of what she'd said. My brain was trying to follow a dozen trails at once.

"Thank you for your help. I appreciate your honesty."

"Find her. And tell her to call me when you do."

"I'm going to give it my best shot."

Graham and I kept quiet until we were back in the truck.

"She left in a truck," he said.

"It looked from the scene like Jerry was taken in a truck."

"Not like there's a shortage of them around here." Graham started the truck we were sitting in like he was punctuating the thought.

"She said this truck was red."

"You've seen a red pickup?"

"The other day at the mall," I said. "Buster Beauchamp drives a cherry red Silverado."

27

"My chances of getting you to go to sleep now are pretty much zero, right?" Graham pulled the truck into my driveway and killed the engine.

"We have to get to the bottom of this, Graham," I said, flinching at the memory of joking about how easy it would be to pinpoint Buster as a suspect earlier.

"Faith, Buster was in the hospital this evening. He didn't pick Rosie up at the diner. You can't swing a bat without hitting a red pickup in Central Texas."

I jumped out of the truck, shivering in the chill that crept into the late evening air this time of year. Graham met me at the steps and laid an easy hand on my shoulder. "You need sleep. We weren't wrong earlier—that bumbling little fool is no master criminal. He probably doesn't know a pancreas from a pinky toe. We will figure this out, but it's going to take longer if you don't take care of yourself."

"What if they're in danger?"

"What if Jerry is the small-time criminal his brother said he is and he owed the wrong redneck money? What if Rosie is still turning tricks and didn't want her friend to know since she clearly disapproves? There are easier explanations for what we've seen and heard the past couple of hours, if you take a step back from the mess we've been mired in all weekend and look. They're not even that hard to see."

I rested my forehead on his shoulder. "Why do you always make so much damn sense?"

"God-given gift, I guess?" His chest rumbled with soft laughter.

"We have to get this guy."

"And we will." He put one finger under my chin and turned my eyes to meet his. "You know if I thought for one second someone was going to die because we went to sleep, I'd break out the Red Bull. But there's too much doubt here for me, and you know we'll both do better work tomorrow on a good night's sleep."

He was right. I could well be seeing what I wanted to see, and exhaustion wasn't helping me figure out which lead to follow.

I trudged up the steps in boots that suddenly weighed forty pounds each, and unlocked the deadbolt on the front door. I sent a quick text to Corie Whitehead apologizing for the hour and begging her help with the victims in the local lab in the morning. By the time I got the phone plugged into the charger she had replied: *I'm still up, and I'm always happy to help the good guys. I'll be there bright and early.*

I thanked her and went to brush my teeth.

Falling asleep in Graham's arms, my last thought was that I was still missing the one thing that would make this whole damned thing make sense.

Spring sunshine peeked through the blinds as I rubbed caked mascara from my lashes eight hours later. I glanced at the clock on the night table and groaned, feeling Graham stretch behind me.

"Why is it morning already?" he grumbled.

"The Earth spins on its axis, you see..." My teasing voice was rough with sleep.

"Smartass."

"It's after seven. We have to get our smart asses in gear."

"Five minutes."

"Zero minutes." I sat up and grabbed the jeans I'd left on the foot of the bed the night before. "Remember when Jerry's brother was telling us about his shady doings?"

"I do." He pulled the covers over his face when I bounced out of bed and opened the blinds.

"Who was he doing his criming with and for?"

Graham's green eyes peeked over the edge of the quilt, squinting at me. "Beauchamp."

"Jerry is a small-time criminal, like you said last night. But what if Buster is the bigger fish—but not the biggest one?"

"I haven't had any coffee yet. Just tell me why you're so excited."

"I want to explain so you can do the thing you do where you blow holes in my theories if I'm running too far ahead with them."

His eyes crinkled at the corners with a smile. "Your theories are usually sound."

"I was thinking about that camera in the maintenance closet, and how Jerry came to know Ellen..."

"And you think Buster is your common denominator." Graham threw the covers back. "I still don't think that guy is smart enough to pull off something like this, but it's not the biggest stretch I've ever seen work out, I suppose."

"If Jerry did communications setups for the military in middle-of-nowhere Persian desert, I bet he could figure out how to make a camera talk to the internet in a building with no wifi if Buster asked him to." I buttoned my shirt and tucked it into my jeans before I perched on the edge of the bed and yanked my boots on. "I'm trying to see actual possibilities and not the ones I want to see. And I admit freely that Jerry's brother got to me last night. Like as much as I wanted this road to lead to Skye's creepy doctors, that's how much I don't want it to lead to Jerry."

"There is still a lot we don't know," Graham said.

"Yes. And looking at it a certain way, the things we heard yesterday were pretty damning for Jerry. But I'm thinking: remember how Buster sounded almost excited to tell us Jerry was involved with Ellen the drug dealer?"

"Right. Like he wanted to get him in trouble. Very tattletale vibe."

"I thought so, too. But what if there was more to it than that? Like what if Buster knew Ellen was in that freezer and he wanted Jerry already associated with her in our minds?"

"But how does that explain what you just said about the camera? Or these women being stitched up?"

I sighed. "I don't know." I stood and paced the length of the room to the door and back. "Tommy said Jerry liked helping people. What if he sewed them up because of something to do with that? Jim did say the sutures weren't exactly top shelf. And Corie said the same thing last night."

"Corie? Did I miss something?"

"She called last night. Chester Henning the car dealer got himself murdered by his wife for sleeping with his secretary. But Corie found a kidney that didn't belong to him during her autopsy, and she said he wasn't healthy enough to qualify for a transplant this recent."

"No shit?" Graham sat up.

"And his wife is sitting in the county jail."

"Hopefully hating old Chester enough to talk to us?"

"That's what I'm hoping." I hurried to the bathroom and grabbed my toothbrush while he got dressed.

"So, you think maybe this whole thing was more shitty grunt work Jerry did for Buster and he was trying to make the best of it?" Graham leaned against the door frame as I rinsed toothpaste out of my mouth.

"Possibly?" I shrugged. "I wish I could get a good bead on what the hell is happening here. It's like two and two is nine all of a sudden."

"Which usually means there's something we don't know."

I raised one finger. "Yes. But everything so far that we've found out seems to make the case murkier instead of clarifying anything."

"Corie's dead car dealer sure sounds like proof that someone bought an organ they couldn't get any other way," Graham said.

"Sure. But who sold Chester the organ? I don't think Buster is smart enough to be the mastermind behind some kind of statewide black market organ syndicate. Do you?"

"I do not." Graham rubbed at the scruff on his chin. "Not entirely, anyway. But I think he's just connected enough and just stupid enough to be a good middleman for something like this, maybe. And there are probably a lot of ways he could have strong-armed or blackmailed Jerry into helping."

"Maybe," I consented. "But why would an organized crime syndicate put Jane Doe in that closet at the old mall?"

Graham tipped his head from side to side. "I don't know."

"And the camera in there with her is super weird. And the body theft. All of that is more personal—and pathological—than a business-only organ theft and sales ring."

"And more risky," Graham consented. "When people are making serious money doing something shady, they don't look kindly on anyone taking stupid risks that might draw attention to them."

"Like attacking a state medical examiner?"

"Exactly like that."

"Could that be why someone yanked Jerry out of that Trans Am last night?" I asked. "He looked skinnier than the guy on the lab security video, but the cameras are pretty shitty."

"Could be. Boone is on it; if there's something there, he'll find it."

I secured my ponytail and put the hairbrush back in the drawer. "So really...we're better rested, but we still don't know anything."

"Well. We don't know what we don't know, anyway. This doesn't fit together neatly, that's for damned sure."

I nodded. No matter how I tried to make this equation balance, I had a variable out of place. "The weirdness of it almost makes me more determined to figure it out," I said. "We have a brazen, violent criminal—or maybe criminals—carving people up for some reason that clearly isn't a good one. Serial killer, syndicate, or something we haven't thought of yet, we have to pursue this and put whoever is responsible someplace they can't hurt anyone else."

He stepped out of the doorway. "Shall we pursue it in the general direction of the Goliad County jail?"

I plucked my phone from the nightstand and texted Ruth. *Were you able to get in touch with Dr. Whittaker or his wife?*

"If Ruth got us in to see Dean Whittaker, I'd still like to talk to him. But that's on the way," I said as I moved down the hall to the coffeemaker in the kitchen and stuck a travel cup under the spout. "But that's kind of on the way to Goliad, so if you want to drive, I'll see what the internet can tell us about Buster."

He grabbed my keys off the counter and waved a ladies first in the direction of the door.

Seatbelt fastened, I opened my laptop as Graham pulled out of the drive and turned toward the highway.

"For starters, Buster cannot be a given name," I said, pulling up the state's incorporation records and searching for the property management company. "So who are you, really?"

Incorporated October 29, 1987 by David Wayne Beauchamp. Remembering what Tommy said about Buster's dad, I copied that to a notes file and clicked current officers.

Ernest Lyle Beauchamp was listed as President and Chief Financial Officer.

"Buster's legal name is Ernest Lyle Beauchamp," I said as Graham turned the radio on.

"I might choose to go by Buster, too," he said.

I nodded, copying the name to my notes and going back to Google.

I scrolled past ads for a dozen "people location" services, looking for real results.

A story in the *Herald* archives listing Buster—apparently he'd had the nickname a long time—in the state track and field finals in shot put in 1991, and David Beauchamp's obituary.

That was it.

I double-checked my spelling and ran the search again.

Sipping tepid coffee, I furrowed my brow. "Google has almost nothing on this guy."

"Google has something on everyone, don't they?" Graham asked. "They're kind of like the IRS that way."

"Buster went to the state track finals in 1991, and lost his father three years ago." I tapped two fingers on the edge of the keyboard. "That's it."

"You run his criminal record?"

"About to. I'm just surprised that I didn't find more here."

Criminal records access is helpful, of course, but the most interesting personal information usually comes from Google.

I opened a new tab and logged into the state records database, checking the spelling of Buster's name twice before I clicked "search."

Four results found.

"He's got more in here than he does in Google," I muttered, clicking the oldest charge.

"Misdemeanor drug charge right after he got out of high school, no help," I said, going to the next one, which was dated a decade later. "Oooh, aiding and abetting."

"That might go somewhere." Graham fished a packet of trail mix out of the console and handed it to me.

I opened it and popped a handful into my mouth before I handed him the rest of the bag and entered the case number on my screen in the McLennan County court records. When the search returned a file, I clicked the attached documents, locating the police report.

"So it seems Buster has never done anything but work for his dad," I said as I skimmed the officer's narrative. "It says here that as a property manager for his father's company in 2007, he was taking money under the table to lease a vacant strip center space to a meth cooking operation, which was of course busted when they blew the back wall off the center and two people died."

"Damn," Graham said.

I went back to the court documents, searching for Buster's last name.

"He was arrested as an accomplice on a manslaughter charge," I said. "The lawyers pleaded him down to aiding and abetting on the drug charges, he got off with probation and community service."

I scrolled back up to the first page of the document. "This is interesting, though—the attorney who represented him back then is listed as the only shareholder in the property management company today besides Buster."

"Probably his dad's lawyer," Graham said.

"Sure." I went back to the incorporation papers. "Yep. Same guy filed the original papers to incorporate for David Beauchamp in 1987."

I opened a new window and searched the lawyer's name. "He works at an office down by the courthouse, looks like a one-man show." I copied the address and returned to the criminal records.

"I just don't see bumbling old Buster as a serial killer," Graham said.

"And so far, the methodical way our guy is going about this still makes me think we're looking for a one-man show."

"I agree with that to an extent." I looked up from the computer. "But there are things that don't fit that scenario—not well, anyway—all over the place, too. The women attacked in the nightclub bathroom. The stories Skye told us about those doctors." I waved one hand at the windshield. "A dead car dealer with a kidney UNOS wouldn't have given him. I can make some things fit a serial. A fucking weird serial, because what is a single murderer doing with these organs if he's not selling them? And how is he getting them from unwilling donor to wealthy recipient if he is?"

"Maybe Chester's wife can help us out with that."

I glanced at the GPS. Forty minutes out.

"What are the actual chances Buster jumped from looking the other way when people were cooking meth to facilitating victims for selling human organs on the black market?" I asked. "Greed is one thing, but you know as well as I do that murder is quite another."

Graham shrugged. "I can't tell. All I know for sure right now is that he knows some shady people and he's not above breaking the law to pad his bank account, even when people get hurt. Do I think he's willing to get his hands dirty? Not necessarily. But I'm beginning to wonder if it's possible that there's more than one guilty party here. It just doesn't seem smooth enough in places for organized crime. You heard Skye. Her guys have been selling organs for years. People running a well-oiled machine don't make the kind of mistakes that pulled us into this in the first place. But people like Buster do."

"His dad's attorney keeping him out of real trouble for being shady his whole life probably didn't help."

"Probably not. And it's weird as hell that the lawyer owns part of the company his father left him, too. You'd think an attorney wouldn't want a connection to someone like Buster. Especially not one with a paper trail. So what kind of law does he practice?"

"General family law according to the website."

"Which means just about everything."

I pulled up a ramshackle website someone had slapped together with a basic online tutorial. "Seems like it. Wills, custody, criminal defense...This dude is like the last of the old country lawyers."

My phone buzzed with a text from Ruth.

They're in Paris on a second honeymoon. She says he can see you next Tuesday.

So much for the dean's insight. I read the text to Graham, typed and sent *thank you*, and looked over the other two criminal charges on Buster's record. The way the case had turned in the past 24 hours, I was only half sure the dean might get us anywhere anyway. "These are both DUIs, and both from the past year," I said.

"Maybe old Buster hasn't always been such a drinker?"

"Maybe he's looking to drown some guilt?" I arched an eyebrow as I opened a new browser window and started typing.

"Still wondering how they're getting from A to B?" Graham asked.

"How do you do that?" I clicked a link to an article about organ transplant surgery.

"Because I've been wondering since you said that, and I'm a little perturbed that we didn't think about that before."

"This isn't exactly our wheelhouse," I said. "Most of the organs we deal with are usually rotting by the time we get there." My eyes skimmed the screen. "There's a chemical solution called Celsior that they have to be packed in. Plus they require coolers that measure the temperature and keep it in a pretty tight tolerance."

"And where would one get those things?" Graham asked.

"Hospital supply companies." I was already in another search screen. "Of which there are seven just inside the state lines."

GPS estimated thirty-three more minutes of driving to the jail. I reached for my phone and dialed the first number on the list on my screen.

"Good morning, Ronnie, this is Faith McClellan with the Texas Rangers," I said when I got through the labyrinthine automated system to a person.

"Like the TV show?" he interrupted.

"Kind of, sure," I said.

"Wow, okay. I thought they made that stuff up."

I didn't need Ronnie to understand that Chuck Norris wasn't a reality

TV star, I just needed him to get me to someone who could answer my questions. I added a dash of drawl to my voice and smiled as I spoke.

"I am up to my ears in a very strange death investigation—"

"Like you mean a murder?" His voice dropped a full octave.

"Probably. Do you think you could help me out with something?"

"Me?" I could practically see his spine straighten—in my head, his hair needed some shampoo and a comb and his shirt had seen better days—and his chest puff out. "You can count on me, ma'am."

"I need to know if y'all have had any new or unusual shipments of Celsior or organ transport coolers ship out lately," I said. "Maybe to a new account, or possibly extras above a facility's standard order."

"I only have access to place new orders, I can't look at the order history unless you have a number for me to put in."

My shoulders drooped.

"But I have a buddy who can. Let me get him on the line."

I sat on hold with my fingers crossed for about a minute and a half before Ronnie's voice came back.

"I mean for real, a Texas Ranger like the guy who kicks people on TV," Ronnie said. "But it's a chick."

"I don't see any Celsior orders in here at all for the past three months," the other guy said. "And the last replacement cooler we sold was to Harris in downtown Fort Worth in November."

"Thanks for your help, gentlemen, I appreciate it." I hung up and went to the next.

Nothing unusual.

Four more places had the same answer, and I punched the number for the seventh into my phone so angrily I hurt my finger as Graham parked in the Goliad sheriff's office parking lot and rested a hand on mine. "Let's go in first."

"It's one more call." I hit the talk button, launching into my now-rehearsed spiel when a woman with a soft, deep-South accent who identified herself as Kim answered on the third ring. That meant this was a smaller company. I checked the address on my computer screen.

It was less than twenty miles west of where we sat.

"I'm not sure I'm allowed to talk about customer orders," Kim said, her voice tinged with more than a pinch of unease.

"I'm sure your employer would approve of you cooperating with law enforcement in an active murder investigation." I paused and let that percolate for a second. "Or I could always go to the trouble of getting a warrant. But that will take valuable time that we don't have to spare in an investigation like this."

A tapping echoed in my ear, probably her fingernail on the back of the telephone handset. "I don't know," she said finally. "I think that information is confidential, and there's no one here for me to ask."

I stared in the front window of the sheriff's office at a blonde dispatcher who was filing her nails and chatting with a lanky deputy. "I understand," I said, ending the call before I pocketed the phone and met Graham at the hood of the truck. "I'll get a warrant. But I'm not telling her that right now."

"You can spot a liar over the phone now?" He gestured to the front door.

"Something wasn't right. She was nervous, and as accommodating as every other larger company on the list was? There's a reason." I nodded to the door. "Let's go see what Chester's wife is willing—or not willing—to share and go from there."

If Desiree Henning had been old enough to drink for more than a year, I'd eat my Laredos.

Her skin had the sort of glow only youth coupled with an exacting (and expensive) skin care routine produces, and everything about her was a touch over the top. Even after a night in jail, her hair was perfectly teased, her makeup barely smeared, and her pursed lips, rod-straight shoulders, and piercing green eyes could've walked straight off a catalog page.

I watched through a small window in the door for a few beats, trying to get a read on her mood before I opened the door. She was popping the gum in her mouth, staring at the wall opposite her chair, her hands resting on the table, her color even and breathing normal.

Corie said she'd shot her husband dead not 24 hours ago, and she looked calm and flat as Lake Travis on a still summer afternoon.

"We are talking about the guy from the car commercials, right?" Graham murmured.

"Looks like this wasn't his first rodeo—maybe with marriage or a mistress, either one." I turned the doorknob.

I made it three steps into the seven-step-wide shoebox that served as the interrogation room, Graham closing the door behind us, before Desiree flipped her folding chair shut, jumping to her feet. "Holy shit, you're Miss Texas."

She bent at the knees and waist as much as her painted-on jeans would allow, in what could only be described as a denim-encumbered curtsy. I blinked, my face going slack, but she didn't see it because she had bowed her head, eyes on her stiletto-heeled Jimmy Choo motorcycle boots. Committing murder didn't get her worked up, but a decades-old pageant crown did?

"Not in a lot of years now," I said, recovering with my best runway smile and putting my hand out. She closed both of hers around it, and for half a second, I thought she was going to kiss my engagement ring. I shook her hands the best I could and tugged mine free. Graham picked her chair up and opened it before he pulled mine out and took the remaining one for himself.

"I'm Faith McClellan, this is Commander Graham Hardin of the Travis County Sheriff's Office," I said, leaning back in the seat and letting my arms rest, open, in my lap. "We're investigating a murder case with the Texas Rangers and we have some questions about your husband."

"He had it coming." She said it flatly, with a matter-of-fact coating to the words. "Cheating pig." She tipped her head to one side. "Why do the Rangers give two shits about this? I already told the sheriff I shot him—I mean, not like there was a point to lying since his whore didn't die. Is it a slow week for you or something?"

"That's not the murder I was referring to." Not sure I'd ever had cause to specify during a witness interview.

Her forehead wrinkled. "Chester never hurt anybody. Not physically."

Graham took out a notebook and started jotting things down. I knew he found it as interesting as I did that she had jumped straight to that when no one said anything about Chester hurting anyone.

"I didn't think he had," I replied. "But I do think he knew someone who has—who might again, even."

"We have a lot of friends, Officers. I'm sure not all of them are the kind of people we'd trust with our children, but that doesn't mean we know anything about their secrets."

Half-hooded eyes said two comments had turned her from gushing and talkative to guarded and wary—usually a sign we were on the right trail. But I wasn't sure how to navigate from where we sat to what we needed her to tell us.

Graham cleared his throat. "How many children do you have?" he asked.

She blinked at the change of subject. "Two girls."

"How old?"

"Four and seven." The words were halting, her tone uncertain. She didn't know where he was going. I wasn't sure I did, either, but I was sure he was trying to catch her off guard.

"Was your husband what you would call a good father?" Graham asked.

Ah-ha. Graham had an idea of why Chester might've bought a kidney. I folded my hands in my lap and leaned back in my chair.

Desiree's eyes filled with tears, her voice dropping to a whisper. "Chester was a shitty husband. But he was a great father. The sun rose and set on those girls." Her hand went to her forehead, tears falling quickly and spattering her hot pink top with mascara-tinged spots of deep magenta. "My girls. God forgive me, they're going to miss their daddy."

She sniffled, looking up. "I wasn't thinking. I was just so mad. Stacy ain't prettier than me, she's just stupid enough to do stuff I won't. And Chester was lying to me—to me! Like I didn't know when he hired a blonde bimbo to answer his phones that he had other ideas. I used to answer his goddamn phones! He thought I was stupid, too, I guess."

Graham leaned forward, his voice low and soothing. "We don't think you're stupid, Desiree. A lot of people make big mistakes in life. It sounds like Chester was guilty of that, and in turn, you were as well."

"How am I ever going to explain this to the girls?" she asked.

"Your older daughter is in school already?" Graham asked.

Desiree nodded. "She's in the first grade."

"This will make the local news, so you should tell her the truth, and you should do it yourself. As soon as we're done here," Graham said. "I know you don't want to do that, but it will be better for her to hear it from you than from a kid at school whose parents were talking about it."

"I can't have her come visit me in jail." Desiree's chin dropped to her chest.

"What if we can arrange it so you don't have to?" Graham asked.

"Why would you do that? You don't even know me." Hope poured from her eyes and her voice as she hung on Graham's every breath.

"I need to know where Chester got his new kidney. And where to find any papers or computer files that relate to the transplant."

Her shoulders fell with a heavy sigh. "Am I going to be in more trouble?"

More trouble than first degree murder and assault with a deadly weapon, which she was already facing? Not a chance.

"Not if you help us," Graham said.

She nodded. "You can let me see my girls outside this place?"

Graham nodded. The sheriff had seemed like a good guy, and it wasn't like she had a shot at overpowering us and taking off.

"He started having trouble with his kidneys years ago, before we were even together," she said, her eyes on the metal table between us. "He was on dialysis three days a week by the time Kaity—that's our baby—was born, and the doctors said they weren't sure how long he could go without a new kidney. But the problem was, nobody would give him one."

"And his doctor told you that? Do you remember that doctor's name?"

"Sure, that was Dr. Davenport, he even appealed to a review board somewhere—he called it the 'God committee'—on account of the fact that we had young children, and Chester's been giving him great deals on Cadillacs for years. We waited weeks to hear back, but they said no, too. His heart wouldn't hold up and it could be a waste of an organ, they said. And all that time, Chester was getting sicker and sicker. He could barely last half a day at work by the time he got hooked up with Doc Pendergast."

Neither of us so much as flinched when she said the name.

"And how did that happen?" Graham asked.

"I'm not really sure. Someone told him that he should call Doc Pendergast, that he might be able to help him. A lawyer, I think he said. Came in to buy a Vette and got to talking—Chester could talk to anybody."

Graham made a note without looking away from Desiree. "And Doc Pendergast was able to get him a kidney even though the God committee said no?"

And even though Pendergast didn't have a license to practice medicine. But I didn't say that out loud.

"Sure did. In like a week's time, too. Chester said it was the advantage of being able to pay for a private doctor instead of going through insurance."

Graham just nodded. "Do you know how much the bill for that was?"

"Seventy-five grand." Her eyes skipped between us. "I thought you said you were looking into a murder. Does one of you need a kidney or something?"

I offered a half smile that wasn't quite a lie.

"How long was Chester in the hospital?" Graham asked.

Desiree shook her head. "He wasn't."

"He wasn't in the hospital? For a kidney transplant?" Graham's eyebrows shot up.

"They said there wasn't enough room." Her brow furrowed. "That's what Chester told me. There wasn't enough room."

She glanced up at Graham, biting her lip. "That can happen, right?"

"Hospitals do run out of beds." He didn't say the part where surgeries get postponed if that happens.

Desiree nodded. "They sent the stuff to the house instead."

"What stuff?" Graham asked.

"The people from the hospital came to the house the day before with all this stuff and set up our bedroom just like a hospital room. Bed, IV, heart monitor. The doctor brought Chester in that night after his procedure, and he showed me how to change the IV and give him the pain medicine, and how to change the bandage. Left me his card with his cell phone number in case we had any trouble. The medicine mostly kept Chester knocked out. Took about a week for him to be up and around and they came back and took all the stuff away."

Graham's hand moved so fast making notes as she spoke I was sure we'd have trouble reading them. I focused on her words so I could help him decipher later, admiring his interrogation technique for the thousandth time. Graham was a big man, and could be intimidating when he wanted, but he knew exactly when to lay on the charm and kill a witness with kindness to get the information he needed. Helping her get to see her kids to get her cooperation was a brilliant touch. And from the look on her face, he had her trust now, too.

"Where did he go for the operation?" Graham asked. "Was that at the hospital?"

"No. He said he didn't know exactly where they were, but it was a really really big room with a lot of bright lights, and a lot of concrete. Floor, walls."

"You didn't take him?"

"They wouldn't let me," she said. "They said it was safer if only the patient and the doctor were there. Germs and such."

It took effort to keep my face blank.

"He wasn't able to see where they were going on the way there?" Graham asked.

"He was pretty sick," she said. "The doc, he gave him something to help with motion sickness when he picked Chester up that morning."

Motion sickness. Sure.

"When did he have the surgery?"

"November 12th. Day after Veterans Day, because they do a big sales event at the dealership for the military on the 11th and he wanted to see the numbers at the end of the night before his operation."

"Did the doctor tell Chester anything about the kidney donor?"

"Healthy young man who worked in construction," she recited. "It was on a paper."

"And do y'all still have that paperwork?" Graham asked.

"It's in the drawer on the right side of Chester's desk in our study."

Graham stood. "Thank you for your help, Desiree."

She looked up at him. "My girls are with my sister. I didn't have nobody else to watch them."

"I'll work it out with the sheriff so you can see them." Graham closed his notebook and slid it into his pocket. "We have a few things to do, but we'll be back later today. Sit tight."

He held the door for me and I waited until we were around the corner before I spun to him with a grin. "Brilliant."

"I'm glad she loves her kids so much," he said. "Sad for them, but..." He shook his head. "Pendergast is dirty. Firsthand witness."

"I believe it's time to pay the good doctor a visit," I said. "With a detour by Chester and Desiree's place."

Graham pointed to the sheriff's office door, which was open, at the end of the hall. "Thirty seconds."

I nodded, leaning against the wall to wait for him. We were getting somewhere. This case was a weird jumble of things that just flat didn't quite fit, but thanks to Chester and his mistress—plus one pissed-off wife and some smart police work by Graham—I finally felt like we'd found a thread that might unravel the whole convoluted thing.

28

"I guess there's good money in selling cars," Graham said as we ducked under the yellow tape strung loosely between two of the massive white pillars fronting the Hennings' wide brick front porch. I waved to a young officer at the front door, who glanced at my badge and stepped aside. After Graham spoke with him at the station, Sheriff Munoz radioed ahead to tell his deputies Graham and I were on our way to the crime scene at Desiree and Chester's home.

Inside a rotunda-style foyer with a ceiling that soared to probably thirty feet sporting a crystal chandelier about the size of a small sedan, Graham stopped, his eyes on a painting in an art niche on the wall adjacent to the front door. "Is that an actual Picasso?"

I snapped a photo with my phone. "Looks like these folks could afford one, so probably."

He pointed to another niche on the opposite wall—this one empty. "So where'd its mate go?"

We walked over and studied the wall, the interior of the framed-out area papered in heavy navy paper with a subtle jacquard pattern. I clicked the flashlight on my phone. "There."

Graham nodded as I pointed to a faint line where the sun had slightly faded the paper around a frame that once hung there. "It hasn't been gone long," he said, running a finger along the wallpaper outside the line and pulling it away to show off the grayish-white tip. "No dust."

I took a couple of pictures of that, as well, thinking about the seventy-five grand Desiree said they paid for Chester's new kidney. There couldn't be but so many pieces of high-end art sold in this area in a year.

I peeked into the room between where we stood and the Picasso. "Study." I pointed.

We pushed the double doors open more and walked into a massive wood-and-leather-lined room with three walls of ten-foot bookshelves loaded with everything from actual leather-bound encyclopedias to adventure novels and thrillers, some with well-worn spines.

Crossing the plush red and gold oriental rug to the desk, I pulled open the top right-hand drawer where Desiree said the medical papers lived.

Paperclips, scotch tape, and a cell phone charger.

I opened the rest of the desk drawers.

"Someone took them." I tipped my head back and stared at the ornate scrolled woodwork on the ceiling, trying to swallow a scream.

"Assuming that happened after Chester died, someone from the SO has been on the door the entire time, so it shouldn't be hard to figure out who," Graham said.

Walking back to the door, he paused and bent to retrieve something from under an end table next to a leather club chair by the fireplace.

Fingers on the edges, he held it up and looked at the back, grinning. "Pendergast's card—the one she said had his cell number on the back."

"We need a warrant to get his location data on the 12th," I said, voicing what I knew Graham was thinking. Not that we couldn't have gotten the number from his carrier, but it takes so long to petition each company and get it through their attorneys that it's almost never worth it because we get the numbers weeks after we've solved a case.

He took photos of both sides of the card and returned it to the floor under the table.

We stepped out of the study and Graham turned for the front door. I laid a hand on his arm. "I want a peek at the bedroom."

I followed a hallway off the massive family room, barely pausing to marvel at the huge stone fireplace. A box of gloves rested on the floor outside the door at the end of the hallway next to a box of shoe coverings. Donning both, I pushed a dark cherry door open and stepped into Chester and Desiree's bedroom.

No one was working in the room. I checked my watch. "How is it nearly two o'clock already?" I muttered, figuring everyone was at lunch.

"I'll say one thing for this mess—it's making the week fly by a lot faster than I thought it would." Graham smiled and I nodded.

"That's a whole lot of blood," I said, surveying the stains on the bedding and the floor as I stepped around markers for footprints and shell casings.

Graham went to the door leading to the bathroom and whistled. "It looks worse on all this white tile and marble." He pointed to prints left in blood by bare feet. "Looks like the girlfriend fled into the bathroom when Desiree started shooting."

"I wish they didn't have her sedated," I said.

"You think Chester talked to his mistress about the new kidney he bought?"

"I think Desiree said she was his secretary at the dealership."

Graham nodded. "Which means she knows a good bit about his schedule and who he was meeting with during the day."

"Bingo."

My phone buzzed. I pulled it out and tapped the talk button when I saw Corie Whitehead's name on the screen.

"Thank you so much for coming up to help," I said by way of hello.

"Think nothing of it," she said. "Anything I can do, especially on this one."

"Jim is going to be okay," I said.

"Glad to hear it. And I'm still in for helping. If I've ever seen remains this damaged, I've blocked it out. We're only an hour or so into these, and I have about ninety lines of notes in my speech-to-text program."

"Good Lord. Were you able to get an ID?"

"That's what I called to tell you—I figured you'd be waiting for it, and the PD just put in the results from the fingerprints. The woman in the bottom of the freezer is Ellen Helmsley, Caucasian female, age twenty-eight. She was the resident of the property where the remains were found, I understand. The one in the top is Marcy Finelli, twenty-three, address unknown."

"Anything else worth noting yet?" I asked.

"Nothing I want to say until I'm sure," she said. "We're going to be a while. Might even be tomorrow. But I'll call you."

I thanked her and ended the call, opening the top drawer on the night table to the left of the Hennings' bed. The flowery Lancôme lotion on the tabletop said this was Desiree's side, and what people keep in their night-stand drawers is often pretty revealing.

I rifled through: two baby photo albums, one chronicling each of her daughters' first months of life. A stack of letters tied with a length of blue satin ribbon. I tugged one free and opened it, scanning small but neat penmanship as Graham disappeared into the closet. "Chester was married before, to a woman named Angie. He wrote Desiree love letters about how he wanted to leave his wife."

"And she kept them?"

"In the night table." I waved the packet when he stuck his head out of the closet.

He pulled out his notebook and jotted the ex-wife's name.

"Other than that there's just pictures of her kids, a...um...toy of sorts, and..." I spotted something in the back of the drawer and reached for it. "A flash drive." I held up a silver stick.

"That's usually a promising thing to find in there." Graham left the closet. "Nothing in there but clothes."

I snagged an evidence bag from a box near the foot of the bed and dropped the thumb drive in.

"We can't take that," Graham said.

"Why not? I guarantee you they won't search these drawers. And she confessed already. This has way more of a chance of being material to our case than it does theirs."

His forehead furrowed the way it did when something made him uncomfortable.

"If I'm wrong I'll return it to Munoz myself. I'll even dust it for prints for him."

Graham sighed. "Yeah. Okay."

"That card have an address for Pendergast, too?" I asked.

"On Fifth Street."

"Let's see what the not-so-good doctor has to say for himself."

The building at the address on Pendergast's business card was a massive, aging Victorian-style home. A wrought-iron fence fronted the street, and the driveway was on the side of the corner lot. We parked at the curb in front and started up the walk, pausing to read a small, tasteful sign posted on the porch railing.

"What does private medical consulting mean?" Graham asked.

"I think that's an excellent opening question here." I jogged up the steps and tried the front door. It swung open to a wood-paneled foyer that, like the rest of the house, was a little worn around the edges, but clean.

"Do you have an appointment?" a small woman with bright red, close-cropped hair, heavy blue eyeshadow, and several pieces of chunky gold jewelry asked from behind a simple Queen Anne-style desk stationed opposite the door, near the foot of the stairs. "The doctor is on lunch, and I didn't think he had a two o'clock today..." She pulled a pen from behind her ear and flipped a page in an appointment book before she looked back at us with slightly raised brows.

"You won't find us in there." I flashed the kind of wide, saccharine smile only a former pageant queen can. "But I'm sure hoping I heard correctly that Dr. Pendergast can help me." I let my shoulders droop as the smile faded, putting a hand out like I needed Graham to steady me.

He laid an arm around my shoulders and leveled a pleading look at the woman behind the desk. "We're getting married Saturday. Does he have time to see her?"

She hurried around the desk, patting Graham's arm and leaving a cloud of flowery perfume in her wake as she went by. "I'm sure we can do something, y'all wait here for just a moment."

I stood up straight when she disappeared into a room off the right side of the foyer. "She didn't even flinch at our badges," I said.

"Maybe she doesn't know who she's really working for here?" Graham murmured. "What's your plan? Because if he's smart enough to run a black market organ operation, he's smart enough to wriggle out of charges by way of an entrapment defense if we lie to him."

"It's not entrapment if he offers," I said.

"All he has to do is convince a judge we might have done something to coerce him The burden of proof would be on us, not him." Graham shook his head. "This will get us past the receptionist, but we do a better service to our case by playing it straight in there. We know he did it, Desiree told us he did. We have a witness. We don't need him to offer to sell you a liver or something."

"A witness who confessed to murder won't impress a jury," I whispered.

"Chester's death has nothing to do with what she told us about this guy." His mouth set in the straight line that meant he was done talking about this, and I nodded, drooping back against him when the door to the office started to open. The receptionist appeared, beckoning us to the door.

"If you don't mind him finishing his lunch, y'all may come on in."

"Thank you so much," I said as we stepped past her into the office.

Pendergast looked like an older version of the headshot Skye had shown me, his thinning dark hair combed and carefully sprayed, starched shirt and tie visible under his open white lab coat. A plastic takeout bowl with about half a salad left in it sat on the leather blotter covering the center of his desk.

"What...can I do...for you?" The words were halting and almost breathy, Pendergast's tone flat, his face expressionless as he gestured to the leather chairs facing his desk.

We crossed the floor and I stood over the desk, keeping my face neutral as I stuck out one hand for him to shake. "Faith McClellan, Texas Rangers. Are you Dr. Douglas Pendergast?"

He nodded, not offering a flicker of reaction to either my tone—which wasn't my nicest—or my title. "Yes."

His monotone, almost-winded voice was unsettling—goosebumps popped up on my arms as I released his hand and took a seat next to Graham when Pendergast pointed again to the chairs.

"My assistant said you...have a medical concern," he said, giving me a quick once-over. "I suspect...she may have been...misled."

Was he pausing because he needed to in order to breathe? I'd never heard anyone speak that way save for my granddaddy, and only when he was using an oxygen tank. I watched Pendergast's nostrils, but didn't catch any telltale flares in the gaps between his words.

"We have some questions about Chester Henning. I believe he was a patient of yours," Graham said.

"I'm afraid...confidentiality laws...prohibit me from...confirming that." Pendergast's hands folded on the blotter, pushing his salad bowl back. His nails were neatly trimmed and shiny, the beds pink. I'm not a doctor, but lack of oxygen didn't seem to be a problem for him.

I watched his eyes for a minute—they darted about but never quite met anyone else's gaze.

"Mr. Henning is dead," I said. "Confidentiality limitations no longer apply." Even if they would have prior to Chester's death, which I was unsure of given that Pendergast lacked a medical license.

His jaw slackened, but he recovered quickly. "I hadn't...heard that. I'll need to call...his wife."

The more he talked, the less I noticed the peculiar cadence, though it persisted.

"She's in the county jail," Graham said. "She killed him."

"Oh dear." Pendergast could have been saying his desk was brown.

"The autopsy revealed a kidney that was not...well, original equipment, per se, to Mr. Henning," I said, watching him carefully.

His eyebrows lifted ever so slightly.

"Was he a...transplant patient?"

"We were hoping you could tell us," I said.

"I haven't performed...a surgery...in years now." His gaze settled on his hands.

"So what exactly does a private medical consultant do, Doc?" Graham asked.

"I help patients make...decisions regarding care. Offer my...medical expertise...to guide them. Connect them with former...colleagues."

"And did you connect Mr. Henning with a colleague?" I asked. "Perhaps with Dr. Bryce Little?"

Pendergast's flat, dark eyes met mine for the first time, and I could've sworn on my granny's family Bible someone doused me with ice water. I swallowed hard, feeling my chin jut out as I met his gaze and held it despite my every instinct trying to propel me from the chair and the room itself.

"I did not." The words were less breathy and more forceful.

I didn't blink, but my heart had picked up enough speed that I could hear it pounding in my ears. "Did you perform a surgery on Mr. Henning?"

"I am sure you know...I'm not licensed...to perform surgery. But I still... believe you need...a warrant." He didn't blink either. "That's private information. If it happened."

"I can come back with a warrant," I said. "If you'd like to get a judge involved."

"You...do that."

Graham stood, lingering at his full height, shoulders back, over Pendergast's seated form. "This isn't over."

"We'll see." Pendergast didn't look up, reaching for the salad and spearing a bite to put into his mouth.

I slammed the door on the truck and cranked the engine, cutting a hard U-turn and lead-footing it back toward the highway.

"Hey, Dale Earnhardt, we're going to miss your mother's party if you get us killed," Graham said. "That is one creepy dude, and we have plenty to justify a warrant. We got this."

"Creepy isn't even the right word," I said. "I need some miles between us and him, and about ten showers. I have sat in rooms with some of the most heinous monsters mankind has to offer, and I have never had such a strong urge to run away from another human."

"For me it was more of an urge to deck him and then run," Graham said. "The guy is so dirty there should be a cloud of funk around him. Maybe he's our killer, maybe not, but he has to be guilty of something. We just need to build a case. This is what we do."

I hooked the right onto the highway and laid on the gas, speeding back north, where maybe with a little luck, what we'd learned on this day trip would help turn up some answers.

By the time we arrived at the courthouse, the building was locked and the surrounding parking lot and streets devoid of cars.

"We'll come back first thing tomorrow," Graham said.

I turned out of the square toward my house, drumming my fingers on the steering wheel. The whole drive back to Waco, I'd been turning the conversation with Pendergast over in my head. "Just because Corie said he was at the Rotary Club the morning Jim was attacked doesn't mean he's not the killer," I said. "Hiring someone to steal the body while he's in a public place is actually great cover for him."

Graham nodded. "I had the same thought. But whoever it was didn't think Jim would be there."

"Because no one else who does what Jim does would be there that early on a Saturday morning."

"Which brings me back to an employee," Graham said. "Someone who knows how the lab works, and has a key to the door. Have you heard anything else from Cortez?"

I parked the truck in my driveway and shut off the engine, pulling my phone out to check.

"Nope." I opened the contacts and touched Cortez's name.

"Ranger, your ears must be burning," he said by way of hello.

"You were talking about me? Good things, I hope."

"I talked to every patrol officer who regularly patrols the area around Bluebonnet Hills, and one of the guys remembers seeing a vehicle there sporadically lately."

I reached into the console for a pen and mimed writing at Graham. He shoved a notebook under my hand.

"Define lately."

"Past few weeks, maybe a bit longer. He barely noticed it, but when I pressed for evidence of people in the area he remembered. Said there was never anyone in it."

"What shift does he work?"

"Second."

I scribbled that down.

"He didn't get a plate number by any chance?" I knew the answer but had to ask anyway.

"Nope. But he said he'll keep an eye out and he will if he sees it again."

My gut said he wouldn't.

"Any description at all?"

"Older model small hatchback. Gray. He said he thinks it was a Honda but he can't be sure."

"Thanks." I jotted it down. "Any leads from the lab employees?"

"Not yet, but I still have four more people to sit down with in the morning. How was your day?"

"I am going to try for a few warrants in the morning—I'm interested in a lawyer here in town named Gilchrist, as well as some records at a medical supply company and a quasi-doctor's office down in Goliad. Do you know anything about Gilchrist?"

"He's a piece of work, that guy. Keeps more slime out of trouble than anyone in the county. Slippery, too. You think he's tied to this?"

"I think there are a lot of arrows that seem to point to Buster Beauchamp, who is Gilchrist's biggest client. I am doubtful Buster is smart enough to pull anything like this off, but wondering if his attorney might be smart enough to help him hide any possible part in it. So I want to see their business papers."

"Good luck. Let me know if we can help."

"Will do." I ended the call and let my head drop back against the seat, closing my eyes. "Buster, Pendergast, Jerry...Everything almost fits, but nothing quite does. We can't even decide if we're working a serial, for fuck's sake."

"It's a serial," Graham said. "The care taken with the victims and the method of hiding the remains clearly points to a serial."

I pulled in half a breath and then let it out again. I couldn't bicker with him anymore. Hell, maybe he was right. Graham was a good cop, and he'd worked more than a few serial killers.

I could convince myself of his theory, too, as long as I didn't think about Pendergast.

"Except for the changes in venue and M.O.," Graham said. "Those don't fit the serial profile."

Finally, something we could agree on.

"But the 'except' always turns up with this one." I sighed. "It was a personal attack on Jim at the lab, except the killer used Jim's scalpel and probably had a key; there's a single culprit, except I'm as sure as I've ever been of anything that Pendergast is up to his weirdly devoid of all emotion face in this, and he couldn't be doing it alone. I'm going to start calling this case the exception to all the rules."

"Convoluted is an understatement," Graham said. "But we'll figure it out."

I opened the door on my truck, my eyes landing on a small black sports car parked under the wispy, dancing branches of my neighbor's soft green, budding willow tree, the light from the street lamp just barely filtering through.

Graham rounded the front of the truck and saw it, too.

"I've never seen anyone who drives an Eclipse visit the Riveras," he said, taking a step toward the curb.

I laid one hand on my sidearm, still snapped securely into its holster, and followed, Pendergast's odd voice and flat gaze flashing through my thoughts. A shadowy movement in the car had my thumb flipping the safety strap loose, but I didn't draw my weapon.

"Please don't shoot my dog." The voice, at least an octave high, came from my front porch and I whirled, rolling my eyes when I saw wannabe Skye Morrow from the hospital and the body recovery in Ellen Helmsley's garage.

"You have about ten seconds to get the hell out of here," I said, finding my voice—a loud version of it, anyway—after I let go of my gun. "Whatever misguided idea brought you here, reporters do not just show up uninvited at an officer's home. Even Skye hasn't ever stooped so low." That I knew of, anyway.

She descended two steps, reaching her hands out in front of her. "Please, you don't understand. I've combed police reports and I have an injured medical examiner and a missing corpse that was discovered under strange circumstances, and Skye's news story says the thing linking it all was that the body is missing organs."

She stepped off the bottom step and into the light of a streetlamp, the glow glittering off a tear hovering on her lower lashes.

I opened my mouth to yell again and paused. "What's with the waterworks?"

"I thought I knew enough about investigations to figure it out for myself, but I can't, and I just need an answer. Is a serial killer going after transplant patients? Because my dad is one."

I shook my head. "We have no comment on open investigations," I said. "But your dad isn't in any danger."

Her shoulders dropped when she sighed, the lone tear streaking mascara through her on-camera makeup.

I watched relief break across her face. If she was lying, she was good at it. Or maybe I was just too jaded after years of dealing with Skye.

"Covering murders is never fun, but this one has had me unable to sleep." Her blue eyes were wide, her smile TV-bright.

I still wasn't telling her anything.

She held my gaze without blinking, flexing her jaw and standing perfectly straight and still. "Is someone...stealing organs? Like from people who aren't dead?"

Maybe she had managed to dig up something.

I shook my head again. "No comment."

"Where did your dad have his surgery?" Graham asked, his voice easy and almost uninterested.

"At Parkland in Dallas," she said. "It'll be a year in April."

I nodded. "I hope he's doing well. Have a safe drive home."

She pinched her lips into a line and waved, muttering something that sounded like "worth a shot," as she hurried past us to her car.

Graham laid an arm across my shoulders as we climbed the steps and I righted a pillow she'd knocked over in the rocker.

"Chocolate, shower, bed?" he asked. "And up early to go back to the courthouse?"

"Commander Hardin, you know me too well." I smiled.

"Just well enough, I'd say—for instance, I know Judge Stevenson is always in the office early, and I know he likes your nerve and determination."

"Let's just hope he likes it enough to issue a couple of easy warrants in the morning."

29

A lanky deputy with dark hair waved us through the security checkpoint at the courthouse when he saw our badges at seven-thirty the next morning.

"Morning," Graham said.

"Morning, sir." The young deputy smiled. "Getting an early start today?"

"Hoping that saying about getting the worm applies to criminals, too," Graham quipped.

I strode to the elevators. Stevenson was on the fourth floor. He was the kind of judge Chuck McClellan despised: smart, observant, fair, and not for sale.

Which was exactly why I wanted to speak with him.

When the elevator doors whispered open, I forced myself to walk instead of jog down the long hallway papered in navy and white. Rounding the corner with Graham on my heels, I found the front office empty as expected. I knocked on the closed walnut door to the judge's chambers.

"Yes?" his deep baritone came from the other side of the door.

I opened it far enough to stick my head in. "Faith McClellan, Texas—"

"Rangers," he finished for me, flashing a wide smile. "Come in, Ranger. What do I owe the pleasure to this early in the morning?"

I pushed the door the rest of the way open and stepped into the sparsely decorated room. While most of his peers relaxed in practically palatial studies cloaked in dark earth tones, lined with ornate shelves, and dotted with artwork, Stevenson had taken his office decorating allowance and donated to a program for at-risk teenagers the day after he was sworn in. The built-in shelves and heavy drapes were the only thing that remained of his predecessor's lavish taste. He sat in an orange-upholstered rolling desk chair behind a scratched, dented metal desk—he'd unearthed both from the basement storage room.

"It's nice to see you again, Your Honor," I said. "This is Travis County Commander Graham Hardin. He's working with me on a case I'd like to ask for your help with this morning."

"Isn't he also marrying you on Saturday?" The judge's lips pursed, his tone amused.

"You saw the announcement in the paper."

"I did, and congratulations." He slid his glasses off, tucked them into a pocket under his robe, and folded his hands on the Office Max brand calendar blotter on his desk. "My first hearing isn't until ten today," he said. "Talk to me."

I wanted to ask why he was being so nice to me, but I was afraid to. Gift horses, and all that.

"We're working on a strange murder case," I began.

Stevenson waved his hand. "Stolen body, nearly dead medical examiner, and Skye Morrow on TV talking about black market organs. Doesn't take a genius to piece that together. Someone is killing people and taking their organs. It's ghoulish. And if anyone can cut through bullshit and put a stop to it, it's the woman who managed to take down Chuck McClellan from inside his own house. I have a lot of respect for you, Ranger. It couldn't have been easy to lock your own father up—especially with the kind of money and connections that he has. Just tell me what you need."

Oh.

I'm not often at a loss for words, but damned if that didn't do it.

"I'll be damned." Graham whispered it too low for the judge to hear him.

"Well, sir, I'm in serious need of a whole host of warrants this morning."

The judge pulled a legal pad from a desk drawer and picked up a pen. "Who and why?"

I pulled out my phone and read him the name and address of the medical supply company.

"I called all seven authorized providers of transplant equipment in the state yesterday," I said. "This was the only one that refused to release delivery records or orders for the items I'm interested in."

"By what legal precedent?"

"I spoke with a receptionist, who claimed everyone was out of the office and she couldn't release them."

Stevenson shrugged. "You don't need a warrant for that, there's no statute they could stretch far enough to claim privilege. But if it'll help you get what you need to wave my signature around, I'm happy to lend it."

I grinned. "Thank you, Your Honor."

"Next," he said.

"There's a doctor down in Goliad County who lost his medical license a couple of years back, and is now running a practice as a 'private medical consultant,'" I said.

Stevenson raised one hand. "A...?"

"So it's a new one on you, as well?" I asked.

"That sounds like trying to skirt the medical licensing statutes," he said.

Graham and I nodded. "It wouldn't surprise me," Graham said.

"Name?" the judge asked.

"Douglas Pendergast," I said, finding the photo of the card and reading him the address.

He noted it. "What do y'all need from Mr. Pendergast?"

"Any patient records, electronic or other format, relating to Chester Henning of 5739 DuBois Lane, in his possession for reasons professional or personal." I chose words carefully, trying not to leave a loophole.

"You sure you're not a lawyer, too?" Stevenson chuckled. "So he treated this Henning fellow?"

"Henning's widow told us yesterday that Pendergast arranged or possibly performed a black market kidney transplant on Chester," I said.

"But he's dead now?"

"His wife shot him. Caught him with his secretary in their bed, sir."

"I've seen that a few dozen times in my career." Stevenson shook his head. "Granted. Patient confidentiality doesn't apply to self-styled 'consultants.' Anything else?"

"One more, sir. I'd like a look at the list of clients of a local property management company, and a list of the properties managed by that company."

"The one Gilchrist is wrapped up in?" Stevenson's eyes narrowed, his graying brows drawing down.

I slid a glance sideways at Graham when the judge mentioned Buster's lawyer. We were onto something there. I just hoped this time it was actually the right something.

"That would be the one."

"Granted. With pleasure."

I watched him make notes. He seemed to like me a lot more than I'd expected when I came here solely because we'd had a couple of pleasant conversations the summer before and I knew money didn't sway him.

I could probably put a toe over the line of strictly professional. "Sir, what do you think of Gilchrist?" I blurted.

Stevenson snorted. "He's a clever bastard, but crooked as a fencepost after a tornado. I have an intense dislike for people who bend the law to their benefit and that of their clients with a general disregard for public welfare." He smiled. "Professionally, of course, I tolerate Sonny, and I decide every case that comes before me as fairly as the law allows. Personally? I think the guy is a slime ball and it wouldn't surprise me a bit if he was involved in something so hideous."

"Do you think he's capable of murder?"

"I think he knows a hell of a lot of people who are. The kind of people who owe him their freedom."

Oh, shit. Maybe we were getting somewhere.

I needed a cause of death on these victims. I checked my watch and hoped Corie was already in the lab helping the local ME.

Stevenson opened his laptop and smiled at me. "You might as well serve Gilchrist himself with the warrant. Buster Beauchamp will just call him if you waste your time driving it over to him. If I give them six hours to produce the documents you need, can you work with that?"

I checked my watch. "That would be two-thirty." I thought it'd take days at minimum. "Yes, sir, I think that would be just fine."

"Say three o'clock by the time he's served." The judge winked. "I'm sure he'll waste some of it trying to argue, but there's no chance these records aren't accessible to him at the literal push of a button. I've done enough digging myself on Gilchrist to know old David Beauchamp left him a minority interest in that company so his idiot son wouldn't run it totally into the ground after he died. I suspect Gilchrist did some lobbying for that when the old man was sick, but he and Buster are birds of a certain kind of feather, that's for sure."

He pulled the laptop closer and started typing. I tried to keep my jaw properly shut. I'd grown up with judges who were friends of my father's, but I'd never heard one speak so passionately—or freely—about an attorney or their personal disregard for red tape.

"Records of the sale of what items from the medical supply?" he asked.

"A chemical preservative called Celsior and organ cooler boxes," I said.

His head bobbed, his fingers flying over the keys, eyes flicking between the legal pad and the screen.

"You said clients and property addresses for Gilchrist?" the judge asked.

"Yes, sir."

His fingers hitting the keys were the only sounds until the printer on the shelf behind him hummed to life. Pulling a handful of pages from the tray, Stevenson picked up a pen and signed three of them before he stamped a seal of the court under his signature and handed the papers to me. "Let me know if you need anything else."

"Yes, sir. Thank you, sir," I said as Graham and I stood.

"Thank you, Officers," Stevenson said. "I am often disappointed by how many people choose the justice system as a career for reasons other than wanting to see justice done in their communities. You have a long track record of putting that above all else—which I strive to do in my own work as well. Anything I can do to help you with that, I'm happy to."

Graham and I let ourselves out, neither speaking until we were in the elevator with the door shut.

"Those have to be the easiest warrants we've ever gotten," Graham said. "He didn't even ask for evidence."

I swallowed hard. "I'm not going to say I'm not grateful for it today, but it was almost unsettling, wasn't it?"

"I've never met a judge who didn't make you work for a warrant."

The doors opened again and we waved at the deputy on guard as we crossed the lobby and walked outside. I scanned the perimeter of the square. We could work outward from here. I wanted to speak to Gilchrist myself, and if Graham and I got busy we could find deputies to serve the other two warrants.

"There's Gilchrist's office." I pointed to a low building jutting off Columbus Avenue, about a block from the square proper. "I'd like to meet the lawyer who could push a judge to issue a warrant at the bat of an eyelash."

"Stevenson did say he doesn't like the guy."

"He also said he'd done his own digging on him. Maybe he found more than he let on to us."

"Why do I feel like today might be a whole lot less frustrating than yesterday?" Graham started down the steps and I thumped him on the shoulder as I followed.

"Hush up before you jinx us."

We crossed the courthouse lawn and jogged to the other side of the narrow street, making our way down the less-traveled side road and stopping a few yards short of the door to Gilchrist's office.

"What the hell?" Graham squatted and plucked a chunk of glass off the sidewalk, looking at the surrounding buildings—all of which were vacant.

I pulled out my phone and snapped photos of two bullet holes in the frame of the door, as well as the broken window glass.

"See? Jinxed."

30

"We've really got to stop meeting like this," Officer Miller said, hopping out of her WPD Forensics van a few minutes after Graham placed a call to local dispatch about the law office. "I'm beginning to think you two are bad luck or something—I can't remember the last time we had a week this busy."

"We follow the bad luck, not the other way around," Graham said with a smile.

She tipped her head to one side. "You think a lawyer's office being shot up by vandals is related to those dead women?"

"Or something." I pointed to the door and the window. "I count six shots, if we assume one shattered the glass in the door. Two in the window glass, two in the frame, and one in the door frame."

She waved Officer Schaefer over and he raised a large DSLR camera and started snapping photos. Another young officer I couldn't remember seeing before strung yellow tape from the lamppost on the corner down the front of the sidewalk past the far corner of the building, tying it off on a rain gutter that hung looser than it should on the vacant building next door.

"Did y'all just come upon this?" Miller asked. "Or were you going to this office for some reason?"

I let my eyes roam the front wall of the building. A small bronze plaque engraved with *Leonard J. Gilchrist, Esq.* had been nicked by something, though there was no way to know if it was a bullet or debris. I examined it and pretended I hadn't really heard Miller's question. Cops are nosy by nature—it's a job requirement—but I keep my cases close as a general rule, even with local officers. Working in the field with people I don't really know well has taught me that I never know who they might know—or who they might talk to—that could add complications to my investigation. Before the pause stretched to officially awkward, a strangled gasp came from behind my left shoulder.

"Jesus, what now?" A woman's voice, the kind of rough that comes with a pack-a-day habit, had me turning on my heel.

"Good morning, Miss…" I let it trail with a small, expectant smile.

Her eyes were stuck on my badge. "The fucking Texas Rangers? Are you kidding me?" She took a step backward. "This is so not what I signed up for."

She was the kind of petite that verges on waifish, with teased, Texas-big bleached hair, YouTube tutorial smoky-eye makeup, and ruby red lip gloss. Her knees swayed on the three-inch heels on her feet with every step, a plain black pencil skirt that came to mid-thigh and a ruffled pink blouse completing the look.

"Do you work here?" I asked, keeping my tone friendly.

She nodded slowly, staring now at the bullet holes in the glass. "Right there on the other side of that window."

I looked through and saw a polished walnut desk in the lobby.

"For how long?"

"Two months now. Almost," she said. "But I'm rethinking my options."

"I didn't catch your name," I tried again. "I'm Faith. This is Graham, and Detective Miller. Do you know how to get in touch with Mr. Gilchrist? We'd feel better knowing he's okay."

"I'm Missy. Melissa, but everyone calls me Missy." She pulled a cell phone from the large canvas tote over her shoulder. "Let me see if I can get ahold of Sonny."

"He doesn't go by Leonard?"

"He wouldn't answer to it if the call came with a million-dollar check," she said. "Everyone calls him Sonny."

Everything about her was wary, and with Judge Stevenson's words repeating on a loop in my head, I was damned curious about what she might've seen in two months working for Leonard "Sonny" Gilchrist that would cause this reaction to police officers inspecting his office—after it had been shot up, no less. But if we didn't tread carefully, she wouldn't tell us anything. I had to get her to trust me, which might take more time than I had to offer, given her demeanor.

"I appreciate your help," I said.

She touched her phone screen and put it to her ear. Frowned. "Weird. Straight to voicemail."

"Maybe his phone isn't on," Graham said.

"Sonny's phone is always on. I think he sleeps with the fucking thing in his pocket." She shook her head. "Clients call him at all hours and he always answers."

I turned to Miller. "Can y'all send a squad car to his home for a welfare check?"

She was already on her radio asking dispatch.

I looked back at Missy. "Address?"

She turned her phone screen around so Miller could read it to the dispatcher, smacking her gum faster. Probably the nicotine kind.

I went to the police van at the curb, pulled on gloves from a box in Miller's front seat, and turned for the door, trying the knob first. Locked.

All in all, that was probably good. A vandalized office is better than a burglarized office.

"Still locked," I reported over my shoulder before reaching through the broken window to turn the latch.

Graham and I stood aside to let the forensics team enter first. Missy stepped closer to us for the first time since she walked up. "Can I go in? There's some personal stuff in my desk I want to check on."

"It doesn't seem anyone breached the door, but sure. Just let them do a sweep of the building first to make sure I'm right about that."

"So what do y'all want with Sonny, anyway?" she asked.

I contemplated my answer for just long enough to wear through her patience. She tapped a long scarlet nail on the papers in my hand. "I've worked here long enough to know what a search warrant looks like. You were coming to give him that and found this mess, huh?"

"Correct," I said, catching and holding her gaze. "What do you think Sonny might know that a search warrant would come in handy for?"

"How much time do you have?"

"As much as we need."

She flinched at my serious answer to her quippy question. "I'm sure if you have a warrant there, you know that Sonny has some clients who aren't the nicest people around," she said.

I watched her eyes because they were her most expressive feature. She was torn between telling me what I wanted to know because she was a little bit afraid of me, and protecting her boss because she was probably a little bit afraid of him—or maybe some of his clients—too. But I was standing right in front of her, so I won out after a ten-beat silence.

"Can I see that?" she asked. "I probably know better than he does where to find whatever it is that you want. He doesn't know how to file anything. I spent three weeks just getting the place organized."

I pulled the warrant from my stack and handed it over. Her blue eyes skimmed it, her head bobbing as she read.

"Have you met Buster?" she asked when she looked back up at me.

"We have."

"He's the client who spends the most time here in the office." Her face didn't give away whether that was a good or bad thing.

"Can you find these records for me?" I asked.

"Sonny keeps all of Buster's stuff in his office," she said. "I can look, but it will take a little more time." She bit her lip. "Should I wait and ask him before I give you anything? I mean, that's probably a stupid question to ask you, but I don't really know how this works except that on TV when cops show up with a warrant they get what they're asking for. He knows some characters, but this is the best paying job I've ever had and I don't want to lose it." She glanced at the bullet holes. "I don't think, anyway."

"The judge will make Sonny produce these records. There's no chance he doesn't have access to them as a part owner of Buster's company and Buster's attorney, so if he refuses to give us copies, he will go to jail for contempt of court."

Missy handed the warrant back to me. "Okay then."

I stepped through the door to a small square of tile flooring with a rug that marked the entranceway. "Are we clear to come in?"

Reynolds and Schaefer appeared in an arch that led to a hallway, nodding as they pulled their gloves off. "No evidence of entry, burglary, or other forms of foul play. Just damage to the front of the place. Schaefer will write up the report this morning."

I waved Graham and Missy inside and she flipped a switch near the door to turn the overhead fluorescents on.

As she put her bag down on her desk, Miller's radio crackled. "Hey, Detective?" a man's voice said. "Jimmerson here, I ran the welfare check you asked for. House is empty and quiet, no signs of forced entry or foul play."

She glanced at me before she thanked the officer for his help. "Sorry, Ranger," she said after she clicked the radio off.

"I appreciate the effort. Missy, do you know what Sonny drives?"

"A silver Corvette with purple flames up the sides," she said. "Everyone knows his car."

"You want an all-points on it?" Miller asked.

I looked around the office. "Just a welfare check," I said. "Don't pull him over, but radio in if anyone spots the vehicle."

"Will do." She raised one hand and waved. "No offense, but I hope y'all have a lovely wedding and that I don't have cause to see you again beforehand."

"Thanks for your help."

Missy shut the last drawer on her desk as the door closed behind the Waco officers.

"Are y'all going to stay here until I find these papers?" she asked. "It might take a while, I could make you some coffee or something."

My turn to be torn—I kind of wanted to watch over her and make sure she was actually looking for the papers. On the other hand, how would I really know if she wasn't? If she just made a show of looking for them and then told us she couldn't find them to protect her boss, I couldn't argue. And the warrant was limited in scope—it didn't give us permission to search the office, it only required Gilchrist to produce any documentation pertinent to Buster's properties and clients that was in his possession as of seven a.m. today.

On the other hand, time wasn't exactly on my side, and Graham and I had other avenues for investigation on this case. I pulled a card from my hip pocket and handed it to her. "My cell number is on the back. Whatever you find, can you fax it to the number on the front, marked to my attention, and then call and let me know you sent it?"

"Sure thing." She waved a shaking hand at the front of the building. "You don't think whoever did that will be back, do you?"

"I can't say for sure. But shooting up an empty office in the middle of the night and attacking an innocent young woman in broad daylight are two very different things. We can have the PD put a patrol car in the area, just have an officer driving by every few minutes today if that will make you feel safer until this is all sorted out."

"That would be wonderful." She flashed a grateful smile full of teeth colored yellow by nicotine. I looked at her hands, which were still shaking.

"I've never wanted a cigarette so bad in my life," she muttered, folding her hands behind her back. "Sonny says it's a low-class habit and he doesn't like the smell. I've been trying to quit."

"Keep trying. I'm almost a year out myself, and I can tell you for what it's worth that I sleep better and running people down on foot is a hell of a lot easier."

"Thanks," she said. "I'll send you what I find. Can you make sure Sonny checks in when you know where he is? It's really not like him to not be at work first thing, and I'm a little worried."

"No problem."

Graham and I let ourselves out.

"Back to your office?" he asked.

"I'm beginning to think everything we need to know is here, but it's all so tangled together that it's hard to separate out what's good and what's bad. I'm hoping the whiteboard will help with that."

31

I stopped short when I rounded the corner to my desk at the F Company offices and saw Archie in my chair. "I didn't expect you to still be slumming it here with the regular folks," I said.

Boone was in my guest chair, his legs stretched out in the aisle. "Consider it a wedding gift, McClellan. I know you and Baxter make a good team, I know you have your hands full with this case, and I also know I'd really like to find whoever this is before they cut up any more women in my city."

"I drove back up this morning," Archie said. "Boone said you needed more hands on deck, and it's possible that I needed to get away from wedding central for a day or two. My house has been swallowed by silk and crystal and hand-lettered place cards."

"Better yours than mine," I said, grateful for maybe the first time in my life for Ruth's party planning prowess.

"So the Jane Doe that was stolen from the crime lab now has two friends?"

"We're waiting for confirmation from the lab, but that was the general consensus of forensics, yes."

I held up the two remaining warrants. "I need someone to serve these at the listed addresses, preferably before lunchtime."

Boone put out a hand and I laid the papers in it, watching his eyes skim them. "Purchase orders aren't privileged information."

"There are seven companies that sell that stuff. That's the only one that wouldn't tell me what I wanted to know."

He flipped pages, reading the one for Pendergast's office. "What the hell is a private medical consultant?"

"Google says it's an unregulated, relatively new side industry that purports to help patients navigate specialists and get access to the care they need," Graham said, holding up his phone. "There are only a handful of folks who offer this service in Texas, and their fees can run thousands upon thousands of dollars."

"No state oversight?" Archie whistled. "Nah, there's no potential for kickbacks and grift there."

"How about potential for illegal organ sales?" I tapped one finger on the edge of the desk.

Graham went to work on his phone, flipping the screen around with a list of a dozen or so names. "Like maybe we've found Pendergast's syndicate?" He grinned.

"I thought you were looking for a serial killer, Commander?"

"I'm looking for the truth, and what you said about every avenue looking like the right one except for one thing bugged me all night. It's true —and I'm not one for trying to make a case be something it's not. This one is weird, maybe the weirdest we've seen, even—so let's figure out what it is. All of this shit has to fit together somehow, with nothing out of place."

Boone tapped the edges of the warrants on the desk. "Give me ten minutes, I'll find a couple of guys I can pull in to serve these." He disappeared into his office.

I grabbed my laptop and pointed to the conference room. "Let's see if we can dig some sense out of this mess, gentlemen." Archie and Graham waved a ladies first.

Flipping the lights on, I grabbed a marker from the box and put the laptop on the table on my way to the board.

"At this point my assumption is that Ellen Helmsley and Marcy Finelli are the fourth and fifth victims," I said. "But it is only an assumption, given the oddities that impact forensic ability to provide time of death."

"We have to just pick the best assumption there," Archie said, settling into a chair and reading what I had on the board so far. "And how much does the order of the crimes even matter, really? If we have no way to pin down actual time of death, we have no way to search area video feeds for leads on who was there at the time. So whatever order they were killed in, the important point is the manner and the commonalities. The electronic surveillance avenues your generation is used to relying on don't help us here."

Graham opened the laptop and pulled out his phone, clicking and typing on the computer. "Maybe not all of them," he said.

I turned back to the board, knowing he'd elaborate if he found what he was looking for. "Fair enough. So we have three dead, two assaults, but with one assault victim missing and one fading in and out of a coma, we can't talk to them about what they remember."

"And one victim was assaulted, recovered, and was later killed, correct?"

I pointed to Marcy Finelli's name. "This woman."

"What do we know about her?" Archie asked. "Sometimes the way to the heart of a weird case is to pick at the weirdest thing about it. Speaking of—lab folks all over the state are shaken and pissed off about what happened to Prescott, pretty much in equal measures. As such, Jessica Knepp in Austin worked around the clock to run the DNA—and there was DNA—you got from under Jim's nails. No match in CODIS. They'll keep trying the smaller databases, though."

"How does someone go from no record at all to hacking parts out of people?" I asked.

"Desperation," Graham said. "This is the crux of what we've been bickering about: you've been focused on greed as a motive because of what Skye told us about Pendergast so early in this case, but I kept going back to a serial because the greed was the exception for me—I don't see it. Greedy ghouls don't sew a woman up and wrap her carefully and place her in a closet with a damn camera. They dump her in the nearest ditch and move on. The women in the freezer are kind of the same—why hide them? Why go back to the same person as a victim? Hell, why let her live in the first place?" He shook his head, sighing, and spun the computer screen, showing off a map with points marked all over the state. "These are the first nine addresses on the list of private medical consultants. It sure as shit looks like they're pinpointed in strategic locations to me, which points right to your theory of an organ harvesting, black market syndicate. And maybe they do have someone with some medical training doing the actual harvesting—someone like Jerry. I know he has a record, but does he have DNA in CODIS?"

I wrote Jerry's name on the board and added the bullet points. "I don't hate that. And it's not like there aren't other possibilities out there," I said. "Medical school is expensive. People who go because they want to help others graduate mired in the kind of debt you measure in fractions of millions. It's not hard to see the lure of easy money, even if it is dirty money."

"These are all small towns in counties with limited resources for criminal investigations," Archie said, leaning over Graham's shoulder.

"How do you know stuff like that off the top of your head?" I asked.

"Places that regularly ask us for help," Boone said from the doorway. "When you've been around as long as we have, you know the frequent fliers. Johnson and Marquette are headed south with your warrants and instructions to keep us updated."

I added a note about the small town locations under Pendergast's name and glanced at Boone. "Thank you, sir."

"The very least I can do," he said. "Any epiphanies in here yet?"

"We're wondering why Finelli was carefully sewn up and left alive after the first attack, then hacked up and left with Ellen in the freezer after another." I surveyed the board. "Finelli was a self-described sex worker, which isn't the safest profession, but this clearly seems like she was targeted."

"The syndicate would've known her blood type and such from the kidney theft," Graham said. "It's possible she had a rare one they needed for someone else."

I added a bullet point for that under her name. "Excellent. And speaking of prostitution, we don't know anything about Jane Doe because we never got a chance to ID her." I flipped my notebook open. "But the landlord said men coming and going at all hours from the other assault victim's apartment irritated the neighbors. And Cortez said Finelli told him herself she was trolling that club for johns. Perhaps the assumption of pros-titution is warranted."

I pulled the white envelope with the thumb drive of the security footage from the Gray Goose out of my back pocket. "The thing I didn't understand the other day was how the attacker got out of that bathroom. The camera on that hallway is pointed squarely at the end of it, and the back entrance to the place isn't off the same hall. No one came out after the victim went in until the other woman found her and they called the paramedics."

"He went somewhere," Archie said, opening my laptop and moving aside. "Could he have hidden until the place was closed?"

"Maybe. But that doesn't help us, because the interior cameras shut off when the last employee leaves."

"Let's have a look at the aftermath of the attack and see what we see," he said.

I plugged the drive into my laptop and opened the file dated for the most recent assault, pulling the slider at the bottom to the point where the victim disappeared into the hallway.

"There she goes." I pointed, letting it run at single speed for the next ten minutes of footage. "How did he know he wouldn't get interrupted in a public bathroom?"

"I'd bet he locked the door and then just got lucky," Archie said.

The wet floor signs.

"Or he made it look like the restroom was out of order until he was done," I said. We watched minutes tick by on the screen, the mouth of the hallway empty all the while.

"There's the second woman going in," I said, giving it a ten count, "and here she is coming out all freaked out."

We watched the medics go in and then come out with the victim on a gurney.

"Damned if I can see anyone else here. Could the ceiling be attached to another business?" Archie asked.

"Cortez looked when we were there. Said the clearance was low and it was stuffed with HVAC ductwork. So not likely, but not impossible. We can ask them to send officers to collect footage from the neighboring business-es." My eyes stayed on the screen as I spoke, a flicker of motion that could've been static on the shitty camera feed catching my eye. I slid the slider back to where the medics emerged from the hallway into a crowd that had formed after they arrived.

Stopped playback. Clicked slow motion forward.

"What?" Graham leaned into the screen.

"There's something there." I pointed to the barest halo of gray blob slipping between a medic and the crowd. "Right here. Someone followed them out."

"I don't see it," Archie said. "And how could the medics fail to notice?"

"There's a men's room in that hall too. Jim said his attacker was male. What if they just didn't think anything of it? And then right here, he's gone."

"He knew where the camera was," Graham said. "He stayed perfectly hidden. That's damn near impossible to catch just watching this footage."

"They're mounted right on the ceiling, though." I shrugged. "Everyone who's ever looked up in that place knows there's a camera there."

"So he was smart enough to use the crowd to slip out unnoticed," Archie said. "But brazen enough to attack someone in a crowded nightclub."

"What else has he been smart about?" I asked. "He's picked victims unwilling or unable to talk to the police."

"Which buys him time," Graham said.

I tapped the marker on Ellen Helmsley's name. "We have from three sources that Ellen is a dealer," I explained to Archie and Boone.

"Someone who'd be reluctant to go to the police," Boone said.

"Or the media," I added. "It's hard for even Skye to make people care about prostitutes and dope dealers."

"So he's banking on the fact that they won't make a fuss or that people don't care about what happens to them?"

"Sure looks that way," I said slowly.

I read the notes on the board over and over. After three days of chasing one lead after another with precious little time to think about anything except the next interview, having a few minutes to consider the scope and details of each crime felt like it was giving this case a story to tell. I just had to listen.

I rested the marker on Marcy Finelli's name. "This woman's kidney was taken, but she was knocked out, and then stitched up and left alive. At least for a while. Jane Doe was missing several organs, but also stitched up and placed carefully in a closet where no one should've found her."

"And there was a camera in there, probably to alert the killer if someone did," Graham added. "Which is likely how they knew to go steal the body."

"And we still don't have a way to find out who put the camera there?" I asked.

"WPD says the whole room was devoid of prints, like it was wiped clean. None on the camera, either, and it was using the wifi from the Waffle House in the parking lot, with an extender plugged in behind the HVAC unit in the closet," Boone said. "So no. There's not a way to trace it to a specific person."

I tapped the marker, a thought I'd had the day before trying to float back up. "There was something about the body the killer didn't want us to see."

"Pretty obvious since he took it," Archie said. "And he thinks Prescott did see it, otherwise why would he attack him?"

I shook my head, not wanting to remember the scene we'd walked into at the lab but knowing I needed to. "I don't think so. I think he was caught off guard by Jim being there." The nurse I'd spoken to.

"She said he knew where to cut but didn't know that he shouldn't go that deep," I said.

"Another point for a doctor," Graham said.

"But the doctors Skye tipped us off to were in a public room with a hundred other people when Jim was attacked."

"You said this morning that there might be more than one culprit here and I don't think that's a bad theory. They could have someone else working with them," Graham said. "I mean it makes sense that they wouldn't want to do that kind of dirty work themselves, and this way they have an airtight alibi."

"Missing one organ and sewn up." I started with Marcy again.

"But murdered, maybe months later," Graham said.

I kept going to Jane Doe. "Missing multiple organs and sewn up and hidden."

"Did he think by closing the wounds he was somehow absolving himself of the sin?" Archie mused.

I wrote it down and moved to the nightclub assault victim, Courtney. "Knocked out and left with weird bruising on one arm."

"Like this?" Boone rolled his sleeve up, revealing purple splotches.

"Yeah," Graham said, walking over to examine the lieutenant's arm. "That's pretty much what I pictured. We figured someone maybe tried to take blood from her, though why the fuck you'd do that in a nightclub bathroom is beyond me."

"Yep. I had a lousy tech at the lab yesterday," Boone said. "I'm having some trouble with my cholesterol."

"A blood draw?" Archie looked from the board to Boone to the video footage on the computer and back to me. "Someone attacked a woman in a nightclub bathroom to take blood from her?"

I wrote it on the board, Skye's voice in my head as much as I didn't want it to be. "That fits with what Skye found about online organ sales. The blood types have to match, among other factors."

"What other factors?" Graham started typing again. "All of our victims are white women who are in decent physical shape, at least to look at them," Graham said. "Skye said most of the other victims she'd met were women of color from socioeconomically disadvantaged communities, but she had that one post where someone was specifically asking for a Caucasian female."

My eyes jumped from one thing to another on the board. "But he'd have to have access to a lab to be able to analyze the blood sample, right?" I asked.

Everyone agreed.

My marker moved to Ellen Helmsley and Marcy Finelli, the victims from the garage freezer. "They were well hidden, but not sewn up."

"Maybe he's getting messier as he goes? More desperate because he knows we're looking for him?" Graham offered.

I pointed to him. "That. I think that's it. Or maybe he's both more desperate and more comfortable with the act now."

"If we take that trail, it's easy to try to put them in order." Graham stood. "That would be Marcy here having her kidney stolen months ago, but being left alive. Then Jane Doe in the closet, also sewn up. Courtney from the nightclub bathroom is attacked after that—"

"And then disappears, so maybe she's dead and we just haven't found where he hid her yet," I interjected.

Graham nodded. "Then Ellen the drug dealer is murdered and stuffed in her freezer roughly two weeks ago, and Marcy follows suit sometime between then and now."

"How do you know the dealer was killed first?" Archie asked.

"She was in the bottom of the freezer," Graham said.

"Ah-ha."

I drew a timeline across the bottom of the board, marking the names in order but leaving off dates.

I went back to Pendergast, checking my watch. Marquette and Johnson hadn't had time to get there yet. "This Pendergast guy is a strange little man. I wouldn't put murder past him, but I don't see him wanting to get his own hands dirty in it." I glanced at Graham. "Maybe this is where our exceptions to the rules keep coming in. This guy is running an organ market, but he has one trusted henchman doing the dirty work…"

"Who's doing the dirty work like a serial killer would," Graham finished for me.

"Any idea who that might be?" Boone asked.

"Jerry," Graham and I said in unison.

"How is he connected to the doctor?" Archie asked.

"Not obviously," I said. "He's a dishonorably discharged vet who does odd jobs off the books for the property manager at the Bluebonnet Hills mall and maybe also for his lawyer-cum-business-partner."

"Any of those three could've had access to the closet at the shopping center," Archie said.

"And Jerry had some basic medical training years ago in the military," Graham said.

"But that's the guy we think was dragged from his totaled car last night, right?" Boone asked. "Do we have any more leads there?"

I shook my head. "Did the PD come through with the property records you asked for?"

"I saw them come in right before you got here," he said. "I didn't open them yet, though."

I added Sonny, Jerry, and Buster to the bottom left corner of the board while Boone went to get his laptop.

My phone buzzed with a number I didn't recognize. "McClellan."

"Officer, this is Missy at Sonny Gilchrist's office. I just wanted to tell you I'm faxing those records now. I hope they help you."

"Have you seen Sonny today?" I asked.

"No, ma'am."

"Thank you for your help, Missy." I moved to the door and snaked steps through a maze of desks to the fax machine, stopping in front of it just as it started printing something.

"Hell I didn't even know that thing still worked," Boone said from behind me.

"I'm glad it does." I skimmed the pages, none of the client names jumping at me.

I grabbed the other papers as they printed, rushing back to the conference room and dividing them up.

I passed sheets to everyone. "These are all the properties Buster Beauchamp manages in the area. Look up these addresses and see what's located there," I said.

The room fell silent for a stretch as everyone worked.

"I've got the Bluebonnet Center, the old Ridgeway mall, and a few multi-unit residential buildings downtown," Archie said when he put his phone and the paper on the table.

"I have a handful of apartments, two strip centers, and a nightclub," Boone said.

Graham and I exchanged a glance. "Where is the nightclub?"

"On Bosque. Sign says Gray Goose."

"That's the place two of the victims were seen right before they were attacked," I said. "Son of a bitch."

Graham tapped at his phone screen. "What's the address, sir?"

Boone read it to him.

Graham looked up from his screen a minute later. "The Gray Goose is owned by Leonard Gilchrist. That the legal name of the lawyer who's Buster's partner?"

My hand went to my forehead. "Brian the bartender did say Sonny. Remember, he said the owner of the club didn't want to call the cops?" Maybe that's what had been trying to fight its way to the front of my thoughts.

"They're too tangled up in this to not be guilty of something," I said. "Can we find out if Buster was released from the hospital last night?"

Boone picked up his phone, holding up one finger. It took him less than a minute to get his answer, thank the nurse, and hang up with a nod. "Discharged at four-fifteen this morning."

He touched the screen twice and put the phone back to his ear. "I need a patrol unit to pick up Ernest Beauchamp," he said, reeling off the addresses of Buster's home and business. "Consider him possibly hostile and take precautions accordingly...Just put him in an interrogation room and notify me. Thank you." He hung up.

I dialed into dispatch and put a real all-points out on Sonny's Corvette. Hanging up the phone, I finally got the elusive thought.

"Missy said Sonny drives a Corvette with a custom paint job," I said, locking eyes with Graham.

"Oh, shit. A Corvette he bought from Chester Henning?" His eyes popped wide as Archie reached for the computer and logged into the DPS database.

"Chester who?" Archie asked.

"Henning," I said. "His wife told us he got hooked up with Pendergast through a lawyer he sold a sports car to—I would bet everything I own it was Sonny Gilchrist. There's the missing link." I turned to write on the board and caught Graham's eye. "Maybe we were both right?"

"Seems like it. I suppose I should get used to you never being wrong. Not entirely, anyway."

Boone and Archie chuckled. "Smart, Hardin."

I popped the cap off and on the marker in my hand, studying the board and drawing lines between names we knew were connected.

"Can someone run a criminal history for Gilchrist?" I stared at the board. I had a pretty intricate web there, with all the connections between the names and places in this case. But I still couldn't see clearly which ones were the key to solving the murders.

"Gilchrist can't have a felony and a license to practice law," Graham said. "And Buster didn't have anything huge. Drunk driving, most recently."

"That shows a lack of concern for others," Boone said.

"It's not enough to hold him on suspicion of anything, though." I stuffed my hands into my pockets. My fingers hit something with a rough edge and I pulled it free.

Buster's keys.

"I think it might be time to head back to the scene that started all this, y'all."

"The mall?"

I waved the key. "We've been running nonstop almost since we left there Friday, chasing off in twenty directions after every lead. But this is the key for the mechanical closet from Buster's keyring. Remember the shiny door-knobs? Before we go any further down this trail, we ought to go see if Buster's key still fits that lock. And maybe why Marcy Finelli met someone there recently. Do we know if it's still an active crime scene?"

Archie picked up his phone. "I'll check."

"If someone's setting Buster and Sonny up, they're doing a really fucking good job of it," Graham said. "I've never had an actual key be responsible for figuring out a huge chunk of a case."

"First time for everything," I said, my eyes still on the board. "Remember what Jerry's brother said about how he liked helping the doctors in Afghanistan?"

"Sure," Graham said. "He never felt as useful as when he was over there."

I pointed to Marcy's name for the tenth time since we walked into the room. "The organ harvester here started off not wanting to kill his victim, but he wanted her kidney badly enough to go to a lot of trouble to get it."

"Seventy-five grand is worth trouble to a lot of people," Graham said. "A little piece of fifty grand would be worth trouble to a guy like Jerry."

That was true. But given the state of the other victims when we found them, the fact that Marcy was put back together and left alive the first time she was attacked was truly extraordinary. It stuck out. And things that stick out deserve to be scrutinized, which is why Archie had told us to start with her over an hour ago.

"Why her, though? Why this woman in particular?" I murmured.

"Wrong place at the wrong time?" Graham asked.

I shook my head, thinking about the organ request post Skye had shown us.

"Archie, can you get a doctor on the phone? The kind of surgeon who does organ transplants. I want to know how many things have to match up for a transplant to be successful." The board had worked its magic. I finally had a handle on the thing I'd been trying to see.

"On it." Archie left the room without question as I started pacing the length of it.

"What is it, McClellan?" Boone asked.

"When she paces, she's thinking," Graham said. "Sir."

Boone waved off the formality. "Will she tell us what she's thinking?"

"The respect for the victim, the reluctance to kill her, the missing finger-prints, all of it so easy to overlook or dismiss when faced with something this horrifying—what if it had more to do with who she was than a general desire to avoid committing murder? What if Marcy was killed after we found Jane Doe in the closet? Or what if the killer stole Jane Doe from the lab because simply knowing who she was might lead us to him?"

"How?"

"I don't know. Exactly. But I have an idea that's at least not any crazier than anything else we've seen here."

"Don't keep us in suspense, McClellan," Boone said.

I pointed to Graham. "Marcy Finelli was adopted, you said?"

He dragged one hand down his face. "Yes? It feels like eight thousand years ago that we talked about that."

"She was. A family in Oklahoma, but she left home young."

"So?"

"So how did she end up there and what kind of blood relatives might she have come here looking for?" I tapped the marker against my leg, the idea feeling more plausible the more of it I said out loud. "Who moves to Waco on purpose? No offense, sir," I said to Boone.

"None taken." He sounded intrigued. "Organ transplants among family are statistically better matches."

"Wait. I thought we settled on the black market syndicate thing," Graham said. "I conceded defeat on the serial killer. And now you think maybe whoever killed Marcy wasn't looking to sell a kidney, he was looking for a kidney for a specific person?"

"I know it sounds far-fetched, but I keep getting pulled back to her. She's the odd victim out, left alive once, attacked twice. I think she's the key. And this makes at least enough sense to check out."

"It's almost 10," Graham said. "Who wants to call an adoption agency in Oklahoma City?"

Boone arched an eyebrow. "I have seen some things the past few days that I've never seen in my career, but are you asserting that someone is buying organs from an adopted child's blood relatives?"

I paused. "Not from them, as in paying Marcy for her kidney. The woman was picked up at a bar and attacked, I don't think anyone paid her off. And if someone had approached her before that about buying her kidney, surely she'd have mentioned that when she talked to the cops."

"So this person is stealing organs for a specific recipient? Why?"

"I mean...they're expensive, right? Can't it just be as simple as they can't afford a transplant someone is going to die without?"

"This kind of disfigurement and murder doesn't strike me as simple," Boone said. "But it's worth seeing what we can run down while we wait for the locals to turn up the property manager and his lawyer."

"How would they figure into this train of thought?" Graham asked.

"They seem to be more interested in money than anything else, if Jerry's brother was telling the truth. Perhaps they helped facilitate it somehow, put someone in contact with an unscrupulous doctor or found the adoption records or something," I said.

Boone excused himself to call the adoption agency, pointing to his laptop. "Those property records are open on the screen."

Graham sat down in front of the computer and started scrolling. "Hey baby?"

"What?"

Graham spun the screen. "Pendergast owns a place about five miles west of where Jerry's car was last night. Looks like a hunting cabin."

"Hunting means plenty of weapons." I dialed WPD dispatch on my cell phone. "We need all units in the vicinity to proceed with caution to 5491 Wortham Bend Road," I said. "Suspected kidnapping in progress. Establish a perimeter and wait for further instruction. Anyone on site should be considered armed and dangerous. The Rangers will have personnel on site soon." I clicked off the call.

"I thought we were going to the mall," Graham said.

"We are. Boone can send someone to supervise the WPD. I'm hedging bets on Jerry's whereabouts at the moment. His brother said he and Rosie needed a place to crash, and if he had keys to the building at Bluebonnet Hills, it wouldn't suck—plenty of space, and at least some working plumbing."

"Covering all our bases usually goes well for us, and Boone and Archie will call us if anyone finds anything more pressing," Graham agreed. "Lead the way."

32

Corie Whitehead called as we pulled into the parking lot at Bluebonnet Hills. Somehow the signs hanging off the building at odd angles in places, overgrown brush, and boarded-up doors looked more ominous than sad in the morning sunshine.

"Good morning, Corie. I'd ask how it's going, but I'm guessing you're about to tell me anyway."

She laughed, fatigue and stress coming through in the peals. "I am indeed. This case is an interesting one, Ranger."

"We think so too, but we're very interested to know why you do," I said.

"Well, just like we talked about a few days ago, they're not exactly all here."

"Why do I hear a 'but' coming?" I asked.

She sighed. "I think I know why you were asking me about Dr. Pendergast, as much as I wanted to pretend I don't, and I can't even really disagree based on what I know. And if I were going into the black market organ sales business, I would probably do a lot of what this person has done," Corie said. "They were in a chest freezer, so the remains were preserved, which buys him time before someone thinks to report them missing, even if the police go check out Ellen's house, most likely. The incisions are smooth and professional, and though we can't be a hundred percent certain, we're pretty sure these were made with a scalpel."

"The one that was used on Jim was stolen," I said. "But Jane Doe was also surgically cut up."

"So either way, we're probably right about that."

"So what pieces are they missing?"

"That's the weird part. For this scenario anyway. Marcy is missing both kidneys, and her stomach was damaged in the removal best we can tell. Ellen is just missing her liver."

"Oh." My teeth closed over my bottom lip. "Is there anything wrong with the rest of their organs?"

"Other than them being dead?"

"I mean, did y'all find any evidence of disease or some reason their organs wouldn't be viable or desirable?"

"Not visible ones. I'll let you know what the blood tests show."

"No evidence that anyone took blood from them?"

"Before they died? Like in a lab? No."

"Cause of death?"

"The gaping incisions to their abdominal walls are leading that race at the moment, but we haven't made an official determination yet. The freezer storage makes it harder to identify what bled when and if clotting occurred before or after they were cut up."

I shuddered at the idea of anyone being sliced open alive and awake, let alone having their liver or kidney removed. The bloody handprint on the freezer interior would likely haunt my nightmares for months.

"Thank you, Corie. Let me know if you find anything else that stands out."

"Will do."

I ended the call and relayed the update to Graham.

"One organ from each victim kind of goes with your theory of a specific recipient," he said. "And at least presumably, they'd used a kidney from Marcy before."

"But why would they not take the other organs to sell? It makes no sense that they took several from one victim, but only kidneys from another, and Ellen is dead, but I'm pretty sure a transplant can be done with, like, part of a liver. Isn't that the one people can donate a piece of when they're still alive?"

"I seem to have forgotten all my medical training this morning," Graham said. "But on the surface, I'd say what if the syndicate bought Jane Doe's organs, but their organ runner took a few pickings from these other women for his own gain? Like maybe Jerry was selling them off the books, maybe he had his own connection to whoever wanted them?"

I nodded. "That would be reason to drag him out of his car bleeding. Multiple reasons, actually, if you're the syndicate boss."

"Something happened between the first assault on Marcy and the others, but especially the one on Ellen. It's a safe assumption that the actual organ removals were the work of the same person. But one victim who could live without what they took was left alive, at least at first, and one wasn't. Why?"

"Opportunity? Time? Comfort level with taking a life? There are a lot of possibilities."

"Corie said Ellen might have been alive when she was cut open."

"That's...gross. And intense."

"And makes me wonder why nosy neighbor Mark didn't hear her scream." I grabbed my phone and called Cortez.

"Good morning, Ranger," he said. "What can I help you with?"

"Do y'all have any recent calls for a welfare check or disturbing the peace on Dunbar Avenue?"

"Stand by." I heard computer keys clicking.

"Looks like we have a crime scene there that wrapped early this morning."

"Before that. Maybe two weeks ago, same address or right around it."

More clicking ensued.

"No. Sorry."

"Thanks."

"Anything else I can do from here?"

"I'm guessing if you'd turned up anyone promising from the lab's employees, I would've heard about it?"

"No one without an alibi. We talked to everyone on the current payroll and ran down every alibi to check veracity."

"The attack on Jim wasn't personal—I don't even think it was premeditated."

"Because they used his scalpel?" Cortez asked.

"Right. Which means our guy had a key. He didn't go up there and park out of camera range and sneak to the door on the off chance that someone would be working before dawn on a Saturday."

"So are you saying someone is lying to protect our suspect?" Cortez asked.

"I'm saying if it wasn't a current employee who provided the key, maybe it was a former one. Can you go back six months, looking for anyone who used to work there, and see if that turns up anything?"

"I'll get right on it."

"Thank you." I touched the end button and put the phone down.

"No suspects?" Graham asked.

"The answer to at least part of this is tied to the lab." I hammered the steering wheel with the side of one fist. "But the answer to part of it is also tied to Pendergast. And the old mall."

My thoughts went back to poor Ellen, filleted and stuffed in her own freezer. "She didn't get sliced open and not scream."

"So either she didn't get sliced open while she was awake, or she didn't get sliced open where we found her."

"The blood in the backyard would argue for the former. Nosy neighbor Mark was pretty sure there are drugs in the house. What if she was dealing more than your garden variety pot and pain pills?" I grabbed the phone again and texted Archie.

When you're free can you go to this address and search the house?

He replied almost immediately. *Adoption agency in Oklahoma is sending records on the woman you asked about. Boone has a team headed to that hunting cabin. We can go now. What are we looking for?*

I wish I knew. Hoping you'll know it when you see it. A way for someone to know if she was a good organ donor and a way for her to get sliced up without making any noise?

On it. We'll let you know.

Tucking the phone into my pocket, I hopped out of the truck, jogging to the door under the food court sign and unlocking it with the number 49 key Buster said would work. It did.

I pulled the door open and looked over my shoulder at Graham.

"We've done a lot of crazy shit I've had the fleeting thought would make me scream at people in a horror movie for doing. This might be the worst one yet, though."

He waved a hand and followed me inside. "The place was crawling with cops until yesterday. It's probably the safest abandoned building in the state." The click from the door closing behind us reverberated through the hollow space. "Creepy as all hell, but safe."

"I wish I felt as secure as you sound," I said.

"I'm perfectly secure," he said. "I even have a bodyguard—my fiancée can kick anyone's ass. I've seen it."

I laughed and started for the hallway that held the closet.

Stepping through the hole where the first door had been a few days before and out of reach of the mall's hundreds of skylights, I pulled a flashlight from my pocket. "I should've asked him where to find the light switch," I muttered.

We found the door to the closet tipped against the wall in the hallway, and I pulled the keys out, checking the numbers.

Holding up the 45, I put the other back into my pocket and handed Graham the light. He held it on the doorknob, and I put the key into the lock.

It slid almost all the way in before it stopped, and it definitely wouldn't turn.

"I'll be damned." I jiggled it so hard the door would've fallen if Graham hadn't shot one hand out to steady it.

"Someone did change them."

I yanked the key free and pocketed it, stepping into the closet and shining a flashlight around.

"You think forensics missed something?" Graham asked.

"Just want to see for myself."

I stepped over the area marked around where the body had been wrapped in the plastic, my eyes on an odd angle in the line marking the back of it.

I pointed, crouching. "There's not an indentation like this in the other side," I said.

Graham squatted across from me, examining the flat line on his side of the outline. "It looks like something was pushed up against it on that side for long enough to leave an indentation in the shape."

"Doesn't it?" I stood and turned, examining the wall behind me.

Stepping closer, I put out one hand, touching a faint coppery line on the wall, then another running parallel.

Graham stepped across and stood at one end of the marks. I stood at the other, each of us putting a foot out toward the lines on the floor.

"That looks like a pretty rough outline of a dorm fridge," he said.

I pointed the light at an outlet nearby. "And nobody would notice these lines on the wall, they're too faint unless you're really looking for something right here."

"But where did the fridge go between when she was put here and when we found her?"

"Another question for the already long list." I moved the light around the rest of the space, but didn't see anything else out of the ordinary.

"So now what?"

"We've confirmed a suspicion, but I'm not sure it rules anyone out necessarily," Graham said. "I mean, playing devil's advocate, it would be pretty damn clever of Buster to change the locks and then give the cops the old key."

"I'm not sure he's that clever, but someone he knows might be."

I huffed out a sigh as my phone buzzed, wondering if we'd just wasted half an hour we couldn't really spare confirming this hunch I'd had since Friday.

"The trip isn't wasted if it gives us a fact we can use," Graham said as I raised the phone to my ear.

I pulled out my phone. Archie sent a photo.

I clicked it.

"Oh shit."

Graham leaned over my shoulder.

"Is that a blood donation card?"

"I sent them to Ellen Helmsley's house," I said, my eyes on the line listing her blood type as AB negative. "And this looks like it's stuck to her refrigerator with a magnet."

"Where anyone who went into her house could see it?" Graham asked.

"How bad will it suck if doing a nice thing for her fellow man by donating blood got this woman hacked up?" I asked.

"Pretty bad," Graham agreed. "Let's go circle up with them?"

I followed him to the truck, texting Archie. *That's very interesting. Get WPD forensics to dust for prints and check for fluids?*

On it.

My phone rang before I got it into my pocket, the number on the screen unfamiliar.

I put it to my ear. "McClellan."

"It's Marquette from crisis investigation," a deep bass rattled out of the speaker. "We're at this doctor guy's office with this warrant and he's not here, but there's a secretary in the office with a very large shredder and a very small stack of paperwork. A look in the recycling can out back tells me we're too late for whatever you were looking for, it's half full of shredded paper."

"Goddammit."

"We told her to cease and desist. Johnson is in there with her. You want us to bring her in?"

I bit my lip. She might know something.

"Take her to HQ in Austin, it's closer. Someone will be there to question her as soon as possible."

"You got it," he said. "I'll serve the other warrant while Johnson babysits her."

"Let me know if anything goes weird there?"

"Yep."

I thanked him and hung up, sliding into the truck.

"Pendergast had the secretary there shredding files probably since the middle of the night, and probably starting with Chester," I said. "And he's gone."

"Making himself look really innocent, that guy." Graham started the truck and drove toward the north parking lot exit. Staring out the window, I considered all the winding, intersecting threads of this case—there were enough of them to make a hell of a blanket. Buster who ran the building where a body was hidden and his ethically-bankrupt attorney who owned the nightclub connected to several of the attacks. Ellen stuffed into her freezer with Marcy, who had a note in her car about this building. As I tried to find the thread that would bind it all together, I saw a flash of moving metal in an alcove on the building.

"Graham, stop," I said, my eyes on a loading dock door that was still falling shut.

He obliged. "You okay?"

I kept my eyes on the door, a padlock hanging loose from it and a gray Honda Civic parked behind a ramp a few feet from it. The car Cortez's patrolman said had been hanging around. Brian the bartender's voice rang in my ears.

"I think we just found the women Brian was talking about yesterday," I said.

33

"We should call for backup," Graham said.

"So the sirens can alert whoever's in there that the police are coming? No thanks."

"We found human remains in that building three days ago," Graham said.

"The person I saw just now is not the person who attacked Jim. It was a woman. A small one, at that. I just want to go look around. I even had the thought earlier that Jerry might hide out here because it had running water and a roof. Squatters should've occurred to us way before now."

He stared at me for long enough to see I wasn't going to let it go.

"Fine." He reached for the door handle.

I put a hand on his arm.

"Maybe let me go in first with you outside for backup?"

"You know nothing about who's in there!" He didn't shout. But I got the feeling he wanted to.

"Like you said, I can take care of myself," I said. "I believe 'kick anyone's ass' were your words?"

"That was when the building was empty," he muttered.

"I know how to handle myself, Graham. And you'll be right outside." I unsnapped my holster safety strap and squeezed his hand.

He stepped out of the truck and waved me forward, staying close on my heels as I crept quietly up the ramp for the loading dock.

Pulling the door open, I smelled the scented candles that lit the space before I saw them. I counted seven women reclining on various pallets made of threadbare blankets spotted around what looked like an old department store stockroom.

The two closest to the door scrambled to their feet, while others watched with interest from their posts on the floor. Their faces looked worn and weary far beyond their years, every set of eyes fixed on me dull and resigned.

"I told you the fucking cops would be back," a brunette said in a flat tone that expected the worst from the universe, probably after years of knowing little else.

I showed both hands. "Nobody is in trouble. I just have a few questions about the body in the boiler closet near the food court. I don't care about anything else." My eyes stayed on the brunette, her hair falling in soft waves and her knees hugged tight to her chest. The candlelight was dim, but I wouldn't put a single person in the room except myself over 25.

"Body?" A redhead, her slight frame swallowed up into a purple sweatshirt that would've been big on Graham, stepped away from the pallet two from the door and into more light. "Like dead person? We don't know nothing about dead people."

In the light, I could see her eyebrow twitching.

"Young woman, pale skin, dark hair, party clothes?" I cast an eye around the room. "Wrapped in plastic?"

Every eye was on the floor. The brunette rested her forehead on her knees, her shoulders hitching.

I stepped closer to her and the redhead slid herself into my path. "She doesn't feel well." She was clearly the leader of this ragtag pack.

I stared down at her, noting the hands resting on her hips, the defiant set of her jaw—and the flicker of fear in her eyes.

They were sex trade workers. It was painfully obvious from the second I stepped into the room, punctuated by the condom boxes littering the space and the disproportionate proliferation of sequined clothing in the laundry piles next to each pallet.

I lowered my head and my voice. "I don't give one damn what you ladies do to earn a living. Truly. I have a corpse that was taken from the morgue and a friend lying in a hospital bed that a whole lot of folks with badges are interested in right now. Other folks might not be as single-minded as I am. If you know anything, it's really in everyone's best interest for you to talk to me."

She didn't blink. "Why the hell should I trust you?"

Neither did I. "What choice do you have?"

She held my gaze for four beats. Sighed. Stepped backward. "We can find somewhere else to go."

Her chin fell to her chest, her small shoulders slumping under the weight of caring for her friends.

The other women watched her for cues.

I turned a circle, stopping my gaze on each of them. "My name is Faith. I can help you if you'll talk to me."

Nobody said a word for a full minute before a small voice came out of the darkness. "The law is never going to take the word of a bunch of whores over a doctor."

"Doctor?"

"Shut the fuck up, Lizzie!" The redhead leapt at a curvy blonde, and I barely managed to get a good enough hold on her to keep her from landing a blow.

"Let's keep it civil, ladies." I let a warning edge creep over the words, tightening my grip on her arms until I felt her relax a little.

"What's it to you, Dana? Did you fucking hear what she said?" The blonde's voice was high as she jumped to her feet, pointing into the darkness. "They found Rachel here. In this building. That motherfucker knew enough about us that he hid her here. We went crazy trying to find her for weeks, and she was right fucking here. If you're still thinking there's a way our asses are not going to prison behind this, you're crazier than your mother was."

Dana's head whipped up at that last, her whole body going rigid as she fought me anew.

"Shut up, bitch!" she snarled.

"Whatever you do to me can't compare to the shit we're all going to catch on the inside. My brother says it's no joke," Lizzie shot back.

I pulled Dana's shoulders just shy of too far behind her, the pain making her wince. "For the third time. I'm listening. Right now. But y'all need to tell me what the hell happened here before I get tired of trying to fill in holes. I can help you."

"Straight into the pen, maybe." That came from the brunette, her face still pointed at the floor.

"My business is solving murders, not busting people for trying to survive," I said, leaning closer to Dana. "Right this minute, I don't think you killed your friend, but if you don't tell me what you know about who did, hand to God, I'll take you all in and file every charge I can think of. I don't have time for games."

Dana's shoulders went totally slack as she craned her long neck back to look into my face. "What other women?"

"You really think your friend was the only one?"

Her eyes popped wide. "I guess I kind of hoped it was an accident, you know? Like something just went wrong, maybe he was into choking her and he went too far or something. Buster said it was safe. The guy was high class. A doctor." She twisted in my hands. "I'm good."

I let her go and she turned to face me. "Buster said?" I asked. "Y'all know Beauchamp?" I couldn't even pinpoint why I was surprised.

"Sure," Dana said. "He lets us pay whatever we've got each week to stay here, keeps the bathrooms on even if they are kind of far away, sometimes he introduces us to people."

"And he introduced y'all to the guy Rachel was with the last time you saw her?" Having a name for Jane Doe made the idea that we would find out what happened to her more real, somehow.

"Just her. Buster came by that afternoon and said he needed to talk to her," Dana said. "She told us he said she was supposed to show up at the Goose at 10 wearing a rose in her hair."

"It was weird, remember?" Lizzie chimed in. "Like usually he would come in and say a guy wanted a blonde or a redhead or whatever. That time he went straight to Rachel and said the guy wanted her."

"Did he tell her how much she was going to get paid?"

"Buster always kept some of the money if he made the introduction."

I added pimp to my mental list of reasons to dislike Beauchamp.

"And then what happened?" I asked. "She never came back?"

"It's not like we don't know there are sick fucks out there," Lizzie said. "We try to look out for each other. She had her phone with her when she left with him."

"But not after she disappeared?"

Lizzie pointed to an older model iPhone resting on a box she'd made into a night table next to her pallet. "We used the locator app to find it. In a dumpster."

"Where?" I asked.

"Outside. The screen is broken. Like a warning that whoever hurt her knew where to find us, too."

I watched her face carefully. On one hand, her story would've been easy to blow holes in. Their word against that of a respected local businessman and possibly a physician—not many people would believe them. But I did. Lizzie's tense exchange with Dana rang true. They'd kept quiet about their friend going missing because they were afraid of being implicated in her murder.

"When was this?"

"The day before Valentine's Day."

My phone buzzed in my pocket again. I ignored it. "That was more than a month ago," I said.

"We're not lying." There was a defensive edge in Dana's voice.

I shook my head. "I didn't say you were. Just trying to make it fit with what I already know."

I pulled in a deep breath. Rachel went, because that was the world they lived in every day. Danger lurked around every corner, and they did what they had to do to dodge it as long as possible. They knew they were safer together—that was obvious looking around the room—but when there was no other choice, they had to roll the dice. Terrible things happen to sex workers every day. They're sold and traded on the internet. Kidnapped and subjugated and dehumanized. Abused. Murdered. Gutted and rolled up in plastic and left in a closet.

"Did you get a look at this guy? The one she met that night?"

"He was tall. Brown hair, nice clothes. No tie, though," Dana said. "Between Buster's insistence that she go meet him alone and the shit lighting in the club, it wasn't like we could see really good, you know?"

"Have you seen him again?"

"I saw a guy a couple times that looked like him. But I was afraid to ask him what he did with her after they left," she said. "Didn't want to be next."

"And the last time y'all saw Rachel was when she was leaving the club with this guy? No one followed?"

"Yes. I mean, um, correct," Dana said.

"Do you know Rachel's last name?"

"Moses," Lizzie said. "But we always thought it was a little weird that most of the time she told the johns to call her Amber."

That was weird enough to note. "I appreciate your help today, ladies. If we want to find out what happened to your friend, I think I'm going to need you to introduce me to this john."

34

A fundamental truth of almost every murder case—the complicated and therefore more interesting ones, anyway—is that nothing makes sense until everything does. A homicide investigation is never a smooth start, it's akin to learning to drive a stick shift: you work in fits and starts, stall out, grind the gears, and bang your head on the steering wheel occasionally, but if you're stubborn enough about keeping to the road, eventually it all falls into place and it's hard to understand why it wasn't always obvious.

I walked down the ramp from the loading dock after making sure Dana had locked the doors behind me, more than ready to find the sweet spot in this case that would make it all seem like it should've been easy the whole time.

"How'd it go?" Graham asked as my phone buzzed my hip pocket and I pulled it free. Archie. For the third time. I held up one finger and mouthed "Archie."

"Hey," I said, putting it to my ear. "I was talking to a witness. And I have an undercover set up for tonight."

"Waco has Buster in an interrogation room, and I think a traffic check-point just picked up his lawyer." He paused. "You have a what? What witness? When did we find witnesses?"

"Turns out there are squatters in the Bluebonnet Hills mall—in the old Macy's storage room. They knew Jane Doe. Her name was Rachel Moses."

He was silent for two beats. "Jesus, why didn't they come forward? If they live in the mall, they had to have seen all the police vehicles. Did they know what was going on?"

"I'm not sure. But they're sex workers, Archie. They didn't think we'd believe them. And they don't want to go to jail."

"I see." He sighed. "So what'd you get?"

"Get this: they say the last guy they saw Rachel alive with was a doctor. Beauchamp has his sticky little fingers in pimping, too—he set her up with this guy, and her friends never saw her again."

"So you're going with them to the club to see if you can find him."

"Ding ding ding."

"When?"

"I'm meeting them here at nine-thirty."

"So we have 11 hours."

"What's the story with Buster?" I opened the door to the truck and climbed into the passenger seat.

"He's not talking. Says he wants his attorney. But since his attorney is also wanted for questioning, we offered him a public defender. He wasn't happy about that."

"We're on our way," I said. "If Gilchrist comes in, put him in a different room and let me have a crack at him first?"

"You got it."

I ended the call and filled Graham in on what Dana and Lizzie had told me, logging into the DPS database from my phone to run Rachel's name and aliases through the system looking for any kind of information that might tell me why she was dead.

"Waco PD headquarters, please. They found Buster and maybe his lawyer, too," I said, my eyes on my phone screen. "She was arrested for solicitation two years ago, but got off with time served," I muttered, scrolling until I found a link that made me stop. "Huh."

"What?" Graham turned left out of the mall parking lot while I read.

"She didn't just go by an alias for her work," I said. "She changed her name. Legally. About five years ago."

I followed another link to an Oklahoma state site. "When she applied for a driver's license here, she had to provide proof of the legal change."

I clicked the old record in Oklahoma and waited as the page loaded.

"Holy shit, Graham." I stared at the letters on my screen. "They were sisters."

"Who?"

I opened another window, my fingers flying over a text to Archie. *I need the adoption agency in Oklahoma to speed it up. And I need to know if Marcy Finelli and her sister Amber were blood relatives.*

I went back to the other screen, double-checking it against my notes and catching Graham up. "Marcy Finelli, who we found in the freezer last night? Rachel changed her name to Rachel Moses from Amber Finelli. She's a year older than Marcy at twenty-four, with the same prior address listed in Broken Arrow. I just don't know if they were related by blood or not."

Graham gripped the steering wheel tighter, pressing the accelerator. "But if they were, they definitely weren't random victims in this. Someone was looking for them. Like you said earlier, because they knew blood relatives would be a better match."

"All those organs couldn't have gone to one place," I said. "Could they?"

"I don't know." He sighed, gripping the steering wheel tighter. "Every time I think I know what the hell is happening here, the whole damned thing flips again. That Pendergast guy didn't skip town and tell his secretary to shred his whole damned office because he's worried about patient confidentiality. He's in this. We have enough evidence already to convince any jury in America."

"Maybe he found these women and sold their organs to whoever was looking for them?" I asked. "An ailing parent suddenly sorry they gave a kid up?"

"Or a parent who gave two kids up, and then had another that's sick?" Graham asked. "But then, what could Buster Beauchamp possibly have to do with that?"

"No idea. But he's not going home until I find out."

Buster looked smaller than I remembered him, slumped in a metal chair in interrogation room B. I stood with Archie on the back side of a one-way window, watching him fidget. "He sure doesn't want to be here."

"Nope. But in fairness, we already know he's a crook. That would be enough to make him antsy about being here. Is he also a murderer? I couldn't tell you."

"I don't think he's our killer," I said. "I might've wondered enough to try to scare him a few hours ago, but now? The women who knew the victim said a doctor, and they all know Buster, he charges them whatever they can pay him for letting them stay there and takes a percentage when he introduces them to dates."

"He does look the part."

"Yet he won't turn on the plumbing in that part of the building for them, probably because the owners will get wise to his little subletting side hustle."

"Nice. So what do we want from him, then?"

"I'm pretty convinced now that these weren't random acts. I think someone wanted those young women's organs, specifically, and I think when we hear back from the adoption agency they'll confirm that. Buster is tangled up in how the guy found Rachel in the first place; her friend told me today he said this guy wanted her specifically, and they thought that was weird. He and Gilchrist seem to be all about money and connections, and I don't think the killer asked for these women by chance. I think he was looking for them."

"Why do you say that?"

"They were sisters—Rachel, also known as our Jane Doe, and Marcy, the woman who woke up without her kidney and then turned up dead in the dealer's freezer. Since they were adopted I can't be sure if the relation is blood or not, that's why I asked you to light a fire under the adoption people. But I'm betting it is."

"They're short-staffed, but they promised to send me something before the end of the day." He paused. "So you think if they were blood relatives, then their organs were taken for something more than money?"

"I don't know. Maybe it was money. Maybe whoever gave them up got rich and then needed multiple organs, or had multiple sick family members. Here's what I do know: Pendergast's office was a bust, Marquette said he's gone and the secretary was there burning up the motor in a large shredder. And I started thinking about my training with the organized crime unit—in a syndicate, there's a hierarchy, but everything is kept compartmentalized for protection and deniability. Low-level guys only know a little bit, and they deal with go-betweens. Go-betweens know a little more, and they deal with middlemen, but the big players are fairly insulated from culpability. Maybe what we've been seeing here is bits and pieces of a syndicate working, but we haven't considered them as a whole."

He nodded slowly. "I like this track." He nodded to Buster. "Where does he fit that theory?"

"No higher than go-between, I would think," I said. "But I want to see what we can get him to give up."

The door behind us opened and Cortez stuck his head in. "Sonny Gilchrist is across the hall in room D. He's pissed, though."

We thanked him.

"Let him stew for a few minutes." Archie said, jerking a thumb at the closed door. "If Gilchrist knows we've been talking to Buster, he might be more likely to squeal in order to cover his own ass."

"True." I ducked out of the room, pulling open the door to room B with a wide smile. "Mr. Beauchamp! Thanks so much for coming in to talk to me today." I poured a Florida beach week's worth of sunshine into the words, clearly catching Buster off guard. He sat up straight so fast he nearly fell off the chair.

"Miss McClellan...uh...Officer...I wasn't aware you'd be here. Was there something else you needed from me? Were you able to find Jerry?"

"Oh yes, Jerry and I had a nice long chat yesterday," I said.

His brow furrowed. "You...you did?"

"Does that surprise you? You told me to find him and ask him about that maintenance closet." I pulled out the chair across the small table from him and took a seat, laying a file folder between us.

"Of course I did." He eyed the folder the way most people would an angry rattlesnake, his hands working in and out of lacing his fingers together.

He didn't think we would be able to find Jerry. And he wouldn't have sent me off chasing geese if he didn't know something—or if he hadn't done anything wrong.

"When was the last time you saw Ellen Helmsley, Mr. Beauchamp?" I asked.

He raised his eyes to mine, then flicked them back to the folder.

"Why?"

"I'd like you to answer the question, please," I said.

"But I...am I being charged with a crime?" His lower lip trembled and I came closer to laughing than I ever had in an interrogation room. Buster here was the walking definition of "all talk." Whatever the truth was here, I knew in my bones in that moment that he might be a low-rent quasi-pimp who sold women to a butcher, but he wasn't getting his hands dirty in it—at his core, Buster was a coward.

I knew how to work cowardly to my advantage. I just needed to scare him into talking to me.

I flipped the folder open to the photos from the scene in Ellen's garage that had made Officer Schaefer vomit, stills of Marcy and Ellen still stuffed into the freezer with their intestines spilling onto the garage floor.

"This was the last time I saw Ellen Helmsley. After I asked you about her yesterday."

Buster flipped his chair over backward he recoiled so violently.

I stood and rounded the end of the table. Buster was stuck like a cockroach on its back, his arms and legs flailing, his face red. "What in the hell would you show a tax-paying businessman something like that for?"

I put out a hand to help him up. "When was the last time you saw Ellen Helmsley?" I repeated.

Buster's eyes popped twice as wide as normal in his fleshy face half a second before the red flushed to green like a color-changing Christmas light. "You can't possibly think I could have done that to her. The woman was a dope dealer, for Christ's sake. A whole lot of people would have more reason than me to want her dead." He huffed, the crimson flush to his face deepening.

I grabbed one outstretched hand and pulled him to his feet so easily he gave me a puzzled once-over as I righted the chair and motioned for him to return to it.

"I need to know how well you knew Ms. Helmsley, Mr. Beauchamp, and I need to know if you think you might know who did this to her, because I have to tell you, unless you start telling me something that makes some sense, it doesn't look good that women keep turning up all sliced up, all with trails that lead to you somehow."

He pushed the photo away, averting his eyes from the table. "I have never killed anyone in my life! I can't believe you think I could," he shrieked, his voice rising two octaves.

I didn't. Not anymore. But I wasn't telling him that.

The biggest fear a crook who is also a coward harbors, next to being fed to sharks, maybe, is going to prison.

"You have done something here," I said. "That much I know for certain. Unless you tell me what it is, I have no choice but to assume the worst until I have proof otherwise."

Buster raised his hands to cradle his balding head, his shoulders shaking like he might've been crying.

I let him stew for four breaths.

"We are running out of time for you to help me help you, Mr. Beauchamp."

He straightened, dragging one hand across his face. A sigh so deep it had to have rattled his bones washed out of him, reeking of stale whiskey and cheap cheeseburgers.

"Okay listen, that girl, the one who was in the closet, all the guy wanted was to meet her, right? I mean, she was a whore. I thought he wanted to fuck her, not dissect her. That's all I did was make an introduction. That ain't against the law."

"To who?" I stood, raising one foot to kick my chair over, the clatter when it hit the floor making Buster jump. His hands came up on either side of his face.

"I didn't know his name. I sent her to Sonny's club with a red rose in her hair, and he was supposed to take care of the rest." Tears welled in his rheumy eyes. "Hand to God, ma'am, I didn't know he was going to kill her."

"How did you meet this person?" I ignored the crocodile tears. He wouldn't give two shits these women were dead if he wasn't scared half out of his little tiny mind right then.

"Sonny. It was someone who came to Sonny looking for information."

"What kind of information?" I flattened my palms on the table and leaned forward, sharpening my tone.

"I don't know." Buster began to sob in earnest, his shoulders shaking, fat tears rolling down his cheeks and leaving splatter marks on his white linen shirt. "I swear to God I don't know. Sonny said he met the guy through a friend…or maybe it was a client…and the guy was asking for information on this woman who was sleeping at Bluebonnet Hills. He wanted to meet her. All I did was send her to meet him."

He rested his elbows on the table and buried his face in his hands.

I stood there with my arms folded for a full minute, watching him cry.

So how did the "friend of a friend" know to ask Gilchrist about Rachel?

"Sit tight, Mr. Beauchamp," I said. "I'll be back."

35

Sonny Gilchrist was a much more worthy adversary than his most time-consuming client.

He kept his eyes hooded when I walked into the room, not so much as a flicker of a giveaway on his stone-flat face when I smiled and introduced myself.

Damn. I was hoping the name would impress a connection whore like Gilchrist.

He probably knew I was onto him at least enough that it wouldn't do him much good to be nice to me.

"Sorry to interrupt your day," I said, keeping my tone conversational.

"No you're not."

"You're right, Counselor, I'm not. Know what I'm also not today? Very patient."

"Well that makes something we have in common, Ranger," he sneered. "Cut to the chase. You have nothing you can hold me on, so what's say you tell me what you're fishing for, I tell you to go to hell, and then you let me and my client out of here before I tie the Rangers up in so many lawsuits the governor just shuts you down?"

I raised my eyebrows. "Sell it to someone who didn't get the easiest search warrant in the history of mankind for your office just this morning.

You can file all the lawsuits you want, and the court can dismiss them with a flick of the judge's pen."

"Who'd you go to? Stevenson? That old tree-hugging hippie ni—"

I raised an index finger and leaned forward, putting my face about six inches from Gilchrist's.

"I wouldn't finish that thought if I were you," I snapped. "Files get lost. People sit in jail for days because of paperwork errors. Test me if you want to find out how your scumbag clients live firsthand."

He pinched his lips into a thin white line between his straggly mustache and some stragglier chin scruff that wanted to be a goatee, holding my gaze for five beats as his wide nostrils flared with a breath in.

"What do you want to know?"

Well played. He wasn't confessing to anything he wasn't asked about.

"Someone asked you to put them in touch with a woman from the group Buster has sleeping in squalor at the Bluebonnet Hills mall. Who was it?"

"Why?"

"I asked you who first."

"And I didn't answer before I asked you why."

I folded my hands behind my back to keep myself from taking a swing at the smug smirk on his face.

"She's dead. I want to talk to the person who asked you to send her to the nightclub you own, because it's where she was last seen alive and well."

His brow furrowed. "The woman in the mechanical closet at the mall? That was her?" His face took on a faraway look, like he wasn't even sure he was saying the words out loud.

"Yes." I was pretty sure by that point, anyway.

"I can't help you," he said, the faraway look clearing. He folded his hands on the table in front of him.

"I believe you can. Buster Beauchamp also believes you can."

"Buster," he snorted. "He believes what I fucking tell him to, and he wouldn't know his own ass from a hole in the ground."

"He says you asked him to introduce this woman—this woman in particular—to someone you knew from your club."

"See? As usual, he half remembers and fucked up the story." Gilchrist kept his eyes on his own knuckles.

"So how about you set it right, Counselor?" I pulled out a chair and sat down. "There's another woman missing, and at least two more who are dead. I need to understand what's happening here so I can stop it. Tell me what you know."

He stared at his hands.

But he didn't ask for a lawyer.

I studied him for a few seconds, thinking, before I changed tactics. "I met your assistant this morning. She's a nice woman. Worried about you."

"I don't deserve her concern," he muttered.

Bullseye. It seemed Missy's infatuation with her boss wasn't one-sided.

"Don't you want to?" I asked softly. "Help me stop this. Before anyone else dies."

He raised his eyes to meet mine and the despair in them nearly swallowed me whole.

"I wish I could, but I can't."

"Why not?"

"They'll kill me. They'll kill Missy and Buster and probably you, and those women you're so worried about? They'll die anyway." He blinked hard. "I want to talk to my lawyer."

I watched him for a minute, his knuckles and jaw flexing in alternating time, before I stood and went to find Archie in the observation room across the hall.

"Any luck?"

"Someone went after at least Rachel specifically, maybe Marcy too, but I can't tie her case straight back to them, that's just a gut feeling. Whoever it is, they're wrapped up in something Sonny Gilchrist is so scared of, he'd rather request an attorney and spend the night in jail than give me a name."

"Speaking of your victims, the adoption agency called." He waved a legal pad covered with his hurried scrawl.

"What did they say?"

"The two women you gave me names for were in fact biological sisters. They were removed from a home in Fort Worth on order of social services when one was almost a year old and the other was two and a half, and adopted by the same family in Oklahoma."

"Were there any other children in that family?"

"Not that this agency handled or was notified of, but she gave me the parents' names and I called Boone. He's looking. I'm sure he'll have an answer for us shortly."

I sucked in a deep breath and turned my attention to Buster, who was slumped over the table on the other side of the glass. "Is he asleep?" I asked.

"For about ten minutes now. I don't think it's an exaggeration to say he cried himself out."

"I can't believe I thought about fifteen hours ago that this guy might be our criminal mastermind." I stared at Buster's heaving shoulders. "This whole damned case is a study in contrasts. And none of it makes sense."

"How so?"

"Those women were targeted because of something to do with them specifically, and it's sure looking like it was their bloodline. Whoever killed Rachel didn't want *a* heart, they wanted *her* heart." I pointed to Buster. "He's in there bawling himself to sleep while his partner is literally scared silent by whoever this is. I can't figure out how someone evil enough to scare the shit out of a guy like Sonny Gilchrist is stealing specific organs from specific people."

"Selling them, right? I mean, whoever's doing that has to be a pretty cold piece of work."

"But then why sew Rachel up and place her body somewhere so carefully?"

He pinched his lips into a thin line, rocking up onto the balls of his feet. "I got nothing," he said. "They didn't want her found, but I can't even hazard a guess as to why, but I'd love to ask the guy who did it. Let's hope you find a road straight to him at that club tonight."

36

Disruptions inside the human body aren't always dramatic—and the more insidious ones are often the most dangerous.

By the time an excruciating pain and an alarming level of blood in her urine leads to an emergency room visit, only the best doctors will even be able to help.

The first-year attending working the midnight shift suspects dehydration, but fluids do nothing for the pain.

"She has a medical history of systemic lupus erythematosus," the pretty young nurse says, her hand cool and reassuring on his arm as he paces. "Renal complications are common in flares. Don't worry. A quick scan will tell us what we're dealing with. Even if she needs a kidney, we have some of the best surgeons in the state here, and she's young."

A wheelchair ride becomes an hour spent trying not to panic as a massive machine whirs and clicks with his whole world trapped inside. He paces the ninety-seven dingy tiles it takes to make up the length of the hallway, trying not to hear the heavy breath and gnashing teeth of a monster. A monster he should've noticed before today. Before it had time to sharpen those claws and sink them deep into her already weakened body.

When the nurse returns her smile is gone, a small crease between her brows that wasn't there before giving away her hand. The news is bad.

Maybe puzzling even, but definitely bad. "The doctor will be in shortly," is all she'll say, no matter how he begs.

The doctor's somber face reveals nothing as he scratches his head, pointing out the dead tissue in the image on his tablet screen.

"Highly unusual," is all he offers.

Wristbands are printed, admission papers signed.

After a week, they ride a helicopter to a bigger, shinier hospital. A place where miracles happen and gods walk among mortals, their ability to puzzle out medical mysteries snatching brothers, daughters, wives, and grandfathers straight back from the maw of death to the warm arms of grateful, tear-stained families.

Here, answers would come.

Here, the future he'd looked forward to would be salvaged.

The memories of these days would fade into the fuchsia-tinted haze of gratitude, the pain and the needles and the waiting forgotten amid a life full of love and children and laughter.

If only. If only.

The tests took weeks to turn up definitive answers.

High cytokines. Reduced red blood cell deformability.

Very rare complications.

Renal damage. Reduced cardiac function. Possible endothelial dysfunction.

Developing multisystem organ failure.

Poor transplant risk.

No further options.

Palliative care.

Those two words flash in neon in his head as he finishes filling Ellen's freezer, his icebox loaded with a pancreas and a section of liver.

This has to be the last time. A prostitute and a dealer don't matter more than his life, than their future, but every incision takes a little piece of his soul with it. He steps into the cool February night air and carefully re-wraps the chain on the doors. He should've brought a new lock. He'll get one and come back. He nods, moving to the shadow of the hedges lining the yard and creeping back to his car.

Across the street, the orange glow of a cigarette on the porch catches his eye.

The neighbors are used to people coming and going at all hours. Jerry wants the Trans Am, and it'll keep him quiet about what he saw at the old mall—all he has to do is pick it up without drawing attention to himself, which might be a tall order for a guy like Jerry. He double-checks his pocket for the keys and walks confidently to his car.

This is it. Three weeks post-op they can travel.

Three weeks, and they won't ever set foot on Texas soil again.

37

I tugged the black spandex dress down for the tenth time as I stood in front of the mirror, sliding a red gloss wand across my lips and batting long fake eyelashes.

"I don't like any of this. Not one bit," Graham said from the bathroom doorway, where he leaned against the frame and watched as I got ready to meet Dana and her girls.

"I have a Bluetooth mic unit, I know how to take care of myself, and you and Archie will be literally across the street." I gave my teased hair a final pat and two more shots of spray and turned to face him. "I can't kiss you because it'll wreck my makeup, but trust me, I'll be fine."

"It's not you I don't trust," he growled, pulling me into a tight hug and resting his chin on top of my head. "I know you know what sort of men you're dealing with here."

"I do. And I got this." I laid one hand on his face and followed it with a soft kiss I dragged myself back from when his arms tightened around me. "Later."

"I messed up your lipstick." He wiped his hand across his mouth.

"I messed it up myself, because you are one of the best men I've ever known, and I'm really glad we're doing this thing on Saturday."

He stepped back and lifted my hand, pressing his lips to the backs of my knuckles and leaving a faint red smudge. "Me too, baby."

"We just have to, you know, catch Jack the Ripper first."

"I think actual Jack the Ripper might be easier to find at this point."

"Marquette is sorting purchase orders he practically had to pry out of that teeny little medical supply office this morning as we speak." I waved one hand. "And I have a good feeling about this. The doctor Buster set Rachel up with is the most solid lead we've had so far. We know our guy has more than a YouTube video knowledge of anatomy, and Jim said the sutures showed skill. This has promise. We're not sorting through a dozen anonymous guys, I'm simply looking for the one we need to talk to."

"Except that we don't know who he is, or really much about what he looks like? Sure."

"Dana and her girls have seen him. I'll find him."

"They've seen him in fuzzy lighting from far away," Graham grumbled. "And you said that hard ass crooked lawyer was scared of whoever is running this. What if they know we have him in custody? What if they know you're coming?"

"Then I will put my ability to handle myself to good use. I can be scary myself when I want to be."

"I'll be right with Archie. You let us know if you need us."

"Squadron." I smiled as I said the code word. He flashed one back, but it didn't reach his eyes.

"You got this," he said.

"I really, really do." I laid all the emotion I had into the words before I grabbed the little clutch purse that held the transmitter for my microphone and the keys to a battered Honda Civic we'd borrowed from the Waco PD impound lot in case anyone was watching Bluebonnet Hills and had seen my truck.

"See you in a bit." I tucked my notebook into the bag.

"That thing is like a security blanket," Graham teased. "Undercover isn't exactly conducive to taking notes."

"I'd rather have it than not. Have fun with Archie."

Graham waved as I slipped out the door and hurried down the sidewalk to the Honda before the goosebumps became a permanent part of my legs.

Starting the engine, I pointed the car's weak, frosted headlights toward the mall and said a prayer that I'd been telling Graham the truth.

Two hours, a dozen indecent propositions, and too many strange hands on my ass to count later, Dana said the doctor wasn't there yet, and I was almost ready to cut my losses and call it a night.

"At least in pageants people are only groping you with their eyes," I grumbled into my mic. Archie's laugh rang in my ears.

"Hardin's going to storm in there and start decking people if you say much more," he said. "There's a difference between knowing your lady can take up for herself and staying put when people are getting handsy."

"Sorry," I whispered.

"Hey." Dana poked my shoulder, nodding at the door. "I told you he'd show if we waited around."

I cursed the stupid fog machine on the DJ stand for the tenth time since I walked in the door and squinted. The guy she pointed out was probably an inch or so taller than my five-ten, dressed well in a crisp blue shirt that was open at the collar with a gray suit over it, a powder blue pocket cloth folded perfectly and peeking out of his jacket at precisely the right height. He could've been an assistant in the Governor's office, casual after-hours style. His dark blond hair was gelled carefully, his face clean shaven at coming up on eleven o'clock at night.

I could buy doctor.

What I wasn't sure of was how a guy as clever as the one I'd been after for the better part of a week was just prowling the same club for victims over and over.

"You're sure that's him?"

"Sure as I can be from here."

This guy looked nothing like the one from the security footage that the bar manager had said was with the bathroom assault victim on the night she was attacked. There wasn't an awkward thing about him—hell, awkward wouldn't dare get near him for fear of being pulverized by the waves of charisma. Growing up around politicians, I was familiar with the power of charm. Coupled with a face like this one, it would make a pretty strong woman magnet.

The kind that didn't need to pay for sex.

Which meant if Rachel had indeed left with him it was because he was interested in something else.

"Showtime," I murmured as Dana faded into the crowd.

He stopped near the bar and turned, his eyes widening when he saw me before they ran from my big hair to my too-high heels and back to my face. I gave him my best dazzle-the-judges smile.

The look on his face said I still had the dazzle, a decade and a half removed from my last crown.

He pushed past three other guys and leaned on the corner of the bar nearest my stool. "I haven't seen you here before," he said, laying a hand on my bare knee. His palms were sweaty.

"I'm new in town." I stuck close to the story I knew about the previous victims. If the general profile was women they assumed no one would miss, I wanted to fit it.

"Well let me be the first to welcome you to our lovely city."

"Thanks."

"I'm Darren," he said.

"Like from the TV show about the witch?"

"I'm told my mother was a fan." He smiled, lighting up killer ice blue eyes.

"I'm Carrie," I said, blurting the first TV show name that popped into my head.

"Pleasure to meet you."

"Likewise."

"Can I buy you a drink?"

"A vodka tonic would be great." Because I hate vodka and wouldn't be tempted to drink it, but he didn't need to know that.

He signaled the bartender, who wasn't Brian.

Drinks ordered, he turned back to me. "So what brings a beauty like you to our fair city?" he asked. "School? Work?"

"Looking for a place to start over," I said. "I watch a lot of HGTV. Looked like as good a place as any."

"Shiplap fan?" He grinned.

"I love it."

"You know, she designed my office."

I gasped, feigning shock.

"I swear. I'd love to show it to you." He leaned so close I could smell the wintergreen Life Savers on his breath.

"One vodka tonic and one old fashioned." The bartender set the drinks in front of us and Darren straightened, his disappointment showing in the glare he shot across the bar.

I fiddled with the plastic stir stick in my glass and pretended not to notice. Darren sipped his and then raised his glass. "To new beginnings. And new friends."

I touched mine to his with a soft *clink* and pretended to sip it. "Cheers."

"So how about it?" he asked, downing his whiskey in one long swallow.

"How about what?"

"Would you like to see my office? It's quiet. Much better for getting to know each other. And there's a very comfortable sofa."

"Sure." I smiled. He tossed a fifty on the bar and took my hand, heading for the back of the bar.

"Didn't you come in the front?" I asked.

"This is faster." He tugged my hand and I had to hurry to keep up with him, repeating "excuse me" a dozen times as he plowed through the floor with no regard for who was in his path.

Once we reached the far back hallway that led to the back door, he found a corner and pushed me against the wall, keeping one hand on my shoulder as one tried to slide up my skirt, his lips landing on my neck when I turned my head to avoid a kiss.

What the hell was happening here?

"What're you doing?" I asked.

"So no kissing, huh?" His breath was hot on my skin. "Like Julia Roberts in *Pretty Woman*? I got news for you, baby, not many billionaires come through this joint."

My skin crawled right up my arms, and I slowed my breathing, biding my time until he pulled back just enough to give me room to throw a punch.

It was a good left hook, splitting his lip over his teeth and sending him staggering back two paces. I spread my feet into a punching stance and raised both hands.

"What the fuck is the matter with you?" he growled, wiping blood off his lips and widening his eyes when he saw it on his fingers. "Crazy bitch."

I lunged forward and grabbed his wrist, twisting his arm up and back as I moved around him. Two beats later, he was face first in the wall, his cheek pressed against it, his arm wrenched behind his back keeping him still because the more he struggled, the more his shoulder hurt. "Let go of me! I'll call the police and have your ass thrown in jail so fast your head will spin." The words sounded like they were grinding glass.

From just behind his ear, I murmured, "I am the police, asshole. And unless you want to go to jail for the rest of your natural life, you're going to tell me what happened to the last few young women who left this bar with you."

"What the fuck are you talking about?"

"I'm talking about stolen human organs."

His one visible eye went wide, his breath speeding. "I don't know anything about that."

"I think you do," I said. "The only thing I can't tell is if you're taking them yourself or delivering these women to someone who is. So are you really a doctor?"

He whipped his head backward too fast for me to get out of the way, and my chin felt like it was on fire after it took the brunt of the blow, my teeth clacking and grinding together. My grip slipped just enough for him to shove off the wall.

I landed on my ass thanks to my teetering heels, and he buried a wingtip in my ribs before he took off out the back door.

"Archie, Graham, he's on foot out the back entrance," I said, fumbling with the mic and swearing under my breath. "Six-one, one-ninety, dark blond hair, gray suit. I'm not sure he's our guy but he hit me and took off when I asked about the victims."

"We're on it. You okay?" Archie said.

"My ego is bruised. I can't believe that fucker got away from me. But I'm fine."

"Hey, what's all the commotion back here?" The bartender rounded the corner and stopped short. "Oh, shit, are you all right? Goddamn him." He put out a hand to help me up. "I'm sorry."

I let him pull me to my feet.

"Thank you." I met the bartender's eyes. "Boy, the staff here is friendly. Where's Brian tonight?"

He blinked. "I'm Brian."

"Oh, are there two of you? I'm sorry. I met the manager the other day and was going to say hello if he was working tonight."

"Still me. But I'm really sure I'd remember if we'd met before." He let go of my hand, confusion plain on his face.

"Oh shit." I fumbled the keys to the Civic out of my bag and ran for the front door, not stopping when I heard Dana calling me from the dance floor.

38

One handy skill from my pageant days that translated well to my career: I can sprint a marathon in three-inch heels and a skintight dress, and do it with a smile on my face.

By the time the Honda started on the third try, I jammed it into gear and squealed the tires turning out of the lot, searching the cupholders for my phone with one hand while keeping my eyes on the road. The Bluetooth radio was out of range, which meant they were chasing Darren and his fat lip.

"Hey Siri, call Graham," I hollered when I couldn't find the damned phone.

I groped in the passenger seat when I heard the robot voice say, "Calling Graham Hardin, mobile."

Voicemail.

"It was the bar manager, Graham. Or rather, the guy who told us he was the bar manager and isn't. That guy who was there the other day lied to us. I bet he was in that bathroom because he was trying to clean up evidence from the recent assault. He broke in and didn't bother to lock the door because it was early in the morning." The more I talked, the more that part of the story made sense. I shuddered at how easily we'd been fooled. This guy was clever and he was a good actor. And we'd told him half of what we knew over the course of two conversations, I realized as I thought back through it.

I banged my hand on the steering wheel. The card he'd handed me was from the holder on the manager's desk and had the actual manager's name. I didn't know the first thing about where to find him.

The card.

He'd touched the card and I'd tucked it into my notebook so I wouldn't lose it.

I squealed the tires again pulling into the parking lot at Waco PD headquarters. The desk officer's brows disappeared into his hairline when he saw me, and I remembered my outfit. Squaring my shoulders, I let my most authoritative cop voice ring off the 1970s acoustic ceiling tile. "Texas DPS Ranger Faith McClellan, I've been undercover and am aware of what I look like, but I need a print run and I need it now."

He dropped his clipboard, tipping his head.

"Do you want to risk being wrong if you tell me no, Officer?" I asked.

"No, ma'am."

I pulled my notebook from the tiny evening bag, thanking my lucky stars for my borderline-obsessive need to have it with me. Flipping pages carefully, I handled the card by the edges. A door at the end of a short hallway off the lobby buzzed, a young officer offering a smile with her raised eyebrows. "Ranger?"

"Undercover."

"The missing organs thing?"

"Good guess."

"I heard from Cortez that the first vic was a prostitute."

I held the card up by the edges. "I'm sure there are a few prints on this that belong to me. I'm also hoping there's at least one good one from someone I really need to find. Right now."

"Come on back and let's see what we can find." Her uniform nameplate read "Arlington."

I followed her down a hall and through a bullpen of detectives' cubicles to a small room that housed two desks, four chairs, and a laptop attached to a small, specialized scanner.

She pulled a sheet of plastic from one drawer and I laid the card carefully on it, face up.

"Is Brian Maxwell the person we're looking for?"

"No, a guy who told me he was Brian Maxwell is."

She pulled a small black box that looked like every other print kit I've ever seen from a drawer. "You want to do the honors?"

I took the box and went to work, painting the front of the card with reagent and then dusting the surface with silver nitrate powder.

"Five full and a partial," she said. "Not bad."

"As long as one of them isn't mine," I said.

"Let's see." She touched the screen to wake the computer while I lifted the prints one at a time with the tape from the kit, careful to pull slowly and not smudge anything.

When they were all transferred to cards, she took the first one and put it in the scanner, pulling up the Texas DPS database first, since Texas is one of a handful of states that requires all ten fingerprints on file to renew or obtain a driver's license.

Results loaded on the screen.

"Mine," I said, swearing to never touch anything again that I didn't handle by the edges.

I handed her the next card. She repeated the scan.

All five full prints were mine. The partial wasn't enough to get a result.

"Dammit." I closed my eyes and pulled in a slow breath.

"Try the other side," she said. "The partial would've returned on you if it matched the others we had just scanned."

I nodded, using a small tool from the kit to flip the card and dusting the back.

Four prints came up.

"Fingers crossed," she said.

I transferred them and handed her the first one for a scan.

"Brian Maxwell," she said. A driver's license photo of the guy who'd helped me off the floor in the back of the bar a half hour ago loaded. "Is that who you think it is?"

"It is now," I said ruefully. "You'd think this job would make a person less trusting."

"Don't beat yourself up," she said. "You'll get your guy. I've read about you, you always do."

"Thanks." I handed her the next card. "Big money, no whammy."

She laughed. "I used to watch that show with my nana."

"Me too."

We watched the computer screen.

"No results found," she read. "That doesn't happen very often anymore."

"So he doesn't have a Texas ID," I said. "Can you access Oklahoma?"

"They only do the thumbprint. But yes."

"Is this a thumbprint?"

"Maybe, if the guy has small hands."

"He didn't."

I tapped the edge of the desk, refusing to admit I'd run up against another dead end when we were this close.

Wait.

"Is there a database of doctors somewhere?" I asked.

"With the state medical board."

"Do they by chance take prints?"

She grinned. "You bet they do."

She clicked a few times and typed in credentials.

"Please God," I whispered, squeezing my eyes shut.

"Zachary James Porter," she said. "Last position, chief resident at University Medical Center in Austin."

She clicked his name. "Hold on. It says here he was terminated last year after failing to return from a leave of absence."

"He was the chief resident, and he just ghosted?" I shook my head. "People spend years working their asses off for a post like that, which means that kind of surrender would require a damn good reason. May I?"

She scooted her chair to one side and nudged the keyboard my way.

I checked the date on the medical board's last reference to Porter. He'd been gone a year.

Opening windows for Facebook and Instagram, I searched for the medical school. They had accounts on both platforms, but more posts on Facebook. I scrolled back eighteen months. Found a photo of the third-year residents in the hospital lobby and spotted Porter in the middle row when I zoomed in.

"So what happened to you?" I murmured, scrolling back up slowly.

Two days after the group photos, I found his headshot in a post announcing his selection as chief resident. I opened the comments—all 468 of them—hoping for a clue as to why he'd left the job. A whole lot of congratulations, the most liked one in all caps, from a guy whose profile had a lot of photos of him and Porter together. But nothing newer than about two weeks after the original post. Strike one.

I scrolled up until I got to December and paused, the cursor hovering over a photo of Porter in a tuxedo and a young woman who looked vaguely familiar in an elegant black and white gown. "The Christmas ball," I murmured to myself, my eyes lingering on the woman. I didn't know her. But I recognized her. Which didn't make any more sense than any other damn thing about this case.

March 15, I found a headshot of the new chief resident, double-clicking to make the post fill the screen. No mention of Porter or why he left in the statement from the school, just congratulations for the new guy. With almost a thousand comments. Scrunching a brow, I clicked them open.

"Oh my," Arlington whispered from behind me.

Porter's friend with the "hell yeah" all-caps congratulations on the months-earlier post had commented probably...I scrolled. A hundred times? A hundred and fifty? And he was good and pissed by the last one. "Porter's friend seems to think he got fired," I said.

"For caring for his sick fiancée?" Arlington asked, pointing to the words I'd read four times in the last comment. "That sucks. Can they even do that?"

I nodded as my heart fell to my toes. Porter was indeed looking for specific organs, specific matches. Not to sell to a buyer waiting in the wings —to save his fiancée. But who needed a heart, lungs, a kidney, and a liver?

And how the hell was I going to find him now? I clicked to the DPS database, sure before my search confirmed it that he didn't have a current address available. The last one listed was an apartment in Austin a block from the hospital, and I put the chances he was driving stolen organs from

Waco to Austin on the regular near that of a blizzard in August—in Houston.

I tapped the edge of the keyboard. Illegal transplants. Chester Henning. Desiree said they turned Chester's study into a hospital room.

Bingo.

I pulled up a website for the only local pharmacy that rented heavy medical equipment and called the number at the top, right under the "open 24 hours" banner.

"This is Officer Faith McClellan with the Texas Rangers," I said when a young woman answered the phone. "I need to know if anyone has rented a lot of heavy medical equipment in the last six months. Hospital-type things like IV pumps and ECG machines, maybe even a bed."

"Um. I have to ask my boss."

I tapped my fingers through hold music until another voice came on the phone. "Pharmacist, can I help you?"

"I sure hope you can because I'm out of time for things like warrants," I said. "My name is Faith McClellan, I'm a field officer with the Texas Rangers, and I'm investigating a string of homicides and a disappearance. Can you check your records and tell me if a good deal of hospital-grade equipment has been delivered to the same local address in the past six months?"

Officer Arlington looked confused.

I finally felt like I wasn't anymore.

I listened to the pharmacist click around her computer.

"The listing with the most items is from October 24. We delivered a bed, a wheelchair, a toilet chair, an ECG, an auto BP monitor, an IV pump, and two bedpans to 6726 Briar Thorn Court."

"Thank you!" I didn't wait for her to say anything else, hanging up as I scribbled the address before turning for the door.

"Wait," Arlington said.

"What?"

"Don't you need backup?"

I paused. She was right. But I didn't have time to waste. The progression of sloppiness and desperation meant my time was running out either way —the motive was saving his fiancée, who just flat out had to be related to the Finelli girls from Oklahoma. If he did manage to heal her, he was too smart to hang around one second longer than necessary now that he knew we were looking for him. If she died, he had no reason to stay.

I wrote the address down and added phone numbers for Archie and Graham.

"Call and text both of these numbers from dispatch, give them this address, and tell them I went there to make an arrest. How far is this house from here?"

"Ten minutes."

"In fifteen, call an all cars to this address and tell them to assume an undercover officer is inside. If I'm not, I'll let you know before then."

"You got it."

"Thanks."

I ran for the parking lot without looking back. Graham and Archie would get the messages and be there, maybe before I was depending on where they'd chased Darren.

I was pretty sure I knew what had happened.

And as sad as the story might be, it was time to go end it.

39

Every light in the small clapboard postwar house blazed bright enough for me to see a shadow moving in the curtained windows from where I parked two houses down. My breath came fast, sitting in the Civic trying to finish making a plan.

I couldn't go up there and wing it—this guy was far too brilliant. He'd fooled me and my human lie detector from the first moment I'd set eyes on him. Thinking back over the past few days was sure a good reminder that context is just as important as every other element in a murder investigation.

We tend to stitch people and events quickly to the context in which they're first presented to us—it's the factor that can make a person instantly dislike someone else and then have trouble overcoming that feeling later; the same impulse I was currently trying to fight where Ruth was concerned. I'd fully accepted Zac as Brian the bartender based on context, and once the connection was made, little cues like his subtle digs for information about the case at the coffee shop all fell in line with that assumption. He wasn't trying to gauge how close we were, he was worried about the victims and the bar's business—my assumption was an easy and logical one, given the context my brain had interpreted "Brian" in, but that didn't make me any less frustrated with myself in the moment.

I pulled my Sig from the glove box and checked the clip, but I couldn't go in shooting before I asked any questions at all.

I glanced around the quiet street of small, neat houses surrounded by small, neat lawns. It was coming up on one in the morning, so they were all dark save the one I was interested in.

No sirens split the silence. No sign of Archie and Graham.

I took ten seconds to send a pin to each of their phones from where I sat. Not because I thought I couldn't trust Officer Arlington to send a text, but because I was looking through a window at a guy who'd lied convincingly to my face multiple times, and I didn't want to feel stupid again.

The front door opened and Dr. Zachary rushed down the steps and hurled three bags into the back of a white SUV before he ran back into the house.

Fuck. He was leaving. Had someone—like Darren, maybe—called to tip him off that I was at the bar?

I couldn't wait for the cavalry.

Chambering a round in my sidearm, I clicked the safety off and got out of the car while the murderer we'd been hunting for four days rushed around the front room of the little house, his shadow moving between the windows and the now-open door. Under cover of a row of pruned box hedges, I moved to the side of the house and flattened myself against the siding, shivering from the chill and wishing to hell I had different clothes.

The next time Porter came outside, I was waiting for him. "It's over, Zac. Hands where I can see them." I stepped out of the shadows, my weapon raised in front of me.

"Ranger McClellan," he said, not lifting his hands. "I read up on you after we met. The only perfect record in the state. I really thought we'd get out of here before you knew it was me."

"She got sick and you thought you were the only one who could help her," I said softly. "But why? You worked at a hospital. You had a career. You had insurance."

"Not even considering that the non-insurance portion of one organ transplant still costs more than a new car," he said, "what we found out was that none of that matters when you need five transplants. You're not considered a 'good risk,' even if your fiancé is a surgeon who's working his ass off saving other people every single fucking day. They just look you in the face and tell you you're going to die." His hand went into his pocket.

"Show me your hands," I repeated.

He put them up slowly, the light from the doorway glinting off the scalpel resting between his thumb and forefinger. "I put out feelers about buying them, you know. Found a guy down in Goliad who offered me an indentured servitude situation." He stepped forward.

I moved my finger from the guard to the trigger. "Stop right there."

He did, but his posture stayed casual. Unconcerned.

"He deals in them," he continued. "He said if I'd bring him what I didn't use and work for him on the side for five years, he'd help us. What the fuck was I supposed to do? I would've signed my whole life away if it meant she'd get better."

In a way, he had.

He paused, tipping his head to the side. "But you get it, don't you? I saw your fiancé the other day at the bar. Do you really love him?"

I nodded, swallowing hard. "I don't want to shoot you, Zac. I do get it. But you have to know what you did is wrong."

"What, so it's right to sit by and watch her die because the shittiest thing her shitty birth parents did was pass along an autoimmune disease that caused her organs to start deteriorating and failing one by one? She's twenty-nine!"

I let out a slow breath. I thought about Jim, lying in the hospital, trying to channel some of the rage that had kept me going all weekend.

"And that made it okay for you to try to kill a medical examiner who has dedicated his life to catching murderers and serving the public?"

"He wasn't going to die. I heard him on the phone when I walked into the building. You were on your way. I cut the artery clean through." He waved a hand at the house. "I had to get Amber's body back, and he saw me. I just needed him out of commission for a few days, with no chance he'd be able to talk. I wasn't trying to kill him."

I watched his face carefully. No lies detected, though I didn't know if I could trust that right then.

I didn't want to kill this guy.

It was an impossible situation, and damned if I couldn't see the temptation for someone with the skill to do what he'd done.

"So why not just work for Pendergast and Little, then?" I asked.

He didn't even look surprised to hear me say their names.

"Dr. Pendergast got her a kidney, to begin with. They were the first thing to fail. It wasn't a great match, but it was what he could get. Two months later, her body rejected it. So I called up this guy my father used to talk shit about. My dad, he was a lawyer. And his dream was to see his only son be a doctor. He knew Sonny Gilchrist and said the man couldn't find a scruple with two hands and a flashlight. Told me a few stories old Sonny would rather I keep to myself. I needed to know where to find her sisters. She was the oldest of three, and she remembers the social worker taking the little ones away. Siblings are often perfect matches. We were going to beg them, see if one of them would donate a kidney to her."

He kept talking and I kept my grip on my gun, watching the scalpel in his hand and trying not to let sympathy cloud my judgment. It was a horribly sad story. But he'd murdered people.

He'd hurt Jim.

"Her heart went downhill, though, right?"

"You really are smart," he said. "I couldn't be sure her heart wouldn't hold at partially functioning when I took the first kidney from Marcy. I didn't want to have to kill her. I went to a lot of trouble to have one of Sonny's goons who cleaned up well enough to pass for a doctor meet her—and Rachel, later—in the bar and lure them outside so nobody would see me. Sonny told him to do what I asked because Pendergast said to."

"Why did you put her in that closet?" I had to ask.

"I was going to bury her later, but I had to go. We didn't have that much time to get the organs transplanted, and Pendergast was waiting to help me. I don't think he felt sorry for me as much as he thought the case was interesting, but I needed the help. I had the camera rigged up outside to make sure no one came up as I was working, and I moved it to the closet to make sure she was safe until I could move her without being seen. I had changed the locks on that closet so I could store organ preservative and IV drugs in there. Jerry had hot-wired the power to the electric water heater and an outlet next to it with some crazy MacGyver shit he learned in the army, and

I needed a place to keep that stuff near where I was working. Once I was done, I got rid of the fridge, but the women Buster has staying there came back before I could get Amber from the closet. I really did want to give a proper burial to the woman who saved my fiancée's life."

I believed him. Not that it changed what I was there to do.

"That day at the bar, you were making sure there was no evidence left in the bathroom when we showed up," I said.

"Sonny was paranoid that I'd missed something, or that the camera footage was going to give us away. Pendergast wanted white women nobody would miss. We were looking for one who was AB negative. We tried having Darren take the blood the first time and it was a shit show, so I went from then on."

"Why did you tell us about those other assaults when we found you at the bar?"

He pursed his lips. "I knew there was a police report about the most recent one, so I thought it looked better if I offered it up."

"It did."

"But also, I figured if you were looking for those girls, you'd stay distracted for long enough for Dahlia to be able to travel. We're so close. I just needed a few more days to disappear, and then no one would ever see either of us again." His eyebrows went up, his tone taking on a pleading edge. "Just let me get her out of here."

I glanced from the scalpel to his face just in time to see his eyes go to the front stoop.

Too much happened all at once.

"You shouldn't be out of bed, love," Zac said.

Tires squealed.

Someone shouted.

And the night exploded.

———

"Faith!" I realized it was Graham screaming as his shoulder connected with my ribs, which happened roughly the same time the gun fired. For a second, I wasn't even sure whether or not it was mine.

We landed on the grass in a tangle of limbs, something warm, wet, and sticky spreading over my hip.

"Don't move, either of you." Archie's tone had a razor edge sharp enough to slice steel, his weapon pointed at something near the house that I assumed was Zac's beloved. "I'll shoot her, son, and I don't miss."

Leave it to Archie to read the situation in half a second.

I struggled to pull air back into my lungs, wriggling a hand up and between my body and Graham's.

It was blood. There was a lot of it.

But it wasn't mine.

My heart thudded in my ears, simultaneously feeling like it was being ripped from my chest. "Graham! Archie, he's hit! Help me!" My own voice sounded so shrill with panic I didn't even recognize it.

The scalpel clattered to the concrete with a metallic ringing. "I'm not armed," Zac said, moving closer slowly, his hands up and his eyes on Archie. "May I?"

"Help him." My voice broke as I tried to move my unconscious fiancé onto his back.

Archie came closer, still holding his weapon on the figure in the doorway. I looked up and gasped.

It was Jane Doe.

Yeah, they were sisters, all right.

This woman was just as pale in life as the other one had been in death. She barely gripped a gun, dangling at her side, her skin pale, eyes glassy, and chest heaving.

Jesus, the resemblance was downright creepy.

"Give me the gun, miss." Archie put his hand out.

She tried to raise it again. "She was going to shoot Zac."

"I really wasn't," I said around a sob, kneeling next to Graham.

"Dammit, Dahlia, please go lie down." Zac ripped Graham's shirt open, looking for the source of the bleeding. "I need more light."

Archie took the gun from the woman and I clicked on the flashlight on my phone, spotting the hole about halfway between Graham's ribs and his hip, spouting blood in time to his heartbeat.

"Goddammit." Zac saw it when I did, pulling his sweatshirt over his head and pressing down on the wound with his full body weight.

Graham screamed, coming to and flailing his arms.

"Keep him still," Zac said through clenched teeth as one of Graham's fists landed a blow near his ear.

I leaned over Graham's face, stroking it. "Stop, baby. He's trying to help you."

He went still when his gaze locked on mine, his breath fast and ragged. "Hurts."

"I know. Stay right here with me." I grabbed his hand.

"Officer down, repeat, officer down," Archie was saying into his phone behind me. He was on the steps where he could watch Dahlia, who appeared to have gone back to her bed. "Where the hell are we again?"

Zac reeled off the address as he lifted Graham's left hip and put his hands under it, stuffing part of the sweater underneath him. Graham's face went slack before he bit down on his lip hard enough to draw blood.

"Sorry, man," Zac said. "I have to stop the bleeding."

"Is he going to be all right?" I asked.

"It appears this one in the front is the exit wound, and she only fired once, so that's good. But she might have nicked his liver. This blood is dark. That I don't like."

Sirens. Finally.

I rested my forehead against Graham's. "You better be there Saturday, Hardin," I whispered. "I went dress shopping with Ruth McClellan for you."

40

Eight hundred sixty-five yards of ivory Mulberry Silk bunting. Seventy-five pressed white linen tablecloths. Five hundred white lilies and every surviving orchid from either side of the Mississippi artfully arranged into individual masterpieces for every table. Baccarat glasses shimmered, throwing rainbows across every surface, and a designer purple and silver sugar-fondant confection defied gravity as it twisted and turned in sixteen layers toward the fairy lights woven through the top of a canvas tent with a twelve-foot ceiling.

"You weren't kidding when you said your mother knows how to throw a party," Graham murmured, his lips brushing my ear as the band played a sweet, fitting song about careless men and their careful daughters.

I pulled my head back enough to be able to look up at him. "You really are the best thing that's ever been mine," I whispered. "Thank you for saving my life, Mr. Hardin."

"Thank you for making mine, Mrs. Hardin."

I returned my head to his shoulder. "I won't ever get tired of hearing that."

"It has a hell of a ring to it." His breath was still shallow, but steady, his arms tight around me. "So. Am I the only one of us who's been thinking about this damned case all day long?" he asked.

I shook my head. "I can't stop thinking about how he saved you. He knew he was going to go to prison, probably for the rest of his life, and he didn't even try to run or fight. He saved you and surrendered."

"Archie would've killed them both if they'd tried anything else," Graham said.

"Maybe. But still. I can't help but be grateful to him. And their story is so damn sad."

"Don't forget ghoulish. People can justify a whole lot of things to themselves in the name of love." Graham rested his cheek on my hair, his feet barely moving in a shuffle that belied the stitches holding his liver and side together. He'd been released from the hospital Thursday evening with orders to take it easy but clearance for the wedding to go on as scheduled. I had deemed this first turn on the floor one of two dances, with seated breaks in between. Ruth, in a last-minute stroke of brilliance, had a pair of white leather recliners delivered for the head table, so Graham could sit comfortably and enjoy the evening.

She'd offered to postpone, but he wouldn't even discuss it. "Are you kidding? Considering how I got this gunshot wound, it's possible I want to be married more than I did a week ago, and I didn't think then I could want anything more," he'd argued, his hand up to prevent further assertion that a few weeks wouldn't matter in terms of the lifetime we were planning together. "We are doing this now. Just like we planned."

And we had. Ruth couldn't have bought a more beautiful Texas spring day for our wedding—warm sunshine, a light breeze, and the gardens at the Driskill just beginning to bloom. I'd felt my sister nearby all day—Charity was the other thing I hadn't been able to get out of my head in the hours of sitting by Graham's hospital bed watching the reassuring beep of the monitors. If either of us had needed a kidney or a chunk of a liver, there wouldn't have even been a conversation beyond "how soon can they do this?"

I missed her so much it still hurt sometimes, but my wedding week had certainly made me a new kind of thankful for the relationship we'd had.

The song finished and I tilted my chin up, planting a soft kiss on his lips. "I love you, Graham Hardin. Thanks for not dying on me."

"Anytime." He pulled his head back and stared like he'd never seen my face before. "I am so damned glad you married me. I never thought it was possible to love anyone this much."

"Me neither."

Taking his arm, I helped him back to his chair, turning when he was settled and someone tapped my shoulder.

"May I have this one?" Archie smiled.

"I'm good," Graham said. "Go."

The band played a waltz as we walked to the floor, and I smiled. "Do you remember teaching me these steps by letting me stand on your boots?"

"Some of the most fun I ever had on duty," Archie said.

"I'm so glad you're here today." I smiled softly.

"You deserved so much better than you ever got from your dad," he said.

"Lucky for me, he wanted the best for security, huh?"

He glanced at Graham. "How's he holding up?"

"He's tired. But he won't say it."

"And how about you?"

I swallowed hard. "It wouldn't be in your best interest to make me cry, Arch. Ruth will murder you herself if you ruin my makeup."

"She likes me too much to kill me." He winked. "But I don't want to see you cry. Just checking. This was a hard week on you."

"You think they'll get capital convictions?"

"Organized Crime made arrests yesterday at every 'consultant's' office on Graham's list, and the FBI came in today to fan out from there. Pendergast's operation is in at least nine states, and they might find more. That guy is definitely going up for maximum sentencing. I've never seen a jury that wouldn't be flat ass horrified at what he did. I'm not sure we can pin any of the actual murders on Pendergast, but if there's a way to get there, the DA will go for it. Just being in a room with that fellow made my blood run cold. He has no remorse for anything he's done. Pretty easy to see why Sonny Gilchrist was so scared of him. And if the scars on Jerry Blanchard when Boone found him were any indication, Gilchrist was right to be terrified."

The WPD SWAT unit had found Jerry tied spread-eagle to a stable stall doorway behind Pendergast's hunting cabin, a pair of Sonny's redneck goon sometime-clients taking turns at him with a cattle prod and a branding iron and shouting about loyalty over his screams. Sonny had admitted to giving the order to have Jerry "dealt with" after Pendergast threatened Missy's life when Graham and I left his office. Turned out, Missy was Zac's way into the lab—Cortez left me a voicemail while Graham was bleeding on Zac's lawn detailing that she had left the front desk at the lab to go to work for Sonny. Zac lifted the keys she never returned when he noticed them on her desk, just in case he needed to steal some supplies—hospitals are open around the clock, but nights and weekends at the lab usually don't come with witnesses.

"They're still working on putting together how the younger guy, Little, got lured into this, but it's pretty clear Pendergast was using him for access to patients after he lost his license."

"Those bastards I don't even feel a little sorry for. While Zac didn't mean for Marcy to die when he took her first kidney, I'm pretty sure a deep enough dig there is going to prove Little let people die on his operating table specifically so he and Pendergast could sell off their parts. But I keep wondering what will happen to Zac and Dahlia."

"I mean...she shot a police officer and he kidnapped and murdered at least three women. Did we ever figure out why he killed the drug dealer?"

"She was his source for pain meds for Dahlia," I said. "Apparently the liver is the hardest organ to transplant in that it rejects the most often. Even with the sibling match, Dahlia's was starting to reject. He went to get pills and saw a blood donor card on her fridge. She matched, he needed the organ...like we said, he was getting more and more desperate."

Archie shook his head. "Jesus. Makes you glad they were able to repair Hardin's liver."

"I've thought about it so much this week," I said, blinking against tears that welled anyway. "When he was lying there bleeding on the lawn, I'd have yanked out someone's liver with my bare hands to save him, Archie. How is that different?"

"Because you didn't."

"Because I don't have the skill. If I were in Zac's shoes? I can see how it would be so tempting." I rested my head on Archie's shoulder and locked eyes with Graham across the room. "I can't imagine having to live a day without him."

"Hopefully you won't have to."

"I keep thinking Zac went through all that, and the doctors at Memorial say Dahlia will probably be fine, at least for a while, and the best they're going to do being together is maybe the sticky gross conjugal trailers at Huntsville."

"It's such a sad story all the way around," he agreed.

"How easily could it be any of us?" I asked. "Given the right circumstances?"

He planted a kiss on my forehead as the last notes of the song faded.

"That's easier to think than to do in the moment," he said. "I promise. For tonight, Jim is over there dancing with his wife, Graham is the happiest married man on the planet, Chuck is reading in his bunk according to the guard on his cellblock, and all is right with our world."

"Indeed." I took his arm and let him walk me back to Graham, watching his eyes light up when he saw us coming.

Archie was right, as usual.

I settled into my chair and Graham reached for my hand. "Have I told you that you look beautiful tonight?"

"Thanks."

"The dress was worth going shopping with your mother."

"I heard that," Ruth said as Archie waltzed her by our table.

Graham smiled. "It's a great dress, Mrs. McClellan."

"Your bride is a gorgeous woman," she called over Archie's shoulder, her voice lighter than I'd heard it in....maybe ever.

"Thank you." I squeezed Graham's hand.

"I think I feel so sorry for that guy Zac because I get it. I mean, jumping in front of the bullet the other night was easy, because I didn't even think, I just saw her pointing the gun at you and reacted. It was instinct. But if I was in his shoes, with his skills? I'd probably be in a cell, too, because life without you wouldn't be worth living anyway."

I curled my fingers around his, thankful for good health and good friends and a bright future looming with the love of my life.

"Good thing we don't have to," I said.

"Promise?" He smiled.

I leaned in for another kiss.

"I do."

TELL NO LIES: Faith McClellan #6

Faith McClellan tackles the most dangerous case of her career when a string of murders leads her to a smuggling operation at the Texas border.

Get your copy today at
severnriverbooks.com/series/faith-mcclellan

"LynDee Walker is a modern voice in crime fiction with a southern belle's charm...if you like Tami Hoag or Nora Roberts, you will love her work." —S.A. Cosby, New York Times bestselling author of *Razorblade Tears*

"Walker is an accomplished and exciting author who writes procedurals with heart, and this might be her best one yet." —Jennifer Hillier, award-winning author of *Little Secrets*

"Texas Ranger Faith McClellan is a strong and compelling heroine who will keep fans coming back for more." —Laura McHugh, award-winning author of *The Weight of Blood*

"Walker...creates a living, breathing, ass-kicking Texas Ranger who honors the badge." —Brian Shea, author of the Boston Crime Thriller Series

"LynDee Walker...always provides relatable characters and a compelling plot, but somehow she also manages to improve with each new novel released." —Raven Award Winner Kristopher Zgorski, BOLO Books

ACKNOWLEDGMENTS

The biggest thank you this time goes to my son Gabe, who made an offhand comment that grew into this book—proof that I really never know where my next idea will come from, and also that my son is brilliant and imaginative, and I am so proud of the young man we have raised.

As always, taking an idea and turning it into a novel I'm proud to share and add to this series is a group effort: my thanks to my editor, Randall Klein, for making me dig down and see this story the way it should've been all along; my agent, John Talbot, for making me believe I can do things when I don't think I can; Cara Quinlan, thank you for your sharp eyes and ability to keep grammar and hyphenation rules that continually escape me straight so that I look polished to my readers; Andrew, Mo, Keris, Amber, and the rest of the SRP team, thank y'all so much for supporting me, connecting readers with my stories, and being the most amazing people in the industry to work with.

My thanks to my sweet Avery, who loves Faith and Graham and keeps mom on track with their story because she wants to know what comes next, and to Kennedy for understanding when mommy has to pull late nights and work on the weekends to meet a deadline.

My wonderful readers, thank you for loving my imaginary friends and allowing them to be part of your lives, and for your kind comments about the different ways my stories have impacted you—your stories about finding a needed escape in my characters and their adventures never cease to amaze me, and make the parts of this that are hard work worth it.

As always, any mistakes are mine alone.

ABOUT THE AUTHOR

LynDee Walker is the national bestselling author of two crime fiction series featuring strong heroines and "twisty, absorbing" mysteries. Her first Nichelle Clarke crime thriller, FRONT PAGE FATALITY, was nominated for the Agatha Award for best first novel and is an Amazon Charts Bestseller. In 2018, she introduced readers to Texas Ranger Faith McClellan in FEAR NO TRUTH. Reviews have praised her work as "well-crafted, compelling, and fast-paced," and "an edge-of-your-seat ride" with "a spider web of twists and turns that will keep you reading until the end."

Before she started writing fiction, LynDee was an award-winning journalist who covered everything from ribbon cuttings to high level police corruption, and worked closely with the various law enforcement agencies that she reported on. Her work has appeared in newspapers and magazines across the U.S.

Aside from books, LynDee loves her family, her readers, travel, and coffee. She lives in Richmond, Virginia, where she is working on her next novel when she's not juggling laundry and children's sports schedules.

Sign up for LynDee Walker's reader list at
severnriverbooks.com/authors/lyndee-walker
lyndee@severnriverbooks.com

Printed in the United States
by Baker & Taylor Publisher Services